JOSEPH CHAPMAN:

MY MOLLY LIFE

JOSEPH CHAPMAN
MY
MOLLY
LIFE

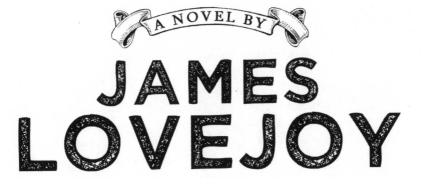

A NOVEL BY

JAMES LOVEJOY

I

WHEN I WAS VERY YOUNG, I assumed I would grow to be a waterman like my father, take a wife, and have happy children, and that my life, despite the usual pedestrian vicissitudes, would be, in the main, pleasant and uncomplicated. But that was before everything else happened instead, far worse and much better than I ever could have imagined.

I was born in London, the thirteenth of February, 1762, as a cold night edged towards dawn. My father, his mother, my three-year-old brother, and a midwife hastily got from the parish were all in attendance with my mother. I came quickly, giving her an easy time. My father looked me over, and, expecting me not to live, sighed, observed there was scarcely enough of me to feed a rat, and went off to his skiff. The midwife, having washed me, concurred. She advised my mother not to become too attached to me.

"I can take him now, if you'd like," she offered.

"We can let him to a beggar woman as easily as you and keep the coin ourselves, thank you very much," responded my grandmother, tartly.

Despite her confinement, Mother communicated her sentiments by means of a pewter mug standing at the bedside, which flew within an inch of the midwife's ear before clattering against the wall opposite. The woman, begging no offense,

---

humbly collected her half crown and removed herself with haste.

I was told this long afterwards, of course. When I was small, my mother would tell it to me as she put me to bed, ending with, "And look how you have grown!" Hearing this, I would wriggle with pleasure. I flourished regardless of my inauspicious arrival, and found myself to be well loved, well fed, and as safe as it is possible in this uncertain world to be.

My parents were unlettered and unpretentious folk of the kind that may be said to be the backbone of England, which would make me the same by rights, but this asseveration has been much disputed, as I shall tell. My father, a round-faced, mostly placid man of steady habits and no small skill at his waterman's trade, deeply loved and was entirely overawed by my mother, whose bright and ready wit tutored us all.

She was every bit as tall as he, black-haired, keen-eyed, with a sharp nose that might have been shrewish on another woman, but given that she laughed readily and often, her visage was deemed handsome. They had met at Billingsgate, where she was sometimes an oyster girl, buying her wares before dawn and peddling them in the streets. This she continued following their marriage. When I was small, I would traipse after her, singing her song.

She left off her other trade of woman fighter upon marrying, despite having won several nice prizes. Owing to her having won a prize of ten pounds, in fact, my parents were able to marry and let lodgings better than their station might seem to warrant, for my father had but little money. His father, also a waterman, had squandered his time and money in the gin shops that flourished in the forties and early fifties, before they were licensed and put down. Rousting his insensible parent from stinking cellars turned my father against spirits for all time, and he foreswore them when he was grown, rarely indulging in aught but small beer, making him very much an oddity amongst his peers.

We lived in a tightly packed neighborhood of close buildings and narrow streets between St. Paul's and the Thames, thronging with many thousands of people all more or less like ourselves, none too poor to wear a clean shirt on Sunday or afraid to wield an opinion, solicited or not. And if the better sort looked a long ways down their noses at us, we returned the compliment full measure, viewing their precious affectations with salty derision.

Our lodgings on Brickhill Lane, two rooms on the uppermost floor of a doddering rent built immediately after the great fire of the previous century, were more salubrious than many, having piped-in water at a common tap on the ground floor, and proximity to the river, which provided breezes that, at times, dispelled the clouds of flies attendant upon the dung wharf hard by.

On fine days in summer when the water was low, we were ofttimes beset by a stench no application of vinegar or soothing powders could quell, this malodorous emanation arising from the river itself and its exposed banks, ripening in the sun. We accepted this as we accepted everything good and bad, for this was simply how life presented itself to us. To quarrel with it would have been mad. And, to be sure, not all was stench and flies. When the water was high and the weather fine, we could swim at any of several stairs leading down to the river, and in the coldest winters had frost fairs on the ice, which exercised our imaginations mightily.

With my parents and I dwelt my Gram, my father's mother, my older brother William, and, in due course, a younger sister, Sarah, who was robust and lively, whether one cared for the din or not. And, of course, several babies died, as babies are wont to do. I don't recall how many, as I was then very small.

Gram died when I was five, and I have but few memories of her. She was a jolly, kind old woman in possession of a full store of stories, lullabies, and rhymes, who excelled at playing the little games beloved by small children. Her death was unexpected despite her age. Giving every appearance of perfect health, and without making the slightest fuss or complaint, she quietly fell over dead one morning whilst sewing. My parents counted it a blessing, as she and we were spared the miseries of protracted dotage and illness, but it felt like no blessing to me, and I cried very hard.

GIVEN WHAT I HAVE WRITTEN thus far, it may be opined, and could not be opposed, that my boyhood was indistinguishable from thousands of boys in the huge and teeming city. I was, to be sure, more happy than not, and I passed many profitable hours in pursuits innocent and, at times, not. But I will confess that I did not feel myself to be much of a boy, as I discovered in myself an unaccountable delicacy. I do not know why this should have been, only that it was. I did not care for most boy's games, and the rougher they were, the less I cared for them, as they seemed little more than pretext for disputation over some daft rule, which often as not led to a fight. Indeed, it seemed to me boys, my own membership in the tribe notwithstanding, were oafish things, oft as not bedaubed with snot or blood, who would sooner argue and fight than do anything useful, and I cared little for their society. I preferred the company of girls, whose games were gentler and more interesting withal. To compound the tendency, I was more welcome in their society than that of the boys, who were contemptuous of my indifferent skills. In providing the requisite father at many a playtime tea and compliantly participating in elaborate, play-acted dramas, I found myself pleasantly engrossed. If only the girls had chattered less, and not schemed against one another so, but they were given to these vices every bit as much as the boys were to dominance and disputation.

Had they not been, I might have decided an inexplicable error had occurred, whereby my sex was belied by my body. In fact, it was not so, as I had no quarrel with my masculine flesh, and though I preferred the girls' games to the boys', eventually found their torrents of talk and petty intrigues as wearing as the latter's brutality. Thus it was that I often preferred my own company to that of anyone else's, and the more so as I grew.

I shared my discomfort but once, with my mother when I was five or six years of age, to the effect that I did not feel quite like a boy, and her response was abrupt: "You look every bit a fine boy to me," said she, hoisting her basket to her shoulder. "If you are less like someone else, you will be more like yourself," which observation bears an admirable cogency. But I have since learned it is not wise to be too much like oneself, if oneself is in contradistinction to the generally accepted model, and I very early on found myself pressed against this stricture. At the age of perhaps four, I applied rouge that one of my female playmates had brought to our little party in the hall, coloring especially my cheeks and lips. I thought it very fine, but when I returned to our chambers, Gram took an instant and utter dislike to it, roughly scrubbing my face and saying, "Now, we will have no more of *that*!"

This epicene sensibility increased with age, and by my early teens I became aware that boys were more interesting than girls, and that some of them were extremely interesting indeed. This raised the yet deeper conundrum: how was it that boys should be interested in girls at all? But now I am getting ahead of myself, as what happened because of my interest in young men is at the heart of my tale.

II

MY FATHER DIED NOT LONG before I turned sixteen, of a fever occasioned by the odorous night air. I remember a barber surgeon returning often and letting more and more blood, which spattered into a dish and was unceremoniously dumped into the bucket otherwise reserved for night soil. My father never complained, but weakened steadily till there was little left of him. This patient, strong man whom I adored, became a slight thing shivering under many blankets, until, at last, he expired one night while I slept. William, my older brother, assisted the parish men in wrapping and carrying the body out, as I looked on. I was too grown by then to show my tears and endeavored in every way to appear manly, which is to say calmly grave and self-possessed. I knew he would have wanted that of me, but it was almost more than I could manage.

Father's death was for me a multiplicity of disasters. I had determined to perpetuate his trade, and became his apprentice at the age of twelve. By the age of fifteen, I had learned about the river's currents, how to handle a boat and read the weather, the locations and names of the many stairs at the water's edge, and how to talk to and cajole the public and especially gentlefolk. With father dead and William securely placed, 'prentice to a boat builder, Mother wanted me to stay near, to help her and Sarah, as she said, just for a little while.

The little money that came from the Waterman's guild upon Father's passing was soon expended. What mother made from peddling oysters was insufficient to maintain our lodging and our bellies, though we happily ate what she did not sell. We then let our second room to a ruined draper, his industrious wife, and their four children, which kept things lively, as access to their quarters was through the midst of ours, but the shillings he gave us at random intervals were welcome indeed. Thus it was that Mother declared she would take up fighting once more, despite our protestations.

"One blow from Bruising Peg, and you'll be done," offered William, to which I added,

"We can all help you sell more oysters and fish, and the fighters can be hanged," said I, and Sarah, so much younger, simply said "Mummy, please don't."

But she wouldn't be dissuaded. "I'll not be a beggar woman, nor the mother of beggars and thieves, and Bruising Peg doesn't scare me. I've had a fancy to fight again for a long time. I have been challenged by several rude women, and I shall be happy to settle their accounts. And where else can I get guineas in a few hours and not be hanged for my troubles? I only stopped fighting because your father asked me to. I was good at it, you know. He said most of the women fighters are whores, and that I was altogether too fine for it, but in truth some of them are not whores, and I'm not so very fine. I enjoyed it, and I want to fight again. Me arms are strong!" She then proceeded to tell us where to make application so that she should fight once more.

And so the next day whilst Mother was peddling, William and I walked to Marylebone, where on Wells Street, Figg's Boarded House featured an enclosed amphitheater for boxing. There we applied to have posted a challenge that Maggie Chapman, Billingsgate Fish Woman, would fight any woman presuming to best her Friday next, 16 May 1778, at 7 in the morning, this date and time being to the convenience of the house and to us. This notice having been read back to our satisfaction, and upon payment of a half crown, was posted among others on a large board visible to the street, with the instruction to return frequently to see whether anyone had accepted the challenge.

"I remember your mother well. She was a strong fighter, but it's been a very long time," said the agent, roosting in his wicket amidst a dishevelment of ledgers, tickets, and receipts. "There is no purse, and she will find few if any to wager on her. We will not make any money on it, but perhaps she shall prosper if she does well."

We thanked the man and walked home, to find a basket of fish and onions on the table, and Mother boxing her shadow on the wall. "How they taunt me," she declared, "and how they shall rue their rash words!"

"The street women are very nasty, now that Father is gone" said Sarah, who was then accompanying Mother on her rounds. "They believe she will take their men away, I think," she said, laughing uncertainly.

"I want nothing of their men!" responded Mother, throwing a series of furious punches in the direction of the wall. "Your—father—was—all I ever! Wanted! And the rest—of them—and their stinking! I say stinking! Women too—can go hang!"

Two days later, William and I returned to Figg's Boarded House where we learned that one Mrs. Stahl, a Jewess and daughter of the celebrated fighter Mrs. Gulko, had accepted the challenge. "The upstart crone Mrs. Chapman shall be laid flat in a trice! So say I, Mrs. Stahl, and I dare any to say it shall not be so!"

"Your mother will have a very pretty fight," opined the clerk, when he read the notice to us. "Mrs. Stahl is but nineteen, but her mother has trained her very well. She hasn't lost a match yet and is hungry for fresh meat."

Mother was delighted. "I will feed her to the dogs," she laughed. "Just as I treated her mother! Her mother may have trained her, and a pretty thing it is, but has she been lifting five stone baskets of oysters?" She flexed a bicep that would have shamed many a man. "Eat your fish, boys. You will need your strength to hold my corner."

When the appointed morning came, we rose early and ate boiled eggs, wheaten cakes, and coffee, extravagances Mother in her confidence had felt were warranted. Sarah was to stay behind with the draper's family, with whom we had become necessarily close, whilst William and I, his master having given him the day's liberty, walked with Mother as she threw jabs at the air. The morning was glorious, and as Figg's was the most well known pugilistic resort in the city, on arriving we saw a considerable crowd had already gathered. Mother went immediately to her corner in the ring, William and I following, where she was approached by the sharp-faced and sinewy Mrs. Stahl, who, despite the pugnacity of her public pronouncements, was almost deferential.

"My mother has told me much of you," she said. "She said you are not given to dirty tricks, and you were the only one she never beat. I will be honored to fight you. And win, of course."

Mother looked her up and down. "Very prettily said, although you are quite wrong about winning. I shall school you in the art of losing as I did her. Now begone, and get ready to fight!"

And with that, the women stripped to the waist. The judge gave each of them two half crowns to hold in their fists. When he gave them the nod, they set to, dancing each around the other in furious movement, sparring and punching. I own that I did not like it one bit, not only because I feared my mother might be injured, but because, too, of that internal delicacy I have previously mentioned, which set me against the very contest itself and, indeed, all who attended. I did not, of course, betray these niceties of sentiment. Instead, I fetched water and linen with perfect alacrity, as did William, and as the fight unrolled, Mother prevailed.

Mrs. Stahl was smaller, more agile and very quick. She did land several punches, but these did no great harm and served only to put Mother into a fine fury. Mother was larger and stronger, and she battered Mrs. Stahl mercilessly. Mrs. Stahl, who began by dancing away nicely whenever Mother would jab, increasingly failed to evade Mother's stout blows, and was soon worn down. Mother finished her off with a great blow to the left eye that sent her bleeding and sprawling before she could get down on her knees for the thirty second count.

She rose soon after, wobbling but eager for more, but as she was quite unable to see due to the blood and swelling in her eyes, the judge declared the fight over, and Mother raised both arms and then bowed to the cheers of the crowd. She then approached Mrs. Stahl in her corner, saying, "I pray I have not injured you too severely. Let it be a lesson not to taunt your betters. And do give my respects to your Mother." This last was unnecessary, as Mrs. Gulko was in the front row next her daughter's corner and could hear every word, but Mother would have her way.

III

THE JUDGE AWARDED MOTHER THE two half crowns she had been given to hold in her fists when fighting, and would have given her the two held by Mrs. Stahl, had the woman been of a mind to relinquish them, but the judge, on being warmly informed by her that he and all his ilk were welcome to be dragged through every last stinking dung heap in London on his way to Royal Flaming Hell, and that she'd be damned if she had not earned every farthing of them, wisely desisted. He told Mother that much better was in store for her if she would forbear this once. Mother graciously assented to this, laughing that she had rubbed Mrs. Stahl's nose in it well enough, and that she was satisfied with the outcome and the guinea she had won on a one crown wager on her own behalf.

On vacating the ring, Mother was approached by a sallow, fat fellow in a soiled red velvet waistcoat and an ill-fitting, unpowdered wig. He introduced himself as Mr. Clegg, Impresario of Pugilistic Spectacles of the First Order. He stated he would be pleased to represent Mother, and would be most happy to arrange for her a succession of contests of increasing severity, each with a guaranteed purse. Mother heard the man with interest, but when he hinted with a wink that she could gain much more by knowing when to win or lose, and that the true art was in the simulation, not the actuality of a hard fought contest, she spat at his feet and walked on without a word. She hastened then to post her next challenge under her own name, for the available date of a fortnight hence, and the three of us walked home in the broad sunlight of a very fine spring forenoon. Mother was exultant, and with a portion of her winnings bought pasties and sweets for a celebratory dinner. William was quite giddy, and I was more relieved than anything, and kept my reservations to myself.

THE FORTNIGHT PASSED, WHEREUPON MOTHER dispatched one Mrs. Sachwell in much the same manner as she had Mrs. Stahl, and, in succeeding weeks, Mrs. Pigott, the unmarried Pugilistic Peg, and Mrs. Molly Minahan, who was a rather more formidable competitor, knocking Mother down several times and quite severely bloodying her nose before succumbing to Mother's bare-knuckled windmill attacks. The house was now attaching prizes to Mother's contests as their receipts were very good, and the oddsmakers piled on a percentage. By August, Mother's contests were advertised in the papers and she was taking home ten, then fifteen pounds per fight. She had not yet been defeated.

Thus it was that in late August, at the close of yet another victorious contest, as mother washed her face in the dressing room basin, Mr. Clegg again approached, appearing to have neither changed his waistcoat nor given any attention to his wig since we had seen him last. His speech was an oleaginous patter. "I do so very apologize for any impropriety in my previous remarks, Madam, and beg to have a word with you."

"Speak, then," shrugged mother, carefully feeling her nose.

"Well, then, Madam, if it please you, I beg to propose a free and open contest with a woman fighter under my management, for a very large purse. Very large. Entirely free and open."

"And who might this woman be?" Mother put on her stays and began to lace them up.

"I speak of the one known as Meg the Madwoman. Very large purse indeed. Might you be interested?"

Mother paused in mid pull. "Out of Bedlam, is she? I didn't know she still fought. I thought she had been banned. I cannot say I am interested, but I will be content to hear how much."

"Thirty pounds, at least. More when the odds makers have chipped in. Could easily be as much as fifty. I will handle all arrangements. Think of the money!"

Mother straightened and looked hard at the man. "Sir, ten thousand pounds would not avail a dead woman. There is reason she is called mad. She has killed more than one of her opponents. She was to have been hung, but it could not be proven that she knew what she was doing in her madness, and so she went to Bedlam. Surely you know this. Everyone knows it. She is famous for her bloodlust and will not stop when told. What say you to that?"

"Very likely more than fifty pounds, I say. And I say, too, that she is entirely reformed. She has learned her lesson and wants to return to the ring, much as you have returned. We have convinced the house there is no chance of the previous regrettable lapses. More, I am myself convinced of it. I give you my word. Very, very large purse. Will it please you to meet her? If you like, you may speak to her. Why not watch her fight? Do come next Tuesday, at four in the afternoon. Make your decision then."

And so the following Tuesday afternoon, Mother and I made our way to Figg's, and, paying sixpence each, found the place filled nearly to capacity. We took our places in the third row, and had not long to wait before the fighters emerged, the first being Mrs. Phepoe, a grim, stout, half-bald thing of pocked face and much soiled linen skirt, whom one would have thought too old for fighting. She went iron-faced to her corner and sat glowering at the floor in front of her feet.

Next, from the dressing rooms emerged Meg the Madwoman to a chorus of hoots and jeers, stripping to the waist as she went to her corner. Meg was a head taller than Mrs. Phepoe, very large in every aspect, and quite pear-shaped. Her shoulders were broad, and her back and arms muscular, but her hips were wider yet, and her arse massive above gargantuan, much-dimpled thighs. Her coarse face displayed small, dark eyes rather too close together, beneath very thick brows. Her nose was much flattened and pushed to one side, and her small, endlessly working mouth displayed but a few overly large teeth set all at wrong angles. Graying hair sprouted stringy and unkempt from a patchwork scalp featuring numerous small sores, while great, flabby breasts descended nearly to her waist; and from her arose a ripe, sickly, and curiously penetrating stench, which soon caused me to think rather more favorably of our neighborhood dung heap. The platform shuddered with each of her steps, and as she went to her corner, she stole glances at the crowd, in a manner at once flirtatious and craven.

Mother was unimpressed. "As big and stupid as that thing is, she'll be no match for a quick and skilled fighter, given a fresh breeze and a bit of luck," but I was not so sure.

The fight was for a long while inconclusive. Mrs. Phepoe easily ducked the wild swings of the Madwoman, who, in spite of her heavy breathing and spastic ejaculations of uninventive cursing, appeared not to be able to see well. If Mrs. Phepoe's blows had scant effect on her mountainous opponent, neither did Meg take any toll on her, as every one of her wild swings went wide, until Mrs. Phepoe, displaying an unexpected agility, succeeded in tripping Meg, landing several sharp jabs to her face as she went down. The Madwoman fell like a load of bricks from an overturned wagon and did not rise until the judge had declared Mrs. Phepoe the victor.

Mother was pleased. "It is just as I said. She is huge and dangerous, but slow and stupid. She is not the fighter she once was. I shall trounce her just as Mrs. Phepoe did." She turned to share her sanguine observations with several individuals seated nearby who were curious to know the perceptions and sentiments of a woman fighter, but I kept my eyes on the Madwoman. It seemed to me she rose none the worse for wear, and rather too easily for one who a moment before had been laid flat. Her small mouth twitched a half smile as she went to the dressing room, taking no notice of the severely pleased Mrs. Phepoe, or of the jeering crowd. I mentioned my concerns to Mother but she dismissed them, saying it did not matter. "I have seen how she moves. That is what is important. I know I can best her."

IV

MOTHER'S FIGHT WITH MEG THE Madwoman was scheduled for noon a fortnight thereafter, and Mother trained hard during the intervening period, carrying ever heavier baskets, dancing many a jig, and punching at shadows. As she now possessed a certain notoriety, woman fighters generally assumed to be of questionable virtue, she was often challenged by saucy young men who wanted only to raise her ire, but she cared nothing for their foolish jibes. "Buy my oysters, as it's plain you have none of your own," she would laugh. "When you are no longer a-sucking at your mother's teat, find me then, and I will show you what it is to be bested by a woman!"

On the day of the fight, Mother and I arrived early. She went first to the wagering office, where she deposited on her own behalf a purse jingling with gold, and learned that in the minds of the bookmakers she was very much the underdog. Meg was not only undefeated, but had rediscovered her savagery of late, pummeling nearly to pieces a series of contenders during the fortnight. None had died, but, said the man at the wagering wicket, "She did sit on one and very nearly smothered the woman."

"I will bite a nice piece out of her bum if she tries any such thing on me," returned Mother, who headed to the dressing room as I went to her corner and laid in water and linen, William's master not having seen fit to give him the day's liberty.

And then the fight was to begin. Mother first entered the ring to encouraging cheers, and then Meg appeared to jeers and catcalls. She paused, and a none-too-fresh fish thrown from the crowd struck her breast. She whirled about and bellowed that they should all go to hell after she had broken them every one in pieces, to which a wag safely in the back row cried out that rotten fish smelled better than she did. Howling, Meg ran for the ropes and began to climb over them in an effort to reach the offender, but she was restrained by two very large and strong men, whom I gathered were employed by Mr. Clegg at the insistence of the house to prevent Meg from doing more damage than might be profitable.

The fight progressed at first much as had that between Meg and Mrs. Phepoe, Mother continually evading Meg's predictable, wide swings, and Mother landing frequent blows which, however, had no discernible effect. Mother danced backwards as the heavier woman doggedly stalked her whilst continually swinging. Mother took but the briefest of instants to look behind her to see how close to the ropes she was, when Meg hit Mother with a full-force blow to her jaw that sent her sprawling to the mat. Mother did not stay down, but had no more than half risen before Meg hit her as hard again full in the face first with one, then the other fist, and would have kept going had not the two guards each seized an arm and pulled her back. Meg almost immediately wrenched herself free, and to the vast and raucous delight of the crowd, forgot Mother, and flailed at and cursed her keepers. It was diversion enough that Mother was able to crawl to her corner where she took water, and I attempted to stanch the flow of blood from her nose and eye. I was hopeful she might concede, but to my dismay Mother would not surrender. The two guards stood between Mother's corner and the Madwoman, who circled, heaving and blowing in the center of the ring, her piggy eyes those of an enraged beast. Mother strode out to face her again.

For a time it did seem Mother might prevail in spite of the early reversal, and she succeeded in bloodying Meg's nose and tripping her down not once but thrice. Each time, Meg rose immediately and stormed ever more furiously, until at last she succeeded in landing a titanic blow under Mother's chin which lifted Mother up and then caused her to fall backwards, hitting the back of her head very hard against an oaken post. She slumped to the mat and lay still. When she did not rise, the judge lifted high Meg's paw and declared her the victor, to which the crowd replied with a chorus of the most vehement and sustained boos and hisses.

V

I RAN TO MOTHER'S SIDE and saw that she breathed, but was dismayed she would not waken. The barber-surgeon employed by the house opined that it was impossible to know if she might live or die, but if she lived, she might continue insensible for a protracted period. Mr. Clegg expressed his most sincere and entirely humble regret and wishes for her speedy recovery, extending to me a leathern pouch containing a number of coins. "There's five pounds here, which you and your mother are most welcome to. A consolation prize, if you will. If she recovers, and if she would like to fight again, please do come to see me. You can always find me here."

There was nothing for it but to hire a hackney carriage, put Mother into it, and take her home. We laid her across the seat, and I sat beside the driver. With the help of the draper and his wife, we carried her up to our chambers and put her to bed, where she lay for a day and a half before coming around. When she could speak, she complained of a very fierce headache and blurry vision, and soon vomited. She wished the curtains kept drawn, wanting no light or noise, which was an impossibility given the perpetual din in the street, but we did try to keep it down by covering the window and keeping all doors shut. "When am I to fight Meg?" she wanted to know. "I must prepare myself, but my head hurts so ..."

I told her what had happened, but she would not remember it from one hour to the next, and would again insist she must ready herself to fight, and wonder anew why did her head hurt so? After numerous iterations, she finally began to recall, and even then the details would again and again escape her. Worse, as her strength slowly returned, she displayed a most uncustomary irritability, which Sarah and myself both became objects of. At other times she would cry, which she had never done. I learned she had wagered thirty pounds on the contest, hoping to realize double, if not triple, the amount, none of which could now be recovered. There was no money other than the five pounds Mr. Clegg had provided, from which numerous expenditures had already been made. If managed very carefully, it would last two months, perhaps a little longer. One piece of luck was that the Waterman's guild retained a physician, one Dr. Goodpenny, a rotund man of about fifty, whose services were available to us without cost, but he was not encouraging. He noted Mother might well survive for years in this condition, but full recovery and restoration of her prior vigor was unlikely. He recommended heavy application of mercury and frequent bleeding, but when pressed could not guarantee their efficacy. As the decision was mine to make, and I had little faith in doctors and less money, the treatment was foregone. I have ever since wondered whether I made the right decision.

The situation was dire, and the more so that Mother was for some weeks unable to return to Billingsgate. When she did return, she had indifferent success and seemed confused by the taunts and saucy remarks, which would anger or dismay her. There was none of the ready repartee at which she had formerly excelled. Soon she began to suffer men to visit her in our lodgings, during which intervals Sarah and I were required to wait in the street below. This soon caused us all to be thrown out. It was a blessing, although of course it did not seem so at the time, when early in the third night of our sleeping for a penny each in a common lodging house in which a score or more slept on the bare floor of a single room, she took a great fit and died. With the last of the funds remaining from her consolation prize, I paid to have her body removed to the parish, where they put her into the pauper's pit. Sarah and I now faced the future, penniless and alone.

VI

ONCE MOTHER'S BODY HAD BEEN taken away, Sarah and I walked the several miles from the lodging house in Holborn to Waterman's Hall beside the Thames just above London Bridge, not so very far from our former home. Applying within, we found Dr. Goodpenny in the act of leaving. He was just setting out to see a waterman who had fallen down the hatch of a lighter and broken an ankle and perhaps more. We followed him as he exited the Hall and walked to his gig, conversing as we went.

"Bugger thought he would help himself to a nice bit of tea and cocoa, but of course he had to do it in the dark, and the hatch having been left open, down he went." Dr. Goodpenny laughed, but neither Sarah nor I were in the mood for levity. I explained our situation, and the Doctor immediately became grave. "I do believe I can make arrangements to see the both of you looked after, but it will take some time. Rather than simply wait here, I insist you attend a church service to pray for your mother's soul." He took his watch from his pocket and looked at it. "Do you know St. Michael Royal?"

Sarah and I averred that we did, as it was very near our former lodgings. We did not mention neither of us had ever been inside.

"There will be a service starting within the hour. Go there, attend the service, and then wait for me there. I expect to return for you not long after noon, if all goes well." And with that, he jumped in his gig, snapped the reins, and headed east to meet his patient.

Sarah and I walked to the church, where, as the Doctor had predicted, services were about to begin. We hesitated, watching a prosperous throng file in, but could not quite muster the resolve to enter. We felt conspicuous in our unwashed and tatty clothes, and unaccustomed as we were to church, nothing would pertain. Grief rendered us numb to the blandishments of pretty music, and I failed to see what good prayers could do, as Mother was dead, and if she did survive in spirit with reason restored, she was more than capable of interceding with God on her own behalf.

Thankful to be ignored, we skulked around to the lee of the building and waited. The weather was typical for November, dank, gloomy, and cold, and we huddled against the damp wind and listened to the muffled sounds of the service coming through the windows. After some time, the service ended and the congregation exited, but there was no sign of Dr. Goodpenny.

A cold, steady rain set in, accompanied by a stronger, fitful wind, and we retired to the shelter of the church's doorway. The church door was now bolted shut, but as it was well recessed we were able to stand, and then sit, as time wore on, out of the rain. Several hours more passed before Dr. Goodpenny returned, by which time we had grown very cold, damp, and hungry indeed. He smelled strongly of spirits and behaved with an unaccustomed alacrity of manner in stark contrast to his previously sober mien. He told us he had had great luck in making arrangements for the both of us, and we were to be settled straightaway. I found myself strangely without curiosity as to my destination, but was shocked to learn that Sarah and I were to be separated.

"There's no help for it, I'm afraid," he said, wobbling. "Your parish workhouse is full to bursting, and nowhere else takes both boys and girls, ah, short of a prison, that is." He essayed a grotesque chuckle, and I hated him. "Sarah could do worse than Bridewell, actually, and they are prepared to receive her. Eleven-year-old girls are just the thing there, but they have no use for sixteen-year-old boys. I have got you another placement, Joe, and it was the devil to do it. No one wants boys your age. Well, you are as much man now as boy, and that's the thing. Short of going straight into an apprenticeship, for which you are rather too old in any case, there are very few opportunities. Very few, indeed, but I happen to know of a charity school that does take older boys and have just barely managed to get you into it."

I heard the man speaking, but his words did not register. Bridewell and a charity school? It was inconceivable. But, having no choice, we loaded ourselves into the Doctor's uncovered gig and resigned ourselves to a long, wet ride through town.

We rode on and on. The streets were quiet, as none were out but those who had to be. At first, Dr. Goodpenny mumbled a bit about what a pity it was, and about God looking out for unfortunate children, but as neither of us answered him, he soon trailed off and took to humming to himself as he drove. We rattled through St. Paul's churchyard and on through Ludgate to Bridewell, where Sarah hugged me, trembling, while I kissed her. Dr. Goodpenny said she would learn useful skills there and go on to service. Losing bright and lively Sarah that day was, among the many losses I have suffered, one of the very nearest to my heart and a poignant source of continuing sorrow, but there was no help for it.

We then turned about and recrossed the city, arriving in the gathering dark in front of a grim brick and timber building of no recent construction in Little Eastcheap. I learned later it had been built after the Great Fire as a foundry, but the improvident owner had lost all in the South Seas bubble, and the building, with lodgings for apprentices and laborers, family quarters for the master, a large yard in the rear which opened on a lane, and several very large rooms which had once housed the furnaces and foundry, had been converted to its present purpose of charity school.

A single lamp shone through a small leaded window. To the left of the door, just above the bell handle, was a small sign. I asked Dr. Goodpenny what it said. He turned towards me and seemed to want to put his arm around me but did not, and his aborted gesture resulted in an awkward feint of no clear purpose.

Fixing me with a rheumy eye, and assuming a counterfeit brightness, he said, "Ah, this, m'lad, this, this here is the Little Eastcheap Free School for Unfortunate Boys, one of which you now are. You are quite a bit older than most of the boys here, but I am assured by the Governor that if you don't mind working hard, they will house and feed you, and very likely even school you some. Now, they are Dissenters, but that is no crime, and if you do well, you may go to a proper apprenticeship in a year or two, despite your age. It is not altogether too late. I did not think I could get you in here, and it's a small miracle, but they have a very few openings for someone older and stronger like you, and, to be honest, there really is no other place for you to go just now."

A charity school, in which one was penned in, force-fed sanctimonious prattle, and called a blackguard if one dared not like it, was the last place I had ever imagined myself. I had seen groups of such boys on Sunday afternoons, the only time they were ever let out, doleful, underfed, and dressed with uniform shabbiness, each one complete with the very badge of utter subservience, all the while suffering the barked instructions of hectoring mentors. I would rather have been sold for a sweep's 'prentice and face black smothering death, than be so imprisoned in body and soul. I seized, instead, on the question of a "proper" apprenticeship, which I was certain was now as unattainable as to hold the moon in one's hands.

"An apprenticeship? How? To what? That takes money! A lot of money. Twenty or thirty pounds for anything at all good. If I'm not to be a waterman, how can I be anything? Mother lost all her money. You know that." I was too deeply in shock to rise above petulance.

Dr. Goodpenny landed his hand clumsily on my shoulder. "You didn't know, lad? Your father deposited a shilling or two most weeks with us for many years, and your mother put a portion of her earnings and prizes in as well. A sixpence here, a shilling there, to say nothing of a guinea now and then, well, my lad, it adds up. This fund has now grown to just over fifty pounds, and it's entirely for that purpose."

I stared at him with perfect stupidity, saying nothing. This was all news to me.

"Didn't know that, eh?" he continued. "Well, that's the kind of man your father was. And your mother too. Er, only she was a woman. Anyhow, the both of them wanted you to rise, you see. Others would have spent it all as it came, but not Tom or Maggie Chapman." I nearly gagged on gales of spirituous stench. "I won't be a minute," he said, getting out of the gig. "They are expecting us, and I just need to make the final arrangements."

In his absence, I looked at the steaming horse and the black rain. I knew better than to argue, or worse, run, although I had the impulse. But I had seen too many ragged, homeless youths sleeping in doorways, or slavering like animals over the dry bread or nearly-turned fish Mother would sometimes toss them. If they lived long enough, they were scooped up by the press gang. If they didn't, it was because they died in the gutter of a fever or by starvation or a knife fight, or, as very often happened, as a result of a little appointment with Jack Ketch, which is to say they were hung because they had been caught thieving.

Recalling the many pointed observations my father had made upon life and those we may be blessed or cursed to share it with, I was determined not to be one of those vanquished by misfortune. What little religious instruction I had been given played into this, and I solemnly resolved that if my parents were indeed looking down on me as I had been encouraged to believe they might, they would not see anything in my behavior to distress them. This thought brought the beginnings of quiet tears, which I accepted with simple grace. I discovered in myself, beneath and behind the tears, an impassive bedrock of resolute calm. I had been shaken to my very foundations, but would discover them sound.

VII

No SOONER HAD I COMPLETED these meditations than Dr. Goodpenny reappeared and indicated I was to follow him inside. Daubing dry my eyes, I brought with me the small bundle containing the remnants of my former life and crossed the threshold. We entered a narrow foyer lit only by a single candle resting on a sconce. Musty and sour odors stole into my nostrils, and the floorboards creaked as we walked. Soon we entered a small office in which we found the headmaster, writing at a large desk near a bright and congenial fire. This gentleman, as I was to learn, was the august Mr. Peevers, Governor of the school, and an important figure in his congregation.

However that may have been, Mr. Peevers was not encouraging in person. Despite our having come in out of the cold and wet, he did not extend his hand or invite us to take off our greatcoats or step closer to the fire. A small, downturned mouth, long, hooked nose, and darting piggy eyes were pasted incongruously onto a broad, fleshy visage of pale and oleaginous complexion. His wig was ill-fitting and in dire want of powder, and his black, tent-like, and not so very clean clothes had a rumpled and chagrined air, as if they knew they could expect no help from him and would have to fend for themselves. Later, I would have ample, if unwelcome, opportunity to observe that his large, doughy frame culminated in an appallingly broad posterior.

Mr. Peevers turned in his seat and regarded us without expression, causing Dr. Goodpenny to become all things obsequious. "Ahem, uh, Mr. Peevers, this here's the lad what I was telling you about. Comes very well recommended, he does. Parents, as I said, were real solid people. Loves to work hard. Joe, say good evening to Mr. Peevers."

"Good evening, sir," said I, to the large, peculiar form.

Mr. Peevers eyed me with a curiously penetrating gaze. "Joseph Chapman," he said, seeming to taste my name. "Joseph Chapman. Welcome. How fortunate that we are able to provide this most necessary haven for you. Are you grateful, young Joseph?" His voice was higher than I would have expected, his tone a curious combination of sanctimony and entreaty.

"I believe I am, sir. That is, I would like to be. What I mean is, yes, sir. I am, sir." There was scarcely a word of truth in it. Mr. Peevers's aspect was unsettling. But I was thinking of the black rain and of the riverside's soaked wharves, where one might sleep with rats and gulls, and I thought of wandering with my mother when she was not herself. Mr. Peevers's fire was warm.

"You shall have ample opportunity to demonstrate that gratitude, Master Chapman. You must give us your all, without holding back." His eyes bore into me. "You will apply yourself to improvement. We trust," he said, rising slightly in his seat and leaning forward to stare at me with a newly discovered intensity of expression, "that you bring with you no evil habits to upset or contaminate our correct and peaceful school?" As he pronounced the word "evil" his voice squeaked and his dark, little eyes bulged.

"Certainly not, sir. I have no idea what you can even mean, sir." I did, in fact, have some idea and wondered what someone like him could possibly know of it.

Mr. Peevers's tone became sharp. "Don't give me that rubbish, young man! Every boy has evil thoughts and must struggle to conquer them. Here you will learn to keep yourself pure and to be Godly."

"I do look forward to that, sir." I managed the facsimile of a small, contrite smile, meaning none of it. Upon my conciliatory reply, he regarded me anew with the same curiously penetrating gaze, and it seemed like a very long time before he spoke again. As he sat, and Dr. Goodpenny and I stood, aromas of a meal being prepared reached us from the kitchen. I realized I was very hungry.

"You will waste no time settling in then," he said at last. "I will direct the Matron to get you started." He gave the bell rope a vigorous yank, and a spindly old woman well into her sixties scurried into the chamber carrying a small candle lantern. This creature was of medium height and, like Mr. Peevers, attired in severest black. Very pale, papery skin creased everywhere by innumerable fine wrinkles gathered itself here and there to form her features, and she regarded Mr. Peevers, Dr. Goodpenny, and me with impartial distaste with her one good eye, even as the other fixed upon the wall.

Avoiding her gaze, Mr. Peevers spoke. "Eh, Miss Strickenwell, I present to you Master Chapman, who will reside with us. Put him in room four, with masters Ranlet, Gorham, and the other older boys." Having said this, and seeming to require no rejoinder or comment from the impatient matron, who gave every air of having been interrupted at some vastly important task, he dismissed us with a wave of his hand.

Miss Strickenwell looked at the back of Mr. Peevers's head a moment, as if she would say something, and then she turned to me. There played about her fissured and thinly compressed lips a series of spastic movements perhaps intended as a smile and perhaps not.

"Eh, very well then, come with me," she said at last, in a clipped voice at once high-pitched and raspy. With an alacrity I would have thought quite beyond one so aged and apparently underfed, she darted through a door opposite the one through which we had entered. I began to follow her, and then thought of my manners. I paused and turned about to take my leave of the two gentlemen, only to see they had already ceased to take any notice of me. Mr. Peevers was dropping several golden guineas into Dr. Goodpenny's hand. Goodpenny was chuckling softly, and Mr. Peevers emitted a short series of spastic snorts, as if he would have liked to laugh, but did not quite know how.

Turning to follow Miss Strickenwell, I regained the foyer, where a large looking glass hung on the wall opposite the entry. In it, I saw a not unhandsome, nearly grown boy with dark hair and large, brown eyes. He was of middling size in a cheap, tatty and none too clean greatcoat, appearing rather anxious. I confess to finding some fascination in it, so as to compare myself to my peers, when I heard, already from a considerable distance, Miss Strickenwell bark, "Hurry up!" upon which I left off and tumbled after her.

VIII

Miss Strickenwell darted down the dark corridor, turned left, ascended two flights of stairs, turned left again, and dashed down another hallway without so much as a backwards glance. It was all I could do to keep up. We climbed another flight of stairs and arrived at an attic corridor having a series of identical doors on both sides. Hauling up short in front of one of these, she looked impatiently in my direction and waited for me.

"You'll have to do better than that if you want to succeed here," said she, regarding me coldly with her one steady eye. Her tone was severe, accompanied by another of her spastic grimaces. "We've no time for dawdlers. Now then, here's where you will sleep. You'll have precious little time to spend here otherwise." So saying, she threw open the door to a small room into which were crammed two large beds and an assortment of rough cabinets. Insects scurried to flee the feeble light cast by her swinging lantern, which weakly illuminated a sloping ceiling, cracked plaster, and a dormer window flanked by two settles running the length of the wall. To one side on a low table stood a wash basin and ewer.

"You shall have this side of this bed," she said, pointing, "and this cabinet for your clothes and other things. Your uniform will be ready tomorrow, so you will need whatever clothes you have brought Sundays only. Now, child, sit down and

I will explain the rules." I sat on the side of the bed and listened. My coat was still on, and I remained damp. Heavy rain beat against the black window. The room was cold, and Miss Strickenwell's breath visible.

"We must have nothing less than your total obedience and a willing spirit at all times. You shall rise at six daily, and at seven on Sundays. Breakfast is at six thirty. Lessons are from seven to eleven, when you may have half an hour for your necessaries, and dinner is at eleven thirty. From a quarter past noon until five you shall card with the other boys. Supper is at five fifteen, and then card again, or as Mr. Peevers directs, from six until nine. We say prayers at all meals and again before bed."

"Ma'am?" I asked. "Card?"

"Card *wool*. Don't be a ninny. Since we don't charge our students, we must keep the place going somehow. Should you prove to be at all able, perhaps you shall be given other duties. Any other questions?" This last was delivered in a tone as unlikely to encourage curiosity as it was possible to imagine. I was beyond caring what the old prune thought, however, and though it rattle her sensibilities would hazard not one but two more questions.

"What happened to the boy who was here before me?" Having in my own instance a fair example of how boys arrived at this place, I was already wondering how they might be caused to depart it, hoping the knowledge would soon prove useful.

"He was an ungrateful, obstreperous boy given to telling sordid lies. Mr. Peevers had to turn him out, and I'm sure that's very much more than you really need to know."

"Oh." I felt a sudden sympathy for the boy, who had been, perhaps, even more unfortunate than I. I went on to the next question, although I did not expect any sort of informative response. "Do you know why Mr. Peevers gave money to Dr. Goodpenny just now?"

"If it was not for a link boy, I'm quite sure I have no idea," she sniffed. "You may be sure concerning yourself with the affairs of your betters will lead you to no good. If you are wise, you will have no curiosity whatsoever about other people and will attend faithfully to your lessons and to your work. Now then, it is nearly five, and I shall leave you. Your room mates will be up shortly to ready for supper. You will pick up the schedule then and carry on from there." She lit a candle from her lantern, placed it, turned, and bolted from the room.

I was alone at last, and so changed into my much rumpled dry clothes that had been wadded up in my bundle, hanging my wet coat and breeches on a peg which seemed suited to the purpose, and then I sat, weary and desolate, and studied the room. There was little to indicate the individuality of the other boys who slept there. I wondered especially about the boys whose bed I would share. Would they smell bad, or toss about and jab me with bony knees and elbows, or sleep with sweet serenity? And would any of them snore or be heavy breathers?

Having no strength for extended speculation, I moved from sitting to lying down on the bed. The mattress was straw, and not fresh. The pillow, though, was stuffed with washed wool and not so bad. As I turned and plumped it, a scrap of paper fell out of the casing, upon which appeared a small amount of writing. I recognized a B and several E's, but could make neither head nor tail of it over all. It looked like this:

BEWARE PEEVERS

Never had I wished more fervently that I could read. I decided to save the paper until I might have acquired a trusted confidant or could read it myself. This dismal place could not entirely avoid imparting knowledge, I thought, and if I did, in fact, learn to read, perhaps the gloom would have been worth it.

At this moment, I heard the sound of a bell ringing somewhere below, soon to be followed by many footsteps on the stairs, accompanied by coughing rather than the sounds of talk or laughter one might expect from a large group of boys. In another moment, the door was opened, and in walked as sorry a lot as I had ever seen. Their frames were spindly, and their faces drawn and dirty. Several were encased in a furry envelope of innumerable woolen fibers, such that they appeared scarcely human. Others bore the marks of service in other occupations.

Their uniforms, such as they were, were simple, but over all rather less offensive than some I had seen, consisting of a pair of dark brown breeches and a white shirt, affixed to which was a small shield-like badge. Evidently, however, the school's wise and moral directors found the custom of allowing a reasonable relationship between the size of one's clothing and the size of one's frame to be an example of worldly vanity which it would improve their charges to forbear, as the sleeves of several reached no more than two-thirds of the way to their wrists, and on others had been pushed up to avoid extending well beyond.

A similar state of affairs could be discerned with respect to their breeches. But it was the badges which drew my eye above all else. Here was the very shame of poverty, trumpeting the school's, and its benefactor's, glorious benevolence, but most of all one's own meanness. I would not have thought it possible, imagining as I did that I was already as low as I could go, but my spirits sank yet further at the sight.

"Ooo, lookit 'im loungin' like a very lord!" This encomium was offered by the first boy through the door, in a voice hollow with fatigue, yet which retained enough youthful strength to apply a liberal coating of taunt. He was a bit taller than the rest, and his frame appeared strong, despite the rigors of undernourishment and overwork. He sported flaming red hair, and his face might have been handsome, but between the dirt and the dim light, I couldn't really tell.

"Shut your trap, eh, Poxy?" came the nearly immediate rejoinder, in an equally weary voice from the next lad, who went about his business without taking any notice of me. This boy had, it appeared, little to fear from Poxy, who, although he occasionally sent me challenging looks, seemed not to have heard the retort. Although most of the boys seemed to interact with a degree of cooperation and forbearance, they studiously ignored Poxy. I took my cues from the greater part of them and ignored him too.

"What's your name, eh? Mine's Chowder." This was from a skinny, dark-haired youth of medium height who lacked the coating of woolen fibers worn by the others. When he extended his hand, I saw his hands and forearms were red and raw as a washerwoman's; and yet, he was not unappealing. His wan face was intelligent, and his large brown eyes struck me as kind and reassuring. He was my age, or perhaps slightly older.

"Joe," I said, sitting up. "Joe Chapman." I gave him as level a gaze as I could and shook his hand, trying to appear at once friendly and as tough as any of them, should they wish to try me. "I don't suppose Chowder's your real name, is it?"

"Naw. Potter Gorham's my real name, and you can have it if you like." He sat upon the bed and pulled off his shirt, revealing a hollow chest and stick-like arms. Turning his head and looking at Poxy, who had been monopolizing the washstand, he inquired, "Going to be all day?"

Poxy assumed an air of offended dignity and spoke in measured tones. "Chowder, I know how much you would like to kiss my arse. Why don't you come here and show your new molly friend how it's done?" So saying, he lowered his breeches and bent over, revealing all. Chowder, rolling his eyes, ignored him. For my part, I had no idea whether this was intended as the gravest of insults or as a lesser, playful, taunt, the sort of thing that went on every day. Nor had I any idea what was meant by the term *molly*. I had but the briefest of moments to wonder, as another boy, of merrily mischievous round face and muscular arms, administered a crackling slap on Poxy's exposed posterior with the tail of his shirt, which he had just removed, and had handy for the purpose.

Wheeling about in anger, Poxy roared, "Damn you, Nails!" and would have lunged at him had his breeches not been about his ankles, which now became a matter of no small inconvenience. As he attempted to run at Nails, Poxy fell full length on the floor. Several of the boys laughed. Nails calmly informed Poxy that there were plenty more where that had come from, should he wish to collect them. Rather than accept the challenge, Poxy fell to muttering threats and curses, and without creating more spectacle, rose and dressed himself.

Suddenly the door flew open, blowing out both of the candles in the room— the one Miss Strickenwell had lit, and the one carried in by the boys. In the doorway stood a severe, spare man in late middle age, dressed as were the others of his station entirely in scholastic black, who bayed at us, very like a hound. "What in the thundering name of God is going on in here? I've heard enough to have you all thrown out!" I wondered how that could be true, as of the six boys only two had made more than a very modest amount of noise. I decided to query the point at some later date, as the gentleman whose ire we now faced made a forbidding picture of offended authority. "Half supper for you all tonight! Have you not those clean shirts on yet? Hurry! I said, hurry!" He threw the door closed, leaving us in the dark.

Where but a moment before the room had been charged with tension, all was now quiet.

"I thought this was a school, not Bedlam," I ventured, never one to be shy when there would be no point to it. "Who was *that?*"

"Damn him," said one of the boys to the blackness. "Damn his putrid everlasting soul."

Another voice spoke, this time directed at me. "It ain't Bedlam. It's worse. There the people what's locked inside are daft and the guards ain't, or so they say. Here it's the opposite, mostly. And you don't get used to it."

"That was Rennet," said another, whose name I later learned was Spithead. "*Mister* Rennet. He's Peevers's head teacher. Teaches and directs, he does. Likes to think he does, anyway. Gawd, but I hate him. Is anybody going to get a light?"

One of the other boys departed and returned momentarily with a small boy bearing a candle. The boy's face bore marks of sadness, and his little frame was partly misshapen, causing him to limp. He lit our candles from his.

"Thanks, Nimbles," said Nails. "Are you feeling any better?" The answer was delivered by a shake of the head, and the little boy withdrew.

Having confronted the collective enemy, a spirit of cooperation emerged, and the boys splashed water on their faces and all dried themselves with the same filthy towel. Clean shirts were applied to dirty frames, and soon a bell rang in the corridor. Out of the rooms lining the hall filed dozens of boys, and I filed along with them, having made myself as presentable as I could. I had but one white shirt, which I had been wearing for days. I hoped it would not excite interest on the part of Mr. Rennet or Mr. Peevers. I had managed to forget about him for a moment, but now remembered with disquiet his queer aspect and patronizing admonitions, and determined to avoid him as much as I could, if I could. As I walked down the hallway in the line of boys, I became aware of a need that had not been attended to. As Chowder was just ahead of me I addressed my query to him.

"Er, Chowder?"

"What's that?"

"Where does one piss around here?"

"There's a W.C. at the other end of the hall. But hurry. You don't want to be late downstairs. Believe me, you don't."

Having so recently observed Mr. Rennet in full cry, I doubted it not a whit, but nature was not to be denied. I turned and worked my way against the tide of boys until I was past them, and I walked to the end of the hall where the reek indicated I would find the desired facility. I had to leave the door open in order to see, as there was but the single lantern in the hall. The stream of boys quickly drained down the circular stairway at the opposite end of the hall, and by the time I finished, I was alone.

IX

I RAN TO THE END of the hall, and followed the trail of the others down the stairs. Strangely, on reaching the bottom, although I was but a minute or two behind, not a soul was to be seen or heard. I stood and listened, hoping to hear the sounds of an assemblage at meal time, but to my rising concern heard nothing.

Not knowing which way to turn, I chose a direction at random, setting forth down yet another dark corridor, which appeared to be in a state of disuse as I proceeded by several turns along its length. Curiosity now led me on, but as I rounded a last corner, I discovered the corridor was blind. I was just on the point of turning around when I heard muffled sounds issuing from behind a closed door at the very end. It sounded at first not unlike the moving of furniture, but soon were added a pair of male voices, one older and the other younger. I realized from their tone, and the more clearly apprehended nature of the other sounds, that I was overhearing the administration of blows upon some young unfortunate, which were far from being passively received. Unable to restrain my curiosity, I moved closer to the door, stood very still, and listened.

"I shan't, I tell you, I shan't! It's too horrible. You can't make me," wailed the younger.

"You shall, damn you, and you shall thank me for it!" bellowed the elder, in contrapuntal response. "Shut up, now, and take it!"

The voices continued in this way briefly, whereupon the younger voice became muffled, shortly following which the older barked in pain, emitting a string of fearsome curses. The sounds of struggle intensified and culminated in a scream from the younger voice as I stood transfixed. Then, suddenly remembering myself, I turned and ran the way I had come. Passing the stairway by which I had descended, I followed the corridor around another turn and emerged at last into the dining hall, where perhaps four score boys aged from six or seven through the middle and even late teens, and half a dozen mentors, sat in stony silence, heads bowed over deal tables and empty shallow bowls of plainest wood.

The hall was hewn of rough timbers dark with smoke and age, and the black ceiling was low. Dingy, lettered banners hung on the walls in places. The boys were all similar, if on the whole several years younger, to those to whom I had already been introduced, and sat eight to a table. These were arranged in rows, soup kettles and cutting boards at the head of each, attended by functionaries closer to my own age. These, too, kept their heads bowed. There was one candle for each table, and precious few more in sconces along the walls, so that the penurious gloom so in evidence elsewhere in the establishment did not fail to obtain here as well. A very small coal fire in a very large fireplace but mocked the want of heat and light.

I surveyed all this and more in an instant. Mr. Rennet stood before a considerably better sort of table on a dais, where sat Miss Strickenwell and several others whom I had not yet had the pleasure of meeting. Nimbles stood in attendance on them, though his chin barely cleared the table. The boys from my room sat together below the dais, at a table of their own. I salivated at the fine smell of roasted meat and baked bread in the air. Sharp pains arose in my stomach, and I felt weak.

Mr. Rennet spotted my entrance, and, looking at me sideways, offered grace. "For all these mercies we receive, we give eternal thanks to Heaven's high King." Near a hundred heads swiveled in my direction, not a one of them overflowing with kindness. Come between a man and his meal and you will see his true nature, I suppose. "Master Chapman, we are indeed pleased by your presence. Kindly seat yourself here in front next your room-mates." As I fulfilled this request, the hundred heads swiveled to follow me. When I sat between Chowder and the glaring Poxy, Mr. Rennet began again.

"Lord, we apologize for these sinners whose example we may avoid, such as this weak and tardy boy, and these improper and argumentative youngsters who sit before us. We pray they may soon see the error of their ways and long remember the inconvenience and displeasure they have caused their peers and betters, to say nothing of their affront to you, O Lord. A-*meh*." He was very clever to make a spectacle of a confused and sorrowing boy, useful as I was for the enhancement of order and discipline in the establishment, but I cannot say I appreciated the attention or saw any necessity for it. You may call me a blackguard, if you like. I don't care.

Mr. Rennet now struck a bell mounted on the table as a signal for the meal to begin. From each table, boys rose and filed to where a small bowl of brownish soup or thin stew, a slice of bread, and a cup of water were dispensed to each. No one stirred from the table at which I sat, however, and I followed their example from necessity, if not from inclination.

"When do *we* eat?" I asked, in a meek and wondering voice, to nobody in particular.

"Shut *up!*" seethed Poxy in low tones, and in lower still breathed "Gawd!"

None of the others would look at me, save Chowder, who stole a brief glance in my direction. I thought I discerned a glint of compassion there, for which I loved him.

We sat in this condition until all the others had been served, during which time a fine joint, a pig's head, roast potatoes, and boiled tripe and cabbage were laid before Mr. Rennet and the others, which they proceeded to demolish with convivial alacrity. Nimbles brought them tea, milk, and bread and butter as they wanted it. I had to force myself to stop watching them, but the smells got to me anyhow.

The boys at the other tables were finished within a few moments of sitting down, as their hunger interfered with the niceties of refined dining. However, the meal of our betters, as they styled themselves, went on for some time. When I thought I really could stand it no longer, Mr. Rennet indicated we were to be served, and we filed over to the nearest soup kettle, from which we were dispensed a meager amount of tepid, watery broth by a sneering youth of wondrously bad complexion, who also bestowed upon each of us a tiny morsel of bread and a cup of water.

We finished these tidbits in an instant. Just as I was mopping up the last drop, Mr. Peevers entered, strode to the head table, and said a few words in Mr. Rennet's ear. If he had been involved in the mysterious altercation I had overheard, he gave no sign of it, being no more disheveled than he had been when I had first seen him. His hair, in fact, was freshly slicked down, and he had a lightness to his step I would have thought unlikely in one so dour and heavy. Facing the hall and plumping himself up, he began to speak in his unpleasantly high and tremulous voice.

"Ah, the pleasure of good food amidst good company. How fortunate we are.

How fortunate, indeed, you are, to have the grace of this haven against the cold world. Fail not to show your appreciation to your betters and to God! This last is most important. Ingratitude against your fellow men is an insult, but against God is a sin. Remember that always." He paused a moment, and his face darkened. "It pains me to report Master Bell has had to be terminated, largely for obstinate ingratitude. I doubt not the Lord will look after him, even as I know we can no longer. Master Bell is at this moment being escorted to the workhouse, where he will not, you may be sure, enjoy the benefits so generously bestowed upon you here by your benefactors."

A number of the boys exchanged looks. "Not grateful? Peevers is daft, 'e is." This was Nails, whose face was dark with anger, speaking in low tones.

"Prayed 'is heart out every day," said Spithead.

"SHHH, Rennet's looking," said Chowder.

Mr. Peevers's face brightened again. "Speaking of our benefactors, Mrs. Winterbottom will visit next week. She is our—I should say, *your*—most important benefactor, as I am sure many of you will remember. She must be pleased by what she sees, so special cleaning will begin straight off tomorrow morning. Captains will meet immediately following supper." Having said this, he sat down and helped himself to large portions of boiled tripe, fat pig, and potatoes, to the ingestion of which he dedicated himself with rapt absorption. As he reached for his food, I saw he had a bandaged finger which had been unharmed during my interview perhaps an hour previously.

Having nothing else to do, we sat in admiration of the spectacle of our Governor at his repast, until at long last he finished and Mr. Rennet rang the bell. The boys stood as one and filed out, depositing their bowls on large oval trays. Most of the sneering youths who had served us strode importantly to the front, gathering before Mr. Rennet who began at once to crackle out a series of instructions. Peering in our direction with her good eye, Miss Strickenwell ordered me to go with Chowder, or Master Gorham, as she called him, to the scullery.

X

CHOWDER AND I WALKED TOGETHER to the rear of the dining hall, and in the bustle and clatter attendant upon the close of the meal, we were able to walk slowly without attracting attention or getting in yet more trouble. Teams of boys picked up trays of dirty plates, bowls, and spoons and carried them with much artful balancing to the rear, while others brushed crumbs onto the floor or pushed spilled soup into table tops with filthy rags.

"You are the lucky one, you know," said Chowder gloomily, much to my puzzlement.

"I'm sure I don't know how," said I, in similar tones. The meal we had just eaten had only aroused a hunger that might otherwise have lapsed unnoticed into dull lethargy. Now, it consumed my attention to the near exclusion of all else.

"You haven't seen it then, have you?" Chowder looked around himself warily.

"Seen what? I only just got here, you know." We were nearly to the scullery door.

"How they beat 'em. Us, I mean, sometimes. Use the cane." His doleful countenance betrayed a guileless heart. "Just t'other day they beat a lad who wasn't as late as you. Right here, before we eat. Rennet holds 'em and Peevers lays into 'em. Enjoy it, they do." He paused and looked at me. His large eyes held both pity and pain. "Where were you, anyhow?"

"I got lost coming down from upstairs. Went the wrong way." I was about to elaborate when a stentorian voice emanated from the scullery.

"Get your sorry carcasses in here *now*!" It was the very youth who had served us our meager portions, dressing them with such liberal dollops of contempt. "You! Chowder! Wash! You!" He was looking at me. "What's your name?"

"Joe," I replied evenly. Here was a troll if ever there was one. His alarming complexion suited his arrogant, sneering aspect well.

"Oho, good enough for a proper name, are you? I think I'll call you Snot! Snot you are, then! I say, Snot, rinse!" He pointed with absurd vehemence to an enormous oaken wash-tub of clear water, then exercised his charm similarly on several other boys, whose task it was to dry and stack the plates and bowls on the shelves which lined the steamy, close room.

I had never before been spoken to in that manner, even among the roughest denizens of the waterfront, as the esteem in which my father had been held radiated to me as his child, but I had already received so many shocks this day that I was insensible to the fresh application of brutality. He was older and bigger but slow and pudgy, and stupid as bullies are wont to be. I knew I could take him, but to challenge him would be unwise, for I was here without station or protector. This was not the time to try him, but to study him instead. So thinking, I complied without retort, which caused him no small disappointment. I would deprive him of his sport, to begin.

As the trays were brought in, the dishes on them were cleared of their very few adhering scraps by our solicitous overseer, who ate the better pieces and grinned at us while noisily sucking his fingers. He then set the well-licked wooden ware into Chowder's washtub, which was full of steaming soapy water. Chowder lifted them out piece by piece, scrubbed them, then placed them in my cold tub, whereupon I swirled them about, lifted them out, and handed them to the boy charged with drying. If there was more to be got off them, which was very seldom, I put them back in Chowder's tub. Periodically, yet another boy brought more hot water to Chowder's tub from a large kettle over a roaring coal fire in the back of the room. It was the first time I had been warm all day, and in the dampness I soon began to sweat.

Washing up took a very long time. As we neared the end of the ordinary ware, the china from Mr. Peevers's table appeared, as did the cooking pots, soup kettles, roasting pans, and utensils from the kitchen. Mr. Rennet peered in, but as we kept our heads down and worked like demons, he found nothing to become upset about and turned to have a word with Stubbs, as our overseer was named. While Stubbs's attention was diverted, Chowder gave me a knowing look and nodded his head in the direction of the freshly arrived, wonderfully substantial scraps on the china, pots, pans, and serving platters, while feigning dropping something, the sense of which I understood in an instant.

I returned my broadest grin in acknowledgment. We worked on, and when Mr. Rennet had been gone but a minute, Chowder, by apparently inadvertent clumsiness, sent not a dish, but an entire tray full of them, crashing to the floor. Half-eaten potatoes twirled and skittered across the floor, even as the remains of the joint and pig's head fell splat amongst the greasy shards. Excessively boiled tripe and cabbage spread themselves beneath us in limp aureoles, and Stubbs became hysterical.

"Again?! Arse-breath! A pox! You're a-going to Hell and no mistake! Clean it! Sweep it! Every crumb and shard! You! Snot-face! Leave off there! Clean this!" His outraged agitation, expressed as was all his speech with rigorous economy of vocabulary, was finely augmented by hysterical tones, no want of flying spittle, and wild gestures.

Chowder made a prolonged show of not knowing where the broom and mop were, complaining they had been moved since the last time, which occasioned further torrents of abuse from Stubbs, who had to fetch them from the kitchen himself.

During Stubbs's brief absence, we were all able to cram our mouths full, and then stuff the better portions of the potatoes into our pockets and shirts. The leftover pig and beef we packed into our breeches by means of a deft loosening of the knee buckles and a quick tuck. Chowder, nearest the door, was able to keep watch on Stubbs's departure and return, alerting us as he approached. After Stubbs had returned with the mop, Chowder proved singularly clumsy in its use, which inspired the rest of us to discover untapped resources of heroic ineptitude, which by turns diverted Stubbs to the benefit of one or another of us. By the time the mess was cleaned up, nothing remained of the feast that was not inside us, or safely stowed for later consumption.

Stubbs was in a state of white-lipped fury, but never once guessed what we were about. I, for the first time that day, felt a sense of comradeship and hope. Actual beef was stuffed into my breeches and potatoes were in my shirt. Although the others and I presented a rather lumpy aspect, Stubbs could not tell in the dim light. I could feel the potatoes against my skin, but as my shirt was full cut and loose, they did not show very much. The sensation of the greasy meat between my skin and breeches is not to be described.

We continued to work until every last tray, dish, and spoon were clean and put away or sent back to the kitchen. The tubs were drained and rinsed, and the scullery fire banked. We then set about preparing for the following morning's breakfast by placing serving utensils and stacks of bowls at each serving station.

No sooner was all done than I heard the infernal bell, and boys and mentors again assembled in the hall, now for evening prayers. Miss Strickenwell shrilled and rasped to God about how thankful and pathetic we were, and wouldn't He forgive our awful sins and put some sense into us obstinate children. Then she read some things that were very nice, about loving God and being his partner in a way by being kind to people. Those parts made sense to me, but I didn't care much for what went before or came after.

There was a lot more about sin and having great blots on one's soul that only God could wash out, which, however, was not as bad as it sounded, because all one had to do was believe that Jesus was God's son, and then everything would be all right, or as well as it might be. I couldn't fathom the connection and thought it simple minded, or perhaps it was just her way of trying to explain it. My head was swimming from exhaustion and the many extraordinary events of the day, to say nothing of the distraction of the meat sliding around in my breeches.

After many amens, we were dismissed to go upstairs. I filed along with the rest and was soon again in that dismal garret, with Chowder, Poxy, Nails, and the other two boys, Diddly and Spithead. Without ceremony, we all began to undress and make preparation for going to bed. It was even colder in the room than it had been earlier. As I began to unbutton my shirt, I saw through the window that the rain had stopped, and the moon was playing hide and seek with scudding clouds. A stiff wind now blew from the northeast, driving the temperature down towards freezing.

Having grown up on the water with my father, I was always aware of the weather, and as I reflected on this, I missed him with a sudden excess of emotion, which, even as I struggled to master myself, further caused me to reflect on the peculiarity of missing him more than anything at that particular moment, when my mother had been buried that very morning. Had it indeed been that very morning? It seemed like so long ago. I continued my reflections as I unbuttoned my shirt, and in my abstraction allowed a squashed potato to fall to the floor.

"Hello?" said I, thinking quickly. "It appears Chowder and I have brought you all a few tidbits."

I hadn't thought much about how we would handle these morsels once upstairs, but in the desperate economy of the place, I knew I couldn't very well keep them to myself. I could only hope that I had read Chowder right and that he held the same sentiments. I looked at him, and saw that he did, or had decided, anyhow, to play this one along with me. I did not expect him to pay me quite the compliment that he did, however.

"Beautiful, he is," said Chowder, coming to the center of the circle of boys to join me, nodding in my direction as he spoke. "Got it straight off, he did." As he said this, he removed his shirt and half a dozen small potatoes in various stages of disrepair fell out.

"Stubbs *is* thick," said I, grinning, while picking up the potatoes. Mimicking Miss Strickenwell, I added, "Thanks be to God." The boys laughed. Nails immediately shushed us.

"Quiet, you nits! Want to have Rennet in here again? Let's eat 'em."

"Wait, there's more," I added, and I began to work off my breeches. As the breeches came off, the slices of beef and pig appeared from their hiding places above my knees. I will own that this is not the very best method of storing or transporting cooked meat, or any other kind of food for that matter, especially assuming one might want to eat it afterwards, but we were not in a position to be particular. I could scarcely distribute it fast enough, but did not neglect to save a fair portion for myself. Chowder, meanwhile, passed the potatoes around. Poxy, I noticed, participated in this rite with good enough grace, but would give Chowder especially, and me occasionally, dark looks that I couldn't fathom.

We drank water from the ewer. Following this it was washing up, trips to the W.C., and, after hanging up our clothes, to bed. I was able to clean myself tolerably well, although the absence of hot water and soap rendered the removal of the grease an imperfect process. The food provided extra heat to our frames, which were unutterably weary. We spoke little as we crawled under the single, thin wool blanket, which bore the marks of much use. With me were Chowder, and then Poxy, in that order. The other three had their own bed. Some of us slept naked, and others wore nightshirts of varying lengths. I didn't have a nightshirt, and neither did Chowder, so we went to bed just as we were.

The candle was blown out, and I lay for a while with my eyes open, listening to the breathing of the others. I took in the room, especially the scene outside, which I could just see if I raised myself up a little. The window overlooked a sea of chimney pots, above which churches and their steeples rose, mystic spires in the moonlight. First one, then another pealed out ten o'clock in an uncoordinated oratorio of great bells, rendered strange by the trickery of the wind. Only the moon and clouds were familiar to me. I watched them race each other and meditated on this day, the likes of which I hoped I would never see again.

I had only sorrows and uncertainties to think on, other than the near presence of my new friend, which was indeed a comfort, but hardly compensation for the grief, disorientation, and loneliness I felt. I felt saddest, however, for Sarah, and quite forgot myself in thinking of her. I was a strong lad of almost seventeen, but she was only a girl of eleven. In my mind, I composed a prayer for her safety and comfort, and attached it to a speeding cloud to be carried to God who, perhaps, might do something for her if He wasn't too busy, and who, I prayed, would forgive the confusion and lack of understanding in a young and weak creature such as myself.

Just as I began to drift off to sleep, I felt Chowder move, and I realized by degrees he was very close to me, and at intervals would move closer. I was already at the edge of the straw mattress and had nowhere to go. I thought that if he were sleeping and continued to move in my direction I would simply push him back, with all due gentleness, of course, and that with a bit of luck he would not awaken. Next, however, I felt his hand very lightly on my shoulder, moving with unmistakable intentionality, performing a small caress. I had no idea what he intended or what I ought to do, but as I did not shrink from him, the hand remained. He now moved his body yet closer to mine, and his lips next my ear.

"It's cold," he whispered, in observance of inescapable fact. "Care to keep each other warm?"

XI

As SOFTLY AND AS QUIETLY as I could I rolled over and turned towards him. Whispering so low as to be scarcely audible, I asked, "Chowder, what is this about?"

All the others were asleep, as could be told from their breathing, or, in Poxy's case, snoring. Chowder had been careful to wait for that. The wind pulled at the roofs and chimney pots outside, causing eerie whistles and creakings. The room was flooded by brilliant lunar light, which waxed and waned as torn clouds flew past the moon.

"No, really, I'm cold. Aren't you? My brother and I used to sleep arm-in-arm on nights like this. Did you?" His pleasant, open face was less than a foot away from mine, perfectly visible in the moonlight.

"I had my own bed since I was four. My brother was a lot older than me. But, I know what you mean." I was careful not to betray my uncertainty, and I found myself relieved he didn't smell bad. In fact, there was something about the smell of him that I rather liked.

"Well, d'ye mind?" Again he touched my shoulder.

The idea that two fellows should lay arm in arm for the sake of comradeship and warmth was, if not an entirely new concept to me, one I had not expected to encounter, and my mind worked rapidly in consideration of it. I was innocent of knowing of any other way to take it than as an extraordinary offer of friendship which held great appeal. I *was* cold. And his touch was unexpectedly welcome.

"We could try it," I whispered, hesitantly. "Why don't you show me just what you mean?" I was prompted by Chowder's pleasant countenance, but most of all by an awareness that the desolation of my mood had lightened, and that this was somehow connected with his touch. I wanted more of it.

"It's a simple thing. You'll just be a lot warmer, that's all. Lie as you were before," he said, "and we'll be the best of friends." He smiled beatifically.

He then draped his arm over mine and put his chest in contact with my back. He nestled his face against the back of my neck, and we lay for some time in this posture. I found the sensation of his skin against mine pleasantly interesting in a way I could not entirely explain. Our shared warmth filled our side of the bed and at last I was comfortable. As I began to drift off, he again whispered to me.

"There's been nobody like you here since I came. They are all coarse or stupid or mean. You are different. I'm glad you are here"

"Thank you, Chowder," I whispered in reply. "But what about Nails? He seems all right."

"Oh, he is, in a way. But he isn't like you. He wouldn't let himself be held like this, I'm sure. He is altogether too manly for that."

"What, then, are you saying I'm not manly?" I was as manly as they came, I was sure, and would be quite certain to disabuse anyone of any notion that I was not, even Chowder.

"No, no, not at all," he hastened to correct himself. "You really are. I like that about you. I really don't know how to put it. He is just not the same as you are. I don't know, I like you better, that's all." His tone was anxious and contained hints of pleading, but somehow this did not put me off. He was as lost and lonely as I was, and I had cried more than once that very day. I would not presume to judge him, and indeed liked him better for the stumble, which had shown him uncertain and vulnerable.

"I like you too. Thank you for being my friend." At this I could feel him relax, and he placed more of himself in contact with me. "Eh, Chowder?"

"What is it, Joe?"

"Is my name going to be Snot now that Stubbs is calling me that?"

"You *are* funny, you know? Stubbs is purest arse-wipe. Nobody listens to him."

I would have laughed had I dared make noise. "You're right, to be sure. Good night, then, Chowder." I couldn't be certain, but I thought I felt something, a feathery moment of slight pressure on the back of my neck. I decided to say nothing about it, as I did not know what he might have done to cause it.

"G'night to you too, Joe."

And thus we drifted off together, me cradled by him. Falling asleep with Chowder's arms around me, I felt Fortune smile for the first time since Mother had fallen in that terrible final bout the previous August, and for the first time in a very long while felt something like peace. I had forgotten about the mysterious altercation in the room at the end of the blind corridor, and I slept a deep and dreamless sleep, awakening but once to hear mice scurrying inside the wall, and to exchange postures with Chowder so that I cradled him, which I thought I liked doing even better. I didn't know altogether what to make of it, but lonely, grieving, and exhausted as I was, here was simple human touch, which, circumventing my reason, felt curiously like love.

XII

THE MORNING CAME VERY EARLY, much before I was ready anyhow, with another bell and the sputtering noises of Mr. Rennet invading the quiet sanctuary of my soul. Out the window was only darkness, save for a single snowflake which brushed the pane as it fell. Chowder and I had long since disentangled in our sleep, and we arose and performed our ablutions, dressing with the careless disregard of each other natural to boys, or to some of them, anyway. I had to work at it a bit, as the memory of Chowder's warm and comforting touch clung to my wakening consciousness like bits of fairy substance too insubstantial to be real, yet curiously persistent. I wanted to look at him, but I dared not.

Dressing was a bit of a problem. My promised uniform had not yet arrived, and my breeches and shirt bore too plainly the marks of the previous evening's adventures. Shiny grease decorated my pants, while my shirt, in a sorry state even prior to the escapade, now presented even more severe challenge to the washerwoman's craft.

"Is it done around here to lend clothing to one in need?" I queried hopefully, to the room.

"The bastards put labels in 'em, and sometimes they check. You can miss a meal or worse for wearing someone's else's clothes or lending yours." This was from Nails, who was already dressed and heading out the door. As he crossed the threshold, he looked back to say, "Don't worry. The more you look a sorry wreck, the more they like it." This was said without sarcasm or rancor, as a simple statement of plain fact.

Chowder looked at me and shrugged a small shrug, as if to say he would help me if he had any clean clothes, but he didn't. He smiled a furtive smile at me and then he, too, headed out, wearing a clean uniform.

"Piss on 'em! Y'can wear some o' mine."

"Why, Poxy, thank—" I was cut short by flying clothes, which I pulled from the air an instant before they slapped across my face. "—you. I'll be sure to repay the favor sometime."

"Stow it, eh? No favor, eh? No sense me having clean 'uns when you've got naught." His expression was unsmiling, neither friendly nor unfriendly. "By the way," he continued, not looking at me, but going about his business, "I knows what you and Chowder was up to last night. You're not the only ones who wake o'nights, or didn't ye know? Now, I ain't sayin' nothing about it, mind, but you'll want to be careful, hear? *Damned* careful."

I flushed. Here was worry and also anger. What we had been up to was harmless friendship, and I said so.

"And I'm the King and all His ministers, or didn't ye know? See you downstairs." With these cryptic remarks he left, leaving me alone in the room with the lazy Spithead, who had lain in bed until the last moment, and who seemed as oblivious to Poxy's remarks as he had been to everything else since Rennet had first rung the bell. Remembering only too clearly Rennet's tender solicitude regarding my tardiness the previous evening, I dressed in a moment and ran down the stairs to the dining hall, where I arrived without a moment to spare. I had not forgotten to transfer the scrap of paper I had found under my pillow from my dirty breeches to the fresh ones lent by Poxy. Spithead, who out of lethargy now fashioned a wonderful alacrity, likewise ran, arriving hard upon my heels.

Breakfast consisted of thin gruel, slopped out with ill grace and yawned over by wakening boys who shuddered at the sight of it. Our betters had freshly baked bread, eggs, cheese, and hot coffee. This was bracketed by yet more earnest exhortations to God to work miracles upon our sorry, backwards natures, delivered by another of Mr. Peevers's minions, Mr. MacCurran, whose name was told me by Chowder as we slurped our watery repast. Mr. MacCurran had short black hair, a round face, and spoke with a very strong Scottish accent, in a tired voice. He had been at Mr. Peevers's table the evening before, but I had not seen him do anything yet. He was skinny like Rennet, but a bit younger and haggard.

Following the meal, though it sullies the King's English to term it such, I saw Stubbs head for the scullery, and thought for a moment I should be sent there again, even as I wondered whether the promise of schooling would be realized. I had not to wonder long. No sooner had I placed my bowl on the tray than Miss Strickenwell summoned me to the front, where she stood crisp and rigid. Next to her stood Mr. MacCurran.

"Joseph Chapman, have you ever been to school?" she asked, in a tone that suggested she knew the answer and did not like it. So might one ask a pig if it had been castrated, or perhaps would like to be.

"No, ma'am."

"Can you read? Did anyone ever teach you to read?" She was impatient, sharp.

"I learned my letters once, but forgot most of 'em. Never did learn to put any of 'em together. Never needed to read."

"They are mostly stupid like that, Angus." Mr. MacCurran seemed to wince ever so briefly, which caused me to wonder to what extent he was of her turn of mind. To me, she said, "Well, then, do you think you need schooling, or shall we just work you until you are done here?"

"I should like to learn to read, I think. I should like to read newspapers and novels." I tried to look bright. I was struck by the importance of the moment. I was determined to be more than a laborer, however I might achieve it, and be worth every farthing of the fifty pounds my parents had set by for me.

"What's this, not the Bible?" Miss Strickenwell was arch. To Mr. MacCurran, she said, "This mean boy says nothing of the Bible." I vowed to myself I would never again try to act bright. Something made her pause a moment. "I don't know why, Angus, but I will let you have him anyway. You have the wee 'uns, but that's no matter. See if you can teach him to read. We'll take another look at him in a month and make up our minds what to do with him then." She left, not bothering to say good-bye to either of us. Tossing admonitions and reminders about, she worked herself out of the room.

Mr. MacCurran actually smiled at me, although it was not quite your broad, welcoming grin. It was more of a quizzical half smile, as if he wished in some manner to be co-conspirator with me. "So, Joe, ye think ye'd like to read. That's good. That's very good. Ye've a bit of spirit. I like that in a lad. Come with me then, won't ye? We'll go to my classroom, now. The others will be there already, as it's time to be starting."

I followed him through a side door and down a hall. Peering through half-open doors on either side, I could see rooms full of boys, most of whom were already hard at work over books or slates, or teaching each other in small groups under the direction of one or another of the mentors or assistants to whom I had been so far introduced. Mr. Peevers appeared to teach religion, striding about before a large slate board on which were written many words perfectly incomprehensible to my youthful illiteracy. I heard him say the words, "elect," "judgement," and "sin" as we passed, each accompanied by severe concentration of expression, bracketed by ominous pauses.

Miss Strickenwell's room was similarly occupied. She seemed to teach geography, or perhaps it was history. As we passed, she expatiated on the moral depravity of some colonists or other to a room full of glazed eyes and slack bodies. Mr. Rennet was in full cry, although the ostensible subject, arithmetic from the sums written on the slate, would seem to offer little pretext for it. He harangued his charges on their moral frailty, providing, as he did so, a descriptive catalogue of wickedness. I thought his might be an interesting course of study, if he did not remember to teach arithmetic very often. I espied Chowder as I passed Rennet's door, and saw him, as were they all, glazed and listless before Rennet's rant. I felt sorry for him, and wondered if I should have to sit there before long.

Mr. MacCurran's classroom was at the end of the hall. As we entered, small boys ran up smiling and chattering, and surrounded him. The man actually chuckled with pleasure, but I was distressed to see they were mere children, not one of whom reached my chin. The moment of optimism I had experienced as a result of the man's kindness evaporated as I realized I was condemned to be freakishly out of place in a cold, dingy classroom of little boys.

XIII

MR. MacCurran PATTED SEVERAL OF the youngsters on the head and made
encouraging noises to as many more, foremost among whom was Nimbles, to
whom he was especially solicitous. The boys crowded around and seemed to
genuinely like him, which was a wonder. Having no idea what was expected of me,
I stood to one side and felt the fool. My gaze wandered, and I looked through the
many-paned and very dirty windows, which but murkily admitted the first light of
a grey and cheerless dawn. Outside, an occasional snowflake drifted past. Inside,
a tiny fire gave no warmth, but I watched with rising interest as Mr. MacCurran,
closely attended by most of the youngsters, placed a wonderfully improvident
shovelful of coal on the fire.

Turning around, he quizzed his youngsters on the date, and when it had been satisfactorily established that it was Wednesday, 25 November 1778, he was happy. This was altogether too childish, and I felt even more the fool. Mr. MacCurran's eyes then fell on me. "Ah, Joe, me lad. Your time is too precious to waste now, isn't it? You'll be wanting to learn your letters straight away, now, won't ye?" Again that half smile. I smiled a small half smile right back at him. "Nimbles here knows his letters, d'ye not, laddie?" Nimbles, who had not left Mr. MacCurran's side for an instant since he had entered the room, nodded vigorously. "I want the two o'ye t' sit by the fire, here, and Nimbles'll go through 'em all with ye. Mind the sounds they make, Joe, mind the sounds. The names o'the letters dinna matter a'tall. It's the sounds they make."

Again the smile. He seemed to hesitate for a moment, and then he patted my head, lingering a moment in the process, fairly stroking my hair. I took it as a kind, fatherly gesture. I rewarded him with my best smile, and he nodded at me before leaving us and calling the other boys to him for their advanced lessons, which consisted of reading aloud from tattered books and drawing words and pictures on slates. Mr. MacCurran seemed not to care much for sitting on the rows of high-backed benches, and he gathered as many boys on the floor around him as he could. A few boys sat on the first row of benches, but none were stuck behind where they couldn't be seen, or could get into mischief, either.

Nimbles and I sat before the grate as we had been instructed, which now began to radiate wonderful warmth. I was curious about Nimbles, as he seemed to occupy a mysteriously favored position, and I was sorely tempted to quiz him about what he knew of the school, and about himself and his own story, but I wished to learn to read and to please Mr. MacCurran even more, so we set about unraveling the great mystery of letters and their sounds without delay.

"This here's a 'A,'" said Nimbles, drawing a rickety capital A on his slate with a lump of chalk.

"I remember that one," said I. "My Gram knew her letters, although she couldn't actually read much." I looked hopefully at Nimbles.

"A makes a couple of sounds, like ay, and ah."

This was puzzling. "How d'ye know which one it's to be?"

"By the word it's in. You just know." Nimbles made an expression of intense concentration as he rubbed off the A and drew a large and loopy B.

"Bee," he said. "Buh. Buh. Say it."

And so we went through all of the letters. We were interrupted but once by Mr. MacCurran as he passed apples all round and stopped to listen to us approvingly. I badgered Nimbles to write the letters faster and made him tell me everything he knew. I nearly wore the boy out, and several times had to tell him how bright and good he was, to keep his spirits up.

By the time eleven o'clock came, I had learned all twenty-six letters, could draw each one upper and lower case, say its name, and tell most of the sounds. I had, moreover, arrived at a dim inkling that strange and unaccountable things happened when letters were put together, which rather worried me, as I couldn't imagine how to figure it out. Even so, I could write the words *cat, bat, rat,* and *rot.* Mr. MacCurran was vastly impressed.

"Joe, me lad, this is wonderful. How did ye come to be so quick?"

I said I didn't know. As the others were putting away their things and straightening the room, I told him some of my past. He was a bit troubled that my mother had been a woman fighter, but listened approvingly as I told him of Billingsgate and how we had always eaten great loads of fish and vegetables and had never gone hungry. As I left the room, I looked out the window, which I had ignored since beginning my lesson, and saw that it was snowing heavily.

Then it was back upstairs to room four, where I waited in line to use the W.C. and received two shirts and two pairs of breeches from Miss Strickenwell. She instructed me in the mysteries of dirty and clean laundry, where it was put and from where it was fetched, and then gave me my work assignment.

"You seem not to have done too badly last night in the scullery. I understand there was an accident, but you were not responsible for it."

"And a terrible accident it very nearly was, ma'am. Chowder and I were barely able to keep the entire counter from tipping over. They never should pile 'em on like that. Lucky it was that we lost but a single tray—"

"Shut *up.* Chowder," she said, pausing to look at Chowder, who had just walked in, "now works in the laundry. You have cost us a fortune in crockery, Master Gorham, and we are not pleased. You, Joseph, will take his place and work in the kitchen when not needed in the scullery. And, mind you, look sharp at your work. The school is over full, and so many more want in. We would be only too happy to be rid of you." This last was said whilst looking directly at Chowder.

To me, she said, "Report to Master Stubbs following dinner," whereupon she abruptly departed. Chowder stuck his tongue out at her back, while Poxy, who had listened intently to every word, incanted an involved curse that the most alarming indignities be visited upon her posterior, privates, and stricken eye.

Chowder looked at me and gave a slow, dejected shrug. "Well, at least it's not the wool. Anything but that." Our eyes met, and through the gloom penetrated a promise of the night's secret sharing. I smiled involuntarily, which provoked a snort of derision from the too-observant Poxy. Thinking I would have to be more careful with my reactions, I changed my clothes and returned to Poxy with many protestations of thankfulness the clothes he had so abruptly lent me that morning. His response was no more committal than previously, consisting only of a grunt and a nod.

Dinner was no different than before, except in small details. We had broth, moldy oranges, and a peculiar-tasting, chalky white bread that upset my stomach. I guessed it was the bread, at any rate, as I had never tasted the like before. Work in the scullery was likewise the same, except we had to do the dishes from breakfast as well as dinner, which took most of the afternoon. I now manned the soapy tub of hot water and had to get on without Chowder. Stubbs watched us every second, and I didn't know the other boys well enough to try anything. The kitchen was more interesting, hot from the stove fires and full of loud voices, banging, and much activity. They had me peel potatoes, which was all right as I could sit down and not have to bother with anyone. I felt weak. My stomach would hurt or flop at times, and my head would swim along with it. I wondered whether I might be falling ill, and what would happen to me if I was.

The simple task gave space for my mind to drift, and I was soon thinking of all that had happened in the brief interval since my arrival at the Little Eastcheap Free School for Unfortunate Boys. I soon worked my way back to Mother and to Sarah. I could not believe I would never see Mother again, and I could only hope I might be reunited with Sarah. Several times I flagged in my work and dropped potatoes as my eyes filled with tears. I was fortunate at those moments not to be under the close supervision of the cruel Stubbs. The cooks and their assistants ignored me as they did the floor they walked on, and I was glad of it.

Supper was unremarkable, except that I had no appetite, looking at the boiled potatoes and weak tea without interest. I don't remember anything about the prayers, other than that Mr. Peevers led them, having arrived on time. He also went on about Mrs. Winterbottom and how we should be wonderfully glad to see her, and he chirped and warbled about the wonderful cleaning projects, and wouldn't God help the boys doing the cleaning do their work even better. I began to feel nauseated, but couldn't tell whether it was the food, a fever coming on, or having to listen to Mr. Peevers, but taken together they conspired to effect a miasma of woe, which I felt most viscerally.

Before going to bed, Chowder and the others said that following dinner they too had felt a bit off, but had quickly got over it. I felt hot, and a heavy weariness, and my head hurt. In bed, Chowder's and my hand met under the cover, and we held on to each other like that, just with our hands, which brought a measure of gladness into my heart. I desired mightily to remain awake so I might again have the delicious sensation of holding him in my arms and being held, but was helpless against my great weariness. Later, Chowder told me I had been the first to fall asleep.

XIV

I AWOKE IN DARKNESS AND had no more idea whether it was before midnight or nearing dawn than I had of life among the idle rich. The window was banked by snow and covered inside by a patchwork of frost crystals, and I could just see an occasional falling snowflake brush past. I was aware of Chowder's nearness but felt no ease, as I had sweat profusely and felt very ill. My skin hurt on the outside and my head on the inside, and I radiated feverish heat. My stomach was most uneasy, and small pains crept their way around and through all parts of me. Just as I began to think I should have to get up and go to the W.C., Mr. Rennet appeared in the hall and strode up and down ringing his damned bell, announcing that worthless layabouts would go to the devil. He burst into our room to light our candle, braying, "If you won't rise early, you can't succeed," and the idiot like. Never had failure held such appeal.

"Mr. Rennet," I breathed through cracked lips. "I believe I am ill."

"Nonsense!" He barked, in fine imitation of a yapping terrier. "You would be a malingerer, and I'll have none of it! Get out of bed! Get up!" And with that he strove on, to harass other boys in other rooms. He paused briefly as he exited to look back at me and shout "And if you're still in bed when I come back this way, I'll tell Peevers to inspect you himself! He'll put you out, to be sure!"

"You all right, Joe?" Chowder placed his hand against the back of my neck. The touch was painful.

"I believe I have a fever," I said weakly. "What should I do?"

"Get up anyway, of course." It was Poxy. His tone was not unkind or mocking, but of one who believes he has made a useful observation. The others stood in a small circle around me, in various stages of dress and undress. Their faces were interested, concerned. "If you're lucky, you'll fall over pukin'."

"Lucky?" I had not the strength or will to ask any more elaborate question.

"They'll believe you then," said Chowder. "Might even let you spend a few days in the infirmary." The others nodded. Chowder was very thoughtful. "Looks bad if too many boys die."

"Ah, thanks. I hadn't thought of that."

"We don't want you to die, Joe." This was from Nails.

"I puked in the hall once, an' the old bat slipped in it. Fell right down, she did. Oh, it was rich. I'd gladly puke every day, just to see the like o' that again," said Spithead, brightly. I almost laughed, but the beginnings of movement in my abdomen elicited a wave of nausea, cutting short any possibility of mirth.

"Most of us've had our turns. Just get up, and we'll help you downstairs." Again Poxy, showing an unexpected solicitude.

I sat up, radiating heat. Chowder walked with me to the W.C., which was fortunately available, although the lack of a queue signaled it was very nearly the time to be downstairs. After I had made in that appliance the most liquid, voluminous, and foulest deposit imaginable, the stench of which very nearly called forth an answering stream from my other end, Chowder helped me back to room four to dress.

"I don't know how to thank you, Chowder."

"It's life, ain't it? One does what one can."

Surrounded by my room-mates, I made my way downstairs and arrived in the dining hall without a moment to spare, where we took our places at table. Miss Strickenwell said a prayer and Mr. Peevers made some announcements, but I was even less interested than I had been the previous evening. The wholesome, comforting smell of bread that had been baked overnight met my nostrils. I thought I might feel better, and when our turn came, I stood and walked as manfully as I could, which is to say with a weave and a wobble, to the serving station, where I waited in line and watched Stubbs work his ladle.

"Hello! Here's Snot! Lookin' a mite peaked this mornin', aren't we?" He attempted to fix me with a malicious grin, but I would have had to have been able to focus my vision and thoughts rather better than I was at that moment capable of to care, or to react. My mind was beginning to cloud over, and then I experienced a moment of perfect lucidity in which I realized Stubbs was but a fly, which is to say he was attracted to humiliation and conflict as helplessly as a fly is to dung. I looked at him and smiled down from a lofty height.

"'E's gone daft, 'e has! Lookit 'im smilin' away! 'E's too daft to know when 'e's bein' shat on!" Stubbs said this with all of the force and volume he could muster, looking about the room in solicitation of approval, of which precious little was forthcoming save from the other youths of his station.

"Lay off 'im, shit face." I had forgotten Poxy stood behind me. He said it quietly, but with vast meaning. My other mates were also near.

Nails chimed in. "That's right. Lay off 'im."

Mr. Peevers and his minions peered over from their table on the dais to see what was the matter. Fly. Dung. I smiled again.

"Bloomin' balmy!" Stubbs laughed in exultant defiance of Poxy, Nails, me, my other mates, and every decent human feeling. With treacherous generosity, he filled his ladle very full of gruel and then slopped it into my bowl with practiced lack of care, causing it to overshoot its putative mark, and spatter steaming over my shirt, breeches, and jaw. I would have been startled to furious rage had I not been halfway to another world, a world in which the image of fresh, hot, fly-covered dung reeking in the summer sun would not leave my mind, and seemed as real to me as Stubbs' pocked and pimpled face.

I began to laugh, and would have laughed long and loud, had not the shaking in my belly initiated a reflex action of a different sort. This unfortunate juxtaposition of tendencies was exacerbated by the near passage of a boy carrying Mr. Peevers's breakfast tray, on which were loaded boiled eggs, bread and butter, and a great pile of smoking hot bacon. The smell of it was too much, and an extraordinary arc of flying puke erupted from my mouth.

At this moment I experienced a wonderful dilation of time, such that I might see every droplet and chunk of my puke dance slowly through the air, and spew over the top of Stubbs's ducking head and back. I saw his face contort and the beginnings of an awful scream escape him, even as my knees gave way. I was next on my back on the floor, with no clear idea of how I had come to be there. My head hurt something awful, and I seemed to be trembling, all in a cold sweat.

"Ach, God, help me! I've been puked on by a turd," screamed the vomit-bedecked Stubbs.

He tore off his shirt and wailed for water and a towel, all the while cursing loudly. Boys that had queued up for their food made gagging noises and fled. Some laughed raucously. Many others rushed about, giving me a wide berth. As I lay looking at the ceiling, the room slowly spun, which was a wonder to me, as I had not been twirling about or doing anything to make myself dizzy. Moreover, where before I had felt roiling nausea, I now felt a remarkable peace. I would simply lie there. I had no reason to get up or strive for anything. All would be sorted out in due time, and whether it was done by me or another was of no consequence. I felt like sleeping, and so closed my eyes.

XV

I WAS FLOATING SOMEWHERE, DISCOVERING how pleasant and easy floating could be, when I heard a voice from a great distance below calling my name.

"Joe. Joe, can you hear?" How disagreeable it was to descend, and pass through however many layers of cotton, if that's what it was, and rediscover this body of innumerable small pains and feverish disease. I re-inhabited it by degrees, puzzling over the inflexibility of bone, and the tender, limiting flesh, as if I had not known it before.

"I think he's coming 'round," came the voice. "Joe?"

"Hhnnnn?" I discerned a sizeable gap between the progress of my intelligence and what my vocal apparatus could manifest.

"Joe, open your eyes, will you?"

"Mmmmmm." Eyes. Which were those? Ahh! Too bright!

"Joe, will ye?"

It was Mr. MacCurran. There was also a pleasant female voice I had not heard before, which Mr. MacCurran addressed as 'love,' and 'dear.'

I saw a hazy outline. Brilliant sunlight streamed through the window, intensified by a thousand reflections from as many surfaces of snow. Mr. MacCurran was beside me, and the woman to whom I had heard him speak was beside him.

I opened my yet-adjusting eyes a bit more, and saw a roomful of beds in which were other boys, some asleep or lying down, and others sitting up. These were variously adorned with plasters attached here and there, and a few sported fat leeches hanging from their temples.

One unfortunate boy lay on his stomach with the bedclothes pulled down, so that the leeches attached to his rear might have ample room to swell undisturbed. The close air was foul with the stench of every unwholesome bodily excretion, little alleviated by the sharp scent of the vinegar liberally sprinkled about. A pale older gentleman of grave mien in a silver wig and many-pocketed waistcoat moved among the sick, talking gently, making adjustments as necessary, and writing in a small book. He interrupted his inspection of a tray of goblets to look up at me as Mr. MacCurran spoke.

"Love, will ye fetch Peevers? Tha laddie's come 'round at last," Mr. MacCurran said to the woman, whom I supposed must be his wife.

"Uhh. Mmmmm. How'd? I? Get? Here?"

"Joe, ye've come 'round at last. I thought we might lose ye. Ye've been out right 'round the clock, ye have."

"What?"

"A day and a night, Joe," he said gently. "This is Friday morning."

"How … ?" Slowly now began the accretion of memory. Closing my eyes. The peacefulness. Falling … and before that? Stubbs! Had I really?

"Ye've had a terrible fever, Joe. Still have. The apothecary, Mr. Urwick, here, says ye'll not be out of danger for a goodly long while. And ye were delirious, sayin' some mighty strange things, too. Scared us all."

"I did? What?"

"Not a lot of it made sense, Joe, but there were bits about flyin', and a great dark bird. And you called for your mother, of course, God rest her soul. And Chowder. It was enough to make one think an evil spirit was trying to carry you off, but of course it was the action of the fever on your imagination, now wasn't it?"

"Chowder?"

"Aye. In your mind, he was helping you fight. So we brought him down here, and he sat up some o' the night with you, as he wanted to so. Saw no harm in it, and his touch did seem to comfort you."

"Oh." Here was food for thought. Kind as Mr. MacCurran was, I knew better than to let him know how I felt about Chowder. "That your wife?"

"Aye. She's the best of nurses. Ah! Here's Mr. Peevers."

Mr. Peevers greeted Mr. MacCurran and Mr. Urwick, who had in the meantime approached my bed. Mr. Peevers looked at me with what appeared to be genuine concern. Positioning his bulk next the bed and tilting over me, he asked, in a not unkindly way, "Feeling a bit better, Master Chapman?"

"I don't know," I replied weakly.

"We'll do our best to take good care of you. Mind not to die, now, will you? If you die, we shall take it as a serious affront." He attempted a chuckle, the effect of which was anything but encouraging. I shrank beneath the covers and looked at him through crusted eye slits. He quickly turned his attention to the apothecary.

"Er, Mr. Urwick, have you modified your diagnosis since the previous evening?"

"I will stand by it. I believe, sir, that we are confronted with an unusually virulent case of inflammatory fever. The sudden onset is especially troubling."

"You do not consider the possibility of malignant fever?"

"No, else last night's leeches would not have brought him out of it, as you may plainly see they have." Turning to me, he asked, "Do you not remember me applying leeches to your temples, or being tied down so that I might do so?"

"No."

"That is unfortunate." He turned to face Mr. Peevers again. "We shall have to proceed cautiously, but proceed we must. The best authorities until very recently have insisted that early bleeding is essential, especially in the young, but some are now recommending cupping with incision. I would add—"

Here I broke in with great urgency, "Please, please don't bleed me!"

"What's this?" Mr. Urwick was annoyed I had had the temerity to interrupt him.

"No, do let the boy speak." Mr. Peevers' solicitude was unexpected, but welcome.

"When my father was ill, he started to get better, and then he was bled he got a great sore full of pus where they let the blood out. Then the fever came roaring back, and he died." I was starting to sweat and wondered if I would puke again. Mr. Peevers seemed interested, but Mr. Urwick only became more annoyed.

"As I was about to say," said Mr. Urwick to Mr. Peevers, with ponderous dignity, "I would recommend we not solely attempt a general evacuation, although his strong pulse would even in the very recent past have indicated that we should, but that we try the most modern approach. No, we shall apply leeches again, and blister, then some hours later cup with incision and administer a purgative clyster, and an emetic. If we aggressively rid his body of corruption, we shall enable nature's own healing powers to come to the fore."

"Your fee, Mr. Urwick, will of course be no more than for the more standard treatment?" Mr. Peevers was of a sudden all business.

"Well, you see, cupping is rather a more lengthy procedure, and I customarily do ask a shilling more for it than for a general evacuation, but if you insist, sir. I would not wish to complicate our newly formed relationship." Mr. Urwick spoke in precisely enunciated tones.

"Ah, excellent," responded Mr. Peevers. "I tell you what, then. I will assist with the cupping and clyster, if you please." He was most eager. "Please keep me informed."

"That I shall. We shall proceed with the boy shortly."

The two gentlemen then went about their business. Mr. Peevers bade me good-bye and good wishes, then busied himself with several of the other boys before leaving. I was surprised to see he was not too proud to serve as a boy's nurse, as he removed the leeches from the aforementioned boy's backside himself, but I thought it peculiar that he then caressed the boy's bottom for an extended period of time, leaving off only when Mr. Urwick would come near.

Mr. MacCurran, who had attended the two gentlemen with grave respect, now felt at leave to introduce me to his wife, whose name was Mary, before leaving to attend to duties elsewhere in the building. Mary was the nurse. She was a brown-haired beauty, appearing to be gentle and kind in every way. I could also see she was with child, although it would be a while before the little one came peeking out. Mary got me out of bed and into a chair, so she could have a maid change the sheets, and then she washed me herself. It did not feel at all good to move about. Standing made me dizzy, and I flopped into the chair like a drunken tar, but not before Mary had me go in a pot, so that Mr. Urwick could examine it. Once back in bed I drank a bit of water to see if it would stay down.

Mr. Urwick was now ready. He had me lie flat on my back, and then he applied plasters to the soles of my feet and upper arms, following which he placed leeches next my temples. The plasters began to generate heat, and then to burn, but the leeches didn't feel like much of anything. What with my headache, nausea, and feverish pains, I was very uncomfortable, but despite that soon fell into a heavy, dreamless sleep.

When I next awoke, the leeches were gone, and Mr. Peevers was beside the bed, looking at me. It was dark outside, and a few of the boys were sitting up, slurping broth. Others were sleeping, and one youngster cried. I realized I had been hearing the boy's sobs now and again since I had arrived in the infirmary.

"Joe," said Mr. Peevers. He looked at me with one eyebrow raised, as if asking a question.

I looked at him groggily, feeling very weak. On a table beside the bed was a jug.

"Water, please?" I asked. Again I had that sensation of extreme heaviness, and to speak required unreasonable effort.

"Here, Joe. Take a sip, but not too much. Mr. Urwick has prepared your treatment. As you may have noticed, we have removed your leeches, and this has brought the heat of your blood down to a safer level." A shudder ran through me. Like any sane person, I was mortally afraid of medical treatments.

My plasters were peeled or ripped off, revealing reddened, raw skin that had blistered in places. It was a difficult procedure, attended with many small cries of pain on my part, and divers exhortations to be manly on the part of the two gentlemen. It had not previously been presented to me in quite so stark a manner that manliness involves a particular relationship to the experience of pain. My ever-active brain worked on the problem even as the two gentlemen each in his own way worked at abusing my flesh.

Was I indeed part girl, then, because to pretend I was not in pain held no appeal? I realized I didn't understand a great deal. Why, for instance, should crying be considered shameful and the weaker course? I could see it might be inconvenient for one's keepers, but what of it? I possessed neither the temerity nor strength to express any of this to the two gentlemen, and held all inside. I suppose I was manly after all, but I took neither pleasure nor pride in it, only fear of shame, which caused me to settle by degrees into grim silence.

Mr. Urwick brought to the bedside table a tray full of goblets, a large candle, and various evil-looking knives and instruments, which inspired wonder and fear. Foremost among these was a bladder with a small nozzle at one end.

Looking at Mr. Peevers, Mr. Urwick said, "You may prepare the patient, Percival." I was bade to lie on my stomach, whereupon Mr. Peevers pulled my nightshirt up as far as it would go, revealing everything. They then worked together. Mr. Peevers held the goblets upside down over the flame while Mr. Urwick made a small cut in my back. As soon as he had done this, Mr. Peevers handed him the goblet, still upside down, which Mr. Urwick placed over the cut. As the goblet cooled, it sucked my skin up into itself, which also had the effect of drawing out more blood.

I bore it as best I could. It helped a bit that Mr. Peevers also ran his hands along my back, which was rather reassuring, although I didn't like his hands lingering in the area of my lower regions. At the time, I supposed it was medically necessary, or else he wouldn't have done it. They continued this until they had cupped me in like manner with eight goblets, following which I had to lie like that for some minutes, during which time Mr. Peevers massaged away and I began to grow lightheaded.

Mr. Urwick then took up the nozzled bladder. He unscrewed the nozzle and poured an oily looking liquid into it using a funnel, following which he screwed the nozzle back on.

"What's that?" I asked, not a little anxious.

"This is a purgative clyster, Joseph," said Mr. Peevers. "It shall not hurt, although you may have some small discomfort. It's very easy compared to the cupping, actually. Have you had a clyster before?"

"No. What does it do?"

"Ah. The clyster assists in the ready purging of toxins from your body. Your sickness is caused by an excess of corruption, and we must get it out. Blast it out, if you will. We've started the process by removing your polluted excess blood. Now we must get to the rest of it." As he spoke, Mr. Peevers's paws carried on. They had become sweaty, and by now I cared not a bit for his touch. I wondered what was taking so long, even as I dreaded the moment when the worst should begin.

"It isn't necessary to prolong this, Percival," said Mr. Urwick, with a touch of impatience.

"I believe it is important for the lads to be relaxed. This isn't the most natural of procedures, you might say. If the boys are relaxed, there is better penetration."

"Yes, but, my God, man, must you caress the boy like that?" Mr. Peevers's hands suddenly left me, and I heard him suck in his breath. I wondered what might come next, and after an interval of some seconds Mr. Peevers erupted in mirth.

"Oh, jolly, jolly good! What a funny rogue you are, Bartholomew," he said, shaking with feigned laughter. "Here, give me that thing." To show what a great joke it was, and that he was every bit a regular fellow, Mr. Peevers rammed the clyster nozzle all the way into my fundament at one go. I howled, but the only effect this had was to cause one of the lads across the room to announce to the rest that I was getting it up the backside, about time, too, and might I see my way to be quieter about it?

Mr. Urwick, I noticed, did not share Mr. Peevers's mirth, and remained grim-faced. The liquid seeped into me until I felt very heavy, whereupon the cups were ripped from my back, blood running in streams. After some time, I was instructed to climb out of the bed and position myself over an enormous chamber pot, into which I unloaded with preternatural capacity. I then had to stand aside as Mr. Urwick examined the contents and made learned pronouncements to Mr. Peevers which were quite beyond my comprehension. Mary, meanwhile, directed a maid to change my bed sheets again and wash me, soiled as I was with sweat and blood.

Following this, I returned to bed, where I was given a draught of an evil-smelling and bitter liquid, the prescribed emetic.

After a few minutes, I began to feel very ill indeed, so ill that it seemed all the world sickened with me. Every thought and motion deepened my malaise until the apothecary's assault on my weakened system produced the salutary effect. Mr. Peevers and Mr. Urwick had long since withdrawn, and Mary nursed me through the next bit, which it would in no wise improve this narrative to relate. Several hellish hours later, the effects of the medicaments began to wear off, and some time deep into the night, drugged and disoriented, I spiraled into fretful, feverish sleep.

XVI

Mary reappeared in the morning. She asked whether I was hungry, to which I replied unsteadily that the thought of food made me ill. I did have a savage thirst, however, and might I have some water or perhaps tea to drink? Rather than sending a maid, she went herself to the kitchen and returned before long with not only a pot of tea and some bread, but Chowder as well. Grinning, he reached over to me and tousled my hair as Mary placed a cup of tea in my hands.

"Joe, drink this and see how you feel. Chowder here has asked to sit with you a spell, and it's a small miracle, but Miss Strickenwell has permitted it. So he may sit with you until dinner." She paused and looked at us both. "Now I must be off. I must visit several of our benefactors and attempt to solicit their continued support."

"Thank you, Mary, and good-bye." As she left, she paused to speak briefly with some of the other boys in the infirmary. I looked at Chowder and met his eyes, which held for me a comfort disproportionate to the brevity of our friendship.

"Wish you weren't sick, Joe," said he.

"Wish I weren't, neither," said I, "but I do believe I'm going to get well. I feel awfully weak but otherwise not so bad, I guess. My back hurts where they cut me. More tea?"

"Sure, Joe." Chowder poured me another cup of tea. "You going to eat this?" he asked, meaning the bread Mary had brought.

"No. I feel as if I shall never want to eat again." Chowder tore the bread and crammed a very large hunk into his mouth.

"Anyhow, this tea is good," said I, slurping up the last. "MacCurran said I was raving in my fever. Were you here when I did that?" I handed him the cup, and he put it on the table.

"If you think that's good tea, then you *are* sick!" he said with a laugh. "No, when you started moaning and tossing they made me leave, but I didn't want to go, you know." He took my hand and added, "I've been worried about you, Joe."

I squeezed his hand in return. In the weak, silver light of that leaden-skied December day, dimmed further by dirty, small-paned windows and enveloped by the infirmary's stench, we exchanged awkward, tentative grins, which became more relaxed by degrees, opening at last into broadest smiles. I will always remember that moment of brightening to his fond gaze. It did not occur to me what I felt was in any way unusual, or that the quality of my delight in this worthy lad would cast me out of the common lot of humanity, and cause me to be execrated by all good men.

I knew only that I delighted in everything about him, and did not doubt my affection was what any young male would feel for a chum. Lost in his gaze, I was only again aware of my surroundings when the maid, sitting at the far end of the room, emitted a raucous sneeze. Unfazed, Chowder picked up a spoon, and tapping it on first one, then the other of my shoulders, said with merrily feigned gravity, "Hold, ye noble lad of grand exploit, I dub thee Sir Pukes-on-Stubbs," following which he collapsed in giggles.

"Oh, that does have a nice ring to it," said I, happily.

"Indeed it does. You are now Sir Pukes, of wondrous fame evermore!" More giggles. It was gratifying indeed to have at last a name worthy of the establishment wherein I was confined.

"How'd you get to be called Chowder?"

"Can't claim your glory, I'm afraid. The first week I was here, we had an oyster chowder for Sunday supper. It wasn't half bad considering what we usually get, although there were precious few oysters in it, to be sure. Anyhow, when I reached over in front of Poxy to get another hunk of bread, he pushed me arm and I knocked over the bowl of chowder, most of which went in me lap. S'pose I ought to have asked him to pass the damned bread, but then nobody else here stands on manners, now, do they? Have to say my dislike of the fellow started then. And today when the old bat says I can come and sit up with you, she puts Poxy in the laundry in my place, of all people. This morning he looked at me like he wanted to kill me. More than he usually does, I mean. I wish she had taken anybody but him. He's one I'd rather not annoy, if I can help it." Chowder was now pensive.

"He's an odd bird, that one. Wonder what he wants," I mused.

"Don't know, but we'll be happier not to find out, I'm sure. I got here three months before you, and he's thrashed four boys since, and has had to see Mr. Peevers privately I don't know how many times."

"Mr. Peevers privately? He does that?"

"Sees boys for discipline, you mean? I'll say he does. There's a few boys he sees all the time. Rennet sees most of the rest of 'em. Uses the cane, he does, and Miss Strickenwell uses the strap on a few more. But with Peevers, no one will say what he does to them, which is awfully strange. You know what's even stranger?"

"No, what?"

"Every other boy what's been in a fight has been turned out right away, put out as the cheapest sort of 'prentice, to a sweep or greengrocer, or sent to the workhouse, some of 'em, including the ones Poxy beat up. But not Poxy. Peevers talks about turning the other cheek, doesn't he, which is daft because wherever you go people fight. I should think keeping Poxy on instead of the boys he beats is a bit much, given all that meekness and mercy claptrap we keep hearing about. It's a bit contrary, eh? Does that sound right to you? I'd like to know what's behind it."

"This whole place is strange. I don't like it one bit."

"Nor do I." Our eyes met again. Chowder was beautiful to me, although so early on I would not have named it such. I saw friendship and comfort, and a curious appeal. There was sweet delight to be found in cultivating small intimacies with him.

"Chowder?"

"Yes, Joe?"

"Tell me about yourself. Where were you raised up? And how did you get here?"

"Oh, it's no great tale." he said, exhaling and shaking his head, I supposed as too many memories returned. I was almost sorry I had asked and was about to tell him not to mind, when he began, looking at the ceiling as he spoke.

"I was born in a house on Lamb Street very near Spittlefields market. Me dad was in the silk trade, though I don't know in just what way, and Mum was a weaver. Only they fought all the time, and he took to drink. Then about the time of the big strike and riot in '68, when I was six, he left her real sudden like. They must have known it was coming, but nobody said nothing, even though everything was falling apart. And he ups and announces he's out, just like that, and three days later is gone, saying Mum could go on living in the house, he didn't care, no one would call him a blackguard for putting his family on the street. That part was all right, I guess, but Mum couldn't own the house, being a woman and all, so it passed to my uncle, her brother, who out of the goodness of his heart only charged her half rent. We never knew where my father went. He never came 'round to see how his own children were getting on or anything. I can't forgive him that. Then Mum worked like a demon, and all us children too, and for a while an auntie lived with us, but that auntie got married and moved on, so we took in lodgers. Things began to look up, but then Mum got sick and died. One of those fever things in your gut, you know? That was when I was eleven. That was hard."

He paused, and we looked at each other again, just for a moment. I desired to hold him again, or at the very least his hand, but was too conscious of the other boys in the room, several of whom, wanting entertainment, were, I was certain, listening to us. I cared not to provide them with more spectacle than perhaps we already were.

"After that," he went on, "my sisters and brother and I were split up among our aunts and uncles. I went to stay with another auntie who lived nearby, and that was all right for a while, but then she had twins, and—wouldn't you just know it—they both lived. So there were too many in the house, and my uncle put me here. None of the other aunties or uncles had room, they said. My uncle said he found Peevers through an advertisement in a newspaper, about free schoolin' for unfortunate boys. That was around the end of last August, I guess, tail end of summer anyways. So here I am. Oh, and I'm just sixteen."

"Your life's a lot like mine," said I, in solemn response, and I told him my story, or what parts I could bear to. And I told him about Sarah.

"That's no good," he said. "My sisters and brother are all still at one or another of my other aunties' or uncles'."

And so we talked on until I was too sleepy to continue. I had experienced a momentary renewal of energy after the tea, but was soon again exhausted and could scarce keep my eyes open. Somewhere around eleven, Mr. Rennet came to take Chowder away. Mr. Rennet was less obnoxious than usual due to the quiet enjoined on those visiting the infirmary, and stayed but a minute checking on some of the other boys before leading Chowder back to the garret dormitories. Mr. Rennet attempted to rouse the crying boy, who he called Roger, but the boy seemed not to know Mr. Rennet was there, or perhaps he had lost the power of hearing or speech, and Rennet had to leave him.

The remainder of the day passed uneventfully. I napped in the afternoon and was interested enough in food to down a reasonable supper. The night, however, was long and difficult. As I was drifting off, a new arrival came who was as sick, or perhaps even sicker, than I had been, and I was awakened several times by his puking and raving. Another maid sat up the night with him, and then he shat the bed, I guessed, from the things said and the commotion caused by changing his sheets and cleaning him up. I was very glad I hadn't done that. At least, I didn't remember doing that. I experienced renewed sweating and nausea, although it was nothing compared to what I had already been through. When I did sleep, I slept heavily and dreamed of Chowder and I, just walking along the embankment together and feeling very peaceful and good, and then of Sarah, and my mother still alive and quite herself, laughing.

XVII

SUNDAY MORNING CAME, BRINGING WITH it densest fog and a thousand dripping icicles. We ate porridge, and Mr. MacCurran and Mary led us in the Lord's prayer, and in the prayer for sick children. The new boy was too ill to join us, and the crying boy cried on.

In the afternoon, Mr. MacCurran provided moral instruction, which principally concerned what not to do with our privates, or anyone else's. I had not realized this was of such consuming importance to God. I had always liked the feel of it when my member would stand, and would pull on it and the like, although I was never so surprised as the first time I spent, when I was thirteen. I found it so wondrous that I frigged myself several times again straight off, until it would stand no more. Even after I got over the novelty of it, I would frig myself regularly, although seldom more than once at a time, but since coming to Mr. Peevers' school I had not been able to for want of privacy. The urge at times had been strong with me until I fell ill, which took the edge off it. It now troubled me greatly to know that such a thing was not to be done, and I couldn't understand why.

"It's the sin of Onan, Joe, a terrible sin."

"What did Onan do?"

"He spilt his seed on the ground. Never, never do that, now."

This was a relief. I had always caught mine in a cloth. But I was not entirely sure if God permitted this, so I asked Mr. MacCurran what he had done before he married. Had he been able to withstand the urge to frig himself, or had he just kept his seed from the ground, and was that all right? I was greatly surprised that instead of answering reasonably, as I had expected him to do, he became angry, telling me I was wondrous impertinent, and that I ought to know better than to speak thus. He never did answer any of my questions, which was a severe disappointment. I had begun to like the man. I could only guess that he had frigged himself and didn't want to talk about it, but this didn't explain his rudeness. I wanted to ask so many more questions. I especially wanted to know why God was so interested in our private parts, but feared Mr. MacCurran would only become angry again, and so kept it to myself. Then he launched into a related topic that troubled me even more, and which would prove even less tractable.

"Now if Joe here'll not perform any more impertinences, I'll tell ye something more. In a place such as this, ye may run across something so foul that I would never speak of it, except to protect ye from mortal sin. It may happen that another boy here, perhaps an older boy, may want to touch you in ways he shouldn't. Never let this happen! Especially in your beds at night. Keep to yourselves, lads, keep to yourselves. Do not dare to become sodomitical!" But he would not, no matter how we pressed him, reveal just what the word *sodomitical* actually meant.

"What happens to a person who does this, Mr. MacCurran?" This was from another lad whose bed was in the far corner of the room. I had been wondering this myself, but was not about to solicit any more information from Mr. MacCurran that day.

"Why, from that moment God hates him, as do all righteous men! When he dies, he goes straight to Hell, he does! He is damned for all eternity, and his eternal soul will rot in unending torment! It's the one thing God cannot forgive, so, lads, beware! Beware!" He added that this was a vice so foul that the Crown, in wondrous demonstration of its partnership with God, was privileged to expedite God's reckoning by hanging any miscreant who would so offend the sensibilities of man and God.

These words affected me greatly. Despite my losses, there had abided with me a faith that in time, given wit and strength, I would fashion a proper life for myself. After all, people died every day, and those who remained behind had no choice but to go on living so long as it should please God. But here was a new thought, that there was a foul, hidden crime worse than murder, that God could not forgive, the retribution for which would extend beyond hanging to all eternity.

It had something to do with boys touching each other, that had been said, but what? And had I, perhaps, in delighting in Chowder's simple touch, already crossed the line? I felt a dark stain spreading through my soul, of a quality entirely more severe than the simple grief I had felt until that moment. I sank into my own thoughts under the weight of it. I wished to talk to no one until I had puzzled this though as best I could.

Having concluded his lesson, Mr. MacCurran left. None of the boys in the infirmary spoke. Each seemed to wish to isolate himself from the others, and think, perhaps, about Mr. MacCurran's words, as did I. I puzzled mightily, taking inventory of my experience and emotions. Could my feelings for Chowder be sinful and forbidden? He had been my one friend, and in his company alone had I experienced relief from the awful melancholy of my current life. His simple, unaffected touch warmed my heart. Finally, I decided that whatever Mr. MacCurran had meant, it had nothing to do with anything Chowder and I had done.

This relieved my mind considerably, but not entirely, as I could not avoid admitting to myself that I had wondered about and tried to imagine Chowder's body. I had even gone so far as to try to catch a glimpse of him as he dressed. With a start and flush of shame, I banished such thoughts from my mind and hated myself for having thought them. I was sure Chowder, being a fine and proper boy, could not possibly have like thoughts. However imperfectly, I reasoned if Chowder knew I had this turn in my mind, he would have to hate me for it. The thought of that was nearly too much for me.

Sunday night I puked anew and seemed to be getting no better. In addition to my general malaise, the cuts in my back had suppurated. Much to my surprise, I was examined by a physician, Mr. Stogdon, an older and yet more dour version of Mr. Urwick, whose tenure had been brief indeed. Mr. Peevers carried on beside Mr. Stogdon as if nothing had happened. I did not fail to notice, however, that he was even more surreptitious about the patting of boy's bottoms than he had been previously.

Mr. Stogdon said the corruption in my body must be very strong for this suppuration to result. He thought it might be necessary to bleed me some more, but I begged and carried on so that he became disgusted with me and said that as I was equally likely to die in either case, I was free to heal myself, and that he would not attend, to which promise he remained true until my discharge, and in which Mr. Peevers did not interfere. That night, although I did not fall to raving, my mind wandered, and in my feverish dreams I was caught between the glowing haven of Chowder's friendship and a disapproving God. Through the night, Mr. Stogdon liberally administered his medical tortures and patent fever powders to the others even as he studiously ignored me. He bled twice the boy who had come in after me, who was now gravely ill and weakening steadily.

Wednesday, Chowder visited again, and in the presence of his kind face and gentle hand, I forgot my anxieties and was comforted. No evil could be associated with such feelings of friendship, I was sure. As for my interest in his body, I would simply forbid myself to think of it.

XVIII

I STAYED IN THE INFIRMARY another week, slowly mending and feeling better bit by bit, to my delight and Mr. Stogdon's annoyance. My appetite became good again, even as I continued to sweat at night. The swelling at the back of my head went down, and apart from occasional headaches, troubled me no more. As the days passed, I could see the snow melt and dense fog persist. It was an extended period of windless chill, not quite cold enough to freeze and no energy in the atmosphere. It made travel on the river difficult, which my father had loathed.

I seemed to be mending rather better than most of the other boys, who were perhaps not as strong to begin with as I had been. Several of them were stricken rather more severely than I, especially the boy who had arrived just after me. His name, I learned, was James. He died two days after Chowder visited me the second time, despite having been subjected to liberal applications of the apothecary's patent fever powder, and having been bled a third time. Each time they bled him, he would cry or moan, and I shuddered.

Perhaps it had been wicked of me to think I knew better than the apothecary, but when I heard the child's blood spatter in the bucket, I knew I would make the same fight again. When James died, Mr. Peevers appeared genuinely upset, as were we all, and he led us in prayers for the boy's soul. Sickness increased throughout the school, and there were more arrivals than departures in the infirmary. The boy who cried, Roger, was taken to Bedlam, as nothing else could be done with him. He would speak to no one and seemed not to hear, and yet cried on, to the distraction of us all. When they hauled him out of bed, I saw that he was a weak and spindly thing, fit for nothing, and yet I felt sorry for him. Another boy who had been there longer told me that Roger had had a great fever, which had taken his reason.

In the afternoons, Mr. MacCurran taught reading or other lessons to those capable of attending. He seemed to bear me no grudge as a result of my impertinences, as he had termed them, but he never visited those subjects again in my presence. I took pleasure in the lessons and discovered in myself a wonderful facility for learning. I never had to be told a thing twice and was usually the first to understand whatever he wished us to apprehend. I learned dozens of new words every day, and by the time I left the infirmary could read any of the children's books he would bring with him. I begged him to bring me a newspaper, but he said they were wicked. He brought me a Bible instead, which I endeavored to read but found incomprehensible, and soon put aside.

"That's all right, Joe," said Mr. MacCurran. "Keep it until you are able to read it. It is God's word, and wondrously interesting it is, too." This sounded like something I ought to know more about. Perhaps I might find some words of comfort to assuage the anxiety I felt over God's difficult and disquieting rules. I promised to myself I would be able to read it soon.

The day after James died, Mrs. Winterbottom, the benefactress spoken of by Mr. Peevers, visited the school as promised and was taken through the infirmary following dinner. She was a formidable gentlewoman, worth, I heard Mr. Rennet whisper, a staggering fifteen thousand a year. I had seen such gentlefolk before, when they would step clumsily into my father's skiff and grumble about the wet, so I was perhaps less overawed than the other boys. She paraded through the infirmary, her eyebrows raised to an absurd height, arrayed in dozens of yards of sky blue silk and bedecked with a towering wig and many jewels, all the while clutching a silken handkerchief to her face, which I supposed had been sprinkled with vinegar.

This creature was more spectacle than human, nosing about with morbid curiosity, asking Mr. Peevers questions about us as if we were not there. Miss Strickenwell accompanied them dressed in her best black silk, as did Mr. Rennet, who, with Mr. Peevers, sported newly powdered wigs and fine waistcoats. None of them spoke to us, but talked among themselves in affected tones of tending their flocks, and of the trials of Christian duty. One would have thought we were no more than a lot of stinking barnyard animals in need of a veterinary surgeon. It was a relief to see the back of them.

Perhaps an hour after the spectacle of Mrs. Winterbottom, I was visited, much to my surprise, not by Chowder, but by Poxy.

"Doin' all right?" he asked, rather gruffly. He stood awkwardly beside the bed and surveyed me.

"I suppose so. I'm gettin' out of here today or tomorrow." I had no idea why he had come but saw nothing to be gained by rudeness.

"Found this in me breeches," he said in low tones so as not to be overheard, and he pulled from his pocket a rumpled bit of paper which I recognized as the scrap I had discovered under my pillow my first afternoon in room four, and which I had forgotten in the pocket of the breeches Poxy had lent me. He tossed it on the bed where I could reach it. "Mr. Peevers warn't too happy to see it."

I uncrumpled the scrap and discovered, where first I had seen incomprehensible shapes, the words "BEWARE PEEVERS," which I could now well appreciate, written in clumsy block letters.

"You showed this to Peevers? Why?"

"Him 'n me are special, like. You'll see. Where'd you get that? You write it?"

"No. I couldn't write until I got here. Still can't, unless you would call 'cat' and 'boy' writing," I replied. "It was under me pillow when the old bat first took me to room four. I didn't even know what it said till now."

I paused and looked at Poxy. He was also sixteen, or perhaps seventeen, and possessed an animal vitality which was not unattractive, but it was marred. The pustules which had inspired his name were too evident. His flaming red hair would have been a crowning glory on another whose bearing was dignified, but on him was a fillip to his anger, which never ceased to work in him. In thrall to it, he lived ever poised on the knife's edge between cringe and attack, except when, exhausted, he would be seized by dull vacancy. I wondered who his people had been, and what they had done to him. I asked the obvious question. "Why'd you bring that here now?"

"Seemed as good a time as any. Came to tell ye that Mr. Peevers will be wanting to see you, that's all. Private, like, when you're out of here, in a day or two. And to tell you there's no reason to beware Peevers. None at all. If you're smart, Joe, you'll go along. Mr. Peevers likes boys what understands they should please their betters." He smiled the most perfectly ambiguous smile I had ever seen.

"Speak Greek, why don't you?"

"Never mind, then. You'll see. But remember, don't let Peevers down. He means no harm, and he'll do ye none, if you're right by him."

"Let Peevers down? Why would I do that? I've given it everything I've got since coming here. Well, apart from being sick, of course. Does whatever you're talking about have anything to do with your not getting thrown out for fighting?"

"Maybe." He paused, and added thoughtfully, "And maybe you're not as smart as you look, neither." He paused again, and his air softened. "Say, Joe." Here he moved a bit closer to the bed. "I like you, Joe." He extended a finely muscled hand in my direction. From it sprang innumerable small, fiery hairs, which put me in mind of what I had seen my first night in room four. In spite of my wariness, I found Poxy interesting, and as not to take the hand would have been an unwarranted affront, I did so and looked at him levelly.

"What is this about, Poxy?"

"Well, I thought, you know, seein' as how I was ready to thrash Stubbs for you that mornin' afore you puked on 'im, and as I leant ye my breeches and all, that maybe we should ..." He paused and swallowed. You would have thought I was the prettiest girl; he had, at any rate, in every atom become the shy boy too nervous and awkward to talk. "You know, swear friendship."

"I, ah ..."

Poxy was looking at me with nakedly entreating eyes, so different from his usual aspect. "Be with me, Joe. No one could touch us if we was together." That his tone was pleading rendered my astonishment complete.

"Poxy, I ... I don't know what to say."

"Say yes, then."

"But I don't even know what saying yes would mean. It isn't that I don't like you, it's just that—" But before I could concoct yet another dissembling word, Poxy's constitutional anger overwhelmed the entreaty that had been allowed so brief a life.

"Just what, then? It's Chowder, isn't it? Say it's Chowder!" He squeezed my hand until the grip began to hurt, and then he broke away. "I can pat your britches as well as he can, you know, if you want. I can do all that, if you want." To my astonishment, I saw he was near to tears. I stared at him open-mouthed as laughter erupted all around us. In his absorption, Poxy had forgotten where he was, and in his anguish had forgotten to keep his voice down. He looked up and around. Bellowing, "Damn the lot o' ye!" he fled the room.

Mocking laughter followed Poxy down the hall as I performed a most exacting inventory of the counterpane, not caring to raise my eyes and so meet those of one or another convulsed in mirth. I did not find Poxy's anguish funny. That he was jealous of Chowder dawned on me with gathering force, and his reference to touching my person startled my imagination, my mind running along a course inspiring no little excitement and fear. And there were his cryptic references to Mr. Peevers. It was as if a door had been opened to a vastly larger new world in which everything was puzzles.

As I pondered thus, one of the other boys called raucously from his bed, "Can you believe that Poxy? 'E's a bloody molly, he is! Think of it!" There again was the pregnant term I had heard Poxy use the first time I had seen him, when he had dropped his breeches to taunt Chowder. To me, the clever one said, with cold mocking laughter, "Aren't you the lucky one? Think he'll bring you flowers next?"

I delivered the only possible reply to this and the other similarly offered witticisms with surly vehemence: "Go to Hell."

XIX

MERCIFULLY, LESS THAN AN HOUR later, an annoyed Mr. Stogdon discharged me from the infirmary, seeming to take it as a personal insult I had returned to health without his aid. Mary helped me wash and gave me a uniform and instructions to report directly to Mr. Peevers's private study. It proved, to my disquiet, to be the very room from which I had heard the awful sounds of the altercation on the day of my arrival. The corridor appeared considerably less derelict, however, as a result of the cleaning inspired by the recent visit of the august Mrs. Winterbottom. I found the door open as I approached, and Mr. Peevers waiting inside.

"Come in, Joe. Please sit in the blue chair." Mr. Peevers indicated a large and comfortable high-backed chair near the fire. I entered the richly furnished study, sat as directed, and marveled. The walls were paneled in very fine carved woods. Several ornate cases held shelves of curiosities, and many handsome leather-bound books rested in shelves along one wall. A large, leaded window adorned with rich draperies looked out on a narrow lane, though which I could see the gathering late afternoon dusk and a fine drizzle. A goodly fire burned in the grate. The room had every aspect of a substantial gentleman's private study, testifying to Mr. Peevers' station. Despite my determination to keep my head, I felt overawed. Mr. Peevers finished with some papers, rose and poured himself a glass of sherry, closed and latched the door, and then sat in the chair opposite mine.

"Well, Joseph, how are you liking our little school?" Mr. Peevers's tone, a precise concoction of officious solicitude, struck me as altogether too contrived.

"It's all right, I guess." I was wondering about what Poxy had told me. And what he hadn't.

"Come now, Joseph. Is that all you have to say? We have taken you in, fed, clothed, and housed you, and, I shouldn't need to add, nursed you back to health from a most dangerous illness. Now you look a fine picture of a young man, quite returned to the pink of health." Here he reached over to pat my knee in a familiar manner, the gesture accompanied with an ingratiating and altogether too eager smile. "I'm sure there's more you would like to say."

I assumed the air of one misunderstood. "I assure you I am entirely grateful, Mr. Peevers. I would not wish to be all alone in this world, and none to care for me."

Mr. Peevers took a sip of sherry and looked at me for a moment without speaking. When he did speak, it was in a more personal tone.

"Joe, have you had any problems with any of the other boys?"

"No. Well, Stubbs isn't one of the boys, I suppose. I can't say I care much for him, but then I did take revenge, perhaps you could say."

Mr. Peevers's tone passed on to the conspiratorial. "Just between you and me, Joe, I thought the whole affair extremely funny. Stubbs is a tiresome, arrogant youth. I couldn't let the Matron or any of the others know it, of course, but I really did think what happened to him thanks to you was rather an appropriate comeuppance." He took another sip of sherry. "Are you surprised I feel that way, Joe?"

"No," I said, dubiously. "I mean, yes. I would have thought you did not like it. Stubbs is in a position of authority, and what I did, not that I meant to, of course, hardly did him honor or me credit."

Another sip. "Surely, Joe, you would agree that authority, when abused, is owed rebuke rather than deference?"

"Perhaps it may be so, sir, but it would be wrong for one without station such as myself to even speculate, I should think. The rebuke should come from above, rather than below." At this, Mr. Peevers nodded and smiled indulgently at me.

"Very well said, young man. Wherever did you learn to speak so well? Mr. MacCurran has said you were uncommonly bright, but now that I am seeing it for myself I am delighted. Really."

"I don't know, sir. Words are easy things for me, it seems."

"And yet, you could not read until last month?"

"That is true."

"And what about now? How well can you read now?"

"I have read all of the alphabet books Mr. MacCurran has, plus a good many other things of his. I would like sometime to see a newspaper to see if I could manage it."

Mr. Peevers finished his glass of sherry, rose, and poured himself another, retrieving a newspaper from an upper drawer of his desk. He handed it to me as he returned to his seat. "Have a look at this. I've saved it because it concerns something that may turn out to be important."

I took the newspaper and saw immediately I had a very long way to go to master reading. It was dated the middle of August of the previous year, and across the top ran a large headline that I puzzled out with difficulty. "AMERICAN COLONIES IN FULL REBELLION."

"What does that mean?"

"Perhaps nothing. Or perhaps a very great deal. It may be the end of an era, and the beginning of a new and very wicked world. This remains to be seen."

"Beg pardon, sir?"

"America. Surely you have heard of America?"

"It's some place across the ocean?"

Mr. Peevers took a large swallow of sherry and gazed into the distance, which here meant the brick wall across the lane. "America, Master Chapman, is a continent as large as Europe, or larger, no one knows. And previously it was inhabited only by savages. For one hundred and fifty years, English men and women have labored there to create newly settled lands, and build towns and cities, and extend His Majesty's dominions. But now, a few very, very, wicked rascals over there have taken it into their heads the King is some kind of despot, and they think they will be better off on their own. It's really quite insane, and their plans are, of course, doomed, but it comes at an unfortunate time. The international situation is delicate. Have you heard of any of this, Joe?"

"Can't say as I have, sir. My life has been unsettled ever since my father died. I've had no time for news. It's not as if it's going to make any difference to me."

Mr. Peevers continued his confidential manner. "Perhaps that's true, Joe, but even here at home, there seems to be a new and very worrisome tenor to the times. As I travel about the city, I increasingly see want of deference, and at times even disrespect for authority. The beggars, especially, are insolent. It is very unpleasant to have to make one's way through a crush of obstreperous mendicants as one goes into and out of the bank. Most distressing." Looking at me again, he assumed intimacy. "Do you ever feel distressed, Joe?"

"I, ah, my mother died just before I came here."

"Oh, of course. I really am very sorry. But the lower orders are inured to suffering, are they not? You can have no idea, I am sure, of the suffering of a refined gentleman?"

I knew better than to object to the remark, it being the sort of thing one might expect a gentleman to say. I was beginning to tire of the interview and could see no point to it, but Mr. Peevers was just warming to his subject.

"I feel enormously lonely," he said, with a theatrical sigh and shake of his head. "You cannot imagine the pressures and responsibilities of managing an institution such as this. You must have some sense of loneliness, I should think." More sherry.

"Indeed I do, sir." I wondered if the fly is ever impatient for the spider to get on with it. I did not doubt Mr. Peevers was engaged in some stratagem, though I remained ignorant of its object.

"Perhaps, then, as two lonely souls we ought to drink to each other. Would you care for some sherry, Joseph?"

"All right. I mean, yes, sir, if it please you, sir." Mr. Peevers rose and placed a second glass beside his own, filling both of them. Together we drank.

"To our recognition of each other as lonely men," said Mr. Peevers. He smiled in a manner I presumed was intended to display his true, lavishly indulgent, and entirely loving, paternal nature.

"Now Joe, as you may have noticed in the infirmary, I have some medical knowledge. And even though Mr. Stogdon has discharged you, he is not responsible for the entire school, now, is he? Because I am, it is necessary for me to make an inspection of you myself before I can vouch for your readiness to return to work and school."

"An inspection, sir?"

"A simple medical examination quite without pain, Joseph. You may trust me. Surely whatever embarrassment may attend is unnecessary, given that I assisted with your medical treatment. Please remove your clothing."

"I am very sorry, sir, but is this really necessary? Mr. Stogdon did say I was perfectly fit."

"I assure you it is quite necessary. Mr. Stogdon is newly employed by me, is he not? What better way for me to ensure that he knows his business than by checking his work, eh? What's more, failure to comply will severely damage the good will I have so kindly extended to you. Now, let's see you." Mr. Peevers, sweating now, and perhaps not just from the fire, betrayed a lack of patience.

His eyes never left me as I disrobed. The fire was warm, and the sensation of being nude before it pleasant. I was startled by the touch of Mr. Peever's hands on my arse.

"You are looking fine and fit, Joseph. Please turn around." I complied, astonished that Mr. Peevers next reached for my member, attempting to grasp my foreskin between his thumb and forefinger. He did touch me, but was unable to get a hold as involuntarily I stepped away.

"Please don't, sir."

Mr. Peevers regarded me with a stern and aggrieved countenance. "It is medically necessary, Joe. I must make certain that you are healed everywhere."

"But I was never sick there, sir. Please don't."

"Master Chapman, I will have none of this. Should you fail to cooperate, the consequences will be dire! Kindly present yourself at once!"

To my surprise, and no small dismay, I found myself complying with the strange request. What did I know of physic? But no one had touched me there other than myself since I was an infant, and that Mr. Peevers should be first in my conscious life struck me as a very sad thing. He knelt, and I endured his touch. I grew increasingly uncomfortable as what I had expected to be a brief procedure went on and on. He rolled my foreskin back and forth with steady deliberation.

"Will it stand, Joseph?"

"What? Now?"

"Yes, now. Will it, Joseph?"

"Whatever for, Mr. Peevers? This doesn't strike me as proper."

Never taking his hands from me or ceasing their motion, Mr. Peevers looked up at me and shook his head. "Joe," he said, with soft familiarity. "Joe. Who decides what is right in this school, you or I?"

"You do, of course, sir."

"Then if I say a thing is right, it is, is it not? You may trust me, Joseph. Now, I want you to relax. Here, have some more sherry." He reached over to the side table and offered me the glass I had drunk from previously.

If this was what was meant by being properly deferential to Mr. Peevers, as Poxy had suggested, I would have none of it. My mind conjured an appalling image of the two of them together in this room, carrying on in this way. Thinking of my parents and their saucy refusal to be overawed by persons of quality, I determined to speak.

"No, sir, I'd rather not, sir. In fact, I'll be damned if I will, sir."

To my surprise, Mr. Peevers was entirely unperturbed. He smiled, in fact, with a kind of idiot serenity. He now had his other hand on my bollocks, even as the first continued its mischief in the previously mentioned location, which by dint of mechanical action was on the point of producing the effect he so fondly desired. "Excellent. It's agreed then."

"Beg pardon, sir?"

"That you're damned, of course." Mr. Peevers continued to smile reassuringly. Still he continued his motions.

"What!?" That he should touch me in this manner was bad enough, but that he should regard my damnation with complacency was altogether too much. I pulled away and ran to the table where I had put my clothes and began to dress.

Mr. Peevers seemed to cogitate a moment as to the best way to proceed, and then said my name entreatingly, using his softest and most ingratiating manner. "Joe. Stop. Please. Perhaps it does seem a bit improper, but is it really so very wrong? Think, what harm? What harm?" As he spoke, I had the sense I had gained the advantage. I kept my eye on him and dressed without speaking. Mr. Peevers remained kneeling in the spot where I had left him, continuing his entreaty.

"Listen to me, Joe. It makes no difference in the grand scheme of things, don't you know? We're all damned. Predestination, Joe, is the word. And a staunchly defended doctrine it is, too." In spite of my newly intensified abhorrence of the man, I slowed my dressing to listen. He could not have known it, but he was speaking directly to my personal dilemma, and his words drew me in till there existed naught else. Unfortunately, Mr. Peevers misconstrued my signs, and rose to approach me, speaking eagerly.

"Yes, Joe, that's the way it is. God already knows who is pure and who will be taken up to Heaven on the Day of Judgement, and it isn't very many. Very, very few, in fact. Oh, and the world is a wicked place. The rest of us may know ourselves by our actions, even by our secret desires. One can pray for grace, but if we will want such wicked things …"

Mr. Peevers was now within an arm's length of me, but I had espied on his desk an inkwell very nearly within reach, which I was about to throw at his face, when an urgent knocking came at the door, and the voice of an anxious and aroused Miss Strickenwell.

"Percival, come quickly!" she called. "There's a terrible row! Rennet and MacCurran are not here to help. I've got some of the young men on them, but please! Come quickly!"

"Yes, yes, I'll be right out!" And more softly, "Damn!" He pointed to me, indicating as he exited that I was to hide behind a high-backed chair, lest Miss

Strickenwell catch a glimpse of me, and said, in a much lower volume, every trace of soft entreaty and paternal indulgence gone, "Your examination will have to wait. Finish dressing and leave as soon as you can. And Joseph—a word of this to anyone, and it's straight to the workhouse with you." He jabbed his soft, pudgy finger in my direction and squinted his piggy eyes. "The workhouse!"

XX

When Mr. Peevers had gone, I emerged from my spot behind the chair, finished dressing, and lingered for a moment before the fire. As may well be imagined, I was in a state of disquiet. In less than two hours, I had been approached by Poxy, with as yet unknown results, and violated by Mr. Peevers, whose remarks concerning the inevitability of damnation had struck me with considerable force. He had confirmed God's distaste for me, indeed for the greater part of humanity, providing a hopelessly gloomy vision of life. His words gave name and context to the malaise I had discovered with Mr. MacCurran's aid, provoking a precipitation of bitterness in my soul.

It may be objected that such considerations are too abstract, too remote, or too incapable of proof, and therefore undeserving of concern, especially regarding one so young as I was then, but such objections are themselves immaterial. Despite my distaste for the man, in my inexperience I believed Mr. Peevers's words to be true. From this point forward, a dejected melancholy and a gloomy anxiety took up residence in my soul, where they would keep company with my grief.

At that moment, I was in the rare position of being at large in the building without specific instructions. It was nearly dark, and I thought I should make my way to room four and square myself away before supper. I left Mr. Peevers' study and walked towards the stairs leading to the garret dormitories, when I heard Chowder's voice, uncharacteristically strained, issue from the dining hall. I secreted myself behind a cabinet in such a manner that I could hear and observe but not be seen.

Seething, Chowder was being restrained by Stubbs, and another of the apprentice youths held Poxy, who seemed oddly composed despite bleeding from a swelling gash in his scalp. Miss Strickenwell and Mr. Peevers glared at them both.

"I was coming up from the laundry with a load of kitchen towels," said Chowder, "when this one attacked me from behind." Chowder appeared to have got the worst of it. He held a kitchen rag to his nose, from which copious amounts of blood had recently issued and become smeared around the lower half of his face. His left eye was blackening, and he was bleeding as well from his ear, which retained teeth marks. Poxy, who was half a head taller, also sported a blackening eye, and blood oozed downwards from the gash in his scalp over the left side of his face, dripping now and again from his chin.

"Why? Have you any idea why?" inquired Mr. Peevers of Chowder. Mr. Peevers seemed distressed and a bit unsure of himself. He kept looking at Poxy, as if to read from him what he should do.

"I'm sure I don't know. Give the sack to the bastard, will you? Everybody hates 'im." Chowder bit off his words.

"That's enough of that kind of talk, Master Gorham."

"If he wanted to fight, he ought to have challenged me properly. There's a customary way of doing that, as you may know. It proves he's a bastard."

"Master Gorham, that is *enough*!"

Miss Strickenwell spoke next. "Daniel," meaning Poxy, "Is this true? Whatever possessed you?"

"He deserved it. I hate 'im. That's all." Poxy shrugged.

Mr. Peevers sighed. "Master Gorham, I am of a mind to terminate you. I recently have been approached by a greengrocer in Spittle Fields wanting an apprentice. It is, frankly, as good as you are going to get."

Miss Strickenwell's eyebrows shot up at this. She appeared to struggle with herself a moment before speaking, and when she did, she was severe. "Mister Peevers, it may not be my place, but I really must object! Most strenuously must I object! Master Gorham was attacked. Daniel does not deny it. Why then do we terminate the boy who defended himself, and not the instigator, who has started many another fight? Master Gorham may not be the very most exemplary of our charges, but he is doing well in his studies and would learn more if we could keep him. Daniel, or Poxy, as they call him, is useless."

Mr. Peevers's uncertainty vanished beneath the weight of his most lordly manner. "You are correct, madam, that it is not your place to contradict me. I am under no obligation at all to justify my decisions to you. I will condescend to tell you, however, that in spite of what you say, I believe Master Ranlet has potential far out of the ordinary." Here the Matron snorted with sharp contempt, which Mr. Peevers pretended not to notice. "I am of a mind to apprentice him to service in our school, so that he might remain here. He is, ah, a most loyal young man. I do believe he will learn to turn the other cheek."

Miss Strickenwell, losing all patience, now spoke very rapidly, her eyes flashing. "This is absurd! How can you call him loyal when he subverts every peaceable custom? Percival Peevers, I am going to the Presbytery with this, and with the many other instances of your incompetence. I cannot stand to watch you ruin this precious institution. There! I've said it, and now I'm going to do it!"

Mr. Peevers's affectedly composed manner hardened. "Madam, your insubordination is intolerable. As of this moment, I am relieving you of your duties. We shall see whether your suspension is to be temporary or permanent. Kindly repair to your apartment and remain until summoned."

Miss Strickenwell was every bit as unfazed as Mr. Peevers pretended to be. "You can't give me the sack, and you know it. I was appointed by the Presbytery, just as you were. I work for them and the Congregation, not for you. And I tell you, when they hear what I have to say, it is you who will be out on the street!"

"And you were appointed as my distinct underling, were you not?" Mr. Peevers may have lost ground, but he persevered in his lordly disdain.

Miss Strickenwell would have none of it. "Don't be a toad, Percival. Matron and not Governor, yes. But I should be very surprised to learn the Matron is to be a blind idiot. Much to my distress, I cannot interfere with your decision, but I can and do take note of it. Beware, sir, and know that the Presbytery will be informed."

She turned on her heel and walked rapidly away, her footsteps making hard, dry, echoing noises in the silent room. As the sounds diminished, Mr. Peevers muttered, "Damnable cunt," causing Poxy and Stubbs to snicker.

When she had gone, Mr. Peevers spoke. "Master Gorham, I direct you to disregard the Matron, who is obviously not herself. The grocer's name is Cudworth. Tobias Cudworth. I have promised him a boy this evening. You will now go to your room and collect your effects. Supper is in three quarters of an hour, and you will take it here. Following supper, you will be taken to Spittlefields. I already have the articles; they want only your name. Stubbs, see him upstairs and then leave him. Master Ranlet, you will come with me to my study." Poxy smirked triumphant, and I wanted to spew.

"Beg pardon, sir?" said Chowder.

"What is it?" Mr. Peevers was very impatient.

"You're going to send me like this?"

"I do expect you to clean yourself. As for your eye and ear, worry not. Cudworth wants your back and arms. If he will take an apprentice for three pounds, he cannot be expecting quality. Now go!"

Stubbs pushed Chowder in the direction of the hall leading to the stairs. I ran on ahead and bounded up the stairs unseen, and hid in the room opposite number four until I heard Chowder enter and Stubbs leave. When Stubbs's footsteps had faded away, I crossed the hall and entered to find Chowder sitting disconsolate on the bed we had shared. He continued to hold the rag to his nose.

"Joe? What are you doing here?" He looked at me wonderingly.

"I, ah, it's a long story. Peevers wanted to see me, then I got loose when Miss Strickenwell came to get him because of your fight. So he forgot about me, and I hid and watched." In spite of everything, the sight of him lifted my heart, and I found myself grinning. "Look at you. Does it hurt?"

"I don't know. I guess. Not really."

I sat on the bed next to Chowder and embraced him with trembling tenderness. To my joy, he returned my embrace until he had to blow his nose, This renewed his bleeding, and we were for a while diverted by that.

We exchanged news as rapidly as we could. Poxy had indeed attacked Chowder at the top of the stairs leading from the laundry to the vacant dining hall. Poxy, having been governed more by emotion than deliberation, and wanting perhaps more to insult and intimidate than grievously wound, had grabbed Chowder's shoulder and spun him around so that he might land a blow on his face. Chowder's response had been to fly at Poxy with everything he had, and they had gone at it until they were on the floor rolling around, which is when Poxy bit Chowder's ear. Chowder managed to scramble away to a serving station, picking up a pewter mug he flung at Poxy with all the force he could muster. The mug found its mark, tearing Poxy's scalp.

"That was a lucky one. I never could throw worth a damn. Used to make fun of me, the other boys did, when I was little. Said I threw a ball like a girl, they did. Bastards."

"No one can say you didn't throw well this time. Then what happened?"

"The Matron came running and shrieking, and next we knew, Stubbs and the other one were on us. Then Peevers came."

"You're doing well to get out of this place," I said. "What point in staying?"

"I could see you."

"Chowder, I will see you again. I will get out of this damned place as soon as I can, and I will find you. I swear it. How many grocers named Cudworth can there be in Spittlefields? And think, it's your old neighborhood. You still have friends and family there."

"Maybe. I don't know, Joe. Except for me mother, I always seemed the odd one out. I don't know why. I do want you to find me, though, that I do know."

We embraced again. This was the moment I first realized I wanted to kiss him, despite his being a bloody mess. It was the best and most joyous feeling imaginable and didn't seem to have anything at all to do with the horrors Mr. MacCurran, let alone Mr. Peevers, had inspired. I was confused beyond telling, but just then didn't care.

Then I told Chowder of what Mr. Peevers had attempted with me. "He said he needed to examine me, but what he wanted was to play with my member."

"What?! What did you do?"

"He tricked me into thinking it had to do with physic, so I'm afraid I did let him at first. Some examination that was. He was so sly, and then he's pulling on it. Damn. But I didn't let him go any further. I had stepped away and was about to plant an inkwell in his face when the matron came a-shrieking."

Chowder looked at me with compassionate wonder. "Oh, Joe, that is too horrible. What are you going to do?"

"I don't know yet. But if he dares try it again, I will cause him to suffer for it, of that you may be sure. You know, I think he and Poxy go at it together. That has to be why he protects him." Then I told Chowder of how Poxy had come to me in the infirmary and wanted to swear friendship. "So that's why he wanted to thrash you."

Chowder shook his head. "Damn. Good luck with that one after I leave. You're going to need it."

We sat and looked at each other. And then, because time was short, I helped him clean himself. He changed his clothes and gathered all his worldly possessions into a small bundle, showing me his few treasured possessions as he did so. Among these was a wooden top he had received from his mother for a birthday when he was small. "It's all I have from her."

And then we heard many footsteps on the stairs, signaling the supper hour was nigh. When Nails and the others entered, sans Poxy, Chowder was the hero of the hour, as word of the battle had quickly spread. I was content to step aside. I had no desire or need to compete for Chowder's attention, knowing I had no equal in his heart, nor did I wish to tell my own story to the others.

Supper, from which Mr. Peevers and Poxy were absent, was over much too soon, and then I saw Chowder leave. In the presence of the others, we merely shook hands, and then he was gone in the direction of Mr. Peevers's front parlor. It seemed impossible, but I had known Chowder a mere three weeks. It was a very long walk to the scullery, and a yet longer night without him near.

XXI

IN THE MORNING, I RESUMED my former routine, which I pursued with dull vacancy. Life became a ceaseless round of school and toil, and I differed little from the boys whose appearance had so startled me when I first arrived. Overwork and malnutrition left me with little energy to contemplate the possibility of life beyond the Little Eastcheap Free School for Unfortunate Boys.

Chowder took his place among the beautiful things I had lost. I remembered having him in my arms and the joy of wanting to kiss him. But at night, I would find myself thinking of him in precisely the ways I had vowed I would not. Although I put little store by it, I prayed to God to cause me to stop thinking of Chowder when my member would stand, but I had to suppose God didn't, or wouldn't, hear me, as the thoughts and my member went on. I could not help wondering why God had made me so, if only to turn his back on me. If I could not help but desire that which God could not forgive, I was not worthy to approach Him, and so I ceased to try, which did nothing to assuage my deepening melancholy, as I could not imagine how to address it. I shared these thoughts with no one, and none guessed the weight I carried, or that I lived in a world which made no sense.

Life in room four was now very bleak. Although Nails was a fair-minded and upright sort, he offered none of the tender solicitude Chowder had, and he and the others went wearily about their tasks without apparent curiosity as to their room-mates, or any evidence of interest in friendship apart from the occasional episode of back-slapping crudity when the subject of young females would arise, which made me feel very ill at ease. We were different species, and I could not help but find them primitive. They seemed content to live isolated from each other, even as they slept in the same beds and dressed side by side. I could not fathom they showed no need of the intimacies I craved.

I had been discharged from the infirmary on a Wednesday. By Friday, it was clear I had far surpassed the reading powers of the small boys in Mr. MacCurran's classroom, and so was introduced to the academic routine of the older boys, in which one learned from the other three teachers in turn through the morning.

I didn't need to take arithmetic from Mr. Rennet, as I could already do all manner of sums, having helped both of my parents make change since I was a small boy, and so began Latin instead. I wished most sincerely to avoid Mr. Peevers's religion and moral instruction classes but could not, and Miss Strickenwell laid into me with the history of England, and the geography of the world. At last, I learned where America is. As peculiarly unpleasant as each of the three were in his or her own way, I will give it to them that they believed in what they were doing. Even Mr. Peevers shoveled learning at us with furious energy, as if it were coal and we the furnaces of Christendom. Only Rennet's Latin classes were tedious.

After several nights of absence, Poxy, wearing a bandage wrapping over his scalp and around his chin, resumed habitation in room four. He seemed to have pulled in his horns and pretended nothing had passed between us, in which pretense I was only too willing to cooperate. Soon another boy was added to our lot to take the place of Chowder.

His name was Randolph Whimple, and he was but ten years of age. His parents had been of some quality, but this had not prevented their drowning at sea and taking their fortune with them. It irked me the other youths would either ignore or tease the lad, and it added to my sense of difference from them that I was the only one who displayed any compassionate interest in him. It pleased me he and Nimbles got on well, once I introduced them. I will own, however, that I was not above conniving to have him between Poxy and myself in the bed.

I still had Stubbs to contend with, but his attitude towards me had changed. Perhaps he now considered me a force to be reckoned with, in part due to our interaction immediately precedent to my illness. Because I worked like a demon and endured the epithet of "Puker" without complaint, he had little occasion to abuse me. Or perhaps Mr. Peevers had told him to direct his tender mercies elsewhere.

His forbearance may, in part, be attributed to my besting him in a series of arm-wrestling contests performed in the free minutes between finishing the afternoon washing up and the laying out of supper. As he was a slovenly, fat sort, better at browbeating others to work than he was at working himself, I bested him easily, though I was shorter and weighed a stone or more less. All that rowing on the Thames, I suppose.

Mr. Peevers was rarely to be seen, but in contradistinction Miss Strickenwell was much in evidence. The week before Christmas, I looked out from the scullery to see her giving several gentlemen a tour. In contrast to the smarmy cant that had surrounded Mrs. Winterbottom, they spoke earnestly among themselves, although the Matron did indulge herself in the occasional theatrical gesture. Her voice fairly squeaked.

Stubbs told me the gentlemen were members of the Presbytery, and therefore all big wigs in the Congregation. I saw them again the following Sunday when we had services in the dining hall. This was an event I had so far missed due to my bout of illness. I was very uncomfortable and felt an impostor, at best, singing hymns to a God who hated me. I wondered if Mr. Peevers felt uncomfortable as he led us in prayer. I vowed that in future I would have as little to do with churches as I could manage, at least until I should understand them better.

Another time I saw Miss Strickenwell escorting a very elderly and somewhat infirm lady through the dining hall. I learned from Stubbs this was her elder sister Emma, with whom she lived in a private apartment in the oldest wing of the building, and whom she tended. Miss Strickenwell had spent the better part of her many years in this place, having grown up in the Congregation after her father, a cabinet maker turned drunkard, had puked blood until he died when she was fourteen. She had begun as a maid and worked her way up by dint of tireless service.

Although I continued to find her spastic mannerisms and abruptness by turns laughable and annoying, to say nothing of my dislike for her tendency to make caustic remarks to boys in positions of dependency, I drew inspiration from her dedication to her work, and from her outspoken courage. I resolved to emulate her better qualities, which resolution was no sooner conceived than tested.

Two days before Christmas, Mr. Peevers called me out of the scullery to his study again. It was early afternoon, but already very gloomy outside. A relentless, cold rain fell heavily.

"Please come in, Joseph." Mr. Peevers seemed just a bit smaller, somehow. "You may sit again in the blue chair, if you like." I sat as invited, whilst Mr. Peevers poured two glasses of sherry. "Would you like some, Joseph?"

"No, thank you sir. I find it gives me a headache."

"Pity. You didn't say that before. Ah, well, more for me." He brought both glasses and placed them on the table next his chair, and sat, as before, opposite me. He looked at me with what appeared to be an earnest expression, which I returned with a steady gaze. "I believe I owe you an apology, Joe." He began to drink.

"Beg pardon, sir?"

"For having to leave so quickly the last time you were here and neglecting to complete your examination." Mr. Peevers smiled a smile of bland insensibility.

"I'm not going through that again, sir." He could put me on the wintry, sodden street with no place to go, if he liked. I remembered how Miss Strickenwell had handled him and was not afraid of the man. In some manner I did not quite understand, my feelings for Chowder also lent me strength. It was time Percival Peevers were crossed.

"Joseph, that is unnecessary. Do you forget my position of authority?"

"I do not."

"Well, then, what is the meaning of this obstinacy?"

"Do you not recall your remark, Mr. Peevers, concerning the abuse of authority?"

"I cannot imagine I would discuss authority and either its prerogatives or its limitations with one such as yourself." When I was a child I saw, once, the Thames above London Bridge freeze. It was not as cold then as Mr. Peevers was now.

"Well, you did. And you can go to hell. I believe you are *sodomitical*." Although I was not clear on what the word meant, I knew it had something to do with improper actions between men, and so wielded it.

Mr. Peevers raised his voice. "That is enough! I will have none of this!" A vein on his forehead stood out.

"Perhaps Miss Strickenwell will have it, then?" I asked mildly.

He attempted to don the lordly manner, but it wouldn't quite come off. "Such impertinence!" He paused a moment, and our eyes met. I held steady. He continued, now nervously. "You wouldn't dare do such a thing. I can get rid of you in an instant, before you can talk to her." Feeling he had made his point, he essayed the conciliatory. "Now, be a good, sweet boy and drop your breeches and come here." So saying, he rose in contravention of his just-issued command and moved softly towards me. I sprang from my seat, grabbed a letter opener lying on his desk, and whirled to face him, thrusting the blade of the letter opener forward.

"I say I shall not!"

Mr. Peevers hesitated, then said, with manufactured calm, "Put that down,

Joseph. You do not frighten me."

"Frightened or not, touch me and I will put it in your heart!"

"Joseph, please."

"Go to hell! I will tell all! I will see you hanged!"

The vein throbbed, and the piggy eyes boggled in their pouches. "You would be held a liar."

"Would the Presbytery think so, if it could find other boys you have done the same to? Are there not records of where each has been placed?" I wasn't certain of that, but it seemed more than likely.

Mr. Peevers retreated to his chair, finished his glass of sherry in one swallow, and downed the one he had poured for me in like manner. "Damn you. You are a most intractable young man. You are too damned smart for your own good."

Putting down the letter opener within easy reach, I remained standing. "Perhaps I am only too smart for you. Would you like to get rid of me, Mr. Peevers?"

"Indeed I would." Mr. Peevers's face now betrayed fear. His hand shook as he poured and gulped a third glass of sherry.

"Then you will apply every penny of the fifty pounds held for me towards the best possible apprenticeship you can find. I wish something having to do with books or with learning in some manner. And I wish it as soon as possible."

"And that will satisfy you?"

"It will, if you do it. If you do not, I will tell all. I know more than you think." Here was more bluffing, but I had seen enough to conjecture.

Mr. Peevers clung to his prerogatives like a naked man might cling to a scrap of dirty cloth to cover himself. "Do not dictate to me. If you will have anything better than a sweep, you will show proper deference."

"I am too grown for a sweep's 'prentice, and you know it."

"But you *will* mind your tongue. I will do as you request, for I wish most heartily to see the back of you. Er, see you out of here. For your part, you will speak well of me at every opportunity and be exemplary in your studies and the discharge of your duties. If I am to place you high, then all must see the reason for it."

"I believe speaking highly of you would be lying, Mr. Peevers, given the reason for our pact. It would scarce become an exemplary youth." What fun to be haughty. "Even you must see that. I will manage somehow not to speak ill of you, if that will do."

Mr. Peevers, having run out of stratagems, did not speak.

"There is one other thing," I said. "Tell Poxy to continue to ignore me. Is it agreed?"

Mr. Peevers had receded deeply into his chair, and studied his empty glass as if it held answer to his private mystery. "It is agreed. Now leave this room at once."

I was only too happy to comply. As I returned to the scullery, I realized I was trembling, and could scarce hold back tears. Three weeks later, I was apprenticed to a Mr. Thomas Jackson, bookseller, who kept premises at number 58, St. Paul's Churchyard.

XXII

MR. PEEVERS DISCHARGED ME ON one of your rare January days in southern England that can seem like early spring. A fresh, cool gale blew from the southeast, scouring away all smoke, and sun and squall competed for place over London. The air was mild, all was bright, and I was full of anticipation.

"Walk west from here," said Mr. Peevers, lofty to the last. "Little Eastcheap will wander and change its name, but the road trends westward directly to St. Paul's. You cannot miss it, and you will see the dome now and then to make for. Once you have gained the Churchyard, you will want number fifty-eight. That is on the north side, directly opposite the entrance to the Cathedral. Good-bye, Joe."

I looked my last at Mr. Peevers's piggy eyes and pear-shaped frame, returned to him the curtest of nods, then turned and stepped out the door. I was free, gloriously free in the teeming streets, and it felt wonderful. Ignoring Mr. Peevers's directions, I walked south to Thames street, with which I was more familiar, savoring all. How good it felt to be back among the carts, horses and drivers, and their varied loads, and to see again all the differing kinds of people—the tatty street children, shifting about and deciding whether it would be more advantageous at any given moment to beg or steal, worried mothers and puling infants, peddlers and piemen of all kinds touting their wares in song, and fine carriages with dressed horses, heavy wagons with teams of six and eight, and rakes and harlots, pickpockets and thieves, and gentlemen and women of quality, honest working men and boys and girls in service, all in a great crush, trying to get past each other without injury.

Carried by the raucous tide, I was borne westward and soon crossed Brickhill Lane, which caused me to reflect on the progress of my life and how I had grown over eight months. The trials that had previously weighed so heavily on my soul were now relieved by the bright prospect of my future, which I approached with every eager step. I had not heard of Thomas Jackson prior to Mr. Peevers's mentioning him, but that his premises were in St. Paul's Churchyard meant that he and his establishment were of a certain quality. Nearing St. Paul's, I walked up St. Bennett's Hill into the churchyard, where the great, dark bulk of the cathedral dominated all. Passing around to the west of it, I soon arrived in front of the gracefully curving row of buildings on the north side, coming to a halt in front of number fifty-eight.

From the street, the shop window afforded view of many pleasingly arranged books and notices, and above the door, a simple painted sign read: "T. JACKSON, BOOKSELLER AND PUBLISHER" in black letters. Another on the door itself said: "Superior Selection of the Latest Scientific, Theological, and Political Works," and yet another in the largest window read: "Wide Assortment of New and Used Books of all Kinds."

This was so much better than I had dared even dream, that I wondered whether perhaps Mr. Peevers had in spite placed me too far above my station or abilities, to ensure my humiliation and ruin. I wondered, too, how he had arranged it. Why would the proprietor of such an establishment condescend to take on an orphan boy of unproven worth? It couldn't have been merely that I had the fee. All manner of boys more presentable than I would have that and more.

Feeling very uncertain, I opened the door and looked about. Shelves of new books of all sizes and in all manner of bindings, from gilded leather to the cheapest board, lined the walls on all sides save that nearest the street, where the clean, south-facing windows admitted the sweetest imaginable glow of pale yellow, winter sunlight. I found it entirely beautiful.

Smells of leather, paper, tobacco, and ink permeated the air. In the center, a large table held yet more books, and to the rear shelves of used books of every description reached from floor to ceiling. Between these and the table was a desk, where sat a young man in his early twenties. He was dressed in the garb of a prosperous shopkeeper, perhaps even that of a gentleman, and wore a finely cut waistcoat and powdered wig of the first quality. His face, if rather sharply angular, was not unpleasantly so, and his hazel eyes were not unhandsome. He had about him the air of intelligence suitable to one presiding over such an establishment, and he smoked a clay pipe. He regarded me with mild curiosity, perhaps mixed with some suspicion. I approached, set down my bag, and stood awkwardly for a moment. As he said nothing, I ventured to speak.

"Ah, would you be Mr. Jackson?"

The young gentleman eyed me dubiously. "Hardly. Who enquires?"

"My name is Joseph Chapman. I'm the new 'prentice."

"Apprentice? Here?"

"I truly believe so, sir. I was sent over from Little Eastcheap, Mr. Peevers' school. He gave directions to me himself."

"I see." The young gentleman did not appear pleased. "This is news to me. Unfortunately, Mr. Jackson has gone to Leeds some days now. He is expected to return this evening or perhaps tomorrow." He paused, and I waited patiently for him to continue. "But what you say is not impossible. Mr. Jackson has spoken lately of desiring to take on a 'prentice. His trade is flourishing, and he is a very, very busy man. I am merely looking after the place during his absence. But I'm afraid I have no idea what to do with you until he does return."

"Is there any sort of job I could do, perhaps?"

He thought a moment. "Possibly. This morning we received a very large shipment from the printer, three cart-load's worth, and it is all sitting in boxes on the loading dock in the lane. They are barely out of the wet and must be taken upstairs as soon as possible. I've engaged some men to take care of it, but they are very slow in coming. I expect they are drunk by now and will not show up today. If you'll do that for your supper, I can dismiss them if or whenever they do arrive. I'd say Mr. Jackson will be well pleased. Do you, ah, think yourself capable?" His manner suggested that he hoped I was not.

"I did not come here to live like a lord." This response, contrived to demonstrate that his query could only have issued from a half-wit, seemed to please rather than annoy him, and I was rewarded with a smile. He rose from his seat to offer his hand, which I accepted with no inconsiderable relief.

"The name is Rowland Hunter. If you are indeed what you say you are and really are up to it, you are rather a lucky young man."

"Ah." I responded in what I hoped was a knowing manner.

He led me through the shop to the rear, where a steep staircase ascended, and a large door opened onto a lane. I had to stow my bag under the stairs and get right to work. He had not exaggerated the quantity of boxes of books or the need to move them. The outer rows had been drenched by the most recent squall, and although the wooden crates were sturdy, they would not keep water out forever.

"These wet ones here will have to be opened as soon as you get them upstairs, and the books taken out. The boxes are lined with oiled paper, and then waste paper. That will slow the water getting in, but it does not stop it entirely. Here, take this one," he said, pointing to a large box on the end of the top outside row. He then led me upstairs to the storeroom and showed me how to open the crates and where to put the books.

It was not quite one o'clock when I started. As I worked, I felt progressively less enthusiastic and more hungry. The heavy boxes of rough wood were difficult to handle and had to be carried one at a time up the steep stairs, barely wide enough to accommodate a person and his load, to the store room. On the first floor, I pulled nails from the box ends with a claw hammer, put the books on the nearby empty shelves Rowland had indicated, and tidied and stored the packing material as I went. In the course of these labors, I dropped a box on my toe and perforated my hands and forearms with numerous splinters. The books, copies of a work on various kinds of air by someone named Priestley, may as well have been bricks. This was not my idea of the pleasures to be gained from literature, but I well knew that as a green apprentice I could expect much more of the same.

During the afternoon the wind swung 'round to the southwest. Tumultuous, crenellated clouds rode in from the sea, and, obliterating the sun even before it set, loosed heavy rain upon the city, creating an enveloping, sodden darkness. But minutes before my inability to see would have been rendered complete, candles were brought by a pleasant, middle aged, and quite round housekeeper who appeared noiselessly on slippered feet. She introduced herself as Mrs. Whidby and peppered me in a genial manner with questions about my origins, recent history, and intentions, which I answered as well as I could. Saying she would return shortly with something to relieve me, she pronounced it very odd I should be laboring thus alone.

Returning in less than a quarter of an hour, she offered me a very sizable mug of beer. "Now then, love, drink up." As I sucked the foamy golden liquid in, she filled my ears with her opinions of drink and its value to the laborer. "Beer's good food," she said. "Used to be everybody drank beer when they worked, and all day long, too. Beer for breakfast starts you off right. Nowadays, they all want tea and coffee. What for? That's not food. I don't know what the world's coming to, sometimes. Ah, well, it isn't up to me, now, is it?" She continued with these and like observations until I had drained the mug, following which she departed, saying it would be a pleasure to know me better. The feeling was mutual.

The beer entered my brain very nearly as quickly as it had my empty stomach, and if I did not thereby feel entirely nourished, I did feel less pain. The remainder of my task passed with indistinct rapidity, accompanied by sundry heartfelt realizations. Mrs. Whidby was indeed a very, very kind woman to have thought of me when she didn't have to. Chowder was the most perfectly beautiful friend I had ever had or could imagine. These thoughts put me in mind of how unused to kindness I had become, behind which I rediscovered my longing for my dead mother, whereupon I spent some moments in a maudlin state, which as quickly passed.

Soon thereafter I discovered I had finished my tasks. All the boxes were safely raised to the first floor, the wet ones broken open, and their contents properly stored, and the dry ones stacked along a wall. Everything was done exactly as I had been directed to do it.

XXIII

I FOUND A BROOM AND was busily sweeping and reflecting on the powers of beer, the final gift of which had been a strong headache, when I heard footsteps on the stairs. These were followed by a striking gentleman in his early forties, of slight stature, who carried himself with the sort of precise self-assurance that cannot be counterfeited. From his cocked hat and excellent wig to his silver buckles, he was impeccably dressed in clothes of the highest quality, conservatively cut. His features, most notably a high forehead and large eyes, radiated intelligence and mildness of temper. Seeing me, he smiled and spoke without the lordly condescension to which I had become accustomed in Mr. Peevers' school.

"Hello, you are Joseph?"

"Yes, sir. Mr. Jackson?"

"Yes. Welcome." He offered me his hand with an appearance of genuine human feeling that impressed me deeply. "I'm terribly sorry about the confusion. My trade has exploded of late, and when I last saw Mr. Peevers, I had no idea I would be gone to Leeds so long. To make it worse, on my return, the carriage broke a wheel, and a day was lost in repairing it. I had expected to be present this morning. Please accept my apologies." He extended his hand again, and I shook it wonderingly. I had never before been apologized to by a person of quality and had no very clear idea how to conduct myself.

"Oh, it's all right, sir. I got all this work done, anyhow."

"Ah, yes, Dr. Priestley's latest opus." He picked one of the new volumes off a shelf and examined it expertly before replacing it. "Where are the others, or have they already left?"

"The others, sir?"

"The workmen who assisted you, of course. Surely, you did not do all this by yourself."

"But I did do it by myself, sir. Nobody helped me. Mr. Hunter said he would put me to it and send the workmen away, if they ever came."

"He did? Most intriguing. That was irregular, Joseph. It is standard procedure here to have a crew of three handle all of these large shipments. I have some very reliable workmen whom I regularly engage. It's easy when you use the hoist." He nodded in the direction of the end of the room, where a large double door stood closed, and to the side, a strange mechanism. I had supposed the double door had to do with moving freight, but that it was disused.

"Hoist, sir?"

"I mean that you and the others ought to have been using the hoist, there. With it, you can load half a dozen boxes of books or more onto a pallet and raise it straight up using the pulley. I've even installed a winch. A child could turn it. When you have it to the right height, the pulley, pallet, and all can be brought into the room right here." He pointed to a sort of rail running along the ceiling, and nearest the door, suspended from the rail, a pulley from which loops of stout rope hung. "Surely you had help getting the boxes up the stairs, at least?"

"I'm afraid I did not, sir. Carried every one of them myself." Encouraged by his approachable demeanor, I added, "I don't mind telling you it was damned hard work."

Mr. Jackson became very thoughtful. He murmured, "Very odd," and then said "I am truly sorry. I will speak to Rowland about this. This is a modern establishment, and I insist even the lowliest 'prentice be treated in a humane manner." If he was really angry at Rowland, he did not show it, however, as his speech continued mild. Later, I was to learn that he was expert at allowing others to see exactly as much of his inner workings as he wished them to, and no more. This was not from any practice of the dissembling art, but from a deeply ingrained habit of privacy. When he allowed himself the liberty, his features displayed a wonderful alacrity of apprehension. He spoke with an admirable firmness completely free of cant. "I am very impressed with you, Joseph. I am, I daresay, rather more impressed with you than I should think you are with me, or have been given cause to be, at any rate."

The thing was, I was enormously impressed with the man. My abused frame was crying for relief, I had a headache, my mind was not clear, and yet one of London's more prominent booksellers was sitting on a box in his storeroom praising me and apologizing to me as if I were a person of worth. I loved it, and I half loved him, though I had just met him. But there I was full of boyish wonder, when some manner of intelligent reply would have been more appropriate. Taking my silence for awkwardness, which perhaps it was, he brightened.

"You must be quite starved. I do believe supper is ready. Come, let's eat."

He led me down the stairs, chattering all the way. "Mrs. Whidby is my housekeeper. She's the best there is, and a most excellent cook, too. I think you will be very content with what she puts on the table. Where are your things? Here under the stairs? Good. Come, we will go across the lane. I live on the uppermost floor of the shop, as does Rowland, but we don't have enough space in the building for Mrs. Whidby, too, let alone for you. So I let lodgings over there for her, and now for you, too. You shall sleep over there and have your own bed chamber. How does that sound? Here, you wait on the loading dock a minute. I just want to have a word with Rowland."

I only had to wait a minute. If Mr. Jackson had had any tense words with Rowland, on his return he showed no trace of it, resuming his chatter as we crossed the narrow lane. "Tonight, I shall dine with you. This won't happen often, of course, but I do want to start you off right and to get to know you. I'm really very interested to learn more about you, Joe."

We entered a small, snugly immaculate and cheerful lodging, which bespoke in every detail the pleasures and rewards of a modest life prudently and contentedly lived. The fire in the large, old-fashioned fireplace was bright, and from the ovens beside it and the pots within issued glorious smells promising hearty food reserved not only for my betters, but for me. Where Mr. Peevers would have had but a single candle, and that a very small one, Mrs. Whidby had three of goodly size in glass holders.

I found Mr. Jackson's attention flattering, but just at that moment was far more interested in the food. I began to salivate so hard I feared I might drool. I felt a painful tension in my stomach, and my head was very light. I credit Mr. Jackson and Mrs. Whidby for their indulgence of what must have been a boorish spectacle. I vaguely recall a little conversation before Mrs. Whidby rose to bring our supper, but cannot say what it was about. When she produced the food, I fell to with titanic zeal. Such good food it was.

Perhaps it was only plain and hearty fare, but after the rigors of Mr. Peevers's execrable school, it seemed I dined at a king's table. What could possibly be better than pea soup and boiled beef and tripe and potatoes, turnips, and carrots? And all the wheaten bread and butter I wanted. Mrs. Whidby offered ale, but I declined it in favor of real milk, the cream standing on top. It was beautiful enough to make one cry. When I finally began to slow down, I realized the two of them were watching me with kindly indulgence.

"You are so very kind. I can't thank you enough." I got the words out awkwardly enough, between bites and swallows.

"Joseph, thanks are unnecessary," said Mr. Jackson. "This meat is yours. You have earned it by means of your labor and honorable conduct today. That you would think to thank me simply shows you were properly raised before you went to that school. What did they feed you there, Joseph?"

And so I told him of the watery gruel and thin broth with its indefinable greasy lumps, the moldy bread, and of seeing tiny bits of real meat only on Sundays. The question was followed by another, and another, and another. Mr. Jackson possessed a genius for conversation and, what was more remarkable, for listening. Under his gentle direction, although I must say I required very little prodding, I soon told him in detail of the Little Eastcheap Free School for Unfortunate Boys, of how I had come to be there, and of my prior life.

He was especially interested to hear of my parents and what had happened to them. The dismal tale of the final summer of my mother's life touched him deeply, as did Sarah's fate. I shielded from him only the tenderness of my regard for Chowder, and Mr. Peevers's inappropriate attentions. I ought not to have thought so, but I felt in some way that Mr. Peevers's attempted abuse cast me in an unsavory light, even though the wrongdoing had been entirely his. And I had promised not to tell. It did appear Mr. Peevers had kept his part of the pact.

Mr. Jackson, to be sure, spoke as well as listened. He was the son of a farmer near Liverpool, but he had been too sickly as a child for laboring there. He was apprenticed to a bookseller when he was fourteen, which was a desire he had conceived himself, and he had built his life on that. Once established, he had gone from selling medical books in Fish Street to contracting with writers and printers to become a publisher of many of the more important books of the day. Had I heard of Dr. Franklin? I had not. Mr. Jackson was immensely proud to be personally acquainted with the great *American* doctor, and would soon publish his collected political writings. Mr. Jackson firmly believed the best was yet to come.

"Books, Joseph. Books contain and disseminate learning. Print renders thought tangible and portable. To bring the best possible books into the world, to provide the works which advance learning, and which challenge ignorance, is a sacred duty and a thrilling privilege. Do you have any sense of what I am talking about, Joseph?"

The moment was critical. My stomach was now full, and I was growing sleepy and dull, but I had enough wit remaining to know this deserved the most cogent reply possible. "I can't imagine any better way to put it, Mr. Jackson. I mean, an evil person could put lies into a book, and foolish people would believe them. I suppose that happens anyway. But if no one bothered to serve truth by putting out proper and good books, then I don't see how learning could grow, or humanity become wise. We owe a great deal to people like you, I should think." Mr. Jackson smiled broadly, and I felt that I had said a very bright thing, even if another might have put it more elegantly.

"Now, Joseph, before I explain our routine here, and what your first set of daily tasks will be, do you have any questions for me?"

"Well, I was going to ask about my duties, but what I really want to know first is, why me, Mr. Jackson? Why would anyone like you take a chance on an orphan from Peevers's rotten school? It can't just be that my parents put by the fee."

Mr. Jackson looked at me hard for a second. "I am very puzzled by what you say about the fee, Joseph. Mr. Peevers has paid me no fee."

"You were not paid fifty pounds?"

"I assure you I have taken you quite without any fee, and that was deliberate. I could have any number of overfed dullards who want to start at the top and think themselves too good for honest labor. But even though their parents might pay several times your fifty in gold, the aggravation they would cause would not be worth it. What I want, Joe, is a boy who reminds me of myself at your age. What I mean is, a hungry and determined boy with plenty of intelligence and a true heart. I saw Mr. Peevers's advert long ago and thought I might look there. I had several discussions with him, and asked for and received a list of names, with yours at the top. He recommended you most strongly, but in general terms. I then interviewed the Matron and teachers to form a picture of the various boys. It was Mr. MacCurran's remarks which swayed me most. He said you were the quickest lad he ever saw. I liked the sound of that, of course, but when he warned me that despite being generally well-mannered, you had been known to ask impertinent questions, I knew you were the one. Without curiosity and a lively spirit, a boy is not a proper boy, if you ask me, and is unlikely to become much of a man. Certainly no bookseller, to say nothing of publisher. And, Joe, I dare say it is starting to appear I have got my gold, but of a kind superior to the metal, if you don't mind my saying so. But, please understand that I am not all kindness. I truly believe that my idea will be very smart business. You have already put in more work since you arrived than most would in a week. Not that I intended for you to have to work quite so hard, you understand."

I delighted in hearing that merit had played a role in my good fortune. That the choice had been Jackson's and not all Peevers' suited me very well, playing as it did to my weakened sense of self-worth, but the question of the money troubled me. With a sick feeling, I thought of the gold I had seen Mr. Peevers pour into Dr. Goodpenny's hand the day I first arrived in Little Eastcheap.

"But if the fifty pounds were not paid to you, where are they now?" I told Mr. Jackson what little I knew of it.

"I did wonder why Mr. Peevers was so very, very delighted when I informed him of my choice. He danced a little jig, in fact, which I don't mind telling you was a rather peculiar sight." I formed a picture in my mind of Mr. Peevers, tightly encased in scholastic black, jiggling his blubber while an idiot smile played about his lips. I hadn't thought it possible to hate him more. Mr. Jackson, who didn't know the half of it, went on.

"It saddens me to think there may have been more to his delight than the thought of helping a boy. And he is supposedly a religious man, too. But there may be something we can do. There will be records at the Waterman's guild. It ought to be a simple matter to see them, and on the strength of that, demand an accounting from your Mr. Peevers, and from Goodpenny too, for that matter. If they have indeed swindled you, it would be an engaging spectacle to see the two of them explain it to a magistrate. You may well see your money, which as your patrimony I should think you are entitled to keep. I will mention it to my solicitor." Mr. Jackson looked at me with a suddenly grave expression. "If Mr. Peevers is in any sort of regular habit of swindling boys, the penalties will be severe."

If before I was sensible of a rising admiration for the man, what I now felt very nearly overwhelmed me. That Mr. Jackson was willing to assist me and bring some measure of retribution to the odious Mr. Peevers allied him in my heart with my lost parents, piercing me through. My eyes brimmed with tears. Although I wished to thank him, I could not speak. Mrs. Whidby, who had busied herself cleaning up as Mr. Jackson and I spoke, offered a cogent observation.

"Ah, look at the lad. He's had enough for one day, don't you think, Mr. Jackson?"

"Right you are as usual, Mrs. Whidby. That he has, that he has. Joe, you can put in a full day tomorrow. I think it wise to allow you the remainder of this first evening to collect yourself. I will leave you, and Mrs. Whidby will show you your bedchamber and all that. Tomorrow is soon enough to learn what tomorrow will bring. Good night, Joseph."

"Good night, Mr. Jackson." I hated myself for being near to blubbering, but Mr. Jackson took no notice of it and gave me a gentle pat on the shoulder before letting himself out. No sooner had he gone than Mrs. Whidby came into her own.

"Now then, lad, you're going to be just fine, you are. This has been a very big day for you, I'll wager. Come, I've something to show you I think you'll like." Now that Mr. Jackson had returned to his shop, I saw Mrs. Whidby as if for the first time. She was perhaps fifty, and as I have said merry, gentle, and round. Her graying hair was pulled back in a bun, and her face was beginning to show wrinkles. I noticed the deepest creases formed where she smiled. She wore spectacles which she was forever pushing back up her nose. "Come along now."

I realized I had been sitting in a kind of daze. "Oh, sorry," I said, rising to follow her. The room was an old fashioned kitchen and sitting room in one, with a large open hearth beside which all of the cooking was done. A broad mantle was affixed above, upon which rested objects of pride mingled with domestic utensils. Settles were on both sides of the fire, beneath windows of many small, leaded panes, arranged in a diamond pattern. Later I was to observe that these windows, unfortunately, looked upon a very near stone wall. A door opposite the fire led to the lane, and another led, I supposed, to her chamber. A third door led to a water closet, and in the corner opposite very steep stairs rose nearly straight up. It was to these we went.

"Up there you'll find a snug bedchamber all ready. I don't get up those stairs so good any more, so you'll be keeping it yourself from now on, but I did want to give you a proper welcome. Here, love, take this candle. I've even put water and a basin and some towels up there for you."

"It seems all I am doing is thanking you or Mr. Jackson. But, really, thank you so very much, again."

"You're welcome, and it's a pleasure. But don't be worrying about ways to show your gratitude, now. Mr. Jackson will get plenty of sweat out of you, of that you may be sure! You never saw such a one for work. I don't think he does anything else. Even his dinner parties are for business, with writers and artists, and dissenters and philosophers, and all manner of high society. You should hear them go at it, sometimes! We even had a lord in here once! I mean in the dining room in Mr. Jackson's premises, not right here, of course. I don't cook for those, though.

He has them catered, thank goodness. Ah, but I'm babbling.

"Poor child, you are so wan. Go on up now, and get to sleep. I'll be shouting you up at six, which I don't need to tell you will come very early. Welcome to your new life." She gave me a great grin, affording a view of many imperfect teeth, and a kindly slap on the back.

"Thank you again." I was so very weary. Later, I would be able to do such work without tiring, but I had come undernourished from Mr. Peevers' school and had no reserves of strength. I crawled upstairs, and had barely enough wit remaining to observe that it was a large and beautiful bedchamber, with not one but two dormer windows, beneath one of which stood a writing desk.

A straight-backed chair faced the desk, and another, large and comfortable chair for just sitting in, and reading, and dreaming, perhaps stood in the corner. A fire burned low in the grate, and the bed seemed wonderfully clean and snug. It was a better and prettier room even than the room of my boyhood, and it was all for me. I marveled and would have stayed awake and savored it, and imagined great imaginings in it, but in my exhaustion I merely washed, undressed, and crawled between the sheets. Just as I pulled a thick down comforter over me, the great bells of St. Paul's struck nine. I wished most fervently Chowder were with me that he might see my luck, and that we might hold each other as when first we met. I cannot say I dwelt long upon it, though, as in a very few moments I was asleep.

XXIV

I DREAMT I FLOATED OVER a gloriously sunlit London, in company of a beautiful young man but little older than I. Together we looked down upon the city and marveled at its greatness. I could see with wonderful clarity and completeness the Thames, a plenitude of steeples, and the dome of St. Paul's. I asked him if he did this often, and he said yes, very often. We alit then, beside the Thames where great leafy trees were waterside next to a small beach. A sward extended away from the river to a knoll.

He led me thither, where stood a wondrously large and beautiful tree, and there drew me to himself with sweet tenderness and kissed me. He knew my most secret desires and loved me for them. I returned his kiss with all the tender love I had in me. It came to me then that I was dreaming, and I asked him could we meet and do this again? "I want to see you again," I said. He was about to answer, as he held me just so about the waist, to intimate that more was to his interest than he had yet shown, when the bubble of my dream burst against the cheerful, raucous voice of Mrs. Whidby.

"Halloo, Joe up there! It's a mornin' as I promised you. The fire's bright and warm, and there'll be porridge and coffee for you as soon as you're down. Come on now love, I know you're no dawdler. Come get this candle from me so's you can dress."

A steady, cold, winter rain fell straight down in the pre-dawn blackness and beat upon the roof. I clung to the shreds of my dream, which disturbed me awake even as it had entranced me asleep, and I went over it in my mind so I might remember it always. Even as I ruminated, I threw off the bedclothes and scurried to the stairs, where I knelt to take the candle from Mrs. Whidby's outstretched hand. Mrs. Whidby, of course, was completely dressed and appeared to have been up and contentedly bustling about for hours. I set the candle in its holder on the writing desk, looked about the chamber and savored it, and then happily threw on my only clothes. The room was nowhere as cold as at Mr. Peevers' school. How very, very much better life was now going to be. In less than three minutes, I was downstairs.

"Here, love, eat this." She put before me a large bowl of steaming porridge, which bore resemblance to the watery gruel in Little Eastcheap as a new guinea resembles a worn farthing. I ate greedily, still mulling over my dream, while she chattered.

"Sleep well, did you?" I nodded while I slurped. "Me, the bells wake me, but I'm so used to it I go right back to sleep, except when it's time to get up, of course. Been getting up at four thirty for so long now, I guess this old body will do it out of habit even after I'm dead. I'm that stubborn, you know. That'll give the lively to the churchyard, now, won't it." She laughed, a rich laugh full of enjoyment that I was to hear often. "Eat hearty, now."

I needed no encouragement. No sooner was I done than she sent me packing across the lane to the bookstore, where I found Mr. Jackson writing at the table Rowland had occupied the day before.

"Ah, there you are. Good morning, Joseph." Mr. Jackson was all smiles and geniality.

"Good morning, Mr. Jackson."

"I'm going to start you off in the time-honored manner, Joseph. For the next six months at least, the most menial tasks in these premises will be yours. You'll have floors to sweep, stoves to feed, coal to bring up, and of course, books, books, and more books. We bring them in and send them out all the day long. You've already seen a bit of that and may as well know now that it never ends. How does that sound?"

I replied I thought it perfectly reasonable, for which observation I was rewarded with a large broom and instructions to sweep the entire shop. When that was done, I brought many bucketsful of coal up from the cellar and filled the bins next to the two stoves that heated the ground floor. I then brought down a score of the books I had carried upstairs the previous afternoon. Mr. Jackson placed several in the window and put the rest among others on shelves labeled: "The Most Recent Scientific Works." Following this, I was sent to the store room to unpack the remainder of the boxes of books I had brought in the previous day.

I was fascinated by the parade of customers, and more than once looked up from my work to watch. Many were people of fashion and even of quality, finely dressed and impatient in their demands. Men seeking gilt-edged and nicely tooled volumes of moral instruction, scientific discovery, or history, and women seeking novels and romances, but occasionally the weightiest of tomes quite equal to any purchased by the men.

One grand woman of heavy, pocked visage, much white paint, and towering hair selected books by their bindings. She couldn't be bothered to know what was in them, she said, but they simply must match her pink décor. She carelessly plopped down thirty guineas, once satisfied with the degree of pinkness and gilt of a great stack of books, which she would have delivered.

I was pleased to see that while Mr. Jackson and Rowland were attentive, they were no more obsequious than I would have been and would not kiss her posterior, if you will, for all that she presented it, in her arch phrases and absurd affectations. There came as well Dissenting ministers, some dour and some lively, seeking bound volumes of sermons and treatises on the many varieties of Dissenting thought and practice. A few were Unitarians, and an eager and daring lot they seemed to be. Yet others, who for all I knew may well have been members of Parliament, came wanting, they said, the "other side" of the argument with America. To these Mr. Jackson would provide pamphlets by Dr. Franklin, Mr. Paine, or any of several others. He did not provide these to all who asked, however.

There also came hungry-looking men and boys, and even a few women and girls, whom I fancied were starving poets or writers of prose. These were such a scrawny lot, literature may well have been their only meat,. They spent hours reading in the stacks of used books, and if another shopkeeper might have shooed them out, Mr. Jackson did not. He knew many of them by name, extending to them the same courtesies he showed the higher-ranking, engaging them in conversation and genteel argument in his free moments. When, finally, these tattered literati would bestir themselves to emerge, they would present to Rowland, who kept the cash box, a worn volume of Swift or Smollet, or Suetonius or Pope, or any of the thousands of cheap used books we stocked, and pay a penny or two.

It was only later, of course, that I had any idea what any of these books were about or who the authors were. As I watched and listened to Mr. Jackson and gained appreciation for his easy familiarity with worlds upon worlds of knowledge and art, my admiration swelled to abject hero-worship.

At noon, Mrs. Whidby brought in a kettle of stew she had made with the remains of the previous evening's meal. Mr. Jackson had already eaten in a coffee house, where he was in the habit of keeping up with the news, and would mind the shop while Rowland and I ate by ourselves in the rear, within a small room I had not noticed previously. This room was in the corner opposite the stairs, and the door to it was hidden behind yet more shelves of books. It featured a small window which opened onto the lane.

We ate without speaking for some time, and I studied Rowland's not unhandsome face as he ate. You might suppose I would bear him a grudge for what he had put me through, but I did not. I assumed it was his right to use me as he wished, and though the work was difficult, it in no way constituted abuse when compared to the trials of many an unlucky 'prentice one hears about every day. And then, it had put me in a better light than him. I wondered if he had wished me not to come, and if so, why. He was evidently performing cogitations of his own, for no sooner had he mopped up the last of his stew with the final hunk of bread, crammed the lot into his mouth, and swallowed most of it, than he spoke. He essayed a casual, offhand manner.

"He just about had my hide because of you."

"Because of me?"

"Well, not quite because of you, actually. It's what I required of you yesterday that he found so much fault with. He's very taken with you now. Look, Joe, I'm sorry about it. The truth is the workmen were on a meal break at a coffee house a few minutes walk from here when you showed up. After I put you to work, I ran over, paid them their day's wages, and sent them home. I thought it a right proper way to break you in. Thomas, I mean Mr. Jackson, has disagreed with me about it quite strenuously. And now I am forbidden to direct you until he will allow me to again. I don't enjoy apologizing, by the way."

"No hard feelings," I replied. "It wasn't so bad. You don't seem at all a rotten sort, actually." I graced him with a genial smile to show that I forgave him. "I rather enjoy having my betters apologize to me, I must say."

"That's good, then, except for that last. Let me explain something very important to you. I'm not any better than you. People must stop relating like that. There's a rebellion in America, and there could be one or two in Europe soon. A lot of it has to do with people insisting on an end to this idiotic business of higher and lower and so on. Either all are gentlemen or none are, Joe. God does not discriminate. Why should we? Ever hear the saying, "When Adam delved and

Eve span, who was then the gentleman?"

I laughed. "No, where did that come from?"

"Four hundred years ago, there was a very big rebellion here in England. A fellow named Wat Tyler led it. Things went pretty far. That was a famous saying then. Have you read Hume?"

I hadn't. I didn't quite let on I'd never heard of the man, although my puzzled countenance must have betrayed the fact.

"Died last year, he did. Wrote the most wonderful history of England. What about Pope? Ever hear of Pope?"

"Isn't he the one in Rome that we're against?"

"Ah, no. Pope was the greatest poet of this century. You're thinking of another one. Very different. Defoe?"

"No."

"Milton?"

"Didn't he put out a lot of chapbooks?"

"Hardly." He rattled off a dozen more names in like manner and to all I said no. I had rarely felt so small. He hadn't needed to go on so.

"I don't want to be rude, Joe, but here you are fancying yourself an apprentice bookseller, and you don't know the first thing."

This provoked in me some heat. "Were you born knowing all those names? I can learn too, you know. If you did it, so can I. I'll read them all. You'll see."

"There's nothing wrong with your spirit, anyway. I suppose I can like you for that. But you're going to have to read like a Turk. It isn't going to be as easy as you think. Mind you," and here he reverted to the conciliatory, "you'll find Thomas is not your everyday master. He will allow you the odd evening for study."

XXV

AND THEN IT WAS TIME to return to work. Rowland would mind the shop, as Mr. Jackson went out for several hours to conduct business. My work consisted of heavy labor in the storeroom, as way had to be made for yet another shipment that would arrive the next day.

As I worked, I pondered my conversation with Rowland. There were thousands of books in Mr. Jackson's premises, and I knew nothing of any of them, or of the worlds of thought they contained. I became consumed with newly intensified lust to learn. Looking over the newly printed volumes in the storeroom, I was at first not in the least encouraged. Such titles! *Natural History of the Human Teeth, An Essay on the Uterine Hemorrhage,* and *Obs. and Exp. on the Poison of Lead* were perfectly opaque to me. However, *An Essay on the Nature of the Colonies, and the Conduct of the Mother Country Towards Them,* by a certain Marquis, I judged as possibly interesting. It was at least a subject of much current debate, or so I had gathered.

I was about to look it over when my eye was caught by a series of volumes in red leather on a high shelf in the next row. *History of the Corruptions of Christianity,* it read, and there again was the name Priestley. Now, that was interesting. Promising as it did insubordination to the likes of Mr. Peevers and his pious cant, I could not refrain from taking the book down. Before I quite knew what I was doing, I found myself sitting on the floor with the thing, puzzling out the words one after another, as well as I could.

The more I read, the more astonished I became. It was far more daring than I had supposed. To think that the sources and tenets of Christianity should be scrutinized to reveal that those who had formed them, apart from Jesus, of course, might have been subject to just the sorts of common vanities and faults of logic that could distract the judgement of anyone, set my mind to reeling. I read on and on, skipping over many a difficult word, until I realized with a start it was growing dark. With a great rush and pounding heart, I finished my work just as I heard Mr. Jackson's footsteps on the stairs.

"Ah, there you are. Getting on?" He was, if possible, even more impeccably dressed than before, sporting understated gold buttons on a blue velvet waistcoat. His cocked hat, too, was enhanced with the most discreet dressings of gold. In an age in which the Macaronis ruled men's fashion, and women of quality sported bejeweled hair rising three feet above their heads, Mr. Jackson's restrained elegance spoke volumes. Nor did he affect the ostentatious plainness of a Quaker.

"Oh yes, thank you, Mr. Jackson. I'm getting on very well. Everything is ready for tomorrow."

"Splendid! Now I must ask you, did Rowland speak to you over your dinner? Did he apologize?"

"Yes, he did. But then we had a very interesting conversation. I ended up feeling very stupid, but it wasn't because of him, not really. There is so much I haven't learned yet. It makes me feel very small. It seems I know nothing."

"The most learned men say the same thing, Joseph. You can't be doing too badly to sound like them."

"I suppose neither they nor I know as much as we would like, sir, but they are on a mountain top wondering at the stars, and I am in a deep and foggy valley. I'd call that a difference, if you don't mind my saying so. I would very much like to know how I may become learned like you."

"You are off to a very good start, Joe, I would say. I am impressed with your wit and without a ready, native wit, no amount of learning will make a learned man. Be curious as you are, ask all the questions you can, and read every chance you get. And never confuse mere learning with wisdom. Knowledge is cheap, wisdom is precious. Knowledge is merely in the head, but wisdom is the head and a whole heart connected. Without the heart's tutelage, knowledge is apt to be grievously misapplied. You must promise never to forget that."

"I promise."

"Good. Now then, as for practicalities, you may borrow any book from the storeroom or shop you like and take it to your chamber. I will allow you evenings free Tuesdays and Thursdays, if you will read in your chamber after supper. And of course you work but half a day Saturday—we are nothing if not progressive here. Saturday afternoons and Sundays you may use as you like, although I hope you will come to meeting with me Sunday mornings. Or if not with me, to another of your own choosing. We could compare notes then. I would enjoy that."

I thought immediately of free afternoons and the opportunity to find Chowder, but spoke not of it. What I said was, "Thank you, sir, very much. This makes me very happy. May I borrow that book there, sir?" I pointed to the volume I had been reading so furtively but moments before.

"But that is very heady stuff, Joe. I fear you may be too young for it. Before you would know where Christianity might have been misled here and there by vain men, ought you not to know thoroughly where it is right, and what it is, altogether?"

"I suppose. But I have learned much of that from Mr. Peevers and Mr. MacCurran, already. Is Dr. Priestley's book one of those that challenge ignorance, as you put it?"

He laughed, a gentle, pleasant laugh, and shook his head at the same time. "You are not any ordinary boy, are you? Poor Mr. MacCurran, and Peevers too, for that matter. I'm sure they had no idea what to do with you. Yes, you could say it was that sort of book. But tell, me Joe, what is your interest in it?"

How could I explain it to him? I would have to tell him of Chowder, and what Mr. MacCurran had said about God, and boys touching each other, and all of that. I couldn't.

"I just find it interesting, that's all."

Mr. Jackson looked at me as if he would peer right into my soul. "Yes, you may borrow it. But let me give you some others to go with it. Bring your book and come with me." I took the volume and followed him downstairs into the shop, where Rowland was just wrapping up a sale for an expensively dressed gentleman. Leading me into the maze of shelves toward the rear, Mr. Jackson gently quizzed me about my knowledge of books and literature. In no time at all, he made the same discoveries as had Rowland, but with less injury to my pride.

"You will need a dictionary, and then I will start you off easy with some wonderful things I think you will enjoy, and one thing to check Dr. Priestley's keg of gunpowder." He handed me the dictionary, two enormous, wide volumes by some Dr. Johnson, and *The Book of Common Prayer, Reformed.*

"This," he said, "represents my own persuasion, which I would describe as a Christianity freed of fairy tales, although not all would call it that, I must add. It is, at the least, a constructive counterweight to Dr. Priestley's argumentation. There is much truth in what he says, but if all you read was his book, you might think there was nothing to do with Christianity but take it apart." He then loaded me up with a number of other volumes, which he picked from the shelves one after another without the slightest hesitation.

"Here's a wonderful thing about a fellow named Gulliver, who makes some rather unusual travels. Dr. Swift may have been a high churchman and a Tory, but he knew how to write. It's all made up, of course, as is this one. He handed me a small volume titled *Robinson Crusoe*, and another by the same Defoe fellow, *Captain Jack*. "You ought to enjoy these. They're great fun. Oh, and this one is wonderful. A woman wrote it near a hundred years ago. It's called *Oroonoko*. Ah, and here's another great tale, full of thought." This one was called *The History of Rasselas*, and again I saw the name Johnson.

"Have you written any books? I asked.

"Oh, dear me, no. I haven't written a thing. It isn't my gift. Now, this Dr. Johnson is a very great man of letters. It's his dictionary, too. Getting well up in years now, he is, and completely stodgy in his views. As arch a Tory as you could find, but very much worth reading in spite of it. But if you ever meet him, you don't want to cross him, I assure you. He takes great delight in squashing lesser wits as if they were insects, and for Dr. Johnston a lesser wit is anyone who doesn't perfectly agree with him. Now, here—you must have this."

He reached to a top shelf and took down the *Arabian Night's Entertainments*. "And here, this is a most marvelous history that was published just last year. Not by me, unfortunately. The fellow's a friend of Dr. Johnson." Here came a great, fat thing by some Gibbon fellow, *The Decline and Fall of the Roman Empire, Volume One*. "No one is learned who doesn't know the ancients, and this is an excellent place to start. The last few chapters will interest you, if you are after unsympathetic portraits of Christianity. Very controversial."

"How many volumes of this are there?" I asked, beginning to wonder how many books I was going to be given, and whether I could carry them all.

"Only the one so far. No doubt Mr. Gibbon is scribbling madly this very moment, working on the next. Oh, and here, Plutarch. These lives of his are just the thing. Now, Joe, is there anything else you can think of that you would like for the moment?

As I spoke, my chin bounced against the top of the stack of books I was holding. "Maybe that Hume fellow Rowland mentioned, his history of England?"

"Of course! Let's see, it comes in six volumes. Which would you like?"

'Whichever one has Wat Tyler in it."

"That would be volume one. There is a chapter or two about the Peasant's Rebellion in the later 1300s, where you will find Tyler. Here you are. Now, Joe, I think these should keep you for a day or two," he laughed. All I ask is that you tell me when you borrow another book, and that we shall talk about what you have read. I want to know what you like and don't like and what you think of them all. Agreed?"

Most assuredly, it was agreed. I felt as if I had been given keys to a great treasure house and clothed in rich vestments.

"You may take these to your chamber now, but return right away. The floor near the door needs to be mopped. There have been a lot of muddy boots in here today, what with the rain."

I thanked him and turned to go, but as I did so Mr. Jackson spoke again.

"Oh, Joe, it nearly slipped my mind. My solicitor made a visit to the Waterman's guild today, and they have provided a statement attesting to your trust of fifty pounds, and that it was given over to Mr. Peevers. We have even seen his signature on the transfer instrument. You will need to write a demand letter to him requesting payment. If you will take care of that this evening, we can proceed with the matter."

"Thank you so very much, sir."

"Joe, you are very welcome." Such kindness in his eyes. What a precious thing it was to trust the guidance of such a man. Damn, I was about to start a-blubbering again.

I carried the books across the lane into Mrs. Whidby's lodgings, where she observed that she didn't know stacks of books could walk about by themselves. I asked whether she would like me to show her the books, but to my surprise she said no. It was all over her head, she was sure, and if I didn't mind, the less she bothered about it, the happier she'd be. Not that she thought it wasn't quite the right thing for me to be doing, mind you. As she spoke, she kneaded dough with a vigorous, muscular rhythm. The fire was burning bright and hot, and I could smell wonderful things baking. I put my books upstairs, returned to the shop and mopped the floor, following which I was dismissed to supper, and to have the evening to read in my chamber. As was to become customary, I ate with Mrs. Whidby after she had taken meat pies and beer over to Mr. Jackson and Rowland. Unlike Mr. Peevers and his ilk, we all ate the same food, even if not together.

Following supper, I took my candles and coal upstairs, brightened the fire, and arranged my books on a shelf next to the dormer window. I now had as pretty a study as one could wish, and, looking about myself, was enormously pleased. The rain had stopped, even as water continued to drip heavily into the lane from many moss-covered slate roofs, and all was dark save for a light which shone through the top-floor window of Mr. Jackson's lodgings opposite.

Discovering paper, quills, and a pot of ink in my desk, I wrote to Mr. Peevers as inept a missive as has ever been penned, blobbed over with drops of ink and littered with crude misspellings, but which communicated with adequate legibility that he wrongfully held my money and must pay up at once.

That night I dreamed of a youth composed in equal measures of Chowder and the mysterious and alluring youth I had met in my previous dream, that I have here recorded. On a glorious summer's afternoon, we walked together beside the Thames, as it might have been had not the wilderness of a distant age been entirely supplanted. Between grand buildings stood copses of great trees inhabited by numerous brilliant birds, which emitted a riotous but pleasing cacophony. Golden barges like unto none I had ever seen sailed the river. None of your ordinary sort of people were about, and, seeing this, we sat upon a stone and took each other in our arms and kissed. The piercing delight of it astonished me, and my pleasure grew until we were interrupted by the ringing of a great bell. We broke our kiss then, and looking into his eyes I wondered if as of old the bell was rung to dispel evil spirits.

"There is evil, but it is far distant from here," he said, and we returned to our kiss. He placed his hand then on my waist. To my amazement, this caused me to spend, even as I stirred awake and discovered that the bell was St. Paul's, and my spending had occurred not only in the land of dream.

XXVI

DESPITE MR. JACKSON'S SINCERE ASSURANCES that I would have Saturday afternoons and Sundays free, practice differed at times from theory. The publication of several new titles and increased custom caused all to work more than had been anticipated, even as Mr. Jackson's enthusiasm and innovative stratagems grew apace. Although I was dismayed, I was not entirely surprised when, at the conclusion of an especially frantic week in early February, he announced that the ground floor of the premises urgently required complete reorganization in order to accommodate more customers and more books. So as not to inconvenience our customers or in any way diminish the flow of trade, the work would be done during the hours the shop was normally closed.

For weeks we labored far into the night, even as we delayed not a whit the hour of rising, working all day Saturday and Sunday afternoons and evenings as well. The task was accomplished in carefully planned increments, the shop altered but remaining serviceable at the completion of each. I worked all waking hours, and when I could work no more I slept, but never enough. Mrs. Whidby plied us with strong coffee throughout, and once encouraged me to drink a large jug of beer, causing me to fall asleep on the floor. Conveyed to my bedchamber, I slept for twenty hours, in which I was indulged by the ever assiduous, but never inhumane, Mr. Jackson.

These rigors were balanced, however. Mr. Jackson did allow me to sleep Sunday mornings when he and Rowland were at church, saying that the liberality which would allow one to pursue religious belief and practice ought to extend in like manner to freedom from it. My Tuesday and Thursday evenings remained inviolate as well, so that my education should not be neglected.

I continued to read Dr. Priestley's opus and strove mightily to make sense of it. Where before it had been enough to know that a book questioning sacred doctrine might exist, and to have the gist of it, I now wanted to understand fully. This presented severe difficulties, as I was far from mastering the art of reading and made slow progress, puzzling over many an opaque word. These set me to wrestling with Dr. Johnson's dictionary, an unequal contest in which I soon wearied of defeat. I put it aside, not to take it up again until much later. If I could make out what word a group of letters wanted to be, I often as not knew what the word meant. If I could not, looking it up served only to expose me to an elaboration of mysteries.

By Spring, I concluded that *The History of the Corruptions of Christianity* shed no light on my dilemma, although the labor was not lost, as I greatly improved my powers of comprehension through its study. And, Dr. Priestley had wandered through a very long discussion of the doctrine of predestination, with which he was singularly unimpressed. This satisfied me that Mr. Peevers' strained justifications for his predatory behavior were without foundation, which meant I could now despise him intellectually as well as emotionally, for me a necessary pleasure. But the nature of Christ's divinity, which so consumed Dr. Priestley's interest, did not attract mine. Jesus's Father, whether or not the Father had a Son, could hate me well enough for both of them, if he had a mind to, and I didn't see much difference in it. The hoped for delineation of the categories of love, and whether and why each might be preferred or forbidden, was missing.

Keeping company with this disappointment were many another. I found no mention of sodomy in Dr. Johnson's dictionary, leaving me to gather anew that whatever sodomy was, it was not to be countenanced. I then began to read the adventures and novels Mr. Jackson had supplied, and was often diverted by the simple pleasures of an intriguing tale. And yet, at the bottom of nearly all of them was the troubling interplay of male and female, founded on an incomprehensible mutual attraction.

It appeared to be universally assumed every male wished to "ruin," as it was said, any female he could, and her duty was to prevent this, unless she could exact the toll of marriage at an appropriate price. Neither love nor pleasure entered into

J A M E S   L O V E J O Y

it, as far as I could tell. And I did not fail to notice that a young man's ability to contest for his desired female formed the basis for judgement of his character. These sentiments, to one whose awareness grew daily that his heart's desire lay in another direction, were opaquest cant, scripted in an alien language. I fervently hoped the mysteries of maturation would enable me to decipher it, but this never happened.

Over time, I read *Pamela* and *Clarissa*, *Tom Jones*, *Joseph Andrews*, *Tristam Shandy*, and even the scandalous *Moll Flanders*, and was, by turns, annoyed, confused, and worried. Even *Shamela*, very funny though it may have been, failed, as did all of them, to question whether, let alone why, a boy might love someone not a girl. And though it gave much pleasure to see many a fictional, vain, and hypocritical parson well skewered, I could only too easily image every last one of them fulminating against the likes of me. Thus my anxieties multiplied.

When I discovered Smollet, the fog lifted just a bit. Here was a writer, who was conversant with the mean as well as the mighty, and even if his Roderick Random was, like so many fictional heroes, tediously obsessed with winning his woman and returning to respectability, the rich pageant of minor characters was in wickedly sharp focus throughout.

When Roderick's manservant, Strap, returns after a perilous absence to cover Roderick's face with kisses, I read with breathless intensity till the candle guttered out, sleeping very little that night. I returned the next day to find that nothing came of it. Later, Roderick is cultivated by a gentleman who discreetly probes Roderick's acquaintance with the ancients. Had he read Petronius? Yes, he had, and damned be the man who first introduced the sodomitical vice to England. Here the gentleman weakly agreed, and desisted in his probing.

Elsewhere, a most peculiar captain of a man o' war is presented, dressed in scarlet silk breeches and all manner of foppery. This spectacle of effete degeneracy remained secluded in his chambers with his male companion during a battle when he ought to have been on deck to exercise responsibility.

In another novel, I read of a hero imprisoned for debt who sojourns in the Fleet, whereupon the six categories of thieving gangs are delineated. The last and most reprehensible of these, trading as they did in what was termed foulest vice, were the sodomitical tribes who entrapped and blackmailed gentlemen so dissolute and unwise as to expose themselves to such dangers. Despite the condemnatory nature of these portraits, my imagination, fired by this intelligence, created a world of handsome, daring sodomitical bandits (I remained unclear as to the precise meaning of the term), each devoted with tender solicitude to the welfare of his brothers, on which theme I invented countless scenarios to play out in my mind.

I read enough among the ancients to learn that their attitude toward sodomitical males was far less severe, and that the Greeks especially considered involvements between mature and younger men natural. This was sufficient to plant in me strident longing to have lived then, and I pored over Gibbon's Roman eulogium with a mourning heart, as if it were my own civilization that had been lost. The ancients were pagans and their souls unsaved, Mr. Peevers had said, but as I progressed in my studies, I waxed independent of that formulation.

I fancied Dr. Priestley would not have thought it reasonable that men who had lived justly should be brutally and eternally punished by a capricious God, whose pretensions to universality could only be weakened by such partisan judgements, and therefore neither did I. I was no less disposed than Gibbon to be outraged at the depredations Christianity had wrought among the virtues of the Romans, and, St. Augustine or no, increasingly saw Christianity, or at least its more virulent forms, as merely another vehicle by means of which the mad might exercise tyranny. I especially could not fathom what the beautiful supplications and refined sentiments expressed in Mr. Jackson's *Book of Common Prayer*, revised in the new Unitarian style, might have in common with the unfair judgements of a spiteful God, who seemed so concerned that a boy, however eager and true his heart, must never love another like himself.

It was by such degrees, then, that the focus of my anxiety shifted from death to life. Given the unresolved contentions of learned men, the fate of my soul was a mystery I was incapable of addressing, but how I should live and find my heart's way was, by contrast, a problem of pressing immediacy.

XXVII

ONE GLOOMY, WET MORNING IN late February, as I squatted shelving books onto a lower tier toward the front, I saw a coupé pull up directly in front of the shop, so near the door that it blocked entry. This was done sometimes to keep the rain off the better sort. The occupant, however, proved to be none other than Miss Strickenwell, dressed as ever in rigors of black. She strode in brusquely, displaying no diminution of her dry and crisp authority.

"Master Chapman," she said, "rise to greet your better." Mr. Jackson had got me in the habit of carrying on with my work no matter who was around.

"Yes, ma'am. Sorry, ma'am." I rose and bowed, slightly.

"Where is your master? I wish to speak to him."

"I believe he's in the rear, ma'am. Shall I show you there?"

"I'm perfectly capable of finding him myself, I'm sure, given that he's here." She made directly for the rear, where she nosed about and quickly found her quarry.

I continued working, despite my curiosity. A gentleman wished to enter the shop, but was prevented from doing so by the carriage. Two others wished to exit, one of whom was a boy no older than myself. They were beginning to display signs of irritation when Mr. Jackson called me.

"Joe, come here, won't you?" The three of us held conference under the stairs. Rowland having gone to Bristol, Mr. Jackson kept watch for customers, interrupting his attention at intervals to put his head out where he could see the desk and cash box.

"Joe, Miss Strickenwell has come to me about your affairs. I thought it best she speak to you directly. I think you will be intrigued by what she has to say."

Miss Strickenwell stood in the landing and nailed me to the wall with her good eye. "Joseph, you were a lazy student and a troublesome charge. However, it is against the wishes of God that anyone, even indifferent boys, should be robbed. Now that I am Governess of the Little Eastcheap Free School for Unfortunate Boys—" Here she drew a deep breath "—I have been sorting out the school's affairs, and have made a number of very unpleasant discoveries. The details do not concern you, but among them is this business of yours. I have brought you this."

The twitchings of her mouth momentarily ceased their downward darting and, for the briefest of intervals, twitched straight across instead. She handed me a small blue velvet pouch in which substantial coins could be heard. Opening it, I discovered six new and shining golden guineas. Rotund King George had never appeared more brilliant or more welcome. I placed the pouch and its contents in my pocket.

"Thank you ever so much, ma'am."

"It is but a beginning. We shall make good the rest over time."

"What's become of Mr. Peevers now?" asked Mr. Jackson.

"Mr. Peevers is in the Fleet. Have you heard of the Fleet, Joseph?" Not a person in London over the age of three had not heard of the Fleet, but I wasn't about to be impolite to the woman just then.

"Yes, ma'am. Some kind of prison, isn't it?"

"It is a nasty, dirty prison for foolish men and women who have made too free use of other people's money. He is there on the strength of your note and several others like it." As she said this, she seemed weary, steadying herself against the stairs.

The news of Mr. Peevers' condition, the partial repayment, and the softening of Miss Strickenwell's tone inspired in me an advancement of trust. Mr. Peevers had no more power to harm me, and if it would bring justice, my pact with him now was as dead as, perhaps, he soon would be. "Has anyone complained about other things he did?"

"As I said, Joseph, the details do not concern you."

"Please pardon me, but I feel you should know Mr. Peevers took very improper advantage of me. I don't just mean the money. He took me to his private study, bade me strip, and touched me where he shouldn't have, in a manner not at all medical."

"Joseph?" They two of them spoke at once. Mr. Jackson's expression was of an equal admixture of surprise and concern, and Miss Strickenwell performed the impossible, becoming paler.

"And you can bet I wasn't the only one."

Miss Strickenwell sank onto the stairs. "Dear God. Joseph, I must ask you to excuse us. I wish to speak to your Master privately." She hung on to the balustrade with a tight grip.

At this moment a large and irritated gentleman came into view. His countenance rearranged itself immediately upon seeing the faltering Miss Strickenwell. "Dear me, terribly sorry. Will the lady be all right?"

"She's had a bit of a shock, but I believe so, yes." Mr. Jackson was perfectly calm.

"Well then, what I wanted to know was whether that blasted carriage is going to stand there all day? I'm a prisoner here and so are several others."

"Joe, go and sort it out if you can," said Mr. Jackson.

I strode to the front. The gentleman and his boy wished to exit, and four others stood outside in the rain, all blocked by the coupé. The driver remained in his seat, loftily uninterested in the drama. It had not occurred to anyone to speak to him, or so I could gather.

I spoke loudly and to the point. "I say, could you move this thing?"

"Sorry. I take orders only from the Miss."

"She's near to fainted. Be a while yet, I suppose. People want to get 'round. Must you be that way about it?"

"She'll snap out of it before long. Always does."

"So you'll not move it, then?"

"Can't. Hell to pay if I do. You don't know the woman."

"I used to be at that school."

"I'm very sorry for you then. So you know what I mean. Door's unlocked," he said conspiratorially.

"It is?"

"Carriage door. Both sides."

Grasping the man's meaning, I opened the carriage door and climbed up and in, through to the other side. The gentleman and boy followed me. I then returned, followed by those wishing to enter. The carriage remained with both doors open, as an overwrought gate through which the sodden public might pass as it wished.

Looking toward the rear, I saw Mr. Jackson motion for me to approach, and I returned to find Miss Strickenwell sitting bolt upright in his chair. She spoke with a softness I would not have guessed was in her. "Joseph, this is an extremely grave matter. I have informed Mr. Jackson of certain particulars and will leave it to him to convey to you what must be done. Obviously, this is not a conversation that you and I can have. I extend to you my heartfelt apologies for what you have endured. We shall make this right, or as right as it can be made." She rose and took her leave of Mr. Jackson, shaking his hand.

Turning to me she said, "Joe, I wish you great success here." She recovered a portion of her crispness and marched to the front, where the open door revealed the coupé with its arms spread wide. As she approached, a large, sopping wet, black dog piled through, followed by an expensively clad and very fat man, his face a sodden assemblage of red cheeks, white whiskers, and dripping gray hair.

"What is this? I say, what is this?" Miss Strickenwell's voice fairly squeaked. Assessing the man as an unworthy target, she drew her bead on the coachman.

"You! Francis!"

"Ma'am?" Francis, obdurately indolent, seemed scarcely to have strength enough to lift his head.

"You are aware, are you not, that the carriage doors are open? The public are passing through. Look at it! Wet and dirt everywhere."

Slowly, then gathering energy, Francis responded with injured dignity. "Had to allow it, ma'am. This great, strapping fellow, he wanted to leave the shop. Became angry when I asked him to wait a bit longer. Lucky thing he didn't damage the door, the way he wrenched it open. Never asked leave. And then the others all piled on. No choice, ma'am."

Looking all around with the severest of expressions, Miss Strickenwell offered a pointed observation. "Cess pit and trial, it is, this life. Isn't it?" We all earnestly agreed, Francis especially. In a moment, she was gone.

Mr. Jackson, having come forward, immediately shepherded me back to the rear. "Now, Joe, I'm afraid I must ask you to tell me exactly what Mr. Peevers did to you. At great cost to her dignity, the matron has confirmed an investigation. The allegations are heinous indeed."

I told him all that had transpired in Mr. Peevers' study on both occasions. I neglected nothing, including my wielding of the letter opener. I also told of the secret altercation I had overheard on my first day, of the boys so frequently dismissed for "want of gratitude," and Poxy's inverted pride. I then told the final details of the pact Mr. Peevers and I had made. It was a great relief to tell someone at last, especially Mr. Jackson. Then I gave him the gold I had received, to be kept safe for me.

He was encouraging and fatherly throughout, but my tale made him darkly angry. "We will take care of this. Stealing from dependent boys is bad enough, but, damn! The Fleet's entirely too good for the man. We'll see him in Newgate, and at Tyburn, too. First, I will see my solicitor, and then you will be called to make a deposition. That's a special legal statement in which you are asked about your experiences, and they are written down in a manner that can be taken to court. As you bravely did not permit him to go very far, I think it unlikely you will be asked to testify, but your statement will add weight to the others and help to show there was a pattern. It may take some time before he is formally charged with these crimes, and the trial will take more time yet, but the matter will be pursued, of that you may be certain."

I thanked Mr. Jackson profusely, and then we returned to work, for which distraction I was grateful. As he had predicted, the matter moved slowly, and over the ensuing weeks it receded to the back of my mind as the unceasing work went on, and I despaired of ever having time to find Chowder.

XXVIII

THE TRAVAILS OF REORGANIZING THE shop occupied us for several months, with the result that many more books and customers could now be accommodated in a space which, if cluttered before, was now utilized to severest efficiency. We increased the number and height of the shelves and placed them closer together, so much so that several very portly gentlemen, good customers all, complained they could no longer fit between them. To this, Mr. Jackson returned that he would be only too happy to provide them with lists of all titles held, and brief descriptions thereof, for their perusal and edification, in anticipation of any orders they might wish to place. The making of the list, which extended to many pages and required frequent recopying, and which was later continually printed, amended, and reprinted, fell to me. But however much it may have improved my script or acquainted me with many a volume I might otherwise never have seen, it continued the pattern of working at all reasonable and unreasonable hours. I was not free to enjoy an entire Sunday at liberty until early June.

On that day, I told Mr. Jackson I wished to attend services at the church of my childhood, St. Michael Royal, and he should not look for me until the close of day as I expected to meet old friends there. To this he readily assented, saying he would expect me at nightfall, which at that time of the year was not until nearly nine. Thus, I set off on foot early on a bright morning, equipped with a sixpence given me by Mr. Jackson for the poor box at church and freighted with equal measures of excitement and guilt, as I had meant none of it. I had never been inside St. Michael Royal, as I have said, and would instead make directly for Spittlefields.

Lying had been far too easy, in which saying I suppose I merely reveal how unused was I to the ways of the world. It would also be easy to strangle a baby, if one's hands could be made to do it, or in any of a thousand other ways create misery and wreak destruction on the fabric of human life and understanding, pouring great, dark stains onto one's soul. Despite my dawning awareness that some argument might be entertained on the subject, I remained largely persuaded I had stains enough already, being so constructed as to settle on inappropriate objects of desire. When I had first met Mr. Peevers, I had lied to him without remorse, but then I had recognized him rightly as an odious miscreant worthy of no trust. This was, in theory at least, precious little justification if one is to hold to an absolute principle of honesty, which I had always believed I would. The stakes of food, shelter, and warmth in that preliminary interview were as compelling as Mr. Peevers was repellent, but the inescapable conclusion remained that I had my price. This realization, added to my persistent belief that God hated me anyway, did nothing to elevate my mood.

Mr. Thomas Jackson, no Peevers, had extended to me every imaginable courtesy and kindness. I had resorted to untruth to protect the sensitivity of my mission, but as I walked eastwards past the many shuttered shops, I hated myself for having done it and wondered if I ought to have taken the man into my confidence instead. I thought of how he would later want to know what had transpired at church and who I had met there, which would necessarily lead to further fabrications and the eventual unraveling of my stupid ruse. Henceforth, were I to maintain my fictions, I would to some degree always be playing a part with him. Thus does one bind oneself.

And yet, his kindnesses and the irrationality of my untruth notwithstanding,

I was unable to trust him with this, my most precious confidence. Having read in Plutarch of the Sacred Band, warriors who were the finer for being lovers, a most unexpected nugget which filled me with desire, I asked Mr. Jackson if he would tell me what he knew of the attitude of the ancients towards the friendships of men, only to see him quickly and nervously change the subject. I had never seen him skittish in that way, and I dared not return to the matter.

Mr. Jackson had in his shop numerous maps of London. One of these, published in a series of sheets nearly two feet by three and showing every building, street, and court, was plastered yards wide across the wall next to the stairs. The map was tilted to accommodate the rising of the stairs, so one had to tilt one's head to get the right sense of it, making prolonged study an ordeal.

Spittlefields, I knew, lay as the crow flies little more than a mile to the east-northeast of St. Paul's, across a mad warren of tiny streets which turned all about and most of which led nowhere. Here, in every manner of habitation from grandest houses to the most miserable and decrepit of rents, piled four and five stories high, lived uncounted scores of thousands. Still, there were a few major roads to help me on my way. On a scrap of paper I had written some directions: "Cheapside—Poultry—left at Threadneedle, left again at Bishop's Gate, walk a long way, look on the right for a narrow entrance to Spittle Square, and follow along to Spittlefields Market." It seemed easy enough, even if I had never been there. I had very rarely ventured north of Cheapside, and had always regarded the street as the border of known and unknown worlds. I was now to breach this barrier, which separated me from him whom I would have for my love.

My thoughts of Chowder were composed of brief impressions formed at odd moments—how fascinating were his hands, his lips, the tenor of his voice, his kind solicitude and patient wisdom, and always, how it had felt to lie in bed beside him and feel his touch. Even though we had done no more than a pair of weary, innocent boys in a room full of others would do, I would never forget it. When I would see certain young men in Mr. Jackson's shop, my interest in them was less vague than it might otherwise have been, because I had been close to Chowder.

How different was Sunday, when the only establishments open were coffee houses, taverns, and churches! It was not difficult to tell whether the god worshipped by a passer-by was of the ethereal or more liquid form, and where he might, therefore, be headed. All the clean and proper people wearing their Sunday best, their bright and dutiful children, and so many elderly widows in black, were all trundling with obedient reverence to the many churches. Others, wearing ill-fitting and ragged clothes as rumpled and soiled as their persons, had slept out of doors or in vacant cellars. These, deep in the poverty of drunkenness, called unsteadily at the better sort for a penny, a ha'penny, a farthing, any coin of the realm, only to disappear once given it, stumbling down cellar steps to gin shops or across the threshold to a tavern. White Lyon, Golden Bear, Black Dog, Daft & Rummy, Cock & Squelcher, Bludgeon and Bedamned, scores upon scores of them, none wanting for trade. Thank God beer only makes me sleep, and I have never had any interest in spirituous drink, or I would very likely have ended my life in such places.

I assumed it would be a simple matter to walk to Spittlefields, and make enquiries there after a greengrocer named Cudworth. Threadneedle was easy to find, narrow and departing at a leftwards angle from Cheapside, and leading then between the Bank and the Royal Exchange, but I became confused a bit farther on where the road forks and Fig Street trends to the left again while Threadneedle jogs to the right. Although streets had names enough, and had always had them, they were secrets held for the initiated. Few signs existed by means of which they might betray themselves. One knew where one was and which way to turn, or one didn't. I didn't, so I mistook Fig and wrongly followed past the Old South Sea House, Gresham College, and the Pay Office, all the way to New Broad Street, where the road left off among the maze of Broad Street buildings just east of Moorfields. I could see a spot of Moorfields by looking down a street-end to the west, which direction I knew only by the angle of the sun, and knew as well thereby that I had lost my way.

I was not dismayed, as I had yet most of the day before me. Thinking it would be a pleasant place to stop and rest, I turned left and walked into Moorfields, which I had often seen on Mr. Jackson's map, to be free of the closeness of the streets and see the sky. Here were trees set in rows about perimeters of large and level grassy fields. I betook myself to a large tree across the way and sat down in the sun beneath it.

Here I drowsed a bit, savoring the brightness and open air, which I had of late too seldom been privileged to enjoy, and reflecting as one may at moments taken aside from life, did not neglect to congratulate myself on having arranged and managed the successful issue of a period of much uncertainty. If I could but find Chowder, things would be all right, and I discovered in myself then an unexpected degree of contentment and optimism, which, giving rise to a small smile, returned to the brilliant morning a portion of that brightness it had so pleasantly bestowed upon me. I nibbled a pie given me by Mrs. Whidby and watched a number of men, gentlemen and others, stroll about in the park.

These men, perhaps a dozen or more of varying station, each of them quite solitary, were behaving with peculiar similarity. Alternately standing and walking about, they seemed in equal parts to be seeking and avoiding one another's eye. An odd, slightly-built gentleman in gold-embroidered yellow waistcoat, scarlet silken breeches and pinkly plumed, cocked hat, would lounge beside a tree and make a show of looking at his watch. Espying a handsome workman of perhaps twenty, similarly solitary and affixed to a tree yonder, he would stroll in the other's direction, passing rather more closely than correct distance would allow, whilst drumming his chest with his finger tips, before continuing on to another tree, where he would again inspect his time piece and cast glances in the direction of the other. Whether he wished to make the acquaintance of the workman was impossible to say, as his pace slackened not as he passed, and in his glance could be found no interest or familiarity of regard, but only the blankness that might be expected from one passing time alone, absorbed in idle thoughts.

I found this curious but, more was my wonder, he was not alone in playing the game. A tradesman, a 'prentice, a young man in the rustic clothing of a farmer, and another whose rakish garb and drawn face had both seen better days, and several others besides, were all similarly engaged in the mime of feigned indifference and silent looks, place exchanging, and secret watching, which went on and on.

I found it an absorbing spectacle, but my interest became signal discomfort when the aforementioned gentleman of scarlet breeches walked now in my direction, and, passing within a very few feet of me, offered a searching look as appalling as it was brief, even as he continued on to another tree, leaving me in peace so that I might construe his passing as I wished. His sharp and narrow face, seen at close range, betrayed a dissipated and premature age. Heavy rouge had been smeared here and there over a thick white undercoat troweled on to level the puffy prominences, creases and pocks beneath, battle scars of a life to which wealth had not lent ease.

Young as I was, I was not so stupid I could not discern the nature of his interest, and in an instant understood the game, even as I was astounded to have stumbled upon it. Not wishing to be mistaken for a player, I withdrew across the street where I found shade in a doorway, that I might continue to observe. I wished to see whether any of them would pursue the thing to its conclusion by leaving together, but as the game went on and on without progress, I determined to set off again for Spittlefields, which I knew lay somewhere not far to the east of me. The only question was, which streets would lead there? This was no idle question, given the recursive nature of London's myriad minor thoroughfares. Standing nearby was an immaculate coupé, so I thought I might avail myself of the services of the driver.

Stepping forth from my refuge, I ahem'd sufficiently that it brought him 'round. He was a drowsy, coarse-faced fellow whose bright livery could not vanquish an elemental untidiness. He barked at me in purest cockney.

"Moind the 'osses, eh? They'll piss on ye. What d'ye want?"

"Beg pardon, sir, but which way lies Spittlefields?"

"Lost, eh? That's too bad, it is. Give tuppence and I might tell ye. Give six and I'll tell ye, all right. Give a shilling and I'll tell ye rightly."

"Haven't got a shilling. And if I did, you'd never see it, I'm sure. A hackney coach would take me there for less. You, sir, are an ass. Good day!"

Taking no notice of my insult, he shrugged, saying, "Suit y'sel'," but did not neglect to add the challenge, "See any hacks?" I ignored this as he had my parry and was about to walk off when the painted gentleman strode up with an energy I had not suspected he might possess.

"Damn you, Xerxes! How dare you practice the beggar's art whilst sitting atop my carriage? You lack the requisite dignity for the trade. Were there a mendicant's office, I should report you to it to be flogged. Imagine, giving offense to one such as this." Here, he eyed me up and down with a too-appreciative regard. "I've half a mind to flog you myself. You are a boil on my bottom, you are." This disdain, expressed in words sharp enough, was severely undercut by the gentleman's fluttery and sibilant manner of speaking, which, laid atop an upper class accent such as only those richly endowed with privilege, education, and money may possess, struck me as ridiculous, as did the florid mannerisms which accompanied it.

"May your precious bottom ever be preserved, sir," replied the peculiarly named coachman impassively, looking directly forward.

The gentleman's eyes flashed at this, but he responded not, and, turning to me, spoke in lighter and, although I would not have thought it possible, yet more effeminate tones. "I would not offend your dignity, young sir, by asking you to excuse my inexcusable servant, however we might observe niceties by doing so. I assure you he is unworthy of it. My name is Sir Reginald Cooper." Here the coachman, unaffected by his master's opprobrious discharge, snorted sharply. "And I am delighted to be quite at your service." Taking his cocked hat in hand, he bowed low before me, brandishing the hat and plume in an exaggerated flourish.

Having seen him at his game in the park, and knowing he could only have mistaken the reason for my sojourn there, I was suspicious of his motives. I had Mr. Peevers to thank for my knowledge that certain gentlemen were not to be trusted with respect to boys. And yet, this creature was as unlike Mr. Peevers as it was possible to be. Despite the unfortunate appearance of his face and the effeminacy of his mannerisms, his wit was not entirely without appeal, and his dress was quite the opposite of Mr. Peevers's dour and ill fitting encasements. I was fascinated even as I was repulsed. At the least, I could see no harm in repeating to him the request I had made of his coachman.

"Thank you, sir. Do you know the way to Spittlefields? I am on my way there from St. Paul's, but seem to have taken a wrong turn."

"Spittlefields? It is not far. I find it the most salubrious of quarters, all those brawny silk weavers. Working the looms all day gives them such shoulders. And I just love silk. I bought the material for my breeches there. Do you like them?"

"Your breeches are very bright, sir, and make a vivid beacon in the sunlight, to be sure."

Sir Reginald, choosing to take my remark as a compliment, smiled broadly, revealing yellow teeth behind his reddened lips, and crazing his white paint. "Ah. And, what is your interest in Spittlefields, if I may be so bold as to ask?"

"I am off to visit a friend recently removed there."

"Splendid. Friendship is the most wonderful thing in the world, is it not? I say there is nothing, nothing better than two chums who care for each other. Would you not say so?" Here he affected a conspiratorial wink, which I chose to ignore. Even if I might hold precisely the same sentiments, they were none of his business. I wondered if, having sodomitical tendencies, one must grow to be like him, and quickly reassured myself that it could not be so.

"Indeed, sir." I was non-committal, but Sir Reginald would have none of it.

"Absolutely the very best thing. I tell you what, I was just going that way myself. May I offer to take you there? I assure you it is no trouble, no trouble at all."

I could see no harm in accepting the ride. If it came to it, I could jump out of the carriage. "If you really don't mind, sir, I would be grateful for it."

"No trouble at all. Please do step in." He opened the door for me himself, as if he were the coachman and I his master.

The interior was finished in padded yellow silk, mahogany, and morocco. Pink roses resting in vases affixed to the forward corners exuded a heady scent; the windows were of glass, and uncommonly large. Reaching upwards, he opened the hatch.

"Spittlefields Market, Xerxes, and be smart about it. We shall show the young fellow we are no mercenary riff raff."

"As you wish, sir," came the laconic reply. Xerxes did not sound as if he were about to be smart or had ever been so. With a jerk a practiced coachman would never have caused, the carriage began to move.

"It isn't far," said Sir Reginald, turning to me. "Pity it isn't farther," he added, again looking me over. "Snuff?" Reaching into his pocket, he retrieved a golden snuff box and inhaled a pinch, sneezing repeatedly and with absurd vehemence into a silken, sky blue handkerchief, which did considerable injury to his paint. His appearance, previously grotesque, was now irredeemably disordered.

"No, thank you, sir."

"Ah, well, I suppose you can't be corrupted." Observing the paint on his handkerchief, he said, "Dear me, I must be a mess." He reached into a miniature cabinet and brought forth a small mirror and tiny pots of paint, which he placed on a little tray and attempted to use to inspect and repair his face. It was instantly apparent that he could not see well, as he squinted and grimaced as he looked at himself in a hand mirror, which he held at various distances in the effort to bring himself into focus. This, and the movement of the carriage, allowed little accuracy in daubing, and small improvement.

"Why don't you wear spectacles?" It may have been an impertinent question, but I had to ask.

"And look like an owl? I should think not. And it isn't as easily made right as that, if you must know." He primped and smiled, to display his composure. "Now then, what, pray, is your name?"

"Menzies, sir. Archibald Menzies." The name popped into my head, and I grabbed it. I desired not even the most superficial of intimacies with this peculiar stranger.

"How very grand sounding. You are an apprentice?"

"Yes, sir, to a printer."

"You shall make an excellent printer. I can just tell. I do so admire tradesmen. I should be quite lost without them. But you are very clean for a printer's apprentice. Where, pray, are your ink stains?"

"I have washed myself, sir. 'Tis Sunday, sir."

"Ah, that it is. But why, then, are you not in church?"

"My master is very liberal. He does not require it."

"Does not require it? Whatever has this Island come to? Tell me, Archibald, how do you take these times? Shall we reinvent Society or leave it as it is?" Here his hand, which he had placed palm down on the seat between us, moved ever so slightly closer to my thigh.

"I'm sure I don't know, sir. People should think for themselves, I think."

"Ah, that they should. You are wise, young Archibald. I admire that in a young man. If people would only to do their own thinking instead of borrowing cant from others no wiser than themselves, how much better off we should be." The hand moved again, another quarter of an inch. "And, perhaps, too, some of them at least might leave off sticking their noses into other people's business. Why, Archibald, do you suppose there are laws against harmless pleasure? What business the Crown's whom we love?"

"I have no idea what you can mean, sir." I knew exactly what he meant. Unfortunately, this statement, which I had judged likely to put him off, had somewhat the opposite effect.

"I cannot believe that. Really, I do believe you know quite what I mean." Here, the hand discovered its purpose, rising from its position on the seat and landing squarely upon my inner thigh, just above the knee, where it began what the gentleman undoubtedly supposed to be ingratiating movements. "Pray, come with me. I have lodgings which I keep for convenience not so very far from here. You shall be richly rewarded, and Xerxes will deliver you afterwards wherever in London you may wish to go. What say you?" He was breathlessly eager.

I grasped the offending member with a firmness made possible by months of lifting heavy boxes, replacing it in its original position on the seat. I replied with more moderation than outrage. "I say, sir, that I have no interest in your attentions."

The painted, rheumy eyes stared approximately in my direction; above them, the querying eyebrows raised absurdly high. I nearly laughed.

"I see. I see how you are, I do." He licked his lips nervously. "Well then, name your price, young Archibald. Perhaps you think me cheap? Perhaps you think I think you cheap?" I thought to myself that I ought to have expected this. He began to inch closer, as before.

"No, I'm really very sorry. You don't understand. I don't want your gold."

"Well then, what the devil do you want? I'm sure I've made it clear enough what I want, have I not?"

"Sir, you have made yourself altogether too clear. I don't want anything."

"Let me see if I have this right. You don't want gold. And you don't want rapture."

"You are very quick, sir."

"And you are an impudent pup. You seek to take advantage of me, do you not, by accepting transport and offering nothing in return? I ought to have Xerxes thrash you."

"Sir, if you will say that, then you were not sincere in your offer. I desire no advantage. And if you set your man on me, I shall have you exposed." The phrase, which I had grabbed as a ready weapon, had magical effect. Sir Reginald compressed his lips into a thin line and furrowed his brow. Dark silence obtained for some moments as the carriage rattled on. Having space to gather my thoughts, I found I felt sorry for the old fool, without quite understanding why.

"Sir Reginald, please understand. I am not entirely without sympathy for a gentleman such as yourself. I can understand how—I mean to say, what you want is not something that I am opposed to. But I believe it ought not to happen between two such as us. We don't know each other and are too different in age. Have you no bosom friend with whom that sort of thing is just for the two of you? It strikes me as very dangerous to be loitering around Moorfields seizing on boys whose purposes you might misunderstand." His eyes grew big as I spoke. He took a moment to respond, and when he did, it was in subdued tones.

"And your chum, whom you wish to visit in Spittlefields, is he—? Do you—?"

"I'd really rather not say, if you don't mind. Possibly." Possibly, indeed. I had no idea. I only knew how badly I wished it to be so.

Here, the carriage came to a stop. We had come to a square surrounded by low buildings of brick, the windows of which were shuttered and the awnings rolled up in honor of the Lord's day. Numbers of working men and women sat on benches taking in the air, talking and eating food they had brought out with them, while a horde of tatty children ran about. A pavement ran around the perimeter of the square, which was filled with vacant fixtures used on weekdays, I supposed, for the purposes of a market. A wonderfully mild and agreeable Xerxes opened the hatch.

"Spittlefields Market, sir. Shall I thrash the lad now, sir?"

"No! You are a disgusting little man, listening to your master's private conversations. I shall have you replaced. Find us a place to wait. And don't speak to me again until I call for you."

"Very well, sir." Xerxes' smiling mildness continued undisturbed.

Sir Reginald turned to me with an expression of exaggerated earnestness. "Now then, young Archibald. I have made a grave error and mistaken you for another sort of boy, a hardened and unpleasant sort of boy, which it is clear to me now you are not at all. Here, take this." He took my hand in one of his, and pushed two half crowns into it. He then closed my fingers over the silver with a shudder of abnegation, finally letting go of me with a movement of sliding caress. It made me intensely uncomfortable.

"I may be a mad old fool," he went on, "but I am not a bad man, really I am not.

I do wish to be kind. I don't know what comes over me sometimes. I was like you once, you know. I would give my estate and all my thousands to be a clean young lad in good health like you, again. Here, take my card, but please do not look at it until I am gone. Should you ever desire to visit me, you will find me at the premises indicated. I stay in town the year 'round, as I find the country insufferable. Should you visit, you shall be most cordially and, I assure you, respectfully received. Now, be off with you. Good bye, Archibald."

I stepped out of the carriage, bidding him good bye. No sooner had I both feet on the pavement than Xerxes snapped the reins and the horses leapt forward at a smart canter. Looking at the card I saw: "Quentin Duckworth, Esq., 12 Sackville St., Piccadilly."

XXIX

As the carriage clattered rapidly away, I alternately looked at it and the gentleman's card, upon which, I could only suppose, was his true name. It startled me to think that while I had been playing a game of evasion with him, he had been doing the same with me. I wondered if I ought to have made more of the encounter, as I found myself thinking rather better of him due to the advancement of his trust. There was much I wished to ask him.

I then reflected dourly on my earlier conduct and meditations concerning honesty, and the inescapable truth that I had resorted to evasion the instant I was confronted with a situation of doubtful issue. This forced my thought, and I sat on a bench and wrestled with it. That I should have so concealed my identity, I reasoned, had less to do with shame than fear, except as the former stands in dependent relation to the latter. I would not be ashamed to declare my love of, or to, Chowder, although I had only hoped, and did not really know, that his affections were of the same nature and degree as mine.

There was, at any rate, in it the trust of two bosom friends and the sure belief he would not betray me. But with a stranger there could only be extremes of reserve, as the stakes were life. I may have been unclear as to what sodomy actually was, but I did know men were hung for it. I concluded that if the Crown, taking it upon itself to act as God's agent, would find the tender actions of my love so odious it must threaten murder to deter them, I might then make the necessary adjustment to sometimes conceal or obscure my identity, and not tax myself overly for having done so.

None of this pleased me, to be sure, and I nearly fell into the pit of thinking that, if being what I was necessitated deception for survival, then I must indeed be evil, or why else would I need the lie. This I quickly threw off, for in taking inventory of my emotions regarding Chowder, I found them associated with the noblest self-sacrificing impulses and strivings for excellence, that I might be worthy of him and his love. And I had dissembled only with respect to my name and occupation to make myself untraceable. That which I believed, I had not feigned, and there was integrity in that. It did not occur to me to praise myself for resisting the gentleman's blandishments. The mere touch of his hand had chilled me. No amount of gold would have been recompense enough for suffering more of it.

Thinking of Mr. Jackson again, I realized with a pang that I had by my dissimulation placed him in league with moralizing murderers, when I very well knew that he had dedicated his life to enlightenment and reform—hardly one from whom one ought to have to conceal oneself, or so I hoped. We had never discussed sodomy. But thinking I should be more like him in general principle and less the rabbity, frightened child, I lifted my head up and resolved to do better. With renewed courage, I stood up, finally to find Chowder at last.

About the square were rows of awninged shops, but none emblazoned with the name Cudworth. I asked several of those sitting on benches nearby if they were acquainted with the name, but received no affirmative reply. I began to walk about, threading my way through the many streets and lanes surrounding the square, in search of the grocer's premises. This occupied me for some hours, during which time the sun drew high and the day warmed. But although I wandered many streets, lanes, and courts through all their turns, I found no Cudworth's grocery, nor, to my puzzlement, did anyone I asked know of it.

Seeing a steeple, I recalled I had failed to discharge my obligation to Mr. Jackson's sixpence, and so made my way to Christ's Church, Spittlefields, for so it proved to be. There I deposited the sixpence in the poor box located just inside, and on an impulse also deposited one of the half crowns I had so recently and unexpectedly come to possess. I didn't suppose I could purchase God's favor so easily, but perhaps it would do somebody some good, and that was reason enough. Services had concluded not long before, and seeing the priest in the nave speaking with a rotund tradesman, I strode forward to make enquiry of him. He, if anyone, would know the district well.

The priest was a thin, wan man in advancing middle age, with bushy white eyebrows and a perpetually startled expression. He listened patiently as the tradesman, shorter, somewhat younger and much rounder than he, complained at length. The tradesman's worn brown waistcoat at some remote date might have supported pretensions to quality, but was now shabby and forlorn. He whined in a rasping voice unpleasantly strident and querulous. Neither took any notice of me.

"And what's worst is the wife, you know. She won't be managed. And now the daughters are taking their head from her. I'm at my wit's end, I tell you. I have no say in my own house. I thought I would force the issue last week and used the strap, but it doesn't seem to have helped. Now they all hiss at me when I enter a room. I've taken to eating and sleeping in the shop."

"Aye, it's the devil's own work, it is, when a woman is headstrong." The priest's reedy voice was infinitely patient, which the shopkeeper decidedly was not.

"Well, what should I do?" He tapped his foot, causing his belly to jiggle. His broad, worn face was framed by untrimmed, bushy side-whiskers. Great shocks of graying hair spread untended below his baldness, making his head appear altogether very wide. His mouth, too, was wide, giving him something of the appearance of a very large bulldog.

"Tobias, I know it isn't easy, but you must not act rashly. Remember our Savior, who taught us to be meek. You ought not to have used the strap, Tobias."

"Christ never married, now, did He? What would He know? Have you no practical solutions for me?"

The priest sighed. "Tobias, love *is* practical. Please. Will you not see whether meekness and contrition bring the result you seek, rather than violence? You can, perhaps and for a time, force people to behave as if they respect you, but it's hardly the same thing as love. Is it not love that you seek, Tobias?"

But Tobias would not be soothed. "Father Snodgrass, I cannot believe you would speak of contrition to me, when those women make my life a misery. Is not woman to be a helpmate to man?" His voice rose. "I ask you, is it not so?" Not waiting for an answer, he turned angrily and began walking rapidly towards the door. The priest, watching the man depart, stroked his beard, then gathered himself and spoke in stern tones.

"Tobias, your inflamed passions become you ill. A helpmate is not a slave. If it's a slave you want, you are free to buy one." But the only response was the crashing shut of the church's door.

Father Snodgrass now noticed me standing in the aisle to one side and spoke in a kindly manner. "May the good Lord teach the man patience. He sorely needs it. Now then, young man, is there something you wish to ask me?"

It was all I could do to wait for him to finish. "I am looking for Tobias Cudworth, the greengrocer. Do you know where I may find him?"

"Why, yes. Yes. That was he, here just now. Still is, actually." Father Snodgrass blinked several times and smiled uncertainly. "Tobias Cudworth, I mean."

"Thank you very much, sir!" I was on my toes, turning and running as fast as I could up the aisle to the door, which seconds before had been so rudely thrown shut. Throwing it open again with equal energy but more care, I raced across the pavement into the street, where I saw the top of Mr. Cudworth's departing bald head bobbing above the throng some distance beyond. Running with all the speed I could muster and weaving madly around one startled pedestrian after another, I was soon abreast of him. He was muttering to himself, and the scowl on his face had, if anything, intensified.

"Hello, pardon me," I panted. "Are you Tobias Cudworth, the greengrocer?"

"That I am. What's it to you?"

"Terribly sorry to trouble you, sir, but have you a 'prentice name of Potter Gorham, previously of Mr. Peevers's Little Eastcheap Free School for Unfortunate Boys?"

"I do. So what?" He strode so rapidly I had to break into a trot now and again to keep up.

"I'm a friend of his, sir. I wish very much to see him."

"What do you want with him?"

"I wish to—to see him, sir."

"That's a damned flimsy reason if you ask me."

"Please sir, it's very important, sir."

"I don't permit my apprentices to have friends. They don't work as hard, always thinking about something else, if you're soft with 'em. Anyway, he's got the day off. Shouldn't, but he does. Stupid business, this no work on Sundays, when there's money to be made. He left the church right after services, and I don't know where he went."

"When do you expect him to return home?"

Mr. Cudworth stopped so abruptly that I almost ran into him. Turning and focusing his bulk and vexation entirely on me, he spat out, "Now look'ee here. I don't know who you are or why you want to see my 'prentice. He's a right proper lad, is that Gorham lad, and I want to keep him that way. Now, be off with you. Be off!" He brandished his cane at me, then strode off with impressive rapidity, even as he punctuated his renewed mutterings with occasional sharp tosses of his head.

I cared nothing at all that the man presented himself as a severe obstacle. I was a step closer to Chowder. I followed him at a discreet distance until he entered a tavern, the Black Eagle, and after some minutes, went in.

Though it was midday, the tavern was filled to capacity, the roar of drunken conversation and the reek of stale beer and cheap tobacco assailing my senses. Narrow shafts of sunlight streamed in through small windows, illuminating strips of dense and curling smoke and splashing here and there over a throng of rough men sitting at tables and in booths. I espied Mr. Cudworth as I entered, and stood behind a post where I could watch him with little likelihood of being seen. He was smoking a clay pipe alone in a corner booth set apart by heavily beamed walls of flaking plaster. Oblivious to the conviviality all about, he sat hunched over a tankard and stared morosely out a window. The light catching his face just so, I could see a tear had run down his cheek. As I watched, he tipped his tankard to the last and called for another in a slow and hollow voice quite unlike that which he had used on Father Snodgrass and me. When the maid came, he fumbled in his pocket for a penny, but came up with naught. A look of distress clouded his face, even as one of impatience crossed hers. He began to plead for credit.

"Ach, ye knows I cain't give ye no credit, Mr. Cudworth. Don't be asking for it, now. Don'cha think it's time to be a-goin' home, anyways? Ye really should be going home now." She spoke with a curious mixture of solicitude and wariness, as if to an extremely large and possibly dangerous child.

"Please, Mary? Just one more?" The voice was slow and thick. "I can't go home yet, you know that. It's only a penny. I'll give you tuppence tomorrow."

"But ye knows the house rules, Mr. Cudworth. I likes workin' here, I does. Don't be askin' no more."

"Thruppence, then. You know I'm good for it. Pretty please?" Mr. Cudworth uncertainly rearranged his features until he had managed the grotesque facsimile of an ingratiating smile. Mary wavered, caught between the allure of copper and whatever sense of responsibility she might be presumed to possess.

"I have to think about it some. I'll be back in a while. But if I thinks not, then it's none you'll have, though you can sit there all the day long, if you like, for nothing." She then moved off, chattering gaily with other patrons.

I placed myself at a booth in her way, the several other occupants genially making room for me, and put my hand on the remaining half crown in my pocket. Seeing me sit, she made her way smiling to my table. She was thin and raven haired, a roving spot of organized intensity amidst the convivial chaos.

"How old are you?" She was mock serious.

"Seventeen."

"Ach, too young t' marry the likes o' me. Now that's a pity." Her merry eyes danced. "I suppose I'll serve you anyways. What'll it be, then?"

I drew forth the half crown. "If you would bring me tuppence worth of meat and a pot of ale, you may keep a penny for yourself."

"Seventeen, you say? Let's get married anyways!" she laughed.

I returned her laughing banter with a broad grin. "I will add you to my list of hopefuls, and I do thank you. And I want to know something."

"Anything for you, dearie."

"Where's Mr. Cudworth's grocery? A friend of mine is 'prentice to him, and I'm looking for him, but I've been all over Spittlefields, and I can't find it."

"Cudworth's 'prentice? Law, I wouldn't wish that on a rat. It's only a little ways from here. Only it's not Cudworth's grocery, it's Bulmer's. That was his wife's name. It was her father's grocery, y'know. She made him keep the name or she wasn't a-going to marry him."

"Ah, that explains it. Tell you what, take a shilling from that half crown and let Mr. Cudworth, there, run an account for nine pence, but don't tell him it's from me." Now that I was not dependent on Mr. Cudworth to find my way to Chowder, it was as well to keep him out of my way, I reasoned. "And do bring me some meat and a pot of ale."

"Well! Teach him to believe in miracles, will you? It's as good as done. Look, love, let me get my orders, and I'll tell ye how to get to his grocery when I come back."

I watched her bustle about. She was a popular maid and kept up a running banter as she moved through the tavern. Mr. Cudworth's eyes grew large when she placed a tankard in front of him, and larger still when informed he needn't make it up on the morrow. He regarded the tankard with wonder and sipped it tentatively, as if it might vanish as unexpectedly as it had arrived. Finally, convinced of its substantiality, he lifted it and drank deeply.

Mary soon returned with my victuals, drink, and change, and revealed the mystery of the whereabouts of Mr. Cudworth's grocery, which was tucked away in an obscure court off an obscure alley, to be known only by those privy to it. A very poor location for a shop, to be sure. Though it was but fifteen minutes walk at best, I might have wandered for days and never found it. I thanked her and quickly ate my meat, but left most of the ale, as I cared not to greet Chowder, should I be so lucky, with a dulled mind. I quickly negotiated the convoluted thoroughfares and minor passages by means of which Frying Pan Alley and its appendage, Hair Court, might be gained.

Here, at last, was Chowder's abode. Hair Court, paved with ancient, very uneven cobblestones, random patches of which were missing, and strewn with trash in every stage of decomposition, was ringed by tottering two- and three-story brick and timber rents presenting a catalogue of the more advanced stages of decrepitude. The afternoon sun, an unaccustomed visitor, illuminated dark streaks of moss and mildew in the corners, where rain water ran down in wet weather.

To one side, just within the entrance to the court, was a small greengrocer's, of most unprepossessing aspect. "Bulmer's" was just discernible in painted letters of considerable antiquity on a warped and decaying wooden sign affixed above the windows. Benches for the display of fruit and vegetables stood empty under the awning, and wooden fruit boxes were scattered upon and beneath them. Looking through the windows I could see boxes of potatoes, Spanish oranges, lettuce, and, perhaps, for it was gloomy indeed within, salt fish and tea, none of which, in keeping with their surroundings, appeared to be in the very best of repair.

My heart went out to Chowder, that he should exist under the inept tutelage of a man such as Tobias Cudworth, in a place such as this. That Cudworth's women would hiss at him spoke well of them, whatever else they might be, and I hoped there was some recompense there for my friend, of whom there was no more to be seen here than anywhere else on that day. I knocked loudly at a door just beside the shop, which I judged as likely to lead to the attached lodgings, but no one answered. Once again, I settled down to wait.

A spindly and emaciated dog rummaged in a pile of refuse, and, finding a bloated, fly-covered dead rat, guiltily sniffed, pawed, and guarded its prize. None of the locals paid it any mind, save a boy of middling size who threw a broken cobble at it. The cobble finding its mark, the dog ran yelping to the farthest corner of the yard, where it emitted piteous howls, leaving the rat to swell in the sun. A second cobble chased the beast from the yard altogether.

In the midst of this drama, a dirty, half-clothed man of minute stature burst from a cellar doorway, pursued by the shrieked curses of a drunken harridan and a hail of shoes, breeches, shirts, and bottles, every one drained of gin. Her aim was remarkably good; his ducking was not, to the amusement of the idle adults and their children, who were out taking the air on a rare summer's day.

The man slunk from the yard, pausing now and again to offer benedictions of rich curses. And a gaggle of grubby little girls played winsome games with pieces of dolls. This one had a much-marred little wooden head atop a stick, that one a headless, broken doll's body to which a wad of dirty cloth had been affixed, and another a mere bit of board on which a crude face and body had been drawn with chalk. Despite its inadequacies, each was animated with rapt absorption, and played its part in intricate dramas of abandonment and solicitude, dispute and reconciliation. A queen, a soldier, a king, then a wealthy merchant, his wife and daughter, small stones standing in for servants, and a cobble a carriage. My heart went out to them all.

Such were my entertainments as the sun dropped behind the rooftops and shadows lengthened. I much consulted my heart, which would not be still. I thought of how little I really knew of Chowder. True, he had expressed every interest in me, and I could not, I was sure, have experienced the sympathy I felt without his partaking of it. And yet, I had known him but a few weeks, and that half a year ago. I had made far too much of very little, perhaps.

My meditations were interrupted by the approach of a woman and a half-grown girl, likely her daughter. These two, if plainly and cheaply dressed, were clean, and what was the more uncharacteristic, sober. Neither was what one would call handsome. The mother's face was deeply pocked, and the daughter's featured an overhanging upper lip, buck teeth, and an overly large nose. Her absurdly thick eyebrows cast a shadow over weak, squinting eyes. The two made directly for the door beside Bulmer's grocery. I was sitting on a box to the other side, watching them intently.

"Hortensia, kindly hold my things while I look for the key"

"Yes, Mum."

"You are a blessing to me, dear."

"Thank you, Mum. I pray I shall never be anything else."

I introduced myself. They were indeed Mrs. Cudworth, née Bulmer, and her daughter. However, I should have to speak to Mr. Cudworth regarding Potter Gorham. They were very sorry, but they couldn't offer me any assistance when it came to Mr. Cudworth. They were not responsible for him or his affairs. They then let themselves inside, closing the door firmly behind themselves.

Perhaps another quarter of an hour passed before a most unsteady Mr. Cudworth appeared, tacking upwind against heavy seas and a strong tide, only able to keep a fix on his grocery by continually taking and retaking his bearings, in each instance a protraction of bogglement. I gathered my jacket around my ears and walked in the opposite direction, away from the entrance to the Court, and down Frying Pan alley. It was time I were leaving, anyways. It was nearing sunset, and I would soon have to be heading back to Mr. Jackson's, a prospect which filled me with anxiety, as I feared having to provide an accounting of my day.

I walked a few score yards, then turned and looked back, and I saw him. Chowder was walking beside a pretty, blonde girl dressed in Sunday clothes, and his arm was comfortably over her shoulder, which sight pierced me with dismay. He appeared older, more grown, and hale. He was beautiful, and my heart leapt, even as it strangled. I slunk into the darkest shadows the narrow street had to offer and waited for them to turn and enter the Court. Neither of them saw me as they rounded the corner.

Creeping forward in stealthy pursuit of the pair, I was just in time to see Chowder tenderly kiss the lass on the cheek before disappearing inside the grocery, the door to which was held open for him by the drunken and glowering Tobias Cudworth. The girl, watching Chowder enter, blew him another farewell kiss before striding away. As she must pass me at the narrow entrance to the Court, I again drew up my jacket about my neck and ears, and shuffled away with leaden steps, a creature of shadows, having a black heart to match.

XXX

I RETURNED ON FOOT WITHOUT incident to Mr. Jackson's. The streets were thronged yet, the fine day having called forth London's multitudes. As in a repellent dream, I was separated from the families and strolling couples as if wrapped in a gauze as invisible as impenetrable. Their happiness and the remaining traces of the brilliant sunset mocked me. I knew I would never be like them, whatever their cares or inspirations.

Those few young men walking alone, like myself, attracted my interest powerfully. What lurked in their hearts? Did any of them harbor secret dreams like mine, of sweetest intimacy with another like themselves? However would I find out? And what were Chowder's inspirations? I attempted to reassure myself I knew nothing of the identity of the girl or what she was to him, but I seemed incapable of listening to my own reason. What I had seen was plain enough, and I could not get out of my head the image of him kissing her. I sensed the possibility of a poisoned and solitary future, perhaps ending up hideous like Quentin Duckworth. Whatever was I going to do?

My steps slowed and became hesitant as I approached Mr. Jackson's. I tried Mrs. Whidby's lodgings, only to discover she was out yet. I would have to ask Mr. Jackson for the key and enter through the shop, which now seemed darkly imposing. Lamps had been lit, and through the window I could see Mr. Jackson at the desk in the rear, going over some papers.

Cursing his cheerful industry, I stopped just outside the door and hesitated, feeling sick in my heart. I tried the latch, but it was locked. Mr. Jackson looked up, smiled, and rose to open the door for me.

"Terribly sorry to bother you, sir." I was cravenly obsequious. I shook his hand weakly.

"No trouble, Joe. Come in. I'm very glad to see you." Mr. Jackson opened the door wide for me to enter. "I was just beginning to wonder if I should start to worry. How was your day? How was it to revisit your church?" He was all smiles and genial grace.

I regarded him with an uncertain look. I should have to lie and hated myself richly for it. But my collapsed heart had deprived me of the power to create fiction. With dawning horror, I realized I was going to tell the truth.

"Are you feeling all right, Joe?"

"Yes. I, er ..." The truth, sharp as a razor, cuts both ways. "You are going to think very ill of me, I think."

"Why, Joe? Whatever for? Please tell me what's on your mind."

"I didn't go to church. I spent the entire day looking for my friend. My best friend from Mr. Peevers' school." I blurted it out in a single breath.

"I see." Mr. Jackson regarded me solemnly. After a pause of perhaps half a minute, during which I looked at my feet, he spoke again. I could not have been less prepared for his smile. "Is that all? I thought perhaps you had been murdering old ladies from the sound of you. And so, did you find him?"

Damn me, I started to cry. "That's the trouble. I did."

Mr. Jackson, to my amazement, responded with a warm solicitude almost feminine and terrifying to behold. He held his arms open to me, and I fell into them. I was very nearly as tall as he and felt absurd. Even as I blubbered on his shoulder, I could not help noticing the lithe perfection of his body. I thought I must be mad, to notice such a thing at such a time.

"You found him, and that is why you cry?"

"He's ... he's my, er, friend. I was going to find him after we both got out of Mr. Peevers' school. He went first, to a greengrocer in Spittlefields. I meant to find him months ago, but we have been so busy here. I couldn't stand it. So I spent all day looking for him. I don't suppose he knows where I am. You wouldn't understand, sir, what it's like."

"My dear Joe. Come and sit in the chair." He led me to the chair at his desk.

I sat as he perched on the corner, inches away. He took his waistcoat off, placing it neatly over the edge of the desk, and put his hand on my shoulder.

"Here, Joe, use my handkerchief. I think, Joe, you might be surprised by what I can understand." He spoke very gently, like a loving father, and gripped my shoulder meaningfully.

"Thank you so very much, sir. I know you're so very learned and all, sir, but this is different."

"Perhaps it's the sort of thing being learned wouldn't help to understand?"

I wiped my eyes and took a deep breath. It was a desperate moment, but I was now sensible of a kind of manic zeal, that had come from somewhere beyond my pain. Mr. Jackson would throw me out, and I would become a criminal. So what? Lots of boys were criminals. They couldn't all be stinking ugly. So I lifted my head, looked him in the eye, and uttered the unholy in as firm a voice as I could manage.

"Did you ever want to kiss another boy?"

He dropped his hand from my shoulder. Mr. Jackson studied a particular spot on the ceiling for a considerable length of time, while I looked at the floor. I can remember that spot of floor yet. After perhaps a year, or maybe two, he spoke.

"Yes."

"What?" I gaped in utter stupefaction.

"Yes, Joe. I said yes." And gently, intimately, "Is that what he is to you?"

I near to whispered. "I don't know. I would like him to be." Renewed tears coursed down my cheek. I blew my nose.

"My dear, dear boy. You have been holding all of this in. God works in mysterious ways, Joe."

"That's for damned sure."

"Do you recall my saying last January when you first arrived, that I had sought a boy like myself?"

"Yes, but—"

"It appears we are rather more alike than either of us suspected until now."

"What? You? Please don't make a joke, sir. How could you be sodomitical?"

"Please, Joe. I hate that word. That word is all opprobrium. A better one should be invented, I think. But yes, I am. I have no idea how or why. I just am. And when I was your age, I was no less so."

"But it's against the law! Are not men hanged for it? How can you live?" These questions burst forth from me in a wail.

"It isn't easy, I can assure you that. But, think, Joe. The law is created by people, really very ordinary people who mean well, mostly. And so the law is as full of their folly as it is their wisdom. I can live because I do not meddle in other people's affairs, and they, despite the law, do not meddle in mine. It wasn't always thought of as so very wrong, you know. Surely you have made some discoveries in your reading of the ancients. And I can live because I have Rowland."

"Rowland? He knows?"

"Yes, Rowland knows. He would be rather disappointed were it not so, in fact."

"He does not hate you for it?"

"Rowland is much more than my assistant. He is my adopted son, but he was nineteen when I adopted him. Now, I invite you to suppose why we resorted to that stratagem. It isn't as if marriage were an option."

Again I gaped like an idiot.

Mr. Jackson spoke slowly, deliberately. "Right. That's how it is, Joe. Now, tell me about your Chowder."

And so I told him, hesitantly at first, and then more easily, of Chowder and how he had been my only friend in that awful place. Encouraged by Mr. Jackson's gentle probing, I told him how we had held each other. The razor of truth, having cut, allowed the matter to flow freely at last. Then Cudworth, the grocery, the girl, the kiss, everything. "I love him, Mr. Jackson, and I shall be damned for it. And doubly damned because he kisses girls. I want him only to kiss me." Mr. Jackson's handkerchief was subjected to very heavy use.

"So the two of you have never declared yourselves to each other. That could be difficult. How do you know he is of the same persuasion?"

"I can't say I do know. Maybe I don't. But he always wanted to be near me whenever he could, and I him. It seemed so natural. And cuddling was his idea."

"Well, few boys not of our persuasion show much interest in nuzzling their chums, it's true. So I wouldn't give up hope, Joe. Not yet, anyway." He said this brightly, but the brightness was quickly displaced by the most serious of miens. "Now, Joe, I must speak very, very seriously. You are quite correct to note men are sometimes hanged for loving as we love. I shall do all I can for you, and will guard your precious secret as carefully as I do my own. In return, you must do the same. I must require of you the very, very strictest secrecy. You must speak of this to no one. No one at all. Everything depends on it. You do realize how important this is?"

"I would rather die than betray you, sir." My heart throbbed with love and admiration of a quality more severe than I had ever felt before.

Mr. Jackson smiled his broadest smile. "Good. Off to bed with you then.

Tomorrow morning will come early."

"Yes, sir. Mr. Jackson?"

"Yes, Joe."

"What will Rowland think? That I know, I mean."

"Leave Rowland to me, Joe. For the moment, I want you to carry on as if nothing has happened between us. There will come a time, fairly soon I should think, when we will let him in on it. You can do that, of course?"

"Of course I can, sir"

"Good. Good night, then, Joe."

"Good night, sir. Oh, here. Your handkerchief. Sorry, I made rather a mess of it." I handed it to him in all its soggy glory. He took it with a smile, and without the least trace of hesitation. I made my way through to the back, and on crossing the lane, found a lamp lit in Mrs. Whidby's window. She let me in, and I was grateful she was not curious about my doings that day. I was soon up the stairs into my chamber.

That night I lay awake in wonder far into the night. Before I slept, I poured forth many tender intimacies upon my pillow. Sir Pillow was not a very good substitute for that which I craved, and must be forgiven for having maintained a very matter-of-fact demeanor despite everything I shared.

XXXI

IN A STROKE, MR. JACKSON had rescued me from the pit of oblivion. By entrusting me with the secret of his life, he provided me with the key to mine. All the better he had Rowland, and I should be indifferent to Rowland and he to me. Simpler that way, it was. I was awed by new awareness of the complexities of this world, and the stratagems by means of which men contrived to live in it. More, the worries instilled by Mr. MacCurran had receded, and the possibility of happiness and fulfillment seemed real, as it had not since before my father had died. Henceforth, I became devoted to Mr. Jackson and his many enterprises with passionate zeal. His interests were now my interests, and his many projects became things of wondrous inspiration to me.

Contrarily, the week's work was marred by a series of small incidents which lent suspicion to my acuity and even to my character. On Monday, a box of books which ought to have presented no difficulties broke apart as I carried it down the stairs. The bottom fell away suddenly, and the lot of new books tumbled out, damaging a number of them. Mr. Jackson accepted this as an unfortunate random occurrence, but the following day, which was rainy and cold, the handle of the coal scuttle broke, dropping coal onto the carpet, which Mr. Jackson found quite displeasing. Wednesday, my book list that I had labored over so long disappeared, causing no little consternation, and Thursday, one pound, seven shillings, and eight pence were missing from the cash box, which I had tended for an hour while the two men were out. Rowland made the discovery of the missing cash, and Mr. Jackson summoned me for an interview in his first-floor office, which I had never before visited. Rowland would mind the shop meanwhile.

"Joe, I am very sorry to have to ask you about this, but there's no way around it. The tally of books sold and the cash in the box don't match. Can you explain?"

"Sir, I have no idea. I counted the money before I did anything else. Here, sir, I even made a list. There were in it one old double guinea, six guineas, nine crowns, five half crowns, thirteen shillings, eight sixpence, three groats, eleven thruppence, seventeen tuppence, eleven pence, seven ha'pennies, and nine farthings when I started. I sold four books whilst you and Rowland were out. There was a better second-hand copy of Swift, that was a shilling. Three of Mr. Paine's pamphlets, eighteen pence. It's all right, I've seen you sell American pamphlets to the same gentleman before. Then some great fat fellow bought your latest volume of Dissenting sermons, best binding, two crowns. And a gentleman came for the parcel you had wrapped for him, I don't know what was in it, but he gave me the guinea you said he would.

"Thank you, Joe. And you didn't turn your back on the desk or cash box when there were customers in the shop?"

"No, sir, of course not."

"I don't doubt you, Joe. I want you to know that. And it isn't the money. But it's a very peculiar occurrence. I don't want it to happen again, of course. May I have your lists?"

"Of course, sir." I handed them over.

"Now, would you go on down and send Rowland up?"

"Of course, sir."

Rowland's expression, when informed that Mr. Jackson wished to see him, was of disgust.

Shortly thereafter, I heard the two men ascend the stairs to their lodgings above. Their muffled voices were sharp. I couldn't be sure what it was all about, exactly, but I did hear Rowland say, far more loudly than necessary, "Well, if you're not going to trust me!" Then the door at the top of the stairs closed, and I could hear no more. They remained there until nearly five, during which time I kept meticulous records of every transaction. It was not a particularly busy afternoon, but even so we took in nearly four pounds, every farthing of which was accounted for. On his descent, Mr. Jackson was pleased. He made no mention of his previous suspicions, nor did he refer to them again. I didn't see Rowland for the rest of the day, nor did I see him Friday, on which day no untoward incidents occurred, to my relief.

The following Sunday, Mr. Jackson suggested I join the two of them at services at the Unitarian congregation Mr. Jackson had been instrumental in founding but three years before. I hesitated, but agreed the instant I was offered the afternoon free, and fare for a hackney carriage to Spittlefields to go with it. Perhaps I would find Chowder by himself this time. Rowland cast me a sour look as we got into the hired carriage, but I was all smiles and determined not to mind. Mr. Jackson had found and won his Chowder. I could only be happy for them both. If the boy I wished to love were better looking and of a more pleasing disposition, so much the better for me.

We poured into the dense traffic of Ludgate, then Fleet Street, and soon the Strand. There, in a newly built hall in Essex Street, I discovered a congregation of hearty enthusiasts, Dissenting scholars, prosperous merchants and tradesmen, and independent proprietors like Mr. Jackson, for whom exaltation was to be found in the rationalization of their religion. Yet they could sing hymns of praise as lustily as any congregation of the Church of England.

There was no mention of Jesus, and, as I sat in the hard, wooden pew, I thought much of Dr. Priestley's book concerning the corruptions of Christianity, and Mr. Jackson's remarks about popular prejudice. That religion should be concerned with this life, and consider its central question to be how we should treat each other, impressed me immensely. The sermon was full of exhortations to moral improvement and the Great Work at hand, but in my mind, I composed an even better one of greater personal significance.

Mr. Jackson was a figure of importance here. At the close of services, he was full of intelligence and good humor as he shared with the minister and interested others the progress of his conversations with Dr. Priestley, who had recently spent several days in London. I was surprised to hear more about gasses than about God or religion. Whatever dephlogisticated air was, endless experimentation on it occupied much of the great Doctor's time. Mr. Jackson was about to publish yet another work of Priestley's, and glowing with enthusiasm as he summed up, asserted that to understand the laws of nature is to penetrate the mind of God. The idea staggered me with its magnificence. I was beginning to understand the exaltation of Mr. Jackson's enthusiasms.

Rowland, incomprehensibly, was ill at ease. The more others gathered around Mr. Jackson, the more strained did Rowland become. He wandered uncertainly around the outskirts of the group assembled about his putative father, and displayed greatest interest in the food brought for the light meal which was soon served.

As I stood taking it all in, Rowland approached. His mien was dark.

"I thought I ought to warn you."

"Warn me?"

"Warn you. Thomas has been talking about you a great deal. It isn't all flattering either."

I didn't say anything.

"He hasn't forgotten about the missing money. Or how you seem to be getting careless lately."

"I'm sure I can't help it if things break." It was a weak response, and I knew it. I added, "He hasn't said anything to me."

"Oh," said Rowland airily, "he wouldn't. It's not his way. You don't know him like I do. But if I were you I'd be worried. Something's going to give way."

With these cryptic remarks, he strode off. I felt as if I had stepped in a dog's mess on a glorious summer's day, because I had looked too long at an eagle crossing the sky. Rowland avoided me after that, ignoring me as the three of us boarded another hackney coach for the return to St. Paul's. Mr. Jackson, oblivious to the strain, placed Rowland between himself and me.

The day, which had begun with an opaque sky, was brightening and promised to turn fair. The passing streets fascinated me as always, but not so much as the contrary ideas which filled my mind. My enthusiasm for Mr. Jackson and his projects burned bright as ever, but Rowland had thrown a pall over it all.

"What did you think of that, Joe?" Mr. Jackson smiled eagerly.

"They are a daring lot. I should like to go back, if it were acceptable to you, sir."

"But of course. I should be delighted." Mr. Jackson was very enthusiastic. I was confused. Rowland shot me a look of contempt. It occurred to me to change the subject.

"Mr. Jackson, why are those colonists rebelling?"

"They wish to manage their own affairs, Joe. It's very reasonable, really. America has a brilliant future. We won't live to see it, but a day will come when it will surpass this Island. And it isn't as if they haven't tried to work things out. Many petitions have been made, and as many unanswered. Our government is sclerotic. Somnolent. It needs a fire lit under it. Not to burn it up, I hasten to add. But enough to cause it to awaken, and reason more clearly."

"But why doesn't the King listen to them?"

"Power knows only to seek more power, Joe. It can't help it. It's a kind of idiot force. But, eventually, there always comes resistance. That very resistance to the sovereign's unlimited power is the glory of our history. It is our very genius, if you will. It will be America's genius, too. Those small works of Mr. Paine's we sell would well reward your study, Joe. They're all about this sort of thing. You'll not read anyone who goes right to the bone like he does. Now, France. There's the final madness of power and a ruined people. That country is headed for a very bad end, I fear."

As we spoke, I witnessed a small, silent drama pass between the two men. Mr. Jackson secretly extended his hand along the seat to Rowland's, who as secretly pulled his away. This occurred several times, until Mr. Jackson stopped trying. A dark look settling on Rowland's face, the conversation between Mr. Jackson and me lost its fire, until silence obtained. I would ask later about the mind of God.

XXXII

I WAS DEEP IN THOUGHT as we entered St. Paul's Churchyard, and Mr. Jackson's premises came into view. To my astonishment, I saw a boy looking very much like Chowder standing beside the door. His head was thrown back against the wall, and his eyes were closed. He seemed to drink the sun into himself. How could it be he? But it was.

"It's Chowder! I can't believe it! However did he find his way here? Excuse me, I have to get out!" I was beside myself with excitement.

Mr. Jackson, smiling broadly, indicated to the driver to stop, even though it was yet some distance to the door of the bookstore, and I tumbled out and ran to my drowsing friend. He looked even better than he had in the previous week's gloaming. He would never have the muscles of a laborer, but had left behind the hollow chest and stick arms, and grown into his own simple masculine beauty in a way that made my heart stop. Having stopped, it ran backwards when the girl he had kissed approached from around the corner, beyond which was a tavern. She carried a basket from which a loaf of bread protruded. She was even prettier than I had feared. This creature, who wore clothes better than average working girls could afford, spoke.

"Chowder, love, I have bought a pie. Hello, who's this?"

Chowder opened his eyes to respond, and in opening them, saw me. I could detect in him none of the excitement I felt but dared not show.

"Joe. At last."

In the presence of the girl, all my enthusiasms withered, and the dismay I had felt so viscerally but a week before returned in force. Mr. Jackson's encouragements and trust were but absurd missives from an alien star.

"Chowder." I extended my hand. He took it in his, and we shook as gravely as two judges. My dreams of joyous reunion evaporated in this painfully stilted tableau. The coach stood by some yards off, Mr. Jackson and Rowland remaining inside for some reason as Chowder, the girl, and I stood awkwardly before the shop.

"Well, aren't you going to introduce me to your chum?" It was the girl. "He is your chum, isn't he? You said he was." She was a bright one, all right.

"Oh, right, sorry. Elspeth, this is Joe. Joe, Elspeth."

"Halloo," I said.

"Charmed," she said. She might have meant it, I couldn't tell.

I looked from Chowder to Elspeth, and back again. He did the same, looking from me to her. She looked the both of us over.

At this moment, an agitated Rowland burst forth from the carriage, which stood yet some yards off. "No, it's impossible!" He was shouting, waving his arms. "You are a damned, bleeding fool! How could you not have consulted me? I won't have it!" Passers-by stopped to stare. He strode rapidly away, in the direction of Ludgate. Mr. Jackson's dignity would not permit him to respond in kind, and he stayed in the coach. I could see through the window he had his head in his hands.

"Whatever is that all about?" queried Elspeth. Chowder merely regarded me with a quizzical look.

"Sorry, not a clue. That is my master in the coach, and his son disappearing into Ludgate, there. Nothing like this has happened before. Come, let's leave the man in peace. My lodgings are in the rear. We can walk around."

It was a brief walk around the end of the street and up the lane to Mrs. Whidby's. We walked in silence. Of the thousands of things I had poured out to Chowder in my heart, I could settle on not a one to say. For his part, Chowder seemed entirely self-possessed, apparently discovering no requirement to speak. The door was locked, but Mrs. Whidby appeared a minute later, having just come from the shop.

"Joe, me boy, I hope you are hungry! And double for your friends! Very peculiar, it is, but Mr. Jackson says Rowland has gone out of a sudden, and that he himself is not hungry. Care to eat?" She had created a splendid midday meal, and we sat down to tea and scones and jam, then salad and roast mutton, potatoes, ale, and coffee.

In an instant, Elspeth and Mrs. Whidby discovered a peculiar affinity. Words poured forth from the two of them in torrents. Neither gave evidence of any need to stop talking in order to hear the other. Contrarily, the awkwardness between Chowder and I only deepened. I had no idea how to begin. And he would fix his eyes on me with a solemn look, and I searched his for that animated kindness I remembered so fondly, and then one or the other of us would look away.

"It's, er, good to see you, Chowder." I squeezed this out against the background of the two nattering females. I wanted more than anything for the floor to open and swallow them both.

"The same, Joe." He paused and seemed to search my face. "But, Joe, well. You said you were going to find me, Joe." His words grew weakest at the end. He looked down.

"I, uh, Chowder. I was not let out for a minute until a week ago. Mr. Jackson's work never ends. It's all hugely important, really. We have been working here all manner of hours and days. I did find you, actually, a week ago. It took me all day, but I made it to Bulmer's grocery in Hair Court, and I saw you come back with, er, her." He brightened.

"But where were you? I never saw you."

"It was already after sunset. I'd given up and was leaving when I saw the two of you walking along. So I didn't hail you." The words came out weakly.

"But, why didn't you?" Chowder's tone was somewhere between interest and pique.

"I ... didn't want to bother you just then."

Chowder looked at me hard. "What, Elspeth and me? You have maggots in your brain, I think." This last was said carelessly, through a large swallow of ale.

"Maggots," I returned, stricken. There it was. He'd called me an idiot. He was just another oaf. He would marry, have children, and die without having ever thought anything.

"She's my bleedin' sister, Joe."

"I'm not a *bleedin'* anything, I'll have you know!" Elspeth, who had not for an instant ceased gabbling with Mrs. Whidby, burst into our fragile conversation. She grinned broadly at me, displaying food stuck in her teeth. "What'd you think I was? A loidy of the streets, eh? Wouldn't I make a nice one!" She lifted and pushed forward her considerable breasts, aiming them square at me in an appalling gesture. She and Mrs. Whidby laughed. Chowder made a face at her, and then he laughed, too.

I choked on a piece of mutton. I suppose I might have died. Mrs. Whidby and Chowder both worked my arms and pounded my back until it came out. It was a while before I had my breath back. I hadn't known it before, but choking can make rather a lot of tears come to your eyes.

XXXIII

WHEN I HAD RECOVERED AND we had done eating, Chowder sent Elspeth packing, to my delight. He should like to have some time with me to catch up, he told her.

"You must come to supper with Chowder and me some Sunday soon," she said. It was all very agreeable. Mrs. Whidby said her own good-byes and without pausing, busied herself with cleaning up. Chowder essayed to help her, for which effort he was roundly teased.

"'Tisn't right for a lad to want to help in the kitchen, now, is it? Next you'll be wanting to be a washer-woman. Wear one o' them big, wide skirts. Wouldn't that be a sight, now?" She laughed the heartiest of laughs. Chowder chuckled weakly.

"Show me about, Joe, why don't you?" And so we crossed the lane to the shop, which we entered.

"Tell me more about Elspeth. And how you found me."

"Elspeth is a wonder, and I love her dearly. She's a blessing, she is. A year older than I am. The rest of my family can go hang, though. They've no use for me at all, nor I for them. But she is devoted to me, and I am grateful for it. She's the only family I have any more, really. She is living with my uncle, working in their factory. Not on a loom, though. I'm not exactly sure what she does. I don't know much about silk. Don't want to."

"I have only my sister, too. She's in Bridewell, though, in the part where they care for orphan girls. Perhaps some time soon we could go there and see if I could talk to her?"

"Of course, Joe. Maybe we can even get her out of there, although I don't know how we would. And I want to see you as much as I can. "

My heart. I thought I should burst from the effort of holding so much inside.

"Elspeth has a very little bit of money from our father. He came 'round to visit her when I was in Peevers' school and tried to buy her affection out of guilt or something, I don't know. Not that it worked. She has helped me look for you ever since last winter. She's even paid for a hackney, more than once. First, we had to track down Peevers. He's in the Fleet, you know. That old bat Strickenwell told us that much, but no more. Oh, it did me heart good to see him there. Was the devil to arrange it, though. Elspeth had to pay the keeper a shilling just to get us in. Paying money to go inside the Fleet, fancy that, eh? And wouldn't you know the old bugger wouldn't help us? Said he had no idea where you were."

"Placed me here himself, he did," I said quickly. Rapidly, I told Chowder of my later experiences and pact with Peevers, and about my coming to Mr. Jackson's. I mentioned my fifty pounds, too. "Wonder what he did with it," I said. We were now well inside the shop, surrounded by shelves upon shelves of books.

"Well, he doesn't have it now. Filthy place. He's a-stewing in the common pit, too. You'd have thought he could have paid for better. Anyhow, we went back to Little Eastcheap and finally Miss Strickenwell coughed up that you were here when Elspeth asked her. She might have told me when I went the first time. She's running the school, by the way. Can you imagine?"

Briefly, I told Chowder of Miss Strickenwell's visit the previous February. "But nothing's come yet of the investigation, that I know of. And to think of Peevers in the Fleet! Suits the man," I said with a grin. "Here, let me show you what all of this is about." I introduced Chowder to the ranks of books and told him of my duties, from carrying coal and wrapping bundles, to making lists of books, and even minding the shop. He was vastly impressed.

"I don't know I could deal with all of these books, Joe. You seem to be getting on well here. Do you like it?"

"It's like home, mostly. Mr. Jackson is excellent. Rowland, though, is something of another story. Mrs. Whidby is the best. What is it like where you are?"

"Could be worse, I suppose. I do have a tiny bedchamber to myself. That's a wonder. But Cudworth is a turd. Must have found a gold piece in the street, last week. I've never seen him so drunk. Threatened to beat me, he did. Passed out instead, right in the middle of the floor. Then the wife, she's even jollier than he is, throws a bucket of water on him. I loved it, except I had to mop it up."

I decided not to mention my spasm of generosity in the Black Eagle. "What's the family like?"

"The mum is solid ice. Dulcibella, would you believe it? Would trip on her nose, from looking down it, if there was justice. She and number two daughter are all cloyingly close, like. Fairly turns your stomach. 'Hortensia, my help,' and 'Mum, dear.' They think theirs doesn't stink. The both of them hate Cudworth with a passion. Won't even talk to him, ever since he tried discipline. That was bad. She turned him out of their chamber, and he bunked in with me for days. Joe, try to imagine it. The man farts all the night long. I thought I would die. Then there's the elder daughter, that's Prudencia. She hates the other three and her father. She's, what, near to sixteen now? She'll be moving on soon. Throws it in their faces every day. Oh, it's jolly, I tell you."

"What's the work like?"

"Rotten fruit, mostly."

"Rotten fruit?"

"Rotten fruit. Cudworth goes to the wholesale produce market and buys the worst they have, cheap as dung. Then he tries to sell it for what a proper store would charge for quality. *Then* he wonders why his trade is so poor. And I carry it in and carry it out. Up, actually. There's a disused lane behind the shop. When it's right covered with flies, he has me carry it up four floors, and I toss it out the rear window. I like doing that, though. I can throw it ever so much farther than I could at the beginning. Then the rats eat it. It's brilliant, it is." Chowder fixed his eyes on me. He seemed to waver for a moment. "Show me your chamber, Joe."

We re-entered Mrs. Whidby's snug and pleasant cottage, where the fire was banked, and all in order. She had gone out visiting and would not return till much later in the afternoon. Chowder and I ascended the steep stairs to my chamber, and I showed him my books and writing desk with great pride. I spoke glowingly of the liberality of Mr. Jackson, which would allow me to become educated. Chowder was overawed.

"Joe, this is too wonderful. But you do deserve it. You are quite the brilliant one. I'm just a greengrocer's boy. Pretty sad, actually." He looked at me with a serious expression, in which some wistfulness had taken residence. "You've changed a lot, Joe. For the better, I would say. You are becoming wise. I'm fated to be forever stupid."

"You're hardly stupid, Chowder. I find you very bright. And if you want to become educated, I'll lend you any book you want. You can read, right? I can help you get better at it. And we can talk about them. Perhaps Mr. Jackson will talk about them with us." I gave him a broad and loving grin.

"I should like that, Joe." He stood just a bit closer to me.

I put my hands on his shoulders and looked into his eyes. "You are my friend. You are my best, and, really, my only friend. If you were 'prentice to a dung hauler, I would—I would still love you, Chowder." My heart beat fast.

He looked at me without speaking, and his eyes, which I had thought collected and perhaps even a bit dour, were brimming with tears. Moved beyond thought, I pulled him closer to me.

We shared an uncertain and gentle embrace, and I experienced all the rush of feeling and awkward tentativity peculiar to young and inept lovers, augmented by the particular uncertainties of not knowing whether or to what extent my feelings were reciprocated. To my astonishment and joy, he returned my embrace as gently as I had offered it. We stood like that for some time, simply holding each other, our cheeks very near but not touching, neither of us speaking. It was enough. In the months since I had last seen him, my imagination had taken the two of us far beyond so simple an act, but here, in the flesh, I was awed.

"Chowder, I—"

"Don't talk. There are no words for this." Here he first demonstrated the innate wisdom of his heart, which I have come to admire in him as one of his greatest gifts. He would discount his own intelligence, and came to stand in awe of what was to become my easy familiarity with writing and books, but I learned of love from him. He held me just a bit closer, then, to my inexpressible joy, brushed his lips lightly against my cheek in a near kiss of unmistakable intention. "You are beautiful, that's all," he whispered.

We held each other for the longest time, neither of us wishing the moment to end, but in contradiction to the impetuosity of our rapidly beating hearts and the rising of our flesh, we were far too shy and uncertain to give way to our mutual passion. Chowder again laid his lips against my cheek, and then I mine upon his. After what seemed at once a very long time and but an instant, we let go and sat on the bed, where in voluble conversation we shared many intimacies, among which were profuse and robust assurances of each other's manliness.

"If you were the least like a girl I would not care for you so," avowed Chowder.

"Nor I you," I returned.

Soon we heard the key in the lock downstairs. Mrs. Whidby had come in from her peregrinations, and set to stoking the fire and making preparations for tea. Her entrance threw a veil of reticence over us, and we talked of less intimate things until Mrs. Whidby called upstairs to see if we were there, whereupon we descended.

"And what have you boys been up to?" enquired Mrs. Whidby, brightly.

"Oh, you know, catching up. Chowder here's got himself a nice situation, he does." I had grasped the first thing to come to mind.

"My situation stinks," put in Chowder. "Cudworth's a drunkard and a turd, if I may say so, ma'am."

"You needn't stand on niceties with me, m'dear. Does he beat you, then?"

"That he does not. I should thrash him and gladly hang for it if he tried."

"That's what I like, a boy with spirit. God knows one needs it in this life. Here, you two, set the table, will you?" We busied ourselves whilst the good woman stirred the pots. Shortly thereafter, Elspeth entered.

"I have had such a fine afternoon, I tell you!"

"And what did you do, then?" asked Chowder.

"I sat in St. Paul's and prayed for all our souls, I did, then I walked Shoemaker's Row, where I found these," she said, drawing from her basket a pair of blue silk slippers, of which Mrs. Whidby was appropriately appreciative. "Then I walked about. The workingmen think I'm very grand, I tell you." Laughing, she told of whistles and catcalls.

"I spotted more than one I wouldn't mind having, dear me. But I left them all a-slavering, I did. You there, Joe, you ought to find yourself a nice girl and have some fun with her. Chowder, well," she laughed again, "I don't know." Looking at me, she said, "What do you think we should do with him? I wouldn't suggest no girl would have him, but really now, what kind of girl do you think might?" Chowder winced and essayed a weak laugh.

"Far be it from me to come between a brother and sister," I offered, "but I should think a great lady worth ten thousand a year would be scarce good enough."

Turning to Chowder, she said, laughing, "Ah, a friend indeed you have here, I see," And offering me the most ingratiating of smiles, she added, "I might just have to fancy him."

"You would find me most intractable, I am sure."

Her countenance discovered the briefest moment of indecision before she brightened and returned, "Well, too good for the likes of me, I dare say!"

Mrs. Whidby laughed and brought tea, sparing us further banter. The meal, comprised of the leavings of our luncheon, was pleasant and all too brief, during which the two women again nattered madly, leaving Chowder and I to ourselves as before.

"When may I see you again?" I asked, daring to look into his eyes, which I had so far avoided in the presence of the others.

"I think it more a question of when might I see you, Joe. I have every Sunday afternoon free and often the evening as well. You are the one whose master will work you a Sunday."

"Right. Here's an idea, then. When I have a day at liberty, I will send a message to you as soon as I know it. Mr. Jackson has deliveries made all over the city, and it would be simple enough for me to send you a penny novel or some sort of book, anyways. You will need only to look inside."

"And I can have moldy oranges sent to you!" he laughed. "Or put a message in the post, perhaps." He smiled at me, and I would have kissed him right then and there but for the presence of Mrs. Whidby and Elspeth.

The meal was soon concluded, and Chowder and Elspeth left. Our parting was of necessity restrained. No thespians were ever more deserving of accolades than we two "ordinary chums."

XXXIV

MY CUSTOM OF A SUNDAY evening was to retire to my chamber to read, but reading held no appeal at that moment. The evening sprawled before me uninhabited, and the elevation of my sentiments urgently required society. I had held Chowder close to me, and he had not pushed me away or called it base. I determined to share my news with Mr. Jackson, despite the uncertain spectacle of Rowland's noisy departure but a few hours earlier. If Mr. Jackson did not wish to be disturbed, his door would be closed, or perhaps he would have gone out, so I was in no danger of imposing. Crossing the lane to the shop and ascending the stairs, I found the door to his office open, and him within, deep in thought. A ledger lay open before him, but he was not looking at it.

"Hello, Joe." He peered at me quizzically.

"Er, Mr. Jackson, sir, I thought I might share with you my latest news."

"I'm not certain that this is the best time for it, as I am somewhat discomfited. Rowland is gone, I know not where." He paused, then went on. "Then again, perhaps this is the right moment for us to speak. He fled because I mentioned to him I had let you into our confidence. I ought not to have done so without first speaking to him, and I am now very sorry for it. He does not share my faith in you, and fears that you might ruin us."

"Do you think he will not return, sir?"

"That I do not know. Perhaps. He is young and, as yet, impetuous. But the situation is unprecedented. It is entirely beyond my powers to divine."

"Well, sir, his fears are without foundation. I would rather die. I do wish he would treat me better, though. And it isn't as if I have ever witnessed anything between the two of you. Not much for a court of law. Unhappy 'prentices prattle all manner of cant that no one listens to, and I am in no wise unhappy here."

"True enough, but the matter typically is less dire. As for Rowland, I do believe he is jealous. It is quite unnecessary, of course, as my feelings for you are of a different kind. I think of you nearly as a son—but not a son such as he is," he added quickly. "You have my full confidence. But, Joe, tell me of your news. It must be better than mine. You had a good afternoon with Chowder, I take it?"

"The very best that could ever be imagined, sir!"

At this, he brightened. "Truly, then? Is he indeed your friend and secret delight?"

"I would say so, sir!"

"And you shared … ?"

"We held each other for the longest time and almost kissed. He is sweetness incarnate. Were he not of a sodomitical turn, I can't imagine he would have held me so close. I felt his heart beating. I love him, sir, with everything that is in me, and he has told me he is very fond of me, indeed."

"Well then, this does call for a celebration," and in so saying, he took a bottle of port from a cabinet, pouring two glasses and offering me one. "To the friendship of men!"

We drank, but I did not fail to discern the progress of a small tear down his cheek, which he daubed away with fine discretion.

"Now, Joe, I must speak to you of a matter most grave. I have already impressed upon you the need for secrecy. I must now redouble that injunction."

"But, of course, sir. I understand perfectly."

"Of course you do. But I speak to you now not out of concern for my own safety, but for yours as well. You and your friend must practice the greatest possible discretion. Were you ever to find yourself in the dock at the Old Bailey, no words of mine would avail, even to the smallest degree."

"I understand." I returned solemnly. "I'm sure nothing like that will ever happen, sir."

"You must never reveal your affection to the world. Never."

"I do understand, though it seem harsh."

"Less harsh than the pillory or noose, my dear boy. So very much less."

"We have already spoken of it, acting the part of two ordinary chums before his sister and Mrs. Whidby."

"Ah, the glorious and good Mrs. Whidby. Excellent. Here's something for you, then. When you and Chowder are in need of privacy, you may use my chamber. I would prefer that you not be intimate with him in your own. Mrs. Whidby comes and goes of a Sunday ofttimes without pattern and, good woman though she be, she is High Church. This sort of thing is quite beyond her comprehension. She has been in my service these many years, and to this day has no reason to suspect anything between Rowland and me other than a proper affection between father and son. I couldn't predict her reactions, and desire greatly not to hazard the chance. Does this suit you, then?"

"I do say so, sir. Thank you, sir!"

Mr. Jackson smiled broadly. For my part, I grinned like an imbecile. Inspired by his confidence and feeling the effect of the port, I would say more.

"And, sir?"

"Yes, Joe?"

"You are like a father to me, sir. Only even better, in a way. I hope I may be permitted to tell you that I love you, sir."

"Why, thank you, Joe. I am humbled and grateful for that, truly I am. Now, be off with you. Morning will come early, and I expect a very large shipment before nine."

"Very good, then, sir. Good night. And thank you again, sir."

"Good night, Joe." As I crossed the threshold and turned to cast a farewell glance, my heart full of gratitude for his loving kindness, I saw him daubing another small tear.

XXXV

THE FOLLOWING MORNING, WORK RESUMED without the slightest diminution of its customary intensity. Mr. Jackson's many meetings, correspondence, and ledger-keeping continued apace while for my part, there were floors to be swept, customers to help, and, workmen to direct, the promised large shipment having arrived. Lacking Rowland to mind the cash, both of us had to be available when the shop grew busy. I but rarely had time to think of Chowder, and yet, the memory of his kind and stimulating presence suffused all with a robust optimism that made no task, however trivial, unimportant or without meaning, nor any customer, however absurd or querulous, irksome. Nothing was beyond our reach if we would but put our minds to it, and we would be, as we already were, happy.

Wednesday morning of the same week, I was summoned to an office deep within the Old Bailey, wherein a Grand Jury at last took my deposition regarding Mr. Peevers. It was a tedious business, and I was asked many questions about my character and habits that to my mind did not pertain. I answered all without complaint or embellishment, and between-times was able to tell my story. There was much discussion among the learned gentlemen of the propriety of my having threatened Mr. Peevers's person, irrespective of the provocation, and the general conclusion seemed to be it showed me to be an unworthy rascal of no repute, as likely to damage as contribute to the Crown's prosecution, and that, further, there was some question as to whether any actual crime had occurred, never mind the impropriety of Mr. Peevers's approach. I was informed that a trial was almost certain, but that my presence was unlikely to be necessary. Despite this, I was treated with courtesy and thanked for my time.

I then left the building and walked the short distance back to Mr. Jackson's bookstore in the brilliant sun of a late June afternoon, to find a weather-beaten horse and cart standing before the door, and Rowland and a lanky, blond creature of stubbled chin, shabby waistcoat, and frowsy woman's bonnet attempting to wrestle a large and apparently very heavy trunk into the cart, in which several smaller trunks and an assortment of boxes were already placed. Neither acknowledged me, but as I had to pass within a few feet of them, I stepped forward and lent my strength to the process, by means of which the trunk was easily hoisted. It did not feel proper not to say anything, so I essayed a pleasantry.

"Rattling on, then?"

"You could say that. Thanks to you." Rowland's face was drawn and his eyes hard.

Here the blond thing interposed. "Please leave us," and added, in contradiction to the scene enacted but a moment before, "We have no need of your assistance."

There was nothing to say. Rowland had invented a demon, and would have me be it. I experienced an impulse to play the part I had been assigned and tip the trunk back into the street, which could easily have been done, as we had but barely got it aboard and a portion yet hung out beyond the end of the cart's bed. I thought, too, it would be fitting to offer a gentle reminder that I had in fact been instrumental, but I thought better of it. I was not displeased to see Rowland depart, and to confirm I was indeed a lout would in no wise enhance the process.

I left them and entered the shop, where I found Mr. Jackson finishing up with a customer. His demeanor was entirely courteous and, as always, perfectly controlled, but he appeared, not surprisingly, uncharacteristically dour. On seeing me, he brightened. Once the customer departed, he wanted to know about the deposition and all that had transpired. This intelligence having been communicated, he produced a small trifold sheet of paper on the back of which was clumsily written "Joseph Chapman, Jackson's booksellers, St Paul's Churchyard." It had been sealed with a spot of red wax. I had never before received a letter.

"I paid the penny, and you are welcome to it," said Mr. Jackson, as Rowland and his friend strode stiffly towards the stairs at the rear, neither looking in our direction.

Breaking the seal, I unfolded the paper to find penciled in an inept, all upper-case hand: "JO MY FREND. I AM SO VERY HAPY THAT WEE HAV MET AGAN. WHEN MAY I SEE YOU AGAN? I LONG TO SEE YOU. I AM FREE OF A SUNDAY ALSO THE MORNING. PLEZ RIT TO ME. I HAVE THE PENY. PLEZ RIT. CHOWDER"

A wagon full of golden guineas, each bearing my own Royal portrait, could not have made me happier or more excited, and I stood rapt, reading and rereading the note until Mr. Jackson interrupted to inquire whether it was indeed from Chowder, breaking my trance. I showed the missive to him, and upon reading it, he immediately and with fine tenderness gave me to understand he would be pleased indeed if I would take the entire Sunday next, and devote it to Chowder, if I would not mind working the extra bit on the days before and after, to make up for the time lost.

"And here, Joe, I ought to have done this long ago, but I will now give to you keys to the shop, your lodgings, and my chamber. 'Prentices usually are not given keys, but, well, you are more than a 'prentice to me, if I may say so. Obviously, I wish you to alert me beforehand any time you and Chowder wish to enter my chamber, and, very important, it must be only on Sunday, when Mrs. Whidby will not come 'round to tidy up, but my promise that you and Chowder may use it for your private resort is good, and I do hope you will have the opportunity to take me up on the offer."

He went to the rear of the shop and, from a drawer of his desk, took three keys tied together, which he gave to me. Two were iron, and a smaller one of silver. I expressed to him the most heartfelt and abject sentiments of utter and eternal gratitude, and assured him I would work happily day and night forever if it would bring me nearer to Chowder, with which Mr. Jackson was indeed pleased. Immediately, I fell to stocking the shelves with new titles.

Over supper I composed a reply, which read as follows: "My Dear Chowder. I long to see you, too. Mr. Jackson has given me all of this coming Sunday at liberty. I will walk to Cudworth's first thing this Sunday morning to see you. We will be together. Your Joseph." For a penny, I purchased from Mr. Jackson a worn copy of *Gulliver's Travels* and placed the note inside, wrapping the whole, to be delivered the following day.

XXXVI

SUNDAY WAS ONLY FOUR DAYS hence, but in opposition to my enthusiasm, time assumed a ponderous inertia, each moment making way for the next only with the greatest hesitation and reluctance. I would work for an eternity, and, asking Mr. Jackson the time, would be told a mere quarter hour had passed since I had last asked. It was almost more than I could bear. Rowland was not seen, and Mr. Jackson kept to himself even more than usual. He spoke of engaging someone to mind the shop, at least on odd days, but I was relieved he did not mention taking on another 'prentice. I had a strong disinclination to share the man, even if to be intimate with him was unimaginable. I had Chowder for that. If time would move, that is.

Saturday night I slept but little and was awake Sunday morning at first light, which was not yet four, it being July. Finding further sleep impossible, I rose, dressed, and fairly jumped down the ladder to the kitchen, where I drank water and helped myself to half a loaf of bread, eating some and throwing the rest in a sack which went over my shoulder. I was out the door in a trice. The dawn was cool, still, and damp, the half-dark sky uniformly grey and featureless, with just the faintest scent of the sea come up from the east, that the omnipresent coal smoke could not entirely occlude.

Believing it would be absurd to show up at Cudworth's at five in the morning, I walked circuitously first towards the river and found myself drawn to Brickhill Lane, where less than a year ago I had lived, first in happiness, then in dismay. I lingered at the foot of the street where it met the river and regarded the water, upon which already watermen were busy ferrying their human cargo. But then, despite my resolve to delay my progress so I might arrive at a reasonable hour, I was drawn to Spittlefields as helplessly as a leaf falls to earth, and found myself standing uncertainly in front of Bulmer's Grocery at a quarter to six, feeling very excited and rather the fool, all at once.

I saw no sign of life in the grocery, and very little in Hair Court other than a starving and mangy stray dog nosing about. The Court appeared almost salubrious, in contradistinction to its prior grim aspect, even though the disrepair and dishevelment, moss, mildew, broken windows, and refuse had not changed, and Bulmer's Grocery was, if anything, even more worn and dismal than when I had first seen it. But I did not give a fig for any of that, as it bore within it a miraculous boy.

I had not to wait more than half an hour before there was movement within the grocery's window, and then the door was thrown open, revealing not Chowder, but an unsmiling Mrs. Cudworth, dressed primly, if shabbily, in what I supposed was her Sunday best. Arms akimbo, she positioned her considerable bulk athwart the doorway in such a manner as to very nearly block any view within, and to command, it seemed, ownership of not only the entryway, but the Court and me as well. A hand rose behind her, enthusiastically waving back and forth.

Dispensing with pleasantries, Mrs. Cudworth spoke in haughty and suspicious tones. "The hour is very early. Just what is it that you want?"

Addressing her as directly as she had me, I responded, "Does not Chowder have the day free?"

"So you are his friend. Interesting." She sniffed, airily. "Whether Potter will be discharged for the day remains to be seen. He has many tasks to perform this morning. It will be up to Mr. Cudworth to release Potter, if he does. I am leaving for church, which is where you ought to be going." Looking behind her, she said, "Come, Hortensia. We will be late if we don't hurry."

Hortensia now appeared, squinting at the sunlight in a gown that at one time might have been worn to a ball, but which was now tatty and absurd, not at all the sort of thing one wore to early morning services. The two of them strode past me, making no further acknowledgement.

The instant they were gone, a broadly smiling Chowder ran out to meet me.

We fell into each other's arms, and though we forbore to kiss, we held each other tightly until I realized Tobias Cudworth, in a much stained nightshirt, was watching us from within the doorway, clutching his pipe. Chowder and I disengaged. Mr. Cudworth's expression was no less grim than his wife's had been.

"Can I go, Mr. Cudworth? I've done everything you asked me to."

"I don't see how that's possible, but begone with ye, anyways. I'm going back to bed, and I don't want to hear you mucking about. You can finish up tonight."

"Thank you, Mr. Cudworth!" Ignoring Mr. Cudworth's dire aspect, Chowder smiled broadly.

"Return before dark, mind, or I will burn your articles and deliver you to the Press Gang!" Mr. Cudworth's voice was a basso rasp, which devolved into a deep, rumbling cough as he spoke.

"Of course I will, Mr. Cudworth," returned Chowder. "You can count on me."

"And stop smiling. Damn it, boy, show some respect."

Chowder rearranged his countenance. "Of course, sir. I don't know what possessed me. I will not let you down."

"I will take good care of him, Mr. Cudworth. I'll make sure he gets back on time."

Not deigning to acknowledge me, Mr. Cudworth coughed again with deep spasms and much protraction, then spat copiously onto the pavement before turning away and closing the door.

I turned to Chowder. "They are a very charming couple, your Cudworths. How do you stand it?"

"I don't, you know," said Chowder. "I pray that he will strangle and die. The way he swills his ale and crams mutton down his gullet, coughing into his pipe all the while, I think some times I will not have long to wait, but then he lives to another day. And she's worse. But what shall we do? I cannot quite believe that we have the day together."

"Nor can I. Come, let's walk together towards the river. I do not care so much what we do, but that I am with you. I have a shilling. May I buy your breakfast?"

"I shall be delighted." He smiled, and my heart leapt.

And so we walked in the direction of Billingsgate, a distance of perhaps a mile, where I bought a great eel pie from a pieman for tuppence and a jug of water for a penny, and we sat on the Billingsgate Stairs, to one side of the ancient fish market where my mother had spent her days, and surveyed the river as we ate. Billingsgate being below the Bridge, we saw large vessels and lighters as well as the many waterman's skiffs, all suffused with an extraordinary silver light, in places shot with gold as the strengthening sun began to burn through the low cloud. Here and there a vessel, or perhaps just its sail, stood forth in effulgent glory, as if to demonstrate that redemption need not wait for the day of judgement, but is here and now before us, the eternal and omnipresent mercy of God, and no one can say it is not so.

My heart was full to overflowing. How lovely to be near him, to sit beside him and not speak while we ate. I delighted in his simple, masculine mannerisms, his open, mobile face so expressive of his every mood, his large, intelligent eyes, and especially his hands, strong and large-veined, and yet capable of a fine, feminine gentleness, as he had and would show me. And yes, there was his manhood, resting quiescent inside his breeches. Perhaps I ought not to speak of it, but it would betray the veracity of this narrative to pretend it was not there or had no significance. His very maleness thrilled me.

"Say, Joe, did you ever find your sister?"

I had not thought of Sarah in many weeks and was startled to realize it. "No, I have had no opportunity."

"Do you suppose she lives yet in Bridewell? Shall we go there this morning?"

"Why, yes. Why not? Shall we?"

It was a walk of perhaps two miles. Chowder and I detoured towards the river when crossing Brickhill Lane, so that I might show him the environs of my former life, and then returning to Thames Street, we turned north at St. Bennett's Hill because it occurred to me to stop back at Mr. Jackson's to fetch more money, in case it were required to enter Bridewell, as Chowder had said was customary at the Fleet. I had not planned the day well, or at all, truth be told, fixated as I had been simply on being with my friend.

Thinking we might find Mr. Jackson in, I opened the shuttered shop with my key, feeling very grand to be able to do so, and that Chowder should witness it. We entered to find Mr. Jackson at his desk in the rear, writing a letter. He explained we were lucky to have encountered him. He had but shortly returned from Meeting and would soon depart for his Club in Holborn, where he would remain until very late, as there was much business to conduct. He was delighted to meet Chowder and engaged him in genial conversation while I went across to my lodgings to fetch the coins. Mr. Jackson had some time ago given me one of the guineas produced on my behalf by Miss Strickenwell, should I require incidentals, and this had been turned into a small pile of copper and silver. It was upon this that I drew, taking five shillings, just in case.

When I had returned to the shop, Mr. Jackson asked Chowder if he might speak to me alone, briefly. Chowder retreated to the entrance, where he examined a stack of books, and Mr. Jackson said to me, "He is utterly delightful. How very fortunate you are, Joe. I do congratulate you."

"Thank you very much, sir. Is he not beautiful?"

"Indeed he is." And with a smile and a wink, "My chamber is available, should you require it."

"Thank you so very much, sir. I confess that I do not know what will happen. We are off to Bridewell to see my sister, if they will allow it. And though we have held each other most tenderly, we have not yet kissed properly, to say nothing of … But, sir, may I take him into our confidence? It feels very odd to speak of it, because I do not know what is to happen, but if or when we do make use of your chamber, it will be difficult to explain without it."

Mr. Jackson hesitated but the briefest of instants before saying, "Why, yes, I do believe you must tell him, if he is to be your love. And you will swear him to secrecy, of course."

With earnest and copious protestations, I assured him, as I had previously, that I would rather die than betray him, and then, having determined that Mrs. Whidby would provide a meal, or the makings of one, later, Chowder and I made our good-byes and walked up Ludgate to Fleet Bridge and then left to Bridewell, less than half a mile from St. Paul's. I wanted to tell Chowder of Mr. Jackson and the secret of his life, and how it had all come out that evening after I had first espied Chowder in Hair Court, but could not find a way to begin. Though I had held him close and felt his heart beat next to mine, we were far from having articulated to each other our Difference. To say, well, yes, Mr. Jackson is sodomitical and so am I, and so are you, was too much. So I said nothing of it and we walked, chatting happily of lesser things. Very soon, we were at Bridewell.

—————— XXXVII ——————

IT MIGHT BE PRESUMED THAT an institution of the magnitude of Bridewell Prison, one of the larger prisons in the city, would present an obvious way for someone not a prisoner to go in, complete with a tidy, easy to find office in which one might make enquiries, but in so presuming, one's mental representations would be at variance with actuality. We walked all the way around the massive, ancient stone structure twice, passing various doorways and gates, none of them sporting any sign or label of direction. And in and out of them, despite it being the Lord's day, passed wagons, tradesmen, bailiffs and their charges, hordes of disputing, ill-clad women and their naked children, and men and boys of every description.

The day promised to be as hot as any a London summer might offer, and though it was yet before the noon hour, the stench from the Fleet Ditch and the open pit in the burying ground was very high. On the second pass, we noticed a gentleman in early middle age and his boy, carrying a bundle of papers, emerge from an unprepossessing opening at a corner of the edifice, and made enquiry of him. With unexpected civility, he informed us that this was indeed the entrance to the business and records office, and that I might learn of my sister therein.

"However, it is an expensive and very slow process. I have wasted absurd amounts of time and money there trying to find out the simplest thing. I do wish you good fortune. You will need it."

We thanked him and entered a dim and narrow passageway, where we were confronted almost immediately by a wicket and small gate blocking the way. We were there informed by a very small and quite ancient woman wearing a bonnet nearly as large as herself that the fee would be a shilling each if we wished to pass. Chowder protested that he would wait outside, but I would have none of it and drew forth from my pocket two shillings, hoping the three remaining would suffice.

Once past the gate, we soon entered a large room lit by a row of small, dirty windows opening onto the courtyard, where groups of women dressed all alike in plain muslin shifts formed and reformed under the direction of divers overseers, performing some rite or exercise, neither the pattern nor object of which could I divine. Inside, opposite the windows, a low counter spanned the length of the room, upon which had been placed a yet higher barrier, in which six wickets appeared. Four were open, hosted by clerks, all very stout and grave women, who moved with cautious deliberation if at all.

It was so ill-lit and gloomy behind the counter that despite the blinding brilliance of a summer noon, lamps were lit, affording view of many bureaus, cabinets, and tables, stuffed with spread ledgers and record books large and small, tottering piles of loose papers and bundles of yet more paper, and folios and pouches of tickets and bills. Long queues at two of the open wickets wound into and around the room, and between the wickets and windows opposite were many rows of benches upon which sat a small multitude of nearly every conceivable sort and station of person, all equal now in the Republic of Torpor. My heart sank. This was not how or where I wanted to spend my day with Chowder, but I did most assuredly wish to learn of Sarah's fate. In any case, it was too late to turn away.

Holding little hope, I approached the one open wicket in front of which was no queue. "Excuse me, Ma'am, I wonder if you might be able to help me?" In response to this, the woman, without speaking or looking up from the very large ledger before her, shook her head and tapped her pencil impatiently against the lower edge of a small sign affixed to the top of her wicket, that I might have seen sooner had it not been obscured with dirt and age, which read: "PAYMENTS ONLY. WAIT UNTIL YOUR NAME IS CALLED," to which was appended below, similarly obscured and written in another hand: "PAYMENT IS NOT MADE ON SUNDAY." She then thrust her pencil, again without looking up, towards the upper portion of the adjacent wicket, where another such notice read: "ENQUIRIES."

I mumbled a thank you, which she did not notice, and took my place at the end of the long and immobile queue and waited, while Chowder sat at the end of a bench facing the window, watching the activities in the yard. The room was now very warm, and a water peddler entered and began to make his rounds, dispensing a scant gill of water for, we were to learn, tuppence, half as much water at twice the price as on the street. From my position in the queue I was now cognizant of the sign above each wicket. The next one, closed, read INVOICES, then, also closed, APPLICATIONS and BIDS, but the next, ENTRY, and last, DEAD, were open. These two also had long queues, but they moved every once in a great while.

"Excuse me," I said to the young gentleman in line in front of me, "If I wish to see my sister, which queue ought I to be in?"

"It depends. To get inside, you need a ticket. That's the entry queue, of course, and that's a shilling. How long has it been since you saw her last?"

"Last November, when she was taken in."

"Well, that's a very long time. She may or may not be here. If you are lucky, she is dead."

"Beg pardon?"

"What I mean to say is that if she is dead, you will most likely have your answer today. Otherwise it will take longer. Now, to ascertain in advance of entering whether your sister lives yet and is here, you must enquire at the enquiries wicket. But since it's a shilling just to learn whether she is here, and then another to get in, you may as well buy a ticket and go in straightaway. You will either find her or not, though it may take much searching, and the matrons are not very helpful.

"And," he added thoughtfully, "if you are the least bit underfoot, they will shoo you out and there goes your shilling. However, in your place I would begin at the Dead wicket, as you know for a fact she was taken in, and so much time has passed. There has been an enormous number of deaths. The gaol fever ran through last winter like fire. Even the senior Matron died. If your sister is alive, you will have wasted a shilling, but if she is dead, you will know it without waiting all day, unless you want a proper certificate, in which case you will have to come back another day. They only do so much on Sunday.

"But yes, at the Dead wicket they have at hand logs of all the deaths here of the past several years, and it does seem that queue moves, quite unlike," and here he sighed deeply, "this one. I only wish to know whether my nephew was ever incarcerated here. He says not, but I have reason to believe he was, and it is very important I know which is the truth. He will or will not receive an inheritance, depending. If he does not, then I do. I need a proper legal statement attesting, but I have been here two days and so far have achieved nothing."

I thanked the young gentleman and went to tell Chowder what I had learned. I gave him a sixpence with which to purchase water, and then went to stand in the DEAD queue. I counted thirty-seven people in front of me.

After perhaps a quarter hour, the elderly, somnolent clerk at the wicket was replaced by a much younger woman who moved, if not with alacrity, then with a well-organized deliberation and efficiency that caused the line to progress every few minutes. Some took much longer, but not a few were turned away almost immediately. Over an hour passed, and as I drew nearer the wicket, it became clear these quickly dispatched individuals were seeking the legal death certificate, which was not to be had.

"May I not at least make the application and return tomorrow, then, for the legal paper?" asked a sweating gentleman, who had stripped to his undershirt.

The response was immediate, monosyllabic, and tart: "No."

"But I have been told the other clerk allows it, for an additional fee."

"She is not to do that, but she does, and pockets that additional fee. My scruples are your misfortune, sir. Now, if you would please clear out. You are wasting the time of every one in the queue behind you."

As for those who had made but the simple inquiry, it was rarely difficult to tell what sort of answer they had received. As I waited and watched, I experienced much anxiety over my sister's fate, and in contemplation thereof, had the awareness that our lives had permanently and most widely diverged. As good as it would be to see her, if she yet lived, I could do little to nothing for her. While I would tell her the objective facts of my new life, it was impossible to conceive of speaking to her of the concerns of my heart. I wondered how she had grown and what she now knew. Another quarter hour passed, and then I was at the wicket.

"Shilling and name, please," said the young woman. Her expression and demeanor, if neither cold nor warm, contained more than a hint of impatience. In common with everyone else, she was sweating. Perspiration covered her forehead.

"Sarah Chapman," said I, proffering the coin.

"When was she taken in?"

"November last."

Without speaking, the woman wrote Sarah's name on a card and began to quickly peruse the very large record book before her, running her pencil down the lengthy list of names. She turned the page and repeated the process again, and yet again. In very little time, she had exhausted the possibilities offered by that manuscript and had turned to another lying open on a table behind her, which likewise she soon exhausted.

Returning to the wicket, she said, "Your Sarah did not die, at least not here, last winter or early spring. I do not find her through the end of April. I do not have the discharge summaries here. Those are with enquiries, so I cannot tell you whether she was sent on, or indeed whether she is here yet, but there is yet one more record to consult for the month of May. I shall be surprised to find her there and do not have records for the current month, so we will see. I shall be but a moment."

I began to think it possible Sarah was not gone, and I had begun to experience the tenderness of renascent hope, when in a very little while the clerk, having disappeared into the dim recesses at the rear, where she pulled on a pile of loose papers, perused several, and paused to add a few words to Sarah's name on the card, now returned, her expression unchanged and inscrutable. She handed me the card folded in half, calling out as she did so, "Next!"

I moved aside to make way, finding Chowder next to me, regarding me with curiosity and concern. Dreading what I might see, I unfolded the card, whereupon together we read: "Sarah Chapman Dead 14 May 1779 age 12 bloody flux."

XXXVIII

I HAD MISSED SARAH BY little more than a month. Chowder placed his hand on my shoulder, a restrained, brotherly, and entirely proper gesture which amply communicated his caring and love. I found myself incapable of speech, and, bless him, he did not require it, but simply said, "I believe the way out is this way," leading me in the opposite direction from that by which we had entered. We were soon again on the street, where the mid-afternoon sun now radiated with rare and brilliant intensity. Heat rose from the pavement as it pummeled down from the sky, and the stink from the Ditch at hand was sharp. He waited for me to speak, regarding me with a tender concern that in no way presumed any weakness in me, but was simply present, offering his heart as balm to my grief.

"I think ... Damn, it is hot!" said I.

"'Tis indeed, my friend."

"I think ... I do not know what I think. Poor Sarah. Had I had any idea, I would not have waited so long. Now there is no help for it. I am a bloody fool."

After some moments, Chowder spoke with much tenderness. "You are not a fool. You could not have known and have been entirely taken up by Mr. Jackson and his affairs."

"But I might have seen her."

"Ah, Joe, don't be so hard on yourself, now. It can't be helped, and you must live. It will sound harsh, but she would be no less dead now if you had seen her. And to enter the gaol when it was pestilential would have been dangerous."

"But to have been so abandoned … She might have known I had not forgotten her." We had retreated to a narrow bit of shade beside the building, and I was distressed near to tears. Passers-by streamed past us, seeing nothing. Chowder placed his hand again on my shoulder.

Avoiding his eyes for fear I would begin to blubber, I said, "I don't know what to do."

After another goodly pause, he said, "My dear Joe, if she is truly in spirit, as we are told, she will know of your love. She will forgive you for attending, as you must, to your own life. You can pray for her if you think it proper, and I will go with you if you like."

I looked at him in wonder, sensing that gratitude which arises when a friend of true heart helps us when we cannot help ourselves. "Yes, we could go to Mr. Jackson's Meeting, perhaps. I am not so interested in the common sort of church, I think. And I would want you there with me, why yes. Thank you."

"I should like that very much." He paused, then essayed, tentatively, "And Joe, what would you do, with the freedom you have here and now, with a day such as this?"

Eyes yet brimming, I said, "I don't know. When it was this hot when I was a boy, we would sometimes jump in the river."

"Where would you go?"

"Any number of places. Three Cranes' Stairs are nearest to Brickhill Lane, but Dorset Stairs are very near to us now, by the Timber Yard. One may get into the water there, and it is above the Ditch, so the water does not stink nearly as much. Or if they are too busy, Whitefriar's Stairs are not much farther on."

"Shall we go, then? To be in the cool water will feel good. I cannot swim, but will be happy to splash about if there is something solid under me."

I supposed to him that, given the heat, and that grief would accompany me whether I were here or there, it was not at all a bad idea. Perhaps, too, I might show him something about swimming, which idea held great appeal. It was not more than a few hundred yards, once again around Bridewell and past the burying ground, where the flies and stench were so thick it seemed we must fight our way through, then to the end of the Timber Yard, where in no time we were at the water's edge.

Here the riverside makes a jog, forming a sort of rectilinear cove facing upstream, behind which the timber yard sprawls. To either side of the stairs, quays present a vertical wall to the water, and at the westernmost, a small ship that would finish unloading the following day lay tied. Here, wood from the hinterlands was brought to the city to be used in building and cabinetry. The timber was fragrant in the heat, a most welcome antidote to the Ditch and the pit. The water was alive with young men and boys, whooping and splashing about. But few of them wore the slightest stitch of clothing. I will confess that the sight of it lifted my heart. Here was healing diversion indeed, and I surrendered myself to its interest, Sarah's soul and my grief receding from the forefront of my mind.

Chowder, grinning, said, "This is splendid! How is it possible that I have lived in this city my entire life and not seen this? Where do we get in?"

The stairs descended narrow and straightaway into the water between the two quays, and upon them parallel streams of naked men and boys descended and ascended. Now and again a lad braver than most, skipping the stairs, would run straight off from the embankment and hit the water with a great splash. Standing at the quay's edge, Chowder and I took off our clothes and placed them beside a bollard, putting them just so, that we might keep an eye on them whilst in the water, as it was not impossible they might be stolen by ragpickers.

And then we joined the queue and descended the stairs. The water was cool enough to give one shivers, and we were soon in it up to our necks. Immediately I pushed off and swam proudly about, wanting to demonstrate to Chowder my prowess, but he was entirely absorbed in not slipping on the slick stones underfoot, looking down rather than in my direction. No sooner did I notice this than he lost his footing. His head disappeared beneath the surface, reappearing in a moment amongst much sputtering and laughter, and then sank again, reappearing once more, now to much coughing. I swam to his side and guided him to a more stable platform nearer the side of the quay, holding with gentle firmness to his arm whilst he recovered himself.

"Damn, I am no good at this," he said, laughing, still catching his breath and blowing his nose. It's lovely to be cool instead of hot, though."

"Swimming is easy if you know how to float. And don't try to breathe the water, you know."

"Listen to you, the Master Swimmer," he laughed, pushing me over.

I turned a somersault in the water and righted myself. "Right you are, young sir! No, really, it is very easy. Take a deep breath. If you fill yourself with air, you will float like a cork. Let the air out, and you will sink. So keep the air in and don't fear it." So saying, I took a very deep breath and held it, then lifted my feet off the bottom and threw my head and arms back, and lay there, supported by the insubstantial liquid. "Now you try it."

Chowder submitted to my instruction to the extent of taking a breath and holding it, but somehow when he would lift his feet from the bottom, he would double up and go sideways instead of throwing his head back, and could not get it right until I placed my arm beneath his shoulders to steady him. "That's rather nice," he said at last. I lowered my arm, intending to show him that he could float on his own, but not having quite learned it yet, he exhaled and sank. I set him to rights. Laughing, he said, "I think if God intended me to swim, he would have given me fins or feathers," whereupon he pushed a great splash of water at me, some of which went up my nose, causing me now to sputter and cough. The only possible response was to give him more of the same, and we were now madly splashing each other and laughing, as silly and happy as possible.

After quite some time at this, we finally had had enough, and climbed the stairs to find our clothing undisturbed. We sat at the edge of the quay beside the bollard, looking over the glittering river, while the sun dried our flesh. I thought of our days at the Little Eastcheap Free School, when I would try sometimes to get a glimpse of him. Now I could see all of him, but I had to be careful not to look too much, lest my uncommon interest be betrayed by a signal from my body which would be most inappropriate in this public place. Several times our eyes met, and in shyness despite our nudity, we looked away. Very soon we were dry enough to dress.

"You know, I think if we return to Mr. Jackson's, that Mrs. Whidby might have that meal ready. Are you hungry? I find myself hungry."

"Why, yes, sounds perfect. I should be delighted."

It was nearing five, but the summer sun was yet high and strong. It took us less than half an hour to return to Mr. Jackson's, where we found the better part of a roasted joint left from the previous evening on the table under a cloth, and with it cold roast potatoes and ale and water in jugs standing by. Taking knives and plates, we soon dispatched the joint and drank our fill of the water. Chowder took a few swallows of ale, but I desisted. "Ale makes me stupid, I'm afraid, and I have few enough wits to spare."

"I don't mind it, but you are right. It tends to put me to sleep."

"Say, Chowder, would you like to sit a bit upstairs in my chamber? It won't be dark for hours, and I don't feel like going out again." Chowder said nothing, but he smiled broadly.

We clambered up the ladder and sat on the edge of my bed. It was very warm in the garret, and my heart was beating rapidly, not solely from the heat. I had intended to follow Mr. Jackson's advice and take him up on his kind offer, but once again words escaped me, and it struck me as a very clumsy thing to pause now, make extended explanations, and then go to another man's chamber strange to both of us, with the express intent of becoming intimate. Against all that, I could see no harm in making use of my own chamber for intimacies. Though Mrs. Whidby might enter her premises, she would not climb the ladder. Provided that we were quiet about it, I saw little sense in Mr. Jackson's requirement. All this passed though my mind in an instant and was as quickly forgotten, as the sight of Chowder pushed everything else from my mind.

Looking at me with an intent gaze and a smile, Chowder observed that it was very warm. "Do you mind if I take off my shirt?"

"Please do. I think I shall as well." This accomplished, we sat a brief moment regarding each other. In the next instant, he put his arm over my shoulder and pulled me close. I felt his skin against mine, and his lips on my cheek, and finding in that tentative instant all that I had dared dream, I dispensed with caution. With tremulous hope, I kissed him fully on the lips, as I had imagined doing so many times. He returned my kiss with full vigor. Inspired by rising passion, we fell to kissing again and again, and lying down, began intimately exploring each other, an enterprise of wondrous delight. How loving and tender were his kisses, and how intent his gaze upon me, and mine on him. Lying beside him thus, gazing into his eyes, is the sweetest thing I have ever known.

Our breeches were soon discarded on the floor, whereupon I discovered his member to be the finest imaginable, standing proud, glorious, and most superbly made, and forbore not to kiss him there and everywhere, as he did me. The scent of him was sweet, and I recalled at moments the wan boy who had befriended me at Peevers's mad school.

"Damn me," I breathed into his ear, leaving off for a moment nibbling on his earlobe and holding him as tightly as I could, "if this be sodomitical vice, I only want more of it. Of you."

He responded by squeezing my bollocks, kissing me again and again.

We frigged each other then, locked in closest embrace, kissing madly. His spending inspired mine, and copious we were, indeed.

"I do believe, dearest Chowder, that you have spent all the way up to my ear," I said, laughing.

"Mmmmmm." He smiled the broadest of smiles and kissed me yet again.

"Here, I'll clean us up." I fetched a washing-up towel from the bureau, dampening it in the basin. Beginning with my ear, I washed the nectar from each of us, lingering over his member, which I found every bit as handsome in diminution as when inflamed. He lay and took it like a lord, tousling my hair and pulling me close to kiss me.

"Will there be any difficulty with the laundry?" he asked.

I had not thought of that, seeing the richly bedaubed sheets. "Dunno! She doesn't do the laundry, though. Sends it out to a washerwoman."

"Ah, then. We're all right."

"'Tis a fortnight, nearly, till they are changed again. It will be sweet to lie upon your seed at any rate."

"Well, provided it's *dry*," he laughed. I wiped the sheets as best I could. "And what is this sodomitical vice you speak of?"

"It's, well, what we just did, I suppose." Leaving the bed unmade to air, we sat and talked. Finally, it was the right moment. "Love between men." I told him then of Mr. Jackson's trust and guidance. "He's sodomitical too, with his adopted son, only Rowland isn't his son. They pretend it to the world."

"Damn me. I would never have imagined it. You have had the most astonishing luck, Joe. Quite unlike Cudworth, I say. Ach, why did I have to think of him? Gawd, I don't want to go back there, but I must. And I can't stay much longer here if I want to be back before the sun goes down. It's better than the street or the press gang, I suppose, although maybe only just." So saying, we rose and dressed. We exchanged one last kiss before descending the ladder. There was no sign of Mrs. Whidby.

I walked with him back to Cudworth's. We spoke but little, having transcended words. In keeping with that, I had to check myself again and again as we walked, not to reach for him, not to take his hand or caress his cheek, not to hold him close to me again, as lovers will. This was made no easier by the heat, which caused us to walk in our undershirts, an experience rare enough in London. And then we were at Cudworth's. "Will I see you again next Sunday?" he asked.

"Most absolutely and definitely, yes," said I. We exchanged the merest and most restrained of hugs, and then he went inside and was gone. Walking back to Mr. Jackson's, amidst fond and fervid replaying of the afternoon and evening in my mind, I realized I had not thought of Sarah since seeing the glittering Thames at Dorset Stairs, and the hours at Bridewell returned to me in a rush. I did not think it improper I had spent my time with Chowder in the manner I had, as whether I had or had not could have no effect upon her condition, but now that I had a moment to myself, I offered my heart fully to her and the progress of her spirit, wherever she might now be.

In the morning, I told Mr. Jackson nothing explicit, to be sure, but left little doubt as to the nature of our activities the previous evening. Mr. Jackson was less displeased that I had entertained Chowder in my chambers than I had feared he might be. But amidst communicating his pleasure at my good fortune, he mildly admonished me to be careful and quiet, and repeated his preference that I resort to his chambers for such activities. He then announced that he had seen Rowland the previous day and was hopeful he might return.

"He had become quite sick of hearing me talk about you, and I must admit I cannot blame him, as I did go on quite without respect to his sentiments. When I revealed to you the nature of his and my relationship without first asking his permission, it was too much for him, despite the fact that you are inescapably aligned with us. I have endeavored to convince him that you are worthy of our confidence and promised I shall be more respectful of his wishes in future. I believe I am succeeding. He and I do care very much for each other, after all."

"For your sake, sir, I pray you and he will reconcile. For my part, I take no interest of any kind in him and wish only for him to leave me alone."

Mr. Jackson gazed at me thoughtfully for a moment. "I am sure that can be managed," he said, adding. "Now then, we both have much work to do, so let us be about it." And with that, I climbed the stairs to the storeroom.

WEEKS PASSED. THE SPASM OF midsummer heat, as rare as it had been brief, was soon replaced by the more usual, much milder temperatures, and the inevitable, occasional rain. Chowder and I reveled in seeing each other every Sunday. If the weather were good, we would spend part of the day walking about the city and taking in the sights, which once included a trip up the river to Vauxhall Gardens, and another time to Ranelagh. When Bartholomew Fair came around in late August, we made certain to go there. We saw a two-headed calf, ate rather more than we ought to have, and exulted in riding an enormous revolving wheel that hoisted chairs, and us, nearly forty feet off the ground. It made us giddy, and though we laughed, we were not sorry to be returned to solid ground.

And, nearly every week we did indeed have occasion to visit Mr. Jackson's chambers, located on the top floor above the storeroom, and which were pleasant indeed, being painted almost entirely in white, having a large white bed and very white bedclothes of finest cotton, and large windows overlooking the Churchyard. Even the armoire was white, apart from the pastoral scenes painted on the panels. And yet, I must confess that despite the luxury and taste, I found it precious, and was never as comfortable there as I had been in my own chamber. It mattered little, though, as Chowder and I did not go there to look at the décor, but at each other. We always remade the bed, and everything was satisfactory.

XXXIX

TOWARDS THE END OF SEPTEMBER, Mr. Jackson received a letter from Miss Strickenwell in which she communicated Mr. Peevers would be arraigned in the morning of the 30th of that month, and she would be pleased if I wished to accompany her to the court. She intimated a second reason for her visit, but did not spell out what it was. I was not so sure I wanted to attend, as the thought of Mr. Peevers made me ill, but Mr. Jackson encouraged me, saying it would benefit me to put the memories of him humbled alongside those of his depredations. I was thus persuaded, and we wrote back to Miss Strickenwell in the affirmative. I asked Chowder if he might come when next I saw him, but Mr. Cudworth would not allow it, saying Chowder might go to the hanging if he wished, but one day off work was more than enough.

Thus it was on the last day of September, Miss Strickenwell reappeared at the bookstore, very early. I was remaking the display of books in the shop window. Looking towards the street, I saw her exit a hackney carriage. She entered the shop very crisp and erect, as always in scholastic black, clutching a large velvet bag of deep violet hue.

"Good morning, Joseph. Is Mr. Jackson in? We mustn't tarry if we are to be in time for the arraignment, but I would like to speak to him, and I have brought something for you."

I averred Mr. Jackson was indeed about the shop, although I was uncertain of his exact location, and offered to fetch him, if that would be all right. Leading her to the rear, where we had sat formerly, we discovered Mr. Jackson descending the stairs. Seeing her, he donned his most ingratiating manner.

"Ah, Miss Strickenwell. A pleasure to see you. What news?"

"And you, sir. I scarcely know where to begin. May I sit?" Without waiting for a reply, she seated herself, grimacing as she did so, in the large chair next to Mr. Jackson's desk. She hoisted her bag onto the desktop, where, in settling, it betrayed its contents by the clinking of many substantial coins.

Speaking to Mr. Jackson rather than to me, she said, "As you know, Mr. Peevers is to be arraigned today. He is accused of heinous crimes. If he is not entirely mad, he will not contest the charges, as proof of his guilt is overwhelming, so I expect he will be sentenced today as well." Here she paused, and as neither Mr. Jackson nor I said anything, took a deep breath and went on.

"He also embezzled from the school, taking from funds meant for its upkeep and operations, and stole from the trusts held for more than a few of the boys," and here she briefly directed her gaze towards me, "such as you, Joseph, as you know. He has, in fact, caused the destruction of the school, and it is no more. The School survives only to sell its property and few remaining assets so as to pay the debts Mr. Peevers incurred. The Congregation is much compromised, too, as the School was an organ of it. Now then, Joseph," and here she looked at me again, "I have brought the remainder of your trust. I have no doubt Mr. Jackson will prove to be a better steward of it than we were able to be." She attempted to smile.

"Thank you so very much, Ma'am."

Mr. Jackson said, "Not at all. I should think you are to be commended for returning Joe's money. I thank you, as well, on Joe's behalf."

"As Governess, I am personally liable. I have never been inside a prison and do not care to start now."

"Of course. Does anyone have any idea what he did with so much money?" Mr. Jackson asked.

"We do not. He squandered many hundreds, even thousands of pounds, and yet does not seem to have gambled or speculated, which makes it the stranger. We suspect it went to very immoral purposes indeed, but it cannot be proven and does not matter now. The money is gone, and naught but the manse will remain. Mr. Peevers's moral crimes will see him hanged, in comparison to which the embezzlement is trivial, so I expect it will never be properly investigated."

Miss Strickenwell then reached into her bag and pulled from it a leather purse of a deep red color that bore a substantial, clinking weight, and handed it to Mr. Jackson. Mr. Jackson immediately gave it to me, that I might look inside. I had never before seen one of the old, massive, five guinea gold pieces, and here were five of them, and many more single guineas, all golden. I found myself quite overawed, offering a stumbling thanks as I passed the purse back to Mr. Jackson.

"You are welcome," said she, "and I am pleased. Are you ready, Joe?" I indicated the affirmative, to which she said, "Come with me, then. I have dismissed the hackney, as one can easily walk the last bit." Miss Strickenwell had lost none of her brisk efficiency.

I thanked Mr. Jackson, who reached into the purse and handed me a guinea and several sixpence, saying, "You may need this." In a trice, Miss Strickenwell and I were out the door. The walk up Ludgate to Great Old Bailey was less than a quarter hour, then a few more steps and we had reached the Central Criminal Court, opposite which was the massive, fortress-like Newgate Prison itself, no less dismal and glowering for having been recently rebuilt.

As we drew near, Miss Strickenwell took a deep breath. "If there is any good to come of this, it is that a young man such as yourself may have it impressed upon him there is justice, and the wages of sin are indeed death."

"Yes indeed, Ma'am. It is very sobering to contemplate. I cannot imagine what possesses a man such as Mr. Peevers."

Very decidedly, she said, "It is madness, and that is all. No sense can be made of it because there isn't any to be made."

A large, muttering crowd was gathered in front of the heavy, curving wall of granite blocks which obscured the entrance to the courthouse. Miss Strickenwell hesitated but briefly. "It has been in the papers, and much news made of it. We shall get in, however, given my position—and yours as well, I should say." She quickly threaded her way through the throng to the gate in the center of the wall where a sentry stood guard.

"Hold, Madam. No one gets in today who has not a pass."

"A pass? Whatever are you speaking of? The people have a right to witness the justice meted on their behalf."

"The people have a right, indeed, but the building is only so large, Ma'am."

"This is absurd! I am Miss Strickenwell, Matron and Governess of the Little Eastcheap Free School for Unfortunate Boys. Or I was, before Mr. Peevers destroyed it. It was my signal displeasure to work under that monster for years. And this, here, is a former pupil, who was subjected to gross indignities." If words had substantiality, given the sharpness of Miss Strickenwell's tones, the man would have been sliced to ribbons.

"Ah, then why didn't you say so?" The guard, who previously had been officiously stern, was now mildness incarnate, yet he made no motion that might be construed as letting us pass.

"I do believe I just did."

"I am very sorry, Ma'am. Why then do you not have a pass? Perhaps you were meant to have one, but never received it? This damned Peevers affair has us all upside down. Look at this mob. They would break him to pieces in an instant if they had him in the pillory, there. They all want inside, to have a go at him. If I let them, there would be riot and tumult within and no business could be done. The people's rights are all very well, but there must be order! Why, I remember when I was a boy ..."

Intuiting what was the matter, I reached into my pocket and fetched the guinea so recently given me by Mr. Jackson, and without making the least show of it, I slipped the coin into his hand, to magical effect. Instantly, the man ceased dissembling, bowed low, and swung wide the iron gate. Taking no notice of the transaction, or perhaps it really had not registered with her, Miss Strickenwell bolted forward, and I followed her.

Once inside, we found a thronged foyer of cramped dimensions, much smaller than I would have supposed, in which we soon located Mr. MacCurran and Mr. Rennet, and perhaps a dozen boys, all younger than myself, but few of whom were the least familiar to me. We also saw several very grave gentlemen who, I gathered, were, or had been, principals in the now much reduced congregation. Assuming command, Miss Strickenwell made the appropriate introductions and led us to the far corner of the foyer, where we were relieved of a sixpence each before we could ascend the stairs leading to the galleries. These were full to bursting, but as some were leaving as we entered, we were able to find places to sit, although it took no little doing, and our group was unable to sit all together.

Miss Strickenwell and I found ourselves squeezed between, on our left hand, several very stout tradesmen of, as we were to learn, quite opinionated volubility, and on the right by a group of rough, and no less garrulous, women, from whom wafted the scent of garlic and unwashed linen. Each of these followed the proceedings below with utter absorption, commenting at every turn. Looking back towards the entrance, I saw Poxy enter alone and stand in the rearmost row, next to the door. He appeared much as he had formerly, if more grown, with a look that was darker and perhaps yet more troubled than he formerly had been. I did not seek his eye, and wished very much Chowder were beside me to see all of this, rather than Miss Strickenwell.

Below us spread the crowded court. To the right, a curving dais ran nearly the width of the room, on which a dozen black-robed and bewigged gentlemen whom I took to be judges sat behind a waist-high barrier. In front of and below them was a large, semicircular, baize-covered table, around which many earnest gentlemen gathered, each with a small mountain of papers. Some of these shuffled or read their papers, while others conversed earnestly. Beyond this was a sort of pen containing a large number of varied individuals, who appeared to be simply waiting.

In front of and opposite the galleries in which I sat were lower galleries in boxes quite separate from ours, containing three rows of four gentlemen each, and off to the right, yet more pens and more people. In the middle of it all was a raised station in which a smirking gentleman stood. On a raised platform nearer to and facing the baize table and judges, another gentleman attempted to speak, but such was the hubbub that he could not be heard.

I strained to pick out Mr. Peevers, finally spotting him in a queue at the rear of the room. He stood slumped against the barrier, looking down. He wore a dun-colored shirt and leggings of very coarse cloth, cheap and simple shoes, also of cloth, and his hands were manacled behind his back. He had lost much weight, causing his once rotund face and frame to be now sharply angular, although he retained his essentially pear-like shape, widest across the hips.

One of the judges at the center of the bench, rapped very sternly with a little wooden hammer on the table-top in front of him, and called out for order, at which the clamor abated, if not entirely, and the gentleman who had been attempting to speak was at last able to finish.

"As I have been attempting to relate, Mr. Blodgett was at my premises at the hour he is supposed to have been committing the thievery of which he is accused. He cannot have done it. I will stake my honor and my life upon it." This was accompanied by the most earnest and entreating attitudes and expressions imaginable.

At this, several of the tradesmen beside Miss Strickenwell snickered, and the women to my right laughed. The judge pointed his hammer in our direction and declared they would be removed at the next such outburst.

"That's Tom, all right. Best liar on the Strand," observed one the of the tradesman, not too loudly, to which several others grunted assent.

"Blodgett and Tom been in it together years now," said another.

The judge enquired of the room at large whether there were any further questions. Finding none, in a trice he summed up the case, which concerned stolen furniture, and gave it to the jury to consider. The jury consisted of the men seated in the box immediately below the gallery in which Miss Strickenwell and I sat, and they now huddled together and began to converse among themselves. I observed a second jury on the opposite side of the room, and later would understand the two juries traded off considering cases, one deliberating whilst the other heard the next several cases. In this manner, with the multiplicity of judges, the court was wondrously productive, speeding through dozens of trials and much other business in a single day.

While the jury deliberated, the judge in the center of the bench left his position and was replaced by another, who nodded to a clerk in a little box at the end of the judge's bench. This clerk now lifted his head and announced in a stentorian voice I would not have suspected one of so diminutive a frame to possess, that there would now ensue a series of arraignments, and those prisoners affected should prepare to present themselves. At this, the queue in which Mr. Peevers stood strode forward and seated itself in the pen behind the station moments before occupied by the accused Mr. Blodgett.

The judge again nodded to the clerk, who called out, in a voice very clear and stern, "Percival Peevers!"

Mr. Peevers ascended the few stairs to the dock and stood with his head down. His complexion was sallow, and his once darting eyes were deeply sunken and still. The whites of his eyes were jaundiced, and a plenitude of small, angry sores clustered about his mouth and nose. Every once in a while, he would be seized by a twitch up the back, which led to a more general shudder and shivering. At random intervals, he emitted a small, stifled sneeze.

"This is going to be good," said the tradesman next to me to no one in particular. "That's Judge Corder. He's a terror, he is."

Judge Corder was sixtyish, thin and pale of skin, but very alert, and to all appearances possessed of an impressive acuity. He wasted not a second, inspecting some papers on the table in front of him, reading one for a moment, then, looking up, said, "We have a very long list here." Staring hard at Mr. Peevers, he spoke with perfect clarity and palpable force. "Percival Peevers, upon the testimony to the Grand Jury of numerous boys, whose tales of your depredations bear a striking consistency, you have taken unspeakable liberties, which we must now detail to our severe disgust. The clerk will read the charges against you. To each, you must tell the court how you plead. Do you understand?"

Mr. Peevers shrugged his shoulders and gave the slightest of nods. The clerk began to read. "Percival Peevers, you are charged with wicked and detestable

---

crimes against the order of nature too foul to be named among Christians, called in lieu of it buggery, upon the unwilling person of one Thomas Calcraft, aged thirteen, in the month of March, 1778, and on repeated occasions thereafter."

"How do you plead, Peevers?" said the judge.

Mr. Peevers trembled, sneezed, looked at the floor, and said nothing.

"Look at me, Peevers. You did not allow your boys any privacy unto themselves, and you will give us your regard, however repugnant it may be." Mr. Peevers raised his head for a moment and as quickly dropped it. Again he shivered, and the judge continued. "Understand, Peevers, that silence will be taken as admission of guilt. If you are to contest the charges, which is your right, you must speak. Now then, let us hear you. How do you plead?"

Mr. Peevers lifted his head a second time and shook yet more. He spoke in a raspy whisper, very difficult to hear. "I am guilty, My Lord. It pains me greatly to speak. I did not mean to do it, not any of it. I am very sorry for it." And here he began to heave and gasp, perhaps to sob, I couldn't tell.

Judge Corder spoke with a fine mixture of exasperation and tutelage. "It's rather too late for that, Peevers. How is it possible to mean not to do something and yet do it?"

Much punctuated by coughing and gasping, he said, "I mean that the urge in me was stronger than my will. I knew it was wrong."

"You knew it was wrong, yet you did it, and having done it, failed to report yourself to a Magistrate. How is that, Peevers? Had you an actual conscience, having conceived a desire of which death can be the only consequence, you would have done something to stop yourself, and thereby spared the children. Had you done it early enough, you might have spared yourself as well."

Mr. Peevers coughed, heaved a sob, rasped, and became, though one would not have thought it possible, yet more miserable. "I thought of it many times, but ... could not ... find ... the courage. I ought to have shot myself. I wish to expiate my sins. To die."

Judge Corder regarded Mr. Peevers as though he were a loathsome insect of peculiar scientific curiosity, said nothing for a moment, then, mildly, "We shall soon provide that impetus which you could not find in yourself." Following this, he nodded again to the clerk, who resumed his stentorian manner of address.

"Percival Peevers, you are, as well, charged with a second such count of unmentionable vice against nature and nature's God, called buggery, upon the unwilling person of Meriwether Bell, aged twelve, also upon repeated occasions in the month of September, 1778 and thereafter. How do you plead?"

Continuing to shake, Mr. Peevers pleaded, "If it please you, My Lord, may I refrain from speaking, as it does pain me so? I will nod my head if that is all right. I am guilty," and here he was seized by a paroxysm of shivering, "of all as charged."

The Judge nodded but made no comment, and the clerk read yet another similar charge, and then another and another, only varying in the names and dates, reading each in full and making no abridgments, until eighteen charges beginning in early 1775 and continuing into 1779 had been read along with seven more attempted crimes of the same nature. To every one, Mr. Peevers, trembling at intervals, raised and lowered his head. As the reading went on, he sank by degrees, so that he was leaning heavily against the bulwark of the dock, and nearly doubled over by the end.

Judge Corder said, "The one and only correct thing you have done is save us the trouble of a trial. You cooperation in ridding us of yourself is appreciated. We will proceed with the other arraignments and come to your sentencing within the half hour." To this, Mr. Peevers said nothing, but, descending from the dock, sank very low into a chair offered by one of his keepers, and dropped his head nearly between his knees.

I turned to the side just in time to see Poxy flee the courtroom, his face dark, and I realized his name had not been among those Mr. Peevers was accused of molesting. Miss Strickenwell, not having noticed Poxy and inspired by what she had seen, turned to me and said, "So you see how it is done. What do you think, Master Chapman?"

"It is a most distressing spectacle, I fear."

"You do not register the majesty of inescapable justice?"

"I do, Ma'am, indeed. It is horrible to contemplate the harm he has done and very distressing to see what a pitiable object he has become."

"No!" she said emphatically. "He is not to be pitied, but condemned! He has brought every bit of it upon himself."

"Indeed he has. There is no disputing it. I only mean to wonder at how he arrived at this state."

"As I have said, it is madness, and there is no sense to be made of it. If he is to be redeemed, it is between him and God, whom he will soon meet face-to-face, and quite beyond our ken. Do not trouble yourself over it."

"I shan't if you say so, Ma'am. The other thing I would like to know, though, is how is it possible that he could have gotten away with it for so long?"

She did not at once answer me this, but offered her best withering stare, meant to communicate, I suppose, that the question was grossly impertinent. For my part, I returned her gaze with uncraven mildness. Out of respect, I would not press her, but neither would I be intimidated. After a very long moment, she left off glowering, and spoke in soft, uncertain tones I had never before heard from her.

"One does not go looking for madness where one assumes it will not be found. As I think of it now, there were irregularities and signs, and I ought to have known something was very wrong. I do believe I ought. And yet, it puzzles me greatly not one of these boys, or you, for that matter, came of himself to tell me or any of the other staff, and when we went to interview them in search of general examples of Mr. Peevers's incompetence, it came out very slowly indeed. I suppose there are reasons, and to be sure it is not the sort of thing that bears speaking of. Perhaps none of you thought you would be believed. I do not know. And you did mention it when I visited your bookseller's the first time, long after the fact. That was very helpful. I have lost much sleep over it and have lain it before God, as there is nothing more I can do now. Be assured we have done everything in our power to provide for the boys affected, to secure them good positions, and we have very much humbled ourselves in apology, though it be Mr. Peevers's crimes, and not ours." She paused, and briefly appeared yet more uncertain, which as quickly resolved. "And now I will speak of it no more."

The half dozen or more other arraignments having been galloped through in little more than twenty minutes, Mr. Peevers was again called into the dock, this time for sentencing. Pausing but for a moment, Judge Corder drilled his intense gaze into Mr. Peevers. "For all of these charges, Percival Peevers, which have been read and enumerated, and to which you have confessed and pled your guilt, it is the will of the Crown, in service of God, that you shall hang by the neck until dead. You may now speak, if you wish to say anything."

Mr. Peevers, who had stood very uncertainly, hanging his head very low, now raised his head, and said, in a most uneven, breathless, and rasping voice, "I believe in God and in God's judgement. I am content to submit to your justice and God's, though I fear it greatly. It will sound mad, but I do not quite know how all this came about. I think, perhaps, that truly I am mad. I sought only pleasure, and at first it did not seem wrong, though in fact it be heinous. And I will say," and here his trembling voice became slightly louder and more firm, "that not all of them objected." Here a murmur swept the courtroom, but the judge waved his hand to silence it. "And when others did, I thought little of it. I thought they would be brought to pleasure and leave off complaining. There is the madness, the cruelty. I forgot it was buggery. I forgot everything about it was evil, from the very beginning. I have done great wrong. I shall now prepare to meet God."

XL

NOT QUITE A FORTNIGHT LATER, early in the afternoon of a still and foggy Monday, Mr. Peevers was hanged. Chowder, having been given the day at liberty, arrived very early and shared our breakfast of porridge, then rode with me in the back of the wagon Mr. Jackson hired to make deliveries, while Mr. Jackson and Rowland rode in front. Rowland had just begun to visit Mr. Jackson on occasion, and sometimes he was seen about the shop, though he had yet to do any work.

We departed early, as Mr. Jackson expected a fierce crush of people and wanted to get in close enough for a good view. A hanging is not unlike a public holiday, and as Mr. Peevers had become notorious thanks to much mention in the papers, it was very much so. Many shops closed for the day, as if it were Sunday. That it was not raining, but foggy and promising to be fair later on, encouraged people to turn out as well.

We were well along Piccadilly and nearing Hyde Park Corner when the crush of carriages and carts became so thick that further progress was impossible. Mr. Jackson turned Chowder and I loose to walk the rest of the way and find our own ways home, saying he ought to have known better than to ride when walking would have been easier overall. "It is five or six miles back to Spittlefields, but you are young enough and will not feel it," he said, and with that Chowder and I tumbled out to follow Tyburn Lane along the edge of Hyde Park, to the gallows.

The mood of the occasion, despite the chill fog and the grave nature of the proceedings to be undertaken, was festive, and it reminded me of approaching Bartholomew Fair, where one looks forward to divers pleasures and amusement. People of all sorts, and many families with children were traipsing in the same direction, talking and laughing in high spirits. Chowder and I were less given to banter, being inured to a habitual reserve when with each other in public, but we were no less curious than anyone else to witness the event.

Piemen and peddlers hawked pies, sweets, drink, broadsheets and ballads celebrating the undoing of the evil Mr. Peevers, and novelties, among which were little cloth dolls dangling from strings around the neck. These were a penny each, three pence more for a miniature gallows, so a child might hang evildoers all the day long.

Eventually, we were able to make out, through the fog, the galleries rising high around the triple tree, where for a sizable fee, one might sit to better see. We had no pretensions to quality and less money, having brought but a shilling so as to be able to eat as the day wore on, and hoped merely to get close enough to see something, if perhaps not well.

The Triple Tree, which the gallows were called, was not a tree as such, but a triangular arrangement of three very stout and tall posts having heavy cross-timbers to join them at the top. These were of sufficient dimensions that a half dozen or more men and women could be hanged from each beam, a marvel of efficiency to be sure. It was high enough, too, that the populace, standing on level ground for a very considerable distance, could see at least the upper half of the structure, and thereby most of the person dangling from it.

Chowder and I secured ourselves a spot near the foot of the largest of the galleries, atop which we could just make out Miss Strickenwell and the other worthies of the Congregation. A very slight breeze had begun to stir the fog, causing spectral wisps to alternately enwrap and release the galleries, the gallows, and us.

We waited for perhaps an hour, when a distant murmuring and tumult could be heard from the direction whence we had come. It very slowly increased until it enveloped us, and we could just see through the fog a group of mounted soldiers preceding a black wagon, its upper sides a cage of iron bars, within which were Mr. Peevers and the others who were to die that day, sitting upon their black coffins. The wagon was surrounded by a crowd of very exercised individuals of both sexes shouting curses and insults, who were kept off by yet more mounted soldiers pacing the wagon at either side. The faces of the soldiers were grim and set, as befitted the dignity of the apparatus of law, court, prison, and armed force that had led to this triumph of order and righteousness.

Mr. Peevers was on the side of the prisoner's wagon nearest us, just within the bars, his head down. He would pause from time to time to look up at the gallows, displaying a most urgent and concentrated expression, then close his eyes and lower his head again, clasp his hands at his chin, and move his lips in prayer. In this, he was assisted by the Ordinary of Newgate, as it was explained to us, whose job was to attend to the spiritual needs of the condemned, and who rode in the wagon with them. But it appeared only Mr. Peevers required such assistance, as when the Ordinary approached any of the others, they scowled, spat, and turned away.

The wagon was now positioned directly beneath the massive gallows. Mounted soldiers stood at the corners, rifles leveled not at the condemned, but at the crowd. All, including Mr. Peevers, wore rather fine clothing, and two young men of not unappealing appearance, highwaymen, Chowder and I were told, waved and smiled to the crowd as if it were a performance, and they celebrated players, for which they received not a little hooting and cheering. But the others, including two women of very worn and haggard countenance, a mother and daughter who had poisoned the younger woman's husband, looked down as if sensible of their shame and impending demise.

Mr. Peevers took notice of nothing other than the gallows and the urgency of his prayers, which he continued without ceasing. Then the prisoners' arms were tied, and much time expended in the measuring, tying, suspending, and placing of nooses around their necks. This was accomplished by two hangmen who went about their business with set faces, but withal no more fuss than if they were slaughterers of cattle, and here come walking in the next load of meat. The hangmen took the greatest care with Mr. Peevers, measuring several times, tying and measuring again and again before suspending the noose from the beam and affixing it to Mr. Peevers, who regarded it with shrinking, abject horror. Meanwhile, the mounted soldiers cleared people away from the area in front of the horses that would pull the wagon away.

Finally, all was ready. The prisoners were arrayed just so beneath the beams. The rear gate of the wagon was opened, the hangmen left the wagon platform, and fog swirled. The crowd, which had been very noisy when the prisoners first arrived, in concert with the zealots who had followed the wagon in, quieted in expectation, until all was silent. Then, of a sudden, came a shout and a shot, and the horses bolted.

The cart pulled away, and the prisoners swung free, those closest to the horses having the briefest of moments to run in place until nothing remained beneath their feet but air. Chowder gripped my arm very hard, and I could not look, not at that very moment when those humans, whatever they had done, were among the living, and then not. But then, a great shout and wild cheering arising from the crowd, and Chowder's grip on my arm not slackening, I did look, and saw not all of them were still.

The smaller of the women, a very slight thing, bucked and writhed as she strangled, her weight, I suppose, not having been sufficient to break her neck as she fell. Mr. Peevers, too, was not yet dead. The hangman had tied his noose rather longer than the others, so when he dropped, Mr. Peevers's outstretched toes for an instant just touched the ground, preventing the snapping of his neck. The tips of his toes but very slightly grazed the grass, and he struggled mightily, but in vain, to find purchase that he might release the lethal pressure on his neck. He could get no air at all, and the more he struggled, the tighter the noose became. His face became very red, then most shockingly purple, his eyes bulging horribly. Again I looked away, this time not looking back until Chowder assured me it was over.

The exultant crowd was in great disorder. "Serves them right!" and "Glory be to God!" was shouted out again and again, not in any organized manner, but by one or another who found himself or herself inspired, and it seemed everyone was shouting, laughing, kissing, drinking, cursing, or fighting. Others stood rapt amidst the chaos, fixed to the spot by what they had seen. Gin peddlers had never ceased to circulate, and many in the crowd were drunk, some very drunk indeed. Some others, having chosen to take not the object lesson so vividly laid before them, but a wallet or purse not their own, and having been discovered in the act, were in the process of being severely beaten.

Parents sternly admonished ashen-faced children to live rightly so they would never find themselves at the end of a rope, preachers set themselves up on little platforms and began to hector and orate, and the many peddlers were in full cry, making the most of their last chances. As the bodies of the dead were taken down and loaded inert into the coffins upon which they had arrived, the mounted soldiers, rifles ready, formed a circle around the gallows to keep the souvenir-hunting mob at bay.

Chowder and I, shaken, looked at each other. "My God," he said. "Let us get away from here." Saying that Cudworth had told him he, Mrs. Cudworth, and their daughters would be at the Greengrocer's Ball and out very late, Chowder asked whether I would care to see the sty in which he lived, to which I readily assented.

We walked the long ways back to Spittlefields, saying little. The fog had lifted, and the day was as bright as it would become in that brief interval before the autumnal nightfall. As we walked, I reflected much on the fragile evanescence of life, Mr. Peevers, and his fate. Who knew whether he existed yet, incorporeal, and was now settling his accounts with God, or whether he had simply ceased to be, his mind and being but a candle blown out as his flesh stilled? How could anyone know? Every one of us will die but live in denial of it, and when this denial is pierced, we are staggered, as if we had never heard it before. I thought much, too, of the precious and excellent young man at my side, whom it was my great good fortune to know. That he was also made of this too-fragile, temporary flesh was almost more than I could bear.

"I think," I said as we crossed Holborn, "that I shall never go to another hanging. I cannot get Peevers out of my mind. I suppose he deserved it, but I wish I had not seen him struggle so."

"It was horrible," said Chowder. "I hope I don't dream about it."

We took sandwiches at a hand and pocket shop on the way, which we ate squatting in a convenient alcove, arriving at Cudworth's grocery near the supper hour, as darkness gathered and the fog reformed. Chowder took a key from under an apple crate near the door, opened it, and we entered. The shop was as I had seen it through the windows, none too well kept, with aged and disorderly produce in piles on shelves and in carts, ready to be rolled out front in the morning. It being October, there were apples and Spanish oranges, potatoes, parsnips and turnips and onions in sacks and boxes, cabbages and dried figs and apricots, and lettuces and boxes of tea and chocolate, all fairly well strewn about, and scales and a till. Leading me to the rear, Chowder passed through another door to the tiny parlor of Cudworth's dwelling, which was very cramped and no more orderly nor clean than the shop.

"Dulcibella believes there has been a great error, and that by rights she is a lady of quality. She will not do the work servants should, never mind that there aren't any, and so has squalor to prove her dignity. The daughters cook but ill, and Cudworth will have me clean when the filth is too much even for him, but as you can see it's a mess." Chowder laughed as we passed through to the kitchen, in comparison to which the parlor was immaculate. Dirty dishes and cooking pots and utensils were piled high, and potato and orange peels and egg shells filled a bucket on the floor, which sorely wanted sweeping.

On the deal table were the remains of breakfast, and cupboard doors stood open at random angles revealing chipped crockery and disheveled packages.

"Cudworth has me work in the grocery, and to spite Dulcibella assigns me to domestic chores but very rarely, as I said. She hates him for this, of course. And here," he said, leading me to a small door off the kitchen, "is my very own, personal sty, where I sleep. This was a broom closet before I came," he laughed. "It's a wonder I can close the door on them, and thanks be to God I can."

He opened this door, revealing a tiny, tidy chamber with small bureau for his clothes, a narrow cot and a shelf, on which were the books I had given him. A little window up high let in a reduced portion of the now crepuscular daylight. "Come in," he said, fussing with tinder, flint, and steel, which yielded a flame after a bit, and he lit a candle.

We sat on his small bed, then lay on it side by side. There was scarcely room for the two of us. The events and lessons of the day, and the agitation my heart had thereby experienced had wakened me from the habitual torpor of existence. I found Chowder inexpressibly dear and could not forbear to hold him close, which embrace he returned. "There is no one about," he said, kissing me. The sweetness of it pierced me through, and we progressed by gentle degrees to a lovemaking of surpassing tenderness. We heard a bit of clatter in the kitchen, but Chowder said it would be the cats, and we thought nothing of it. When I left some hours later, the fog was even denser than before, and it was very dark, and not easy to find my way. By the time I gained Mrs. Whidby's and let myself in, she was gone to bed, and I was exhausted. I crawled into my own bed and immediately fell asleep.

XLI

Two days later, as it was nearing noon on a chill and rainy day, as I was restocking and tidying up shelves of books, Dulcibella Cudworth entered the shop, accompanied by two grim-faced men in the rough dress of the lower sort of working man. I happened to be towards the rear and could just see through the gap between the top of a row of books and the shelf above. Having entered, she stopped, her expression of glowering haughtiness interrupted by a moment's uncertainty as she looked about and saw no one.

"He's around here somewhere, of that there is no doubt," she announced, then, more loudly called, "I say, is there anyone to assist?"

In very little time, Rowland appeared at the bottom of the stairway in the rear. He had returned to minding the shop on days when Mr. Jackson was called away, but he lived yet elsewhere. "Yes, yes, no need to shout," said he, striding towards the front.

Mrs. Cudworth glared at him, and using a very stern and officious manner somewhat at odds with her lower class accent, proclaimed, "We do not come here to buy books. I have sworn out a complaint against your 'prentice here, Chapman." Rowland having reached her, she lowered her voice and began speaking rapidly and urgently, sometimes looking away to glance about the room.

My heart in my mouth, I walked very rapidly towards the rear, not making a sound and keeping to the right side so I might not be seen, then I silently let myself out through the rear door and broke into a run. I was most thankful the door also was set to the right and could not be seen until one was very near to it, that I had recently oiled the hinges, and that Mr. Jackson was for the moment upstairs. I was even more thankful it had not occurred to Mrs. Cudworth there might be a rear entrance, or to place one of her men at it. Once out the door and into the pelting, cold rain, I ran up the lane and around the corner as fast as I could, and on and on, looking behind me frequently to make certain no one was in pursuit, until I was entirely out of breath, thoroughly soaked and chilled, and the better part of a mile away, towards Holborn.

I paused in a doorway out of the rain and tried to think, and the gravity of the situation began to sink in. I supposed Chowder and I were undone. I was soaked and cold, and had no jacket and no money, although I did have my set of keys to the premises, which I always kept about me. But I could see little use for them as I did not dare return to the shop, at least not any time soon. Fear and anxiety dawned in me, and grew apace, but I was determined to think of something.

The situation was grave, but I was not in any immediate danger. I decided I would, very much later in the night, have to take my chances and return to the shop to get my money, my jacket, and my one ticket to the wider world independent of my apprenticeship, Mr. Duckworth's card, that I had kept in a drawer in my desk. I had no idea whether it or he would be of any use, but my alternatives were few indeed, and I thought I should have to try it. How I should support myself, assuming I could evade capture, I had not the slightest idea.

"Will you be wanting anything?" a voice behind me asked. It was the shopkeeper. I was blocking the entrance of a sweets shop.

"Ah, no, sorry." I shivered from the cold as I spoke.

"Well then, perhaps you'd be so kind as to move along." This was said in a manner not so very unkindly, but with enough firmness to indicate he meant it.

"Sorry." I walked on then, again into the rain, and looked for another spot to wait. Had I even a penny, I might easily have gone to a coffee house, but hesitated to hazard it without any money at all. I should simply have to walk about, unless I could find an uncontested spot out of the rain.

No sooner had I thought this, however, than I passed a small, unprepossessing coffee house, the Black Boar, and paused to look in the window. The glass was just steamed enough to make the task uncertain, but I could see the shop was busy, with booths and tables full and many youths standing about. I thought, the worst they can do is send me back outside, and with any luck I will be able to stand about and not be asked for some time what my orders might be.

So thinking, I entered and was met with warm air, fragrant aromas of coffee, ale, meat, and a very goodly fire, along with the murmur of many animated conversations. Hoping to remain inconspicuous, I stayed near the entrance, and over some minutes began to dry out and cease to shiver. The gravity of my situation struck me again and again. I did not doubt everything had been taken away—my situation, my master and mentor, and very likely and worst of all, my beloved. Had Chowder been apprehended? Had Dulcibella and Tobias Cudworth come home early and spied on us? Why had we not heard them? Whatever was I going to do? What was it even possible to do?

"Do you come here often?" My dismal meditation was interrupted by a young man about my own age, of not unpleasing, if somewhat bland, features. His wig and waistcoat were clean and of excellent quality. I had not noticed his approach.

"I, ah, no." I felt as if I had quite forgotten how to talk.

"I see. Well, so much the better, perhaps. First visit? Care to chat?"

"Yes. First. Sorry. Don't mean to be unsociable. I'm … a bit preoccupied, I suppose."

"The name's Dudley. Dudley Bostok." He extended his hand, and with it a broad smile.

"Joe," I said uncertainly, as I took his hand and shook it rather limply.

"A pleasure to meet you, Joe. May I buy you something? A bit of drink, or meat?"

"Why, I suppose no harm in it. Yes, that will do very nicely. Thank you."

He led me to a vacant booth in the rear. I wondered whether a trap were set, and I was walking into it. We sat, and in time ordered beef stew, bread, and tea.

"So, what is your story, Joe? I shall tell you mine in a moment, I promise."

"I am not sure where to begin, nor that I much care to go into it, really. Sorry, I don't mean to be rude. I am rather at a loss. It seems today I have lost my situation, quite suddenly."

"Oh, dear! How disastrous. Stealing, eh? Well, think nothing of it. There are plenty of situations, plenty of ways to make a living. Besides, just about everyone steals, don't they?"

"I don't know. I don't recall saying I had stolen anything. You seem to presume there is no such thing as an honest man. Why is that?"

"Oh, but I do. And I like your answer. Very good." He beamed at me.

"Mind telling me what this is all about, Dudley? You don't know me from

Adam, yet are making a great show of ingratiation, to what object I cannot fathom. Do forgive me, but what is it that you want?"

"Is kindness so very mysterious? You are obviously in some distress, coming in from this weather coatless, soaked, and shivering. Further, you are, as obviously, unused to being in this condition, as you are to all appearances well fed, intelligent, and, until today at least, well cared for. I admit to some curiosity, but withal am pleased to offer you a meal and some conversation."

"I see. You are quite discerning. Is that all there is to it, then?"

"No. You, too, are discerning. I represent," and here he took a deep breath, "the Society for Moral Improvement. This place is a nest of buggery, as rife and foul as can be imagined. I seek to recruit young men such as yourself to help us entrap and expose these fiends. You are very attractive. They will flock to you. When they have made their loathsome advances, you report it to us, and together we make the complaint and have caught another one. Did you hear of that Peevers business? He was hanged but a few days ago."

I fear I gaped at him, open mouthed, speechless in astonishment. It took me some moments to collect myself. "Yes, I have heard of it. Loathsome, indeed. But I am sorry. I am not your man."

"We would pay you handsomely for each one. We have hundreds of old ladies subscribed at a shilling a month for just this purpose."

Mopping up the last bits of stew with a crust of bread, I said, "Thank you so very much for the meal. You must forgive me, but I do not care for your offer, not at all. Sorry again." I rose to go.

"I see," said Dudley, thoughtfully. Then, smiling, "Well, then, what if I tell you I didn't mean a word of it? Would you like to come with me to my apartments?" Here he winked slyly at me to indicate, I supposed, I had passed the test and was welcome to join him in some less than innocent recreation.

If I was appalled at his previous offer, I was stupefied by this one. "Oh, my dear Dudley, I fear you have misread me, or my intentions, at any rate. I am indeed in distress, but not of a kind that would impel me in your direction. Now, do not fear. I shall tell no one. Thank you again, very much, but I must go now." I rose, this time not to be stopped, and made directly for the door.

Once outside, I found the rain had only intensified, and now fell in wind-driven sheets. In very little time, I was again utterly soaked and shivering, and thought to myself as I walked on that I had been a fool. I might have accepted Dudley's offer, and if it came to it, declined any advances without compromising myself. And yet, to trade shelter for a presumption of intimacy that I had no intention of honoring held no appeal. I decided, finally, that I had done the right thing, as I cared neither to trade in falsehood nor complicate my predicament, and soon found another coffee house in which I again waited, just inside the door. This time I was not approached, and stood perhaps half an hour before leaving, whereupon I soon found another, as Holborn was full of them. In this manner, I passed the remainder of the afternoon and evening. I was but once asked for my orders, to which I replied I was awaiting a friend, and would be pleased to tell what I wanted as soon as he arrived, which answer satisfied, and I left the premises not long after.

By degrees, the rain abated and the wind rose as the evening advanced, so that eventually, though it had seemed interminable, the ten o'clock hour neared, and I determined to return to Mr. Jackson's to get the most necessary of my things, if I could. I could not make up my mind whether I ought to speak to Mr. Jackson or not. If possible, I thought I should collect the rest of my money, but if he were very angry, I could not predict what he might do and desired greatly not to hazard it.

It was very dark, as there was no moon, and the wind, now a southerly gale, howled, rattling signs and chimney pots and driving all manner of trash and debris before it. It was no small thing to make my way in the dark and the teeth of the wind from Holborn back to St. Paul's, and very dark indeed in the lane leading to Mrs. Whidby's premises, where I stumbled several times. But, between the darkness and the racket of the wind, I remained undetected. I saw no light in Mrs. Whidby's window, which meant she had gone to bed, but Mr. Jackson's first-floor study was illuminated.

Once at Mrs. Whidby's door, I slipped the key into the lock, and turned it, thankful again I had oiled it but a few days before as I had the others. The door opened, and I entered quickly and closed the door as quietly as I could. I had made no noise, but the wind outside was more audible through the open door, and my heart was in my mouth. I immediately went to the ladder and climbed it. The light from Mr. Jackson's window shining across the lane into my now former chamber was just enough to see someone had been there and made a great mess of things.

My bedclothes were torn off and thrown to the floor, where they lay with my books in utter disarray. The drawers of my bureau had all been turned out onto the naked bed and floor, and my little desk lay on its side, the drawer open and empty. In dismay, I rummaged as quietly as I could through the mess, and in time did find Mr. Duckworth's card, but there was no sign of my purse, which had contained the better part of a pound. Nor could I find my treasure box, in which I kept the few notes I had received from Chowder, and a button, which had come

---

off one of his shirts. I would have to throw myself on Mr. Jackson's mercy. Taking Mr. Duckworth's card, my jacket, and a very few other bits of clothing, I made to descend the ladder, when I heard Mrs. Whidby's chamber door open, and saw, through the hatchway, the light of a candle in the kitchen.

XLII

"JOE, IS THAT YOU UP there? I know someone is up there. I say, if you are not Joe, then you shall answer to my pistol!" Mrs. Whidby's voice was anxious and very determined.

"Yes, Mrs. Whidby, it is indeed me, Joe. I shall be right down," I prepared to descend. "No need of your pistol."

"Oh, Joe, my boy, thank goodness it is you. I am so relieved you have come back. I have no powder for this stupid thing, anyways."

I clambered down the ladder and stood facing her. "Very sorry to disturb you, Mrs. Whidby."

"Disturb me? Don't be silly. Oh, Joe, whatever is this about? That horrid woman! So full of herself! She marched in here like she was the Queen and tried to order me about. You can be sure I told her where to put it, oh yes I did! Whatever does she think she's doing, trying to ruin a fine young man like yourself? And Chowder, too. She must be mad. They demanded to go up to your chamber, and Mr. Jackson said we had to let them, whatever for I will never understand. I'm so angry I could spit nails. I'm so sorry, Joe. They took some of your things."

"Yes, so I have found out. And made a fine mess of it, too. But what of Chowder?"

"She was very pleased to tell us Chowder was taken before a magistrate this morning. She expected he would be in Newgate before night."

"Oh, dear God."

"I want you to know one thing, Joe. I don't believe it of you. It simply isn't possible. Whatever she is after, she will not get it by means of these lies."

"I, uh ..." Here the door to the outside opened, and Mr. Jackson walked in. The wind had masked any sound of his approach. His face was drawn with worry, but I was relieved he did not appear angry.

"I noticed you had lit a candle, Mrs. Whidby, and thought I might look in. Joe, thank goodness you have come back. I must speak to you, and quickly. Please come with me. We will talk in my study."

I thanked Mrs. Whidby, promising I would return to see her as soon as I possibly could, to which she was very surprised I was not home to stay, despite the disruptions of Mrs. Cudworth and her minions. I then followed Mr. Jackson across the windblown lane. He led me upstairs and invited me to sit.

"Joe, I am very relieved to see you. Are you all right? Where have you been?"

Briefly I told him of my adventures, such as they had been.

"The Black Boar? Oh, dear. That might be funny, if the situation were not dire. It is," he paused, searching for words, "a place very well known in certain circles. But as far as I know, the Society for Moral Improvement is defunct. I could be wrong about that, though. Perhaps it has been revived." He paused again, regarding me with an intensity and concern that surpassed any I had before seen in him.

"Joe, you did well to run. I am very glad you did. If you keep away from here and from Spittlefields, there is very little likelihood of your capture. But the hard part of it is, that given the nature of Mrs. Cudworth's accusations, I can have no further association with you. You cannot stay here, as she and her takers may return at any moment, and I must pretend to the world I am as appalled by your purported depravity as is she. If I do not play the part, suspicion might extend to me. In any event, if I am seen to protect you, or it is thought I have knowledge of your whereabouts, I might myself be investigated, and who knows where that might lead. They would have a very difficult time proving anything, but the disruption and taint in and of itself could well prove ruinous to my reputation and livelihood. I am so very sorry, Joe."

I found myself curiously numb, but there remained in me enough wit and sentiment to say the right thing. "I am so very, very sorry, My. Jackson. I have let you down, when I swore I would not. How will you get by in the shop?"

"Rowland has agreed to return to the extent of putting in regular hours. He will sleep in your old chamber, rather than with me, though. It is a condition he required, and I have agreed. Mrs. Whidby does not yet know of it."

"I see. Well, if it helps you out. I don't understand it, though. There was no one at Cudworth's when Chowder and I went in, and we heard no one enter while we were there. We were quiet about what we did, and it was all behind a closed door."

"Mrs. Cudworth—dear God, she is an abomination—did not mind telling us she and Hortensia were lying down in their chambers when you and Chowder came in. She had not gone to the Ball, but insisted Mr. Cudworth go by himself, as he was already drunk, and a turnip-headed fool, as she put it, and she couldn't be bothered. She heard Chowder and you enter, and being a tiny-minded busybody, she sneaked into the kitchen and spied on the two of you through the keyhole in Chowder's door. I will spare you the language she used to describe what she saw. She then dragged Hortensia into it, so she might have another witness. It is most unfortunate. Persecuting the two of you has given new purpose to her stunted life, and she is very determined."

I shook my head in disbelief and dismay. "What of Chowder, then? Mrs. Whidby said he was in Newgate by now."

"I'm afraid it is almost certainly true. Mrs. Cudworth told us she had him taken very early this morning to the Magistrate, where she and Hortensia made the complaint. There is no reason to doubt it. He would have gone from there to the Poultry Compter, and given that he is accused of a felony punishable by hanging, he could not have been there for more than a few hours before the wagon came that transports prisoners to Newgate."

"Oh, my God. What can we do to help him? Is there anything?"

"I have sent a message to his sister, so she knows what has befallen him. I have you to thank for knowing she exists, and it was Mrs. Whidby who told me where. If Elspeth has any money and cares to spend it on her brother, it may be possible for him to be held in a private cell. Very dear, but such as us do not last long in the common pens, if it becomes known why we are there."

"They have made a ruin of my, I mean, the garret, and taken my money and several other things. I need my money, Mr. Jackson. I must help Chowder. And I must know where to find Elspeth."

"Of course, Joe." Rummaging among the papers on his desk, he found Elspeth's information and copied it for me. "And I will contribute, though it must be in a manner that could not be traced back to me. There are ways to do that, of course. I have friends whom I trust who will be willing to serve as intermediaries. But as for your money, it is a bit of a pickle. The very day Miss Strickenwell brought it here, I put your nearly forty-eight pounds into the Bank, under both your and my names. Either of us may withdraw it, except that I meant to take you there to have you sign a card to be used for your identification, but had not yet got around to it. So, really, the situation at present is that only I can withdraw from that account. But if I were to do that, it is a suspicious act, for either I am taking it to give to you, which would mean I know where to find you, or I am taking it improperly for my own use. There is no good way to do it."

I simply looked at him, having no words.

"So, what I will do, Joe, is extend to you the same amount from my personal funds. I make substantial withdrawals and deposits all the time, so this will not arouse suspicion. It will have to wait until tomorrow, however. I have nothing like that on hand, nor is there much in the till. But I can give you this." He emptied his pockets, producing two crowns, a half crown, several sixpence, and some copper. He made a note of the amount, then handed it to me, saying, "Take this. It is plenty enough to get you through the next few hours. If you will be at the Black Boar tomorrow afternoon at four, I will send Rowland to deliver the rest. When this is all over, as it must be eventually, the withdrawal of your funds may occur, and I will be paid back. Will that be all right?"

"I see no alternative, so, I suppose, yes. Thank you. But, sir, Rowland?"

"I cannot go there as it is quite notorious. I cannot be seen anywhere with you, really, even though the risk of detection is slight. The Black Boar has the advantage of being well away from here and known to you, and, as for Rowland, for better or ill, he knows what you look like. I can't very well send someone unknown to you who doesn't. You need not entertain him. Just accept the purse that he will bring and be done with it."

"Very well, then. Thank you, sir. I must be going, I suppose. Sir, do you know a Quentin Duckworth?"

"Duckworth? How on Earth do you know him?"

Briefly I told of my encounter the previous June. "I really have no idea where to go or what to do, sir, and he has given me his card. It's a very long shot, but I am at a loss."

"Quentin Duckworth is a fop and a buffoon. He is very wealthy and has aristocratic connections, or would have found himself at the end of a rope long ago, as his deportment is lamentable. I cannot abide the man. Still, there are worse characters, and I do believe him to be honest where money is concerned, so there is that. He will not cheat you. But keep your wits about yourself and a towel handy. You can expect to be slavered over. What he might require in exchange for protecting you, if he chooses to protect you, I could not say."

With that, I gave Mr. Jackson his keys, thanked him, apologized yet again, and took my leave. We shook hands as if we were no more than business acquaintances having concluded a transaction. I then descended the stairs, where I lingered over the map and was successful in locating Sackville Street, just off Piccadilly, the location given on Mr. Duckworth's card, as well as Elspeth's street, and then was out the rear door and gone, never to return.

Hastening back towards Holborn, I decided to try the lodging house in which we had slept when Mother died, and I ran there, tripping and falling but once, and arrived quite out of breath just as the doors were being locked. I pounded on the door and was admitted with ill grace, being told that those who made unnecessary noise were not welcome, as people were trying to sleep, or didn't I know? However, they did admit me. For a penny, I was shown into a large room in which a score or more of men lay on the bare floor, and told to mind my Ps and Qs, as they didn't mind ejecting folk who broke the rules, never mind that it was the middle of the night. Finding a bit of vacant floor, I lay myself down and arranged my jacket for a pillow. I lay as best I could and turned over Chowder's and my situation in my mind again, as the men about me scratched, snored, and farted. Sleep did not come until well into the wee hours.

XLIII

AT PRECISELY SEVEN IN THE morning, the inhabitants of the room were rousted out by a rotund, red-headed young man of impressive vocal capacity, who burst in, and without preliminary called out, "Up and out! Up and out! Thank you! Thank you! Up and out!" repeatedly, in very precise accents, and with much unnecessary volume, until every one of us had gathered himself up and left. I was informed by an aged denizen the room and several others adjacent to it were used in the daytime for the purposes of a dramatic academy, and classes began promptly at eight. At least they allowed us a few minutes to use the buckets in the corners of the room to relieve ourselves, and to adjust our habiliments before filing out the front door to face the elements.

The morning was raw and damp, but the storm was spent, and the day promised to be bright and mild. Recalling Mr. Jackson's map, I walked down Fetter Lane to Fleet Street, where I turned right, and along to Temple Bar and into the Strand, where I treated myself to a fine breakfast of hashed fish and potatoes and coffee for sixpence in a tavern. It was dear, but I was of the opinion that I deserved it, having not eaten since dining with Dudley Bostok in the Black Boar early the previous afternoon. Then to Charing Cross, where stands the pillory, and to Cockspur, along Haymarket and so to Piccadilly. It was, from Fleet Street on, much the same route we had taken to Tyburn to see Mr. Peevers hanged, until Sackville Street, leading to the right off Piccadilly, where a row of new mansions stood shoulder to shoulder, at that moment splendid in a momentary spot of sun.

Number twelve was halfway up the row, four floors of very fine, blond sandstone, bay-fronted, standing between others of red brick, no less fine, and I hesitated at the bottom of the steps leading to the entry, an imposing, deep blue, double iron door of intricate workmanship, set in a scalloped, white frame. It was not yet nine and very early to be calling on a gentleman. But as I stood and wavered, I saw a dark-haired young man in a night shirt appear at one of the top floor windows, surveying the street and me. Before no more than ten minutes had passed, the door opened, and the same young man, very little older than myself, now more appropriately clad for purposes of greeting the public, addressed me.

"Well, how do you do, Dearie? Have you come to grace us with your presence, or just what is it that I may help you with?" This was said in lilting and delicate tones, which one might not have expected to issue from someone possessed of so robust and masculine a frame. He smiled most ingratiatingly, and I did not fail to notice he was a very fine-looking fellow.

"Yes, right. Thank you. I encountered Mr. Duckworth not long ago. He gave me his card and invited me to call on him, which I thought I might do. I don't mind saying I'm in a bit of a difficult spot, and thought I might ask him for some advice."

"I see," said the young man, suddenly dour. "I hope you are not wanting money. Everyone asks him for money, and he is quite sick of it."

"That is not, in fact, why I have come. I do not need money and will ask for none. But I do seek his opinion on certain matters and will be very grateful to receive it."

The smile as instantly returned. "Ah, very good. Would you care to come in, then? Quentin is here, but I ought to tell you, he sees no one before noon. You will have rather a long wait, or perhaps you would like to come back closer to the time? Personally," and here he looked me up and down, "I think you ought to come in now. You are the first this morning, and if you return later, several others may well be in front of you."

"Now will do very well, thank you. I have nothing else to do, at any rate." So saying, I followed him into the hall, where a row of chairs with their backs against the wall seemed to indicate Mr. Duckworth very frequently received callers. "Shall I wait here, then?"

"Yes, but not for long. I need but a few moments, then I shall return and we will take chocolate together. Quentin desires that his callers," and here he looked me up and down again and laughed, "or at least those as pretty as you, be properly cared for. Have you a card?"

I allowed that I did not, offering the name I had given Mr. Duckworth when riding in his carriage, that of Archibald Menzies. That would help him remember me, perhaps, and if it seemed pertinent, I would offer my true name when the time was right.

"I am Reginald. Wait here, love. I will be but a moment."

I sat as directed. The hallway was expensively paneled, and the floor laid in intricate patterns of woods of varying colors. The chair on which I sat was padded, richly upholstered, and extremely comfortable. I attempted to gather in my mind what to say, and how I should approach Mr. Duckworth, deciding very quickly the simple truth could not be improved upon.

What I needed was a place to stay, at least temporarily, and an introduction to society, in the midst of which I must somehow find a livelihood, and, if he had influence he might bring to bear on Chowder's behalf, persuade him to use it. I was meditating thus when Reginald returned.

"Come with me, love." I followed him down the hall and to the right, through a most well-appointed sitting room, where, despite the hour and the promise of a fine day, a goodly fire burned, and on to the kitchen, where he invited me to sit at a table in the corner. He brought a silver chocolate pot and two china cups and saucers, poured, then sat himself across from me.

"Do tell me, Archibald, how you met Quentin, and of your predicament. He will want to know what to expect." He took a sip from his cup with the precise delicacy of an aristocratic lady.

It was my first taste of chocolate. "This is most remarkably delicious. Thank you. It happened when I was walking through Moorfields one day early last June, on my way to Spittlefields, and he offered me a ride in his carriage."

"Moorfields," he laughed. "That would be Quentin. And what did he want of you in return? May I ask?"

"I didn't take him up on his offer, I'll have you know," I grinned in return, "which rather put him out. The word he used was rapture."

"Indeed. So you got away unscathed." He offered a complex, refined grin at once rueful and jolly. "Not all of us are so lucky. But you will find him more pleasant than not. He does care for his boys and can be very generous, provided one makes no demands. But what of your predicament? June was some time ago. What brings you here now? And if you don't want money, what are you in want of?"

"Until just the other day, I was 'prentice to a bookseller in St. Paul's Churchyard. My chum was with a greengrocer. He is now in Newgate, because his master's wife spied on us when we thought the family was out, and has made a complaint. I am not in Newgate only because I saw her coming and ran. My master and I are at quits. He will have nothing to do with me now, and I am at an utter loss. I have a few pounds, or will have when I collect it this afternoon, but I need a place to stay and a situation. And somehow I must help my friend. So there you have it." Forgetting myself, I gulped the rest of my chocolate. Delicate gestures were quite beyond me at that moment.

Reginald gave every appearance of having been sincerely affected by my tale. "Oh, my goodness me! You poor, dear, thing. You must be in a state of shock. Yes, I am sure Quentin will be very interested. I can't promise what he might do, but you will have his attention, of that I am sure. But I must tell you one thing."

"Yes, please do."

"Very likely, he will ask if he can run his hands up and down you. Do not be hard and refuse him out of hand, because if you do, that will be the end of your visit and your chances here."

I scowled. "Is there no alternative? I do not find that a pleasant prospect."

"He is not a bad man. He will take no liberties that you do not permit, unlike that Peevers fellow. I expect you have heard of that? Horrid!" He shook his head, and I nodded. "If you do not wish it, you may put Quentin off, but it would be wise to leave him hopeful. Tell him you have been so upset by recent events, you can't imagine being intimate, or that you are saving yourself for your friend, though that is a bit of a risk. It might be easier to simply permit it. He will not press you further, at least not today, if you allow him a brief moment."

"I see. Thank you for the advice. I will consider it carefully."

"Not at all. More?" I nodded, and he poured us both another cup. "And I will tell you another thing. If you get nothing from Quentin, which is altogether possible—one cannot predict his moods—do not despair. You are very presentable, and I should expect you will have little difficulty finding a position in service to one or another of the households hereabouts, several of which are very congenial indeed. Assuming you are trainable, and I can't imagine why you would not be, you would make a fine footman, at the very least."

"Thank you. That is most reassuring." It was indeed very reassuring. I wondered that I had not thought of it, and felt stupid, which I admitted.

"My dear Archibald, it is quite all right. You have been giving your all to your bookseller, and then, poof! It is gone, just like that. In your place, I would be utterly flattened. I'd say you are doing very well." His countenance radiated compassion and encouragement, and I experienced a humbling gratitude. Perhaps Fortune had not entirely abandoned me.

A second young man, also of pleasing aspect, now entered the kitchen, very soon followed by another. It was immediately apparent these were the cook and his boy, who was younger and a just bit rougher, but not unappealing, and they set about preparing a varied breakfast of porridge, eggs, toast, bacon, sweet buns, tea, and coffee. It was not a house of early risers, to be sure, nor was it a large household.

Reginald told me there were but eight servants, which it pleased him to enumerate: himself, who served as Mr. Duckworth's secretary, the cook James and his boy, Otto, a German; the coachman Josiah, who also served as groom, Françoise, from France, whom Reginald with a giggle termed the parlor maid, Peter, the chamber maid, which appellation was accompanied by another giggle, then Rudolph, valet, and finally Eugene, a Russian, Mr. Duckworth's footman. "Really there ought to be a butler, but Quentin does not feel the need, as I am able to perform that function. It does keep me very busy, though, and truth be told, we all pitch in at times to help each other fulfill his position, or we couldn't manage. Not the customary way of doing things, but there is very little that is customary about this place," he said with a smile, "and that is how we like it. Will you dine with us?"

I thanked him, but protested that I had not expected such hospitality, and had already eaten. "Tell me, though. What of Xerxes? When I met Mr. Duckworth he had a coachman named Xerxes."

"That was before my time here, but I understand Xerxes was lamentable, and did not work out. Quentin found him very irksome."

"I wondered that Mr. Duckworth tolerated it."

"He did not, actually. It was a dangerous moment. Xerxes found this household very irregular and did not mind saying so. Quentin will never use that agency again, nor take on anyone who does not fit in. We are all quite congenial now. Pity we have no openings. And now, my dear, I must leave you. As you will not be dining with us, would you mind waiting in the hall? The instant Quentin is prepared to receive callers, I will fetch you. Shouldn't be much past noon, as I have said. It's just ten, now."

As we were speaking, the rest of the staff had filed in and taken their places at table in the servant's dining room, which I could just see into, beyond the kitchen. What was extraordinary, not one of these varied young men was uninteresting in appearance, less than refined in demeanor, or appeared unintelligent, and in bantering with one another, they showed a pleasant, easy wit that appealed to me greatly. Mr. Duckworth, if nothing else, would appear to have exercised excellent taste in selecting his servants. Or perhaps it was Reginald who saw to that.

"Yes, not at all. Thank you. I can find my way there, thank you." and I left the kitchen and took myself to the hall, where I sat again in that most comfortable chair. I was not sorry to have time to think. It staggered me to think such a household could exist, in which sodomitical tendencies were not something to be hidden and but whispered of, if mentioned at all, but treated as an unremarkable part of life. How miraculous it would be to be among one's own kind. Yet it was troubling to think of the things Reginald had had to say about Mr. Duckworth's presumptions of intimacy. Did he take liberties with every one of his servants, or what were the arrangements? And how many such households were there in London, and how did they and their society escape destruction, given the Dulcibella Cudworths of this world and the religion and laws that they had entirely on their side? I felt quite out of my depth.

The chair was so comfortable that by degrees I sank into it, and my thoughts growing woolly, I soon fell asleep. I was awakened what seemed but an instant later by a loud knocking at the door, in answer to which Reginald arrived and opened it. After a brief conversation which I could not hear distinctly, he sent whoever it was away, and as he did not address or disturb me, I soon nodded off again.

XLIV

REGINALD WOKE ME WITH A gentle sweetness that betrayed not a hint of judgement at my lack of form. Despite his quiet address, I awakened instantly and followed him to the rear of the hall up a broad, curving flight of carpeted stairs, and through the leftmost door into the library, book-lined, plush, and very fine. I did not fail to notice, however, that while the shelves were lined with handsome, expensive sets of history, literature, and scientific works, their pristine state attested to little likelihood Mr. Duckworth had ever opened any of them. The eclectic collection of well-thumbed volumes such as may be found in the library of a curious and diligent reader was nowhere in evidence, lending to the room an air of sterile artifice. Motley, varied books, however well-loved, would have served only to upset the pattern of décor.

And yet, the room was not unpleasant—quite the contrary. A bright fire burned in the grate, providing warmth and cheer. The carpet was soft, the chairs richly padded and upholstered in complementary hues, and the epicene Mr. Duckworth, in a voluminous, silken banyan of patterned sky blue and a similarly loose, silken blouse of very bright canary yellow, reclined on a plush, velvet chaise longue of royal blue, completing the tableau to pleasing effect, a consideration to which I did not doubt he had given much attention. He wore no wig, and his hair was pulled into a small, bluish-grey bun. His face was freshly painted, the cheeks rouge over white, the eyes outlined in blue of midnight on a mauve field, the lips scarlet. A side table held a teapot and a large bunch of grapes. The walls, where not lined with bookcases, were of a yellow akin to his blouse, and the thick carpet repeated all of the colors in pleasing arabesques of perfect proportion.

Reginald announced me, then excused himself.

"Good afternoon, young Archibald," said Mr. Duckworth, his speech having lost none of its cloying affectation. "What an unexpected pleasure to see you. You may sit, if you please. I had thought you entirely too proper to consider visiting the likes of us, and Reggie tells me you are in some distress, which has provided the impetus. Well, if that is what it takes, we shall not complain. But tell me, how do you like my banyan? It arrived from the dressmaker but yesterday. I had a devil of a time finding this shade of silk, but I find it to have been quite worth the trouble. Do you not agree?"

"It is indeed fine, sir. I recall the scarlet breeches you wore last June. Your taste in clothing is remarkable. I confess I have never before encountered the like."

"You are very young, Archibald. The world is full of things you have not yet encountered. If my breeches startled you, you may expect to be staggered routinely, at least if you spend any time here, which perhaps you may. We will see. But, tell me this. Reggie says you have told him you were apprenticed to a bookseller, and yet I distinctly recall your telling me last June that you were a printer's apprentice. If I am to help you, I must insist on honesty. I have no tolerance for anything less."

I had quite forgotten about the printer. "Yes, sir, and you told me your name was Sir Reginald Cooper."

Mr. Duckworth blinked several times. "Ah, yes, so I did. Well then, perhaps we are even in this game. But I then provided you my card, which bore the true information, and I do not yet have that from you. So, which is it?"

Yes, sir. I was apprenticed to a bookseller."

"May I have his name?"

"I am reluctant to provide it, sir. He wants nothing to do with me now and fears the taint of having harbored one accused of sodomy might ruin him."

"Pish-tosh. I could paper the walls with the accusations made against me, and yet here I am. Give me his name."

"Very well, sir. Thomas Jackson."

Mr. Duckworth laughed long and loud, rather theatrically, I thought, but not without some evidence of genuine mirth. He dabbed his eyes carefully. "Oh, dear me. That is too funny."

"You know him, sir?"

"Oh, yes. We have known each other since we were quite young. We briefly thought we might be companions once, but it did not work out. He is entirely without flair. He does run a nice bookstore, and publishes a thing or two of worth, so I am told. But really," he paused and regarded me with rheumy, blue eyes, "fundamentally uninteresting. Now, Archibald, is Archibald in fact your true name?"

"Ah, no, sir. Joseph Chapman is truly my name."

"Now we are getting somewhere. And you say you and your chum were spied upon by a greengrocer's wife, who has sworn out complaints against the two of you, and that your chum has already been taken?"

"Yes, sir, that is correct."

Mr. Duckworth shook his head and closed his eyes momentarily. A pained expression seized his countenance and then, again regarding me, he said with greater force, "Yes, Joseph, I will help you. We will see how well you and I get on, and that cannot be predicted. You are rather like your Mr. Jackson, dunderheaded, colorless, and true, but it is worth it to me on principle, and you will not be here long. I believe we ought to get you out of the city for some months and place you in service to one of my friends in the country. If we can manage that, and I expect we shall, you would not return to London until the season begins next spring, by which time the affair will have been forgotten. With respect to your friend, we will see if the grocer's wife can be dealt with. When we have finished speaking, you will give her name and location to Reggie. And it would not be unwise to continue to use the assumed name, so Archibald you shall be to us. Does that suit you?"

"Yes, sir, very much. I do thank you, sir. It will be strange to go by another name, but I can see the reason for it surely."

"Very good then. Now, what can you do that would recommend you to service? Having been employed by Jackson, I expect you know a thing or two."

"Yes, sir. I can read and write very well. My hand is quite fine. I can do all manner of sums and can figure any amount of money. I am told I am very presentable and have much experience dealing with the public in Mr. Jackson's shop. I also have a strong back, on a good day a quick wit, and am well on my way to becoming educated, though I confess to knowing but very little Greek or Latin."

Mr. Duckworth stroked his chin in thought, then took snuff, which provoked in him, as it had previously, a great, roaring sneeze, from which he recovered but slowly. "Sorry. I ought to know better, but cannot stop. That is excellent information, Joseph. Would you be so kind as to write something for me, so that I might see your hand? Paper, ink, and a quill are in that secretary, there," he said, wiping his nose and gesturing towards a small writing desk across the room.

I did as instructed, writing my name, Mr. Duckworth's name, and all of "Mary had a Little Lamb," with which Mr. Duckworth was quite pleased. "Very good, Joseph. Can you cook?"

"No, sir. I know next to nothing about it. I am much better at eating than cooking."

Mr. Duckworth smiled. "No matter. You would be wasted as a cook, footman, or maid, none of which require literacy. You are meant for better things. It is possible that, given time, you would make a good secretary or butler, which should serve you very well. It is not easy to find the right man for those positions. Without Reggie, I would be utterly helpless, God knows. Let's see, now. I have a spare servant's chamber off the stable. It is meant for a groom, but I have only Josiah, so the room is vacant. It is tiny, but it will do. You may settle in there. It will be for but a few days in any case, as I have said. I will instruct Reggie to write to several friends of mine—and if they are friends of mine, you may be sure they will be sympathetic to you and your situation. I will also instruct Reggie to find some tasks for you to perform in exchange for your room and board. Will that be acceptable to you, young Joseph? I mean, Archibald?" He peered at me intently.

"Yes, it most certainly will, sir. However may I thank you?" I had become so engrossed in the conversation, I had forgotten Reginald's cautions and immediately regretted having phrased it so.

"Well, now that you mention it, there is something you could do to thank me. Something very pleasant that ought not to tax your sense of propriety. Simply come here, Joseph, and stand next to me."

Feeling very uncertain, I did as he requested. "Sir, I—"

"There will be nothing to it, Joseph. I merely wish to run my hands over you and will not press you for unseemly intimacies. You will remain clothed as you are, and it will take but a moment. Will that be acceptable to you?"

I didn't see how I could refuse. "I suppose so, sir, if you are true to your word."

"You will find me honest in all important respects, Archibald. I have found in this life that in falsity, we betray no one more than ourselves." He placed his hands on my chest and allowed them to descend to my belly and then to my privates, where they lingered, very gently but very thoroughly taking my measure, and then over my backside, and he was done in less than a minute. "And there you have it. Kindly notice you have not been harmed in any way. Even your dignity is intact, I should expect."

"I suppose so, sir. Thank you for requiring no more of me."

"Perhaps a time will come when you wish to make a greater demonstration of your gratitude, but that must wait for time and the growth of genuine affection, if it comes."

"Thank you, sir."

"And now I will ring for Reggie." He rang a hand bell which had lain on the side table. "He will get you situated and, as I said, find some things for you to do. Now, then, is there anything else I should know at this juncture, Archibald?"

"I believe not, sir. Only that I must go out this afternoon, and I was thinking again this evening." Briefly I filled him in on the arrangement with Mr. Jackson for receipt of my trust and my desire to go to Newgate to see if I could help Chowder in any way.

"The Black Boar is a very dangerous place, or it can be to the unwary. Keep your wits about you and do not go anywhere with anyone unknown to you. As for Newgate, that is also dangerous. They will have no sympathy for your friend and may well take your money and leave him where he is. Perhaps if you present yourself as his brother, they will at the very least tell you whether he is in the common pen. We must hope not, although they do make some attempts to keep prisoners alive, at least long enough to try them. The King does not like it otherwise. He prefers the niceties of justice be observed, and if a prisoner is to die, that it be according to His will and by the proper form. I suppose we can be grateful for that. But to be in Newgate without funds is very bad. One does not eat, but they assess a fee."

"Thank you, sir. I will keep all of that in mind. I shall let you know how I get on." I bowed to him, a gesture which appeared to please him.

Reginald appearing, Mr. Duckworth gave him instructions regarding me, then dismissed the both of us. Reginald expressed delight I should be staying, showed me the chamber, as tiny as Mr. Duckworth had promised, and said I would assist the cook prior to supper, when further determinations as to how I should be employed would be made. I thanked him, and it being near to two in the afternoon, refreshed myself and made ready to walk to Holborn and the Black Boar to meet Rowland and get my money.

I was very pleased overall with the progress I had made, and yet Mr. Duckworth's intimate attentions had made me uncomfortable. He had exercised his will upon me, and I did not care for it, despite the ostensible courtesy of his demeanor. I supposed if this were the currency of the place, I should have to get used to it, but I found it had set me at odds with myself. I was very confused as to the propriety of it all. I had been far more comfortable with Mr. Jackson, from whom such behavior would have been unimaginable.

XLV

I STRODE FORTH FROM MR. Duckworth's into an afternoon as mild as the morning had promised. The sun shone weakly through high clouds, offering a modicum of warmth, and as I walked, I attempted to balance my anxiety regarding Chowder and how I might help him with guarded optimism over the adventures of the morning. Mr. Duckworth's offers of assistance did seem reasonable and very much to my advantage, despite his mild depredations. It was an uneasy mixture, served up with a dollop of distaste over the prospect of having to meet with Rowland, even if he bore the funds I needed so badly.

As I was ruminating, I took little notice of my environs and soon found myself at the Black Boar, where I entered to find it as crowded and convivial as it had been on my first visit. Looking about the room, I saw many an interesting young man engaged in conversation, playing cards, or solitary and dreaming, perhaps. Not a few older gentlemen leaned forward and attended with unfeigned eagerness to their younger associates. Rowland was nowhere to be seen. Neither, for that matter, was Dudley Bostok, with whose absence I was not displeased. I found one of the very few vacant spots, at the end of a bench at a busy table, from which I could keep an eye on the entrance. When the boy came, I ordered a dish of coffee, a bowl of mutton stew and half a loaf of bread. Apart from Reginald's chocolate,

---

I had not eaten since the fish hash on the Strand early that morning, and all of the walking about had given me a strong appetite.

I soon finished my meal. The boys and men at the table at which I sat were embarking on an arm-wrestling contest on which substantial wagers were being made. One of the contestants bragged as a stevedore he could and would trounce anyone in the establishment, and his massive arms appeared to give testament to his contention. His opponent, no less stalwart, retorted the ditches he dug required a yet greater strength, and one ought to be careful not to boast overmuch, lest he might fall into a ditch and be buried. It was not the aptest of metaphors, but neither was it a literary contest, and then the last wagers were made and the two men set to, with vein-bulging determination.

Just then, however, I saw Rowland enter and hesitate at the door, looking about. I rose, leaving the contest in progress, to meet him. Rowland's face was grim, but as this was not unusual, I thought nothing of it.

"Have you brought my money?"

"Hold, now, will you not offer a proper greeting?" He lifted one eyebrow but did not smile.

"Lovely to see you again, I'm sure," said I, smiling no more than he had.

He compressed his lips in dissatisfaction and failed to speak.

"Really, Rowland, is this necessary? Are you not here on a specific errand for Mr. Jackson? I would like to conclude our business, and then you may go."

"Yes, I have brought it."

"May I have it, then?"

"It is outside. A friend of mine is holding it. I thought it would be unwise to hand you a large purse here where anyone may see. Very likely you would be robbed of it, and perhaps worse, before you had gone any distance."

I was puzzled that though his words were conciliatory, his mien was very guarded and cold.

"All right."

"Come with me then." Rowland turned, went out the door, and I followed. As I passed through the doorway, I was astonished to see Mrs. Cudworth sitting beside the driver of a stout carriage, looking directly at me with a malign expression of haughty triumph. In the same instant I heard Rowland say, with some volume, "Take him," at which the two rough fellows I had seen with Mrs. Cudworth in the shop earlier appeared instantly at my sides, each taking an arm in a very firm grip. They conducted me to the carriage and fairly threw me in, each taking his place beside me, and closed the doors behind themselves. Through the front window I saw Rowland mount and sit beside Mrs. Cudworth, who gave a word to the driver. He, in turn, snapped the reins, and we were off.

My shocked and speechless state of mind can well be imagined. Surprise, outrage, and dread were coupled in equal measure with an intensified and visceral hatred for Rowland, far surpassing my former distaste. I noticed, too, Mrs. Cudworth's clothing was much finer than before, and that she sported a tall wig of many dressings which included several jewels. It was the sort of thing that, even if the jewels were fake, cost a considerable sum. She now appeared to be, not the embittered, patchwork wife of Tobias Cudworth, but the spouse of a very prosperous tradesman or perhaps more.

With a sick feeling, I began to speculate how she might have paid for it, which caused me to think again of my purse, whether I should receive it, and how much it would contain. If I was to find myself in Newgate, which now seemed inevitable, I would need money more than ever. But the hatch was closed, and it was impossible to communicate with the driver or those seated next to him. As we rode on, and I struggled to keep company with my reason, I thought of Reginald and Mr. Duckworth, who were expecting me to return before supper, and who would now have cause to consider me just another irresponsible oaf.

We pulled up in front of a small, aged, and entirely unprepossessing building of red brick, half-timbered above, the façade of which was much besmirched by stains of smoke and dirt. I had lost track of our route as we rattled on, and had no clear idea where we were. Mrs. Cudworth and Rowland alighted from the driver's seat, and she went into the building. After some time, Rowland told my two keepers to exit the carriage and stand guard at the doors, keeping me prisoner.

I tried to open the door, not to escape, which obviously would have been impossible, but to speak, but no sooner had I cracked the door open the slightest bit than my keeper very quickly and firmly pushed it closed again. I tapped as forcefully as I dared on the glass, and gestured to Rowland that I wished to speak to him. After a delay contrived to demonstrate my subservience, and with an expression of disdain, he approached and allowed the door to be opened less than an inch.

"I say, Rowland, it seems you have forgotten something. Are you or are you not, holding money that is rightfully mine? Or are you thief as well as hypocrite?"

"Yes, I have it. And it shall be given you when I say it shall, unless you have any more insults for me, in which case I may as well keep it. As for my hypocrisy, is this not where you truly belong? I am sure you will find the accommodations congenial." He offered a smirk, and in it was the unjust triumph of a coward and half-wit, as unpleasant an expression as I have ever witnessed. Such are the diversions of those with tiny, frightened hearts and dim minds, who are stupid enough to believe cruelty will make them safe.

Mrs. Cudworth reappeared, indicating we were to go inside. At this, Rowland removed from a pocket of his jacket my velvet purse, and made a show of taking from it a number of coins, which he gave to the driver and the two takers. He then put several into his own pocket and several more again to Mrs. Cudworth.

"What are you doing?" said I, with outrage. "Is that not my money?"

"It was, you fool," said Rowland, his lip curling. "Surely you do not think Mrs. Cudworth or I intend to pay the cost of these thief takers, or the hackney coach, out of our own pockets. And my time, and Mrs. Cudworth's time, is surely worth something, and we and these boys all need fare to ride home again, do we not?"

"May you rot in Hell."

"Let him out, boys, but hold him fast." At this I was made to get out, and here Rowland handed to me my considerably lightened purse, for which I did not thank him. I was then conducted inside, following Mrs. Cudworth, and made to sit on a plain wooden bench towards the rear of what, I supposed, was the hearing room of a magistrate.

XLVI

THE HEARING ROOM WAS AKIN to a small courtroom, with the magistrate in front at a large desk upon a dais, enclosed by a low barrier and flanked by two clerks. Several very large guards armed with truncheons were arranged around the sides, never taking their eyes off the assemblage, and there was a peculiar, fusty odor of closeness, stale air, and decay. The Magistrate, a grave, bewigged man in early middle age, was engaged in conversation with a small group standing about his desk, and the rest of the room was full to bursting with every sort of person. Most of them, I gathered over time, were swearing out complaints, and only a few such as myself, about to be accused of heinous acts. These sat cheek by jowl with their accusers, and no attempt to separate them. Only the guards and their threat of violence ensured order.

Once I was situated, and a guard informed I was not to be permitted to leave, Mrs. Cudworth strode to the front to make application to one of the clerks. She became animated, and above the incessant, low murmur I heard her shrill, "Can it not be sooner? I am a very busy woman!" But the clerk was unmoved and, writing something in a large record book, sent her away.

With a contemptuous toss of her head, she returned, not to sit next to me, but to stand and at times pace about muttering to herself, each time passing in front of and very close to the guard nearest me, who before long instructed her to choose one spot and stick to it. If he needed to use his weapon, he told her, Her Ladyship would prefer not to be between it and its intended target. The possibility he might have intended the honorific ironically quite escaped Mrs. Cudworth, who had at first regarded the guard as a contemptible underling. At his utterance of the magical words, she instantly lost her dudgeon, and with the most gracious of smiles and a refined nod of her head took her position beside the guard, surveying the room with indulgent benevolence. After some moments, she spoke confidentially to the guard, fairly whispering in his ear. I could not hear what she said, but it was no mystery. As she spoke, the guard, looking in my direction, registered first puzzlement, then disgust, and, finally, contempt.

The magistrate soon dispensed with the group that had occupied him since we had entered, but he immediately took up with another, and then another. It was a tedious business, consisting of much impassioned complaining by the aggrieved party, much scribbling by the clerk, and, finally, the magistrate signing his name several times to large legal papers. He rarely asked questions, and only once among the several groups preceding Mrs. Cudworth, did the accused appear, manacled and glowering, protest his innocence. This did him no good, as the instant the magistrate signed the papers, the offender was hustled through a doorway behind the magistrate's desk, a guard on either side.

Finally, after what must have been at least an hour, and perhaps two, Mrs. Cudworth's name was called, whereupon she strode importantly towards the magistrate's desk. I rose to go up as well, but the guard whose ear she had filled intervened.

"Sit down. You can stay right there."

"Is it not required of me to attend? Am I not to contest the lies that viper is telling?" I said this last, I will own, rather desperately.

"If the magistrate wishes to speak to you, you will be called. But don't count on it. You can say your piece at your trial. For now, sit and don't move." He paused and regarded me as one might an insect he was deciding whether were worth the trouble of squashing. "It's no use arguing."

I glared hard at him, in disbelief.

"Someone like you," he said, shaking his head. He fondled the butt of his truncheon meaningfully.

There was no help for it, so I watched Mrs. Cudworth from afar and was able to make out only stray bits of her speech. "… other one what I told you … kissed him … everything … my daughter also … no question …" The clerk scribbled, and the magistrate alternately nodded and shook his head, several times rolling his eyes, but whether at my deplorable conduct or Mrs. Cudworth's breathless mannerisms, I could not tell. Then the clerk presented him with the large legal papers, and the magistrate signed them. As soon as he had done so, he signaled to the guard beside me.

I was instructed to stand up and was then marched past the magistrate's desk towards the doorway behind, a guard on either side, the one to my left holding my arm very firmly. As I passed the magistrate's enclosure, Mrs. Cudworth did not look at me directly, but wore an expression of satisfaction, as at a job well done, and well enough, I suppose. She had Chowder's and my imprisonment, a fine gown, a very fancy wig, and not a few pretty fake jewels to show for it.

I was led through the doorway into a small room where fetters were attached to my ankles, then down an ancient stone stairway to the cellar. In a tiny corridor lit by a single, small lantern in such dire want of trimming it emitted more oily black smoke than light, the guard stopped before a very stout oaken door, let go of my arm, and took a large iron key from his pocket. He paused to address me.

"Will you be wanting supper? The fee is sixpence."

"I ... suppose so. Do you want it now?" Receiving an affirmative grunt, I fished the coin from my pocket and handed it to him. Encouraged by the banality of the transaction and the nascent mildness of the guard's demeanor, I thought to ask a question. "I say, is it possible to send a message to anyone? A letter? I've been brought here quite by surprise, and people are expecting me."

"If you were to be here any length of time, I would expect so, but there is no provision for it. But you will be in Newgate by tomorrow noon and as an Englishman, whatever else you may be, you have the right to some communication on your own behalf."

The guard then unlocked and opened the door to a dim, dirty, and very cluttered little room, weakly lit by but a single lantern on a sconce on the far wall, next to a tiny window that admitted no light. Two score or more men and boys filled the room, nearly all of them underfed and ill-clad, sitting on a divers lot of much-abused, rickety chairs and divans, or standing, not a few sitting on the floor. They were more young than not, a few older, one very aged, and three boys no more than ten years old.

Every one of them turned to look in my direction as I entered, and as soon looked away again. I stood in the only vacant spot, next to the tiny window set up high against the ceiling and painted all over black and nailed shut, so there was no opening it to let air in, or, to be sure, oneself out. The stench, redolent of mundungus, rancidity, and every unwholesome bodily odor, which I had first noticed upon entering the hearing room, was now inescapable, and to it was added a distinct fecal note, I supposed from the water closet that must be somewhere near. Everything in me rebelled at the thought of being stuck in that hole. The air, in very short supply, was near to unbreathable.

My fellows, for such I may style them, stood or sat listlessly, staring at nothing. Several smoked long pipes, adding to the stench and further vitiating the air. The youngest boys played cards on the floor below the lantern, but without energy. No one displayed the slightest curiosity or spoke to me, for which I was grateful. There emanated from the company, not the threat of treachery or violence, but a gasping tedium steeped in exhaustion and melancholy, to which I was not myself immune, and into which I dolloped my own concerns for Chowder and myself.

Perhaps half an hour passed, when a steward opened the door, accompanied by a guard. He dispensed a supper of pea soup and bread from a little wagon. There was no mention of sixpence, and everyone was served, eating avidly where they were. To my surprise, the soup was edible, if little above room temperature, and the bread free of insects. Everyone ate in silence, and the meal was soon concluded. The steward collected the spoons and crockery, trimmed the wick and refilled the reservoir in the lantern, and departed, leaving us to the long night ahead.

As time wore on, I squatted in place, then lay down, my jacket for a pillow, my purse arranged within it to be just beneath my ear. I had as yet had no chance to examine its contents, but as I set my pillow in order, I felt with gentle care a number of coins, one of them of proportions generous enough for me to hope it was a five guinea gold piece, and enough others to suppose there might remain ten pounds or more, if a sufficient portion were silver and not copper.

The room was warm despite the damp chill outdoors, with so many breathing bodies in so tight a space. I had only just enough room to lay myself down, my head between a pair of very worn boots, the feet yet inside, and a set of skinny buttocks in trousers of many patches. I had not enough room to turn over without disturbing the man beside me, and the ancient carpet was full of dust and dirt, causing my head to become very congested, such that I could breathe only through my mouth. This, however, was not entirely without benefit, as in due course the pea soup wrought its effects, which I shall forbear telling of.

After interminable eons, during which I slept very little, the morning came at last, signaled by the arrival of the steward and his wagon, and the attendant guard. The steward dispensed a thin gruel not half as bad as Mr. Peevers had given out, but to say it was any good would stretch the truth. This was accompanied by cups of plain, weak tea. Once these were consumed and the bowls, spoons, and cups collected, the steward again refilled the lantern and trimmed the wick, then departed, and the company relapsed into its habitual torpor.

After perhaps another half hour had passed, the door again opened for a company of six guards, one of whom entered and read out a list of names, including mine, comprising perhaps a third of those in the room. Those of us whose names had been read were manacled, then, bracketed by guards ahead and behind, marched up the stairs and out the rear door of the building and into a chill, pelting rain, where a large wagon awaited us, the windows of which were without glass or covering and set with iron bars. As we were loaded in, one of the younger members of the company queried of the driver, "Where are you taking us?"

"Why, to Newgate, of course. Where'd you think? A pleasure garden? Haw, haw, Ranelagh, driver, and be smart about it! Haw haw haw!" The creature taunted as it brayed. The questioner spat and shook his head, one of the older fellows patted the boy's shoulder, and no one said anything. We sat on bare benches, the door was closed and locked from the outside, the reins were snapped, and we were off, splashing through the cold rain.

XLVII

Traveling from the Magistrate's gaol to Newgate Prison in a plodding wagon which must negotiate a heavy crush of traffic consumed nearly an hour. We came up from somewhere to the southeast of St. Paul's and passed through the Churchyard, where I was afforded a view of Mr. Jackson's premises as we passed. I attempted to reassure myself that as my fortunes had changed so utterly and abruptly several times before, so would they change again, but was only partially successful in reassuring my heart.

And then we were at Newgate, where we entered a rear courtyard off a side street, through a large gate that opened to admit us. We were made to get out and stand in the rain in a queue before a single door set in the sternest of granite ramparts, the entire building having the appearance of a very grim stone fortress, and we were admitted one at a time by a guard. Each person entering consumed several minutes or more before the next one was let in, so that by the time it was my turn to enter, I was very cold and wet indeed.

Upon entering, I found myself in a bare anteroom of diminutive proportions, in the corners of which stood several guards, and before a wicket set with iron bars, which contained a little, bird-like, almost elderly man. He wore no wig, and appeared distracted. "Damn me, I can't find anything today," he said to himself, as

I drew near. "Now then, young man, what is your name? And no tricks! I have the list here, so you may as well tell me. Your name is on it."

"Joseph Chapman."

"Yes, Joseph … Chapman." He ran down the list before him. "Chapman." Finding my name and reading the note beside it, he drew in his breath. Looking at me, he narrowed his eyes. "Well, Chapman, what shall it be? Do you go into the common pen, or have you funds for the master's side? And can you pay for your board?"

"I have a bit of money, not very much. Tell me, what does it cost a person to sojourn in these fine lodgings?

"The smarter you try to be, the more it costs, so you can leave off or we will cut this short and tell you where to go." He glared at me and I said nothing. "Now then, the entrance fee is ten and six, and another three shillings if you want private or semi private on the master's side. A semi-private room, which you share with three others, is one pound per week, and a private room is one pound per day, ten pounds in advance. In either case, your bed and bedding are another two and six per week. If you wish to eat, the rate depends on the level of accommodation, as the food is better or not, depending, also billed a week in advance, and everything on the master's side must be paid in advance. The common pen is simply two and six per week, which, if you cannot pay it now, an account is kept. And I will tell you many a fellow goes to the Fleet upon discharge here due to an inability to pay, and there are the transfer fees for that, so it is much less dear to pay now and stay current, if you can. And you pay the tap room directly for beer."

"I see." As he spoke, I had taken out my purse and gone through it quickly, discovering it indeed contained a five guinea piece, and with the remainder, a little over twenty-two pounds. That was rather more than I had supposed, but it also meant Rowland and Mrs. Cudworth had helped themselves to over twenty-five pounds, more than half of what it had contained to begin with, and there was nothing I could do about it now. "I should like, I believe, the semi-private room. What is the advance fee for that? And meals."

"The advance fee for semi-private is three pounds, and a shilling a day for three meals, payable a week in advance, so that will be four pounds and three shillings." He indicated a little tray just below the bars fronting his wicket, that I was to put the coin in. I dropped the five guinea piece into it.

"Is it possible to enquire about someone else here, and to pay for his room and board, if he has not done so himself?"

The clerk began to count out my change. "To whom do you refer?"

"Potter Gorham."

The clerk wrote Chowder's name down. "I will have to look into it, to find out where he is and the state of his account. I do not have those records here. This is merely an admitting station." He put my change into the little tray and pushed it under the bars towards me, then paused, and added, his eyes narrowing yet again, "Wait a minute. I have your crime right here," he said, nodding towards his list of names. "Would he be the one you … ?" He grimaced and shook his head in revulsion. "That would hardly be proper, I believe. No. I shall tell you nothing of him, and you can go to hell." And nodding towards the guards, said, "Take him upstairs. Cell forty-one."

During this conversation, two more guards appeared, having come down a flight of stairs leading from the left of the wicket, and it was up these I was taken. They did not grip my arm, because fettered, manacled, and inside the prison walls, where could I go? Once atop the stairs, we proceeded down a long corridor of blank stone walls and bare stone floor, then made a left turn into another corridor in which a series of doors of very stout oak, with iron gratings in the upper portion, were set on both sides. It was not unlike the magistrate's gaol, but everything here was larger and stouter, and there was very much more of it.

It was also cleaner and in a much better state of repair, as the building had just been entirely rebuilt, completed within the past year. As we passed the series of doors, fingers wrapped around the bars and faces peered out at us from behind the grates, and then we came to number forty-one, where the occupants, who had also crowded around to look, were told to stand well away from the door. My manacles were removed, but my fetters not, and then the door was unlocked and opened, and I was pushed inside.

I found myself in a dim, cold, granite-walled room perhaps four paces wide and six deep, lit by a single candle on a sconce on the rear wall. Nothing was in it save four low cots, two on either side, a very small table set by four straight-backed wooden chairs, and an oaken bucket with a small seat with a hole in the center. Two men in early and late middle age sat on the cots to the left, while a much younger third stood leaning against the wall on the right, all of them regarding me in a manner neither friendly nor unfriendly. Their dress was of a quality rather better than that of the denizens of the magistrate's gaol, as would befit the station of those who could afford these lodgings, but they appeared haggard and drawn, sorely in want of shaving, and their raiment soiled and appearing as if it had been slept in, as it unquestionably had.

They acknowledged my arrival with the slightest of nods. I returned the gesture in like manner, upon which the youngest one, standing, who was not much older than I, gave another nod of his head in the direction of the rear cot on the right side. "That one's yours."

"Thank you." I went to the cot and sat on it. It was very lumpy and hard, stuffed with horse hair that protruded from numerous cracks in the ancient leather covering. Atop it was a single, dark grey, woolen blanket, showing several holes. I saw no bed sheet of any description, but a small feather pillow of stained linen ticking emitted a sour odor, and I quickly decided I would not use it. It felt unspeakably odd to have no bundle to put down, to have been dropped into that place with nothing I would take with me for even the simplest overnight visit away from home, to say nothing of being so intimately lodged with strangers, quite apart from it being the most dreaded prison in London, where the very worst criminals were kept. I would try not to think overmuch about my condition or fate, but the question of Chowder's welfare was another matter, ever present in my mind.

"What'd ye do?" The question issued from the younger one, whose eyes were dark and constantly looking about. His nose was aquiline and his lips very thin and colorless. I realized he had been taking my measure the entire time I had been sitting on the cot.

"What's your name?" I returned, in a similar manner, neither friendly nor unfriendly, feeling that to hold my own, I should insist on a fair exchange of information.

"John." The gaze was level and appeared to be uncomplicated.

"Joe. I am accused of helping myself from time to time to bits of my master's excess funds, which he would insist on leaving out in a very careless manner. It's all a misunderstanding, really."

"It's all misunderstandings, when you get down to it."

"What did you do?"

"Strangled my mother-in-law."

At this, the younger of the two men on the other side of the room emitted a contrived guffaw, announcing with pompous gravity, "You did no such thing. Why must you toy with the boy?" Looking at me, he said, "His name is David McFee. He is not in the least any kind of murderer. What he is, is a footpad, robbing people on the road at night—and a very poor one, I might add. He was caught within hours of his first endeavor."

"You don't know that." This was said by John, or David, with a mixture of incredulity and pique.

"Oh, but I do. I was told it by a guard three days ago when he walked me to my arraignment. The guards are not above gossiping, you know. He thought it very funny and took great relish in telling me it."

"If I do not strangle her, someone else will," said David, looking into the distance and carrying on as if nothing had happened. "She is the very picture of a harpy. I may well do it yet."

"If you are not hanged, that is." The speaker was round of face and rounder of belly, and his unkempt, shoulder-length, brown locks projected at random angles from the sides of a balding dome. Directing his attention to me, he said, "My name is Crusten, Alexander Crusten. I am guilty of no crime, although there are differences of opinion in this matter, concerning the selling of goods said by some to be stolen. Now, how am I to know the history of every item? People bring me things, and I accept them in good faith. I offer fair value. How else is business to be done? There is not a pawnbroker in London who does not do the same. If the goods were indeed stolen, is not the thief the guilty one?"

At this, the other, older, thinner, and entirely bald gentleman came to life. "So you say, Crusten, but if you accept goods from known thieves and have been caught at it before, just what do you expect? And that's not the half of it. Somehow you always seem to know from whom the goods were taken, so you can pose as the hero of lost property and return the goods to their rightful owners for a fee. It's a very clever scheme, until one of your thieves demands a bigger cut and blabs when you are not forthcoming." This was wrapped in a patrician accent, in condescending tones a schoolmaster might use upon a boy of thick brain, at which Mr. Crusten compressed his lips and shook his head.

Rising and offering me his hand, the gentleman said, "Please allow me to introduce myself. I am Eustace Pegsworth. If you don't mind, I would rather not discuss the reasons why I am here. It resulted from a lamentable lapse of discipline I very much regret."

"He is a coiner, and more likely to hang than any of us. What he regrets is being caught. And his name is Robert Deetham." This was enunciated with triumph by David, who had not moved from his spot next the wall. "Crusten is not the only one the guards talk to."

"Really, David, have you no decency? Must we tell every last bit of each other's dirt? What must Joseph think?" But the air had quite gone out of him, and his complaint was without force.

"I expect he thinks he is in Newgate, and no one here can be trusted. Me, I don't care what anyone thinks, least of all you." Having delivered this pronouncement, David threw himself upon his cot and covered his head with his pillow. Mr.

Deetham looked at the wall and Mr. Crusten his feet, and no one seemed inclined to carry the conversation further. I lay down on my cot, wadded my jacket for a pillow, despite its being yet damp from exposure to the rain earlier, and placed the pocket containing my purse again in the center of it. I thought I might sleep, as I had nothing whatsoever else to do, and I was exhausted from the rigors of the previous two days and nights.

XLVIII

THERE CAME A GREAT BANGING on the door, which awakened me shuddering from a deep sleep, and I hovered uncertainly for a moment above the green vales in which I had been wandering, as the window in the door opened and supper was pushed through, a thin stew containing occasional bits of meat and potatoes, a penny loaf of brown bread, and water. The stew was again but lukewarm, the portions scant and the broth watery, but it was wholesome withal and went down easily. It is true we had paid a price for it that would have fetched much more and better at a coffee house or tavern, but I had seen enough to know in the extortionate economy of that place there was no normal or natural relationship between what was paid and that which one received.

The meal was remarkable only for the sterility of its circumspection. My fellows and I sat at the minuscule table and exchanged banalities containing no hint of the sharp exchanges upon my arrival. I asked whether the fare was ever varied, or did we receive the same thing every day? Mr. Deetham then expatiated on the vagaries of prison fare, which tended towards watery soups, stews, and chowders, as these were more amenable to production in quantity, and the contents of which indeed varied, depending on whatever was cheapest in the city's wholesale markets, but that breakfast was almost invariably gruel, though he had seen an egg once. Mr. Crusten was very fond of eggs and wished he could get them. They both thought the weather uncommonly foul, what they could gather of it, anyways, as they could not actually see it from their current lodgings. McFee ate with energy but did not speak. No one said a word about the one pertinent topic, his offense, trial, or prospects.

When the steward and his guard came by to collect the remains of our meal and supply us with another candle, I asked whether it were possible to obtain writing paper and a pencil, and to post a letter, and was told that for a shilling, and another to post the letter, I might indeed. No sooner had he departed, than Crusten brought forth cards and a cribbage board, and, moving the candle to the table, ran a little tournament, which I was soon out of, as I had to be taught how to play the game.

I then lay on my cot listening to the others and the sounds in the building, which carried up and down the corridor, of occasional speech, banging, and once, shouting that soon quelled. Eventually, the cribbage board was put away, and Crusten, McFee, and Deetham lay upon their cots and soon slept, but I lay awake, listening, and reflected that prison was, so far anyways, more tedium than anything, suffused with desperation, to be sure, that one could do nothing about. I wondered where in the vast stone pile Chowder was, how he was doing, and what would become of us. After a very long time, I slept.

In the morning, the steward brought writing paper and a pencil with the gruel, and after breakfast, I wrote to Mr. Duckworth, telling him what had become of me, so he should not think me shiftless, and I gave it to the steward at the midday meal. I experienced an impulse to write to Mr. Jackson, but forbore, as to get a letter from me, especially one originating in Newgate, might inhibit his prospects.

Three days passed thus, with unvarying routine and tedium, except I got better at cribbage to the extent that one can, so much of it being dependent on the chance draw of cards. Early in the morning of the fourth day, McFee was called to his arraignment, from which he returned in less than a half hour, and shortly thereafter Crusten was called out for his trial, from which he did not return. He was replaced soon after our luncheon by another fellow, Jack Bester, who no sooner arrived than he wished to involve us all in games of chance, but Deetham checked him: "We are not your easy marks in the coffee house and have no interest in your schemes." But would he sit down to a game of cribbage, if that was of interest, to which Bester assented. He immediately wished to wager upon it, which Deetham indulged him in, but for no more than a penny a game.

They were playing thus when the door opened, and an older gentleman of slight stature was admitted, who was at first uncertain whether his business was

---

with me or McFee. He was expensively dressed without ostentation, sporting a precise goatee. His eyes were blue, alert, and, perhaps, kind. My identity having been established to his satisfaction, he invited me to huddle with him in the front of the room near the door, where he spoke very near to a whisper, so as not to be overheard. As he spoke, he surveyed the room, keeping his eyes on the other three, who were doing their best to listen and not show it.

"You may call me Mr. Bartlett. I am an associate and friend of Mr. Jackson's and have been sent by him to give you news and advice. He wishes you to know you are not forgotten. He wishes you to know, most emphatically, he had nothing to do with your capture. It seems when Mrs. Cudworth visited the shop and made her unsuccessful attempt, Rowland offered himself as her confederate, and the errand to give you your purse then presented itself as the perfect opportunity. The evening of the day of your capture, Rowland proudly announced to Mr. Jackson he had solved his problem, meaning you, once and for all. I am here to tell you when Mr. Jackson learned the particulars, he was aghast, and they had a titanic row. He threw Rowland out on the spot and vows to never see or speak to him again."

I was some time absorbing the information. "Ah. That is very reassuring. Thank you. Please tell Mr. Jackson I am most grateful for that intelligence. I could not imagine he had had anything to do with it, but neither could I quite construe how it had come about."

"It is impossible to know whether Rowland was so daft he thought Mr. Jackson would, in fact, be pleased, or whether he wished to do injury to the both of you. Or, perhaps, in his eagerness to be rid of you, he simply had not thought it through."

"Indeed. But what of Chowder? Have you any news of Chowder?"

"Chowder spent two days and a night in the hole, but appears to have held his own and survived with little injury apart from a black eye. He is now in a semi-private room such as this, in another wing of the prison, very near, really, as the crow flies. Mr. Jackson is providing the funds to maintain him, as Elspeth has suffered some reversals. It is nothing so very dire, but she has no money to spare at present, so Mr. Jackson gives the money to me, and I deliver the funds to the front office. Mr. Jackson wishes you to know he will not require to be repaid."

I mumbled a heartfelt thanks to be conveyed to Mr. Jackson as Mr. Bartlett continued. "I have seen Chowder this day, just before coming here, in fact, and told him of your situation. He wishes you to know that he is all right, and nothing will shake his regard for you or his affection. He looks forward to much association with you when this lamentable episode has passed."

I stammered out that I wished Mr. Bartlett to convey the very same sentiments to Chowder as soon as he possibly could.

"That I will do, you may be sure. And am I correct to assume that Rowland, despite his wrongdoing, did in fact convey to you your purse?"

Briefly I gave him the particulars of my purse and the depredations upon it.

"You need make no more expenditures in this place. Mr. Jackson pledges to maintain you at your current level as long as necessary. He feels he must make amends. Even though it was Rowland who betrayed you, Mr. Jackson mistakenly placed his trust in him, which he now greatly regrets."

"That is very kind and generous of him, and I am grateful. Please convey to him my most earnest gratitude."

"That I will surely do. Now then, I wish to provide you with some advice regarding your arraignment and trial, which are not far off, the arraignment especially. I have said these very same things to Chowder. Whether you are charged with sodomy or attempted sodomy, gross indecency, insult to the public morality, however they may style it, you must plead not guilty. I can't imagine you would plead guilty, but I cannot leave it unsaid. It has nothing to do with what you and Chowder may have done or not done, and everything to do with your hide and whether you will keep it. To plead guilty to sodomy would be fatal. Now I must speak very plainly, and you will have to forgive me for it. To convict of sodomy, it must be proven beyond any reasonable doubt and attested to by no less than two witnesses, that one of you penetrated the other and spent within him. Without that, there is no sodomy, and you cannot be hanged. Do you understand?"

"I do. I saw Mr. Peevers in court. He pled guilty, and it was a very quick business."

"Indeed it was. And you understand how sodomy is defined, and what must be proven to convict of it?"

"I do. Your explanation is very clear. I am hopeful now. I know Mrs. Cudworth and her daughter spied on us through the keyhole, but the room was cold, and Chowder and I had a blanket over us. They could not possibly have seen what we did, and truth be told, we did not do so very much. I suppose she might lie, though."

"There is that possibility. Be very clear about your story and stick to it. The trial will go very quickly. Keep your wits about you."

"I shall. Thank you."

"It is my pleasure. Now, here is a letter from Mrs. Whidby, attesting to the excellence of your character, that you may use in court." He removed a sealed, single sheet of trifold paper from his waistcoat pocket and gave it to me. "I wish you the very best of luck." I thanked him again, and he rapped on the door. The guard, who had been standing in the corridor in attendance, opened it and let Mr. Bartlett out. I turned to go to my cot and lie down, and saw that the other three were all sitting up, their eyes fastened upon me.

XLIX

ONCE ON MY COT, I looked at Mrs. Whidby's letter. It had been sealed with wax, and written upon it were the words: "FOR THE COURT." I wanted very much to open it, but as it was addressed to the court and not to me, I thought I should not. I tucked it into the inside pocket of my jacket and had but just arranged myself for a nap when the door opened again, and I was summoned to my arraignment.

I was conducted to the end of the corridor, down several flights of stairs, along another very long corridor, and then up several more flights of stairs, when I came to the same pen within the court in which I had seen Mr. Peevers less than two months previously. There I waited while a number of men and one woman went up into the dock to have their charges read, which comprised in the greater part an enumeration of the many unlawful ways to relieve a person of his property, each of which was elaborated in endless variation. There were as well among these one rape and two murders. All pled not guilty. Each of them went up into the dock and back down again, one after another, with as much rapidity as fetters permit. When my name was called, I clambered up the stairs as quickly as I could, to hear the charges against me.

At the judge's direction, the clerk enunciated, in the loud and clear voice which is the primary requisite of the trade, "Joseph Chapman, you are charged with the felonious, wicked, and diabolical sin, against the order of nature and against the statute, too foul to be named among Christian men, called buggery. How do you plead?"

I found myself speaking in a similar manner, if without the clerk's practiced force. "I am very sorry, but if my crime is a thing not to be named, how am I to know just what it is, or how to plead?"

The judge raised his eyebrows to an absurd height and shook his head. The clerk said nothing more, and the judge, looking first at the clerk then at me, after some seconds said, "You will gain nothing by insolence. Do you mean to say you do not know why you are here?" The courtroom had by now grown very quiet.

"Your Grace, I do in fact have some idea. I mean no disrespect."

"Then you cannot be so stupid as to not know there is but one crime described in this manner. Murder, rape, treason, the very most serious of crimes, are all named, but the one of which you are accused goes beyond any of them in its peculiar repugnance."

"If you speak of sodomy, sir, I did not do it. I plead not guilty."

The judge winced and to the clerk said, "Merely record the plea. Do not write the offending word."

In the next instant, I was down from the dock and the next fellow was going up. In the pen, others moved away from me as I sat down. Shortly thereafter, I was led back to my cell by a guard who, however much some of them may have been given to conversing with prisoners in other instances, said not a word to me.

Re-entering the cell, I was assailed by a foul odor, the source of which was soon apparent as I approached my cot to discover it wet, covered by a mess of soft brown lumps, and the bucket in which we relieved ourselves empty and with the lid off, next to it. Crusten, McFee, and Bester lay upon their bunks, feigning indifference, though the stench was inescapable.

"Why ... What is this?" It was a stupid question, but in my shock it came out.

It was McFee who spoke. "As you are so fond of dung, we thought you might enjoy having a little for your pleasure." He held a bottle containing a clear liquid I supposed to be gin, which he lifted to his lips. "Why, do you not like it?" Looking directly at me, challenge and threat in his eyes, he sucked several swallows from his bottle, then passed it to Bester, who did the same, and passed it on to Deetham, who took a polite sip, but did not look at me. Deetham returned the bottle to McFee, who drank again.

I looked at them, aghast, and asked a second stupid question. "How do you get gin?"

Deetham spoke. "The steward brings it from the tap room. Half crown a quart." His manner was mild, and it was clear he would not challenge the others.

Feeling much distress and not knowing what to do, I went to the door and looked out the little window hoping to see a guard, but the corridor was empty. I banged repeatedly on the door, even though I did not expect it to do any good. It gave me something to do and somewhere to look that was not at my cot, or at the other three. It was also as far away from them as I could get in the tiny room.

After perhaps a half hour, during which I maintained my position at the door, and McFee and Bester progressed towards stumbling incoherence, a guard appeared at the end of the corridor. I pounded on the door and called for his attention.

"It's not necessary to make so much noise," he said with practiced carelessness when he arrived at the door.

"They have poured the bucket out all over my cot. Is it possible to have it taken out and another brought in? The room cleaned? Or is it possible to change rooms? If they have done this, I don't know what else they might do."

The guard stroked his chin and said nothing for perhaps half a minute. His demeanor was unperturbed, very mild, but his words, though spoken softly, were not. "I know about you. Pretty well everyone here does now. You will fare no better in any other cell, once your offense becomes known to your cell mates, as it must. But I will see about getting you a new mattress, and some cleaning done."

"Thank you." The guard turned and walked away in as easy and unhurried a manner as it is possible to imagine. Not knowing what else to do, I sat on the floor in the corner nearest the door. The stone floor was very cold, sucking the warmth right out of my seat. McFee and Bester were now passed out. Deetham lay on his back on his cot, but from his breathing, I did not think he was sleeping. Thus the remainder of the afternoon passed, and then dinner and another bottle of gin were brought. Deetham and I sat silently at the table while the other two slept. The steward agreed wholeheartedly that the stench was appalling, and the mattress must be changed out and the room cleaned.

After dinner, McFee and Bester continuing insentient, I paced the front of the room until I tired, then stood, looking out the tiny window in the door, eventually settling onto my haunches, and at last lay upon the floor, which was very cold. I had no blanket and but my jacket for a pillow, for which purpose it was utterly inadequate. I slept not at all. When too cold to bear it, I would get up and stir about and try to warm myself, and then would lie down again from fatigue, no better off than before.

Very late in the night, McFee and Bester awoke and began to work on the next bottle. Very drunk, they made no effort to mask their contempt, tossing curses and invective at me, when not complaining of their own miseries and everyone who had ever wronged them, of which and whom there were a great many. Towards dawn, McFee rose very unsteadily, and began to lurch in my direction, to show me, he said, just what was done to those of my kind, but on his second step, having forgotten his ankles were fettered, and being very drunk, he stumbled and fell heavily to the floor and did not rise. Bester, no more steady than McFee, made to go to him, but on arising from his cot was seized by a paroxysm of vomiting, and spewed very thoroughly upon his chum, himself, and both of their cots, in which I took but little satisfaction.

The following morning, the steward came and went, inescapably having become aware of the night's misadventures. Perhaps half an hour later, a guard opened the door to admit a woman with a mop and bucket and two men bearing fresh blankets, two mattress, and changes of clothes. Bester and McFee, groaning, were helped out of their soiled clothing, washed, and put into fresh britches and shirts while their soiled mattress and bedclothes were removed and bed frames wiped clean, the floor mopped, and the replacement mattresses, blankets, and pillows put into position. Not one of them displayed the slightest awareness of my existence, and when I spoke to ask whether my cot would receive attention as well, I was ignored.

I continued in this condition many days. McFee and Bester lapsed into sullen silence, drinking heavily every few days, being sick between whiles. They now refused to acknowledge my existence, a blessing of sorts, while Deetham maintained an uneasy, brittle politeness, which may have concealed faint hints of apology, or perhaps it was disdain. McFee was then called to his trial, and like Crusten before him, did not return.

He was replaced by one Chester Fawkes, or so he told us, a colorless fellow who spoke very little. He would neither divulge his offense nor reveal the least thing about himself. To his credit, he did not drink, thus depriving Bester of a companion. Bester, perhaps from want of funds, left off drinking and now spent his time on his cot, face to the wall. The mood in the cell was now perhaps slightly less malign, but nothing was done about my cot, and I found myself shunned yet. I took my meals squatting in the corner and slept on the floor as best I could, which is to say not at all. I grew more exhausted by the day, while my cot, though slowly drying, remained unapproachable, even if very slowly it began to stink less.

L

EVER-DEEPENING FATIGUE FOGGED MY MIND, and I lost count of the days. Worse, I developed a deep cough that troubled me sorely. Every muscle, joint, and nerve in my body ached, and all was as in a most unpleasant dream. Perhaps ten days, or perhaps two weeks, had elapsed when I was advised my trial would take place two days hence, and, truly, two days following, immediately after the midday repast, I was taken to the courtroom to face Mrs. Cudworth and the unreasoning hostility of this world.

The courtroom was as crowded as ever, and I waited in the pen while several trials were dispatched, that of a man who had strangled his wife, a woman who had poisoned her husband, and a man who had married a series of wealthy widows, each of whom he relieved of her property before abandoning her in favor of the next. That he had carelessly neglected to become unmarried to any of them as he went along meant that as he stood in the dock, he was in possession of fourteen wives, a rare achievement which failed to impress the judge, and especially his wives, many of whom were in the gallery shouting invective and abuse.

None of these trials took more than half an hour. Following each, the jury huddled in its box for but a few minutes, before invariably returning the verdict of guilty. It was a discouraging prelude, and though I held fast to Mr. Bartlett's counsel and Mrs. Whidby's letter, I was afraid. I was exhausted and ill, dull of mind and filthy of body, having for some weeks slept in the same clothes, and had had no chance to shave, clean myself, or don clean clothing, all of which conspired to make of me a perfect picture of the depraved wretch I was held to be.

Scanning the gallery, I was very pleased to see Mr. Duckworth and Reggie, which heartened me very much. Seeing me look in their direction, Reggie quietly raised his hand, and Mr. Duckworth nodded, slowly and deeply, with grave dignity. I returned their gestures with commensurate gravity and much gratitude. Mr. Bartlett was also present, seated at some reserve, in conversation with an interesting young gentleman whom I did not recognize, very expensively dressed and of refined comportment.

Mrs. Cudworth, for her part, sitting in the area where witnesses waited, looked as fine as she possibly could in her new wig and gown and freshly painted face, but her heavily rouged cheeks lent a startled, feverish aspect to her countenance. She was accompanied by Hortensia, who also wore an expensive gown and coiffure, which yet failed to alleviate the unfortunate disproportion of her features. Rising but little from my seat, I could see them very well. Mrs. Cudworth was speaking to Hortensia with hectoring emphasis, while Hortensia alternately nodded and shook her head. She appeared to be very uncomfortable. Watching them, one would not quite have said that they were at odds, but neither would one have said that they were in agreement.

The jury, deliberating for perhaps two minutes, delivered the verdict of guilty upon the bigamist, and I was then called to the dock. The judges shuffled their positions, the one who had presided over the previous three trials retiring, and another moving to the center from his position at the side. The clerk retired for a very few minutes, then retook his station. Papers were shuffled and arranged, and the judge nodded to the clerk, who read my name, and, using the same language he had at my arraignment, read out my crime, which, deprived of a proper name, is placed not at the extreme of the moral order, but wholly outside of it, unimaginable, and without referent.

The wizened judge, in wig and robes too large for him, whom I later learned was named Overbury, then began in a reedy, high-pitched voice, which nevertheless bore no uncertain authority. "Now we have before us a case of diabolical wickedness, in which two young men of surpassing arrogance, Joseph Chapman and Potter Gorham, thinking they know better than God and the Law, willfully and with extreme wantonness defied the statute, the order of nature, and Nature's God. They were observed in the act by the sober and upstanding wife of a greengrocer, unfortunate master of Gorham, and her daughter. We will now try Chapman. The clerk will call the prosecutor and first witness."

The clerk barked out, "Mrs. Tobias Cudworth."

Mrs. Cudworth made her way from the waiting area to the witness box, into which she settled with a flounce, looking about the courtroom. The judge then addressed her.

"Do you swear to tell the truth, the whole truth, and nothing but the truth?"

"I do."

"Will you please tell us your name?"

"I am Dulcibella Cudworth."

"And your situation?"

"I am the wife of Tobias Cudworth, greengrocer, in Spittlefields. Mr. Cudworth is master to Potter Gorham, with whom Joseph Chapman engaged in the unspeakable acts."

"Thank you. Now, will you please tell us of the events of this past October eleventh, that are pertinent to the charges today against Mister Chapman?"

"I will be pleased to. But first, may I say that an attempt was made to bribe me to change my story and say it was all a misunderstanding?" She looked about the courtroom, taking in her audience, her strident voice sounding very like a rusty gate hinge, flapping in a gale. "I was offered fifty pounds. A gentleman unknown to me offered me it as I walked home from church last Sunday. I'll have you know I refused it! I am an honest woman. I seek no advantage." She fluttered her eyelashes at the judge and offered an obsequious smile.

"You are indeed to be commended. And if you would now please tell us of the events of October eleventh?"

"Yes, of course. I seek only to do what God and our King have commanded us. I seek only to see the right upheld and the law obeyed." She nodded and smiled, with idiot affectation, I thought.

"Very good. Now, if you would simply tell us what you saw, the court will appreciate it very much."

"Yes. I saw them kiss and pet each other. It was loathsome and horrible. You cannot imagine it. Every fiber of my being rebelled against it. But I forced myself to look, to be certain of what I saw. I thought to myself, I will take it upon myself to bring them to justice. I will—"

"Yes, loathsome indeed. And again, you are to be commended. Did you see anything else?"

"I saw them fornicating, as after the manner of a man and woman. Looking at it, I thought I might faint from the shock, but, as I say, I forced myself to look, so that I might bear witness to their wickedness."

"When you say fornicating, is it possible for you to state precisely what you witnessed? I ask not for indelicacy, but for plain evidence the jury may use to consider its verdict."

"I am a married woman. I have two living daughters and two boys who sleep in the ground. I do believe I know the act when I see it. The motion of the hips. There was no mistaking it. It was this young Chapman, making the motions upon his fellow, who received it with a wickedness I did not know existed in this world. I tell you, it was the most horrible and loathsome thing I have ever seen. How I wish I had never witnessed it! Why, I— "

The judge again cut her short. "Thank you. Is there anything more you can tell us?"

"Well, I, he kept it up until he spent, of that there was no doubt either. The heaving and gasping, there was no mistaking it. I was never so shocked or dismayed in all my life. I have been distressed ever since. I cannot sleep for thinking of it. I am a proper Christian woman. I go to church every Sunday, and I—"

"Yes, yes, very well, and thank you. And your daughter, how much of this did she witness?"

"All of it. I motioned her to come and look and we took turns watching."

"Took turns?"

"It was necessary to peep through the keyhole into his chamber. Gorham's. And not so easy to see, either, as the angle was not quite right, and the room very dim. Chowder has but a single candlestick—"

The judge, hastening to interrupt her yet again, said very firmly, "That will be all, thank you."

Mrs. Cudworth was left gaping, and the judge now looked at me, but it was not clear what he wanted, so I returned his gaze with a quizzical attitude. After a moment he spoke. "Mister Chapman, you may now question the witness."

"Right. Thank you." I had not known of this.

Mrs. Cudworth sat bolt upright in her seat, a scowl of irritation on her face. "Must I be subjected to this? I have given my testimony. He is but a criminal, an object of contempt. He is nothing."

The judge spoke soothingly. "Yes, you must. This is a court of law, and this is England. Until convicted, the accused have rights. Should you ever be accused of a crime, the same rights would pertain to you. Would protect you."

"Me? Accused of a crime? But that is impossible. Why would you say such a thing?"

"Ma'am, if you would simply answer his questions, if he has any for you, it will be over much sooner. He must remain in the dock and cannot approach you. And yes, it is absolutely required."

"I suppose then, if I must." She emitted a great sigh, as if there were no more onerous task in all the world.

The judge nodded to me, and I began. "Mrs. Cudworth, you have said that it was not easy to see through the keyhole, that the angle was not quite right, and that the room was lit by but a single candle. That being so, how can you be so very certain," and here I was taken by a fit of coughing, "... of what you saw?"

"Because I am not an idiot." She tossed her head to indicate she thought I was one.

"The room was cold. Chowder and I were under a blanket the entire time. Was it not late on a chill and foggy afternoon, and were we not under a blanket?"

"I do not recall the weather. I saw no blanket. I saw the two of you very plainly."

"So plainly, you could not discern whether we were under a blanket or not, as I say we were. Very plainly you saw us, but the room was dim, and you have yourself admitted you could not see at all well because the angle through the tiny keyhole was not good."

"Hmph!"

"Now, it is plain that you are very concerned with the behavior of others. Perhaps, as the judge has said, you are to be commended. But I ask you, how can you have so little concern for your daughter's well-being, but you insist she witness what you believe to be depravity? What does it say of you that you apply yourself to a keyhole with the greatest assiduity and must drag your daughter into it? As a loving parent, would you not keep from her the knowledge of such things?"

"If she is to be a solider for Christ, she must prepare herself to endure shock and abuse. If we are to rid the world of evildoers such as yourself, we cannot shy away from the battle. I do not raise her to be coward or fool." Again she tossed her head, to indicate her contempt.

"As a humble greengrocer's wife, how do you array yourself thus, so far above your station? Did you not, with Rowland Hunter, take from my purse, when it was in his possession?"

Mrs. Cudworth's eyes for a moment grew wide, as if from fear, and her mouth opened, but no sound came out. The judge waved his hand. "That is not relevant to this prosecution, though it may be to another. Mrs. Cudworth, you may ignore the question."

"In that case, I can think of no more questions. Thank you," said I.

To Mrs. Cudworth the judge said, "Thank you. You are excused," and to the clerk, "The clerk will call the next witness."

The clerk then fairly bellowed, "Miss Hortensia Cudworth!"

As Mrs. Cudworth made her way back to the witness's waiting area, she passed Hortensia coming forward, and said, loudly enough for the entire court to hear, "Now, mind what I told you and don't forget!" Hortensia said nothing, but scowled and shook her head. She clutched a paper on which many tiny words were written, and seated herself in the witness box simply, without the flouncing her mother had done. She was no more than fourteen, and, as I have mentioned, of overhanging lip, buck teeth, and very thick brow. She squinted at the paper in her hands and seemed to want to shrink into herself.

The judge began, "Now, my dear, do you swear to tell the truth, the whole truth, and nothing but the truth?"

"Well, I, I must, mustn't I? Yes."

She seemed very uncertain, and the judge raised an eyebrow. "Please tell us your name."

"I am Hortensia Cudworth." She spoke very softly.

"You will have to speak up, my dear, if we are to hear you. Now, if you would tell us of your situation."

"My situation?" She spoke but very slightly louder.

"You are the daughter of Tobias and Dulcibella Cudworth, are you not?"

"Yes."

"Very good. And you were present in your home on October eleventh last, and with your mother witnessed something that has led us all to be here in this courtroom today?"

"Yes."

"Will you please tell us what you saw?"

"Yes. I remember very clearly it was the day we were to go to the Greengrocer's Ball. I was looking forward to it very much. But father drank too much at lunch and mother was angry with him, so Father and Prudencia, she's my older sister, went to the ball, but mother and I stayed home. I didn't see why I should not go as well, but mother insisted I stay home with her, which I did not want to do."

"Very well, and did you see this young man in the dock, there, do anything he ought not to have done?"

"Yes. Well, that is, I think so."

"You think so? Pray tell us, what did you see?"

"We heard Chowder, that's Potter, but nobody calls him that, come in with his chum, Joe. I heard Chowder call him by that name. They had been to see Mr. Peevers hanged. Chowder was showing Joe around, as Joe had not visited, or at least not come inside before. So then we heard Chowder say some things about my mother that were not very nice. He said Mum put on airs and would do no work, because she thought herself very grand, even though she is but a greengrocer's wife. I don't know. It's not true, of course, but I can see why he might think so, as Mother can sometimes be very particular. She has very high standards, and why should she not? I like Chowder, or I might if he would say hello to me sometimes, but he never does. He does not know I exist, or he pretends I do not. I don't know. He does work very hard, though, and Father has no cause for complaint."

"My dear, you must get to the point. We do not have all day."

"Sorry. Well, anyway, Mum did not like what Chowder said about her. We heard Chowder and Joe go into Chowder's chamber and close the door, and after some time Mother and I went into the kitchen as we wanted a bite to eat. Mother told me to be quiet, and she got down and peeped at the keyhole to Chowder's chamber. She was a very long time looking. Then she waved to me to come look." Hortensia held the paper very tightly, and her hands were shaking.

"Yes, yes, and what did you see when you looked? That is what we need you to tell us."

"Well, I could not see at all well. But I could see a little bit, and I thought it very odd." She paused and screwed up her face. "They were indeed under a blanket—" At which instant, Mrs. Cudworth called out,

"No, no! They were not! You must read from the paper!"

The judge rapped his gavel and barked, "No outbursts! We will have her testimony, from her, and it cannot be influenced by you!"

Mrs. Cudworth stood up, saying urgently, "But she does not know what to say!"

The judge was severe. "Sit down! Do you not realize it is a crime to influence the testimony of witness? Your outburst is intolerable."

"But—"

"No more! If you persist, I shall remove you from the courtroom. As it is, you risk the charge of tampering with a witness. It makes no difference that she is your own daughter."

Mrs. Cudworth waved her arms, gasped and gaped, a look of astonishment on her face, and sat down only when the tipstaff began striding in her direction.

To Hortensia, who was trembling in the witness box, the judge said, with gentle curiosity, "Now, my dear, what is that paper you hold?"

"It is what I am to say here." Her voice was very faint.

"And who wrote it?"

"Mother did."

The judge sighed, shook his head, and said under his breath, "Dear me." Then to Hortensia, again with gentleness, "May I have it, please?"

One of the gentlemen sitting in the well before the bench rose to take the paper from Hortensia and handed it to the judge, who took it and spent half a minute reading it. He made no remark upon it, however, and again addressed Hortensia.

"Now, my dear, when you were examined by the magistrate, when Potter Gorham was arrested, you agreed with your mother in every detail as to what you had seen. That is what is written on this paper and what your mother has told us here today. Do you now mean to say that, in fact, the truth of what you saw is not the same?"

"Well, I ... I don't know ..." She buried her face in her hands.

"It's all right, my dear. You may have a minute to collect yourself. When you do speak, I wish you to recall that to tell the truth is one of our Lord's commandments. Not only that, but the King is most concerned everyone tell the truth in court, especially in court. I do not presume to come between you and your parents, but your duty to God and King cannot be forgotten. Does not your mother desire you to serve God and your King?"

Hortensia heaved several gasping sobs and struggled to regain her composure. "Yes, of course she does." But where before she had looked frequently at her mother, she now did not.

"So, if we may resume, will you please now tell us in your own words, the very truth of what you saw through that keyhole? And if you would please speak only of what you saw through the keyhole."

She shuddered, then discovered a firmness of tone that had not been evident until that moment. "Yes, well, as I was about to say, I thought it very odd two men should kiss each other. I could see that much. But as Chapman has said, they were under a blanket. I could see motion under the blanket, but I could not tell what they were doing."

"Is that all? You saw them kiss?"

"I don't know. Yes. I saw them kissing, then Mother looked again for a long time. And then she bade me look again, but now they were just lying in each other's arms. Like I say, I don't know. I thought it as pretty a picture of friendship as could be imagined. They were very sweet to each other. I mean, I know it is very horrible and everything, but if one did not know that, one might think differently. Just based on what little I saw, I mean." Now she sat very calmly, looking straight ahead, not at anyone or anything.

"And you saw nothing more?"

"No, I did not."

"Very well. Now I must ask you, why did you say otherwise when examined by the magistrate?"

"Mother said we must bring them to justice, and if I would help her by saying what she told me to, she would be very grateful. She said I should definitely go to the next ball. And then she bought me this dress and wig, that I might wear them today and at the ball later."

The judge shook his head and heaved a sigh. "And what caused you to provide this truer version here this afternoon?"

"I don't know. I suppose it was being sworn. It's very grave and serious, isn't it? But I have been thinking about it anyway. Mother and Father have always said I should be honest, but now Mother is saying something different, really, and it is very confusing. She seems to care more that they are punished than she does about the truth, or at least the truth of what I saw. I don't know what she saw. But I do know what I saw. Anyway, now I have told the truth indeed, and I am glad of it."

The judge nodded, but whether in sincere appreciation or simply for want of another gesture, I could not say. What he said was, merely, "I see. Well, Mr. Chapman, do you have any questions for the witness? I warn you only questions pertinent to your charge will be allowed, nor will indelicate statements be permitted."

"Your Grace, I thank you and her. I do not."

"Hortensia, you may leave the box."

Mrs. Cudworth, rigid with fury, pointedly ignored Hortensia as she, trembling afresh, returned to her mother's side.

Judge Overbury took a large swallow from the glass on his table and now addressed me. "Well, Mr. Chapman, what have you to say for yourself? Have you anyone who will speak to your good character? Can you refute Mrs. Cudworth's testimony? This is your opportunity to be heard."

"Thank you." I spent some time coughing, then, "I believe Hortensia, who is to be commended as very brave, has made my points. Chowder and I were under a blanket, and Mrs. Cudworth has invented her story to suit her own purposes, as she

---

cannot have seen what we were about."

The judge stared at me with a penetrating gaze. "I must ask you, then, just what were you about? Surely if you and he were kissing, you were in the midst of something very wicked and unnatural indeed."

"I do not find my love unnatural," I returned. Here the judge shook his head emphatically and appeared as if he might speak, but I continued. "But I suppose that is not the point. There was no sodomy, sorry, I mean, no buggery. I did not enter him, nor he me, not then nor ever. We have never done that." Here I did depart from the exact and entire truth, as, in fact, there was very little that two male bodies could be made to do together in pleasure that we had not tried at least once, but in fact we had not done it on that day, and I felt no obligation to incriminate myself unnecessarily, and no compunction at failing to do so.

The judge shook his head. "You have made your point with respect to the statute, but I warn you not to trumpet your depravity. It is a grave insult to decency, and we will not entertain a single second of it."

"I have no desire to offend the sensibilities of the court. I will speak no more of it."

The judge regarded me for some moments as if deciding whether to quash me further, or just what to say. When he did speak, he said, simply and with surprising mildness, "Have you anyone to attest to your good character?"

"I have a letter from my master's, that is to say, my former master's, housekeeper." I drew Mrs. Whidby's missive from my pocket. A gentleman rose from the well, took the letter from me and handed it to the judge.

Breaking the seal, the judge looked over the letter, then read aloud, "I am Mrs. Annabelle Whidby, housekeeper to Thomas Jackson, Esq. It has been my pleasure to know Joseph Chapman the better part of this year. In all that time I have never witnessed him do anything dishonest or unsavory. I know him to be of the finest character. He is honest, hard-working, and most considerate. It is simply not possible he could be given to the heinous vice of which he is accused."

The judge looked up from the letter and frowned. "This means merely that you were successful in concealing your unnatural proclivities from her."

"No, she says that my character is of the finest. Had I me a wench, would I expose the good woman to our fumblings? It is no different."

"It is utterly different. It is—you are—at best a repulsive spectacle of failed differentiation."

"Our only failure was in not covering the keyhole, which, had Mrs. Cudworth a proper respect for the privacy of others, would not have been necessary, and none of this would now be under consideration. What one does in one's own chamber behind closed doors is no spectacle."

"Is God not with you even there? And if He is offended, so is the Crown, and the statute. There will be no argument on the subject. Now, how is it that your master does not appear or at least provide a letter of reference? Does it not speak ill of you that he offers nothing on your behalf?"

"There is no doubt he would testify to my good character, as does Mrs. Whidby, but he wishes no association because of the moral nature of the crime of which I am accused. He is in a position of some prominence and cannot be too careful."

"So you say." He took another large swallow. "Well then, is there anything else you have to say or offer in your own defense?"

"I will only repeat Mrs. Cudworth's testimony is not to be trusted. She saw little and invented much, to what end we can only speculate, and in any event is but one witness. Hortensia has given the true account. Beyond that, I suppose I am done."

Neglecting to acknowledge my statement, Judge Overbury now addressed the jury, saying, "The charge is the odious and bestial crime of buggery. The jury must consult its conscience as to whether the charge has been proven. Whatever the jury decides, the defendant is without question an unrepentant degenerate, and in the course of testimony sufficient has been admitted to by him to convict him of a lesser crime or crimes. Now, if you would please be quick about your business, we have quite a bit more to get through before this day is done."

There was a recess of no more than five minutes, while the jury huddled and buzzed, at one point consulting with the judge. I turned to see whether Mr. Duckworth, Reggie, and Mr. Bartlett and his associate were still present, as I had had my back to the galley when in the dock, and they were. Reggie nodded to me to indicate that I had done well, or as well as anyone could have. Then the juryman indicated the jury had concluded its business and was prepared to deliver its verdict. I was sent back into the dock, and the judge made the query.

As a lot, the jury were unprepossessing, appearing in sore want of coffee and a square meal. The one who rose to speak was short, thin, very bald, and wore spectacles. "With respect to the crime of which the defendant is accused, that of buggery, we find the defendant not guilty. We do find him guilty, however, of assault with sodomitical intent and gross indecency." With that, he wiped his brow and sat down.

Judge Overbury said, "There you have it. Sentencing will be at five, following two more trials. Mister Chapman, you may stand down."

I returned to the pen. I asked if I might use the W.C. and was led down the

---

stairs and halfway back to Newgate, where the facility was to be found off the passageway. Following this, I returned to the pen and waited, paying no attention to the goings on around me. I was elated, on the one hand, to be relieved of the fatal charge, and yet very concerned as to just what punishments might be levied for the lesser crimes of which I was now convicted.

The two remaining trials of the afternoon, of an embezzler and a swindler who promoted elaborate, ruinous schemes, had little to distinguish them, and at last it was time to pronounce the sentences. The dock would not hold all of us, so we stood in our places in the pen while the sentences were read by the various judges who had presided over each of our trials. The murderers were to be hanged by the neck until dead, and the bigamist, embezzler, and swindler to be banished and transported. As for me, Judge Overbury read out,

"Joseph Chapman, for the crime of assault with sodomitical intent, and for gross indecency—and, I might add," and here he peered intently in my direction, "for your insolent defense of repellent vice, you are sentenced to stand one hour in the pillory in Charing Cross, at a time suitable to the convenience of the Watch and the prison authorities."

LI

THE PILLORY! IT PROMISES NOT the inevitable fatality of the noose, but the severity of public excoriation, survival of which is not guaranteed, is but little to be preferred. Of all the crimes which might lead one thither, those of a sodomitical nature, even if not involving the very act itself, inspire the mob to its worst excesses, wherein it is liable to leave off throwing dead cats, putrefied offal, rotten fruit, and turds, and take up broken bottles, cobbles, and bricks, with grievous injury, madness, or death sometimes the result. In the days that followed my sentencing, I suffered much apprehension in consideration of it.

Following my trial, I was not taken to my former cell, but to another very similar in a different wing of the prison, where I passed perhaps two weeks amidst indifferent cell-mates, who, like me, had been convicted and were awaiting disposition. In contrast to the insults and depredations I had suffered previously, these three merely refused to speak to me or indeed to acknowledge me in any way, which, as they were very coarse and stupid, drinking every evening and telling pointed tales of fighting and wenching, I counted as a blessing. In every other respect, the routine was as before, but I now again had a cot no more filthy than anyone else's, that one could sleep upon, and it felt like a great luxury. The first night upon it, I slept very hard and long, and as a result of being able to sleep, slowly began to recover from my illness.

Three days on from my trial, in the afternoon, Mr. Bartlett and the gentleman who had accompanied him to my trial visited me, and the three of us were escorted to a small room at the end of the corridor, where a guard waited outside the door, and we were able to sit around a table and converse without consideration of the other inmates. Mr. Bartlett introduced the gentleman as Mr. Broughton, who was very gracious.

"I hope you do not mind my tagging along, and I hope it will not seem presumptuous of me, but since Mr. Jackson first told me of your misadventure, I have been very interested and concerned." He was no more than thirty, and his high forehead and intelligent eyes, gentle demeanor, and impeccable dress reminded me somewhat of Mr. Jackson, but his almost feminine softness was much in contrast to Mr. Jackson's crisp precision. His nose was large and his mouth small, but the effect was not unpleasant. I found him and his gentle comportment very appealing.

"Not at all," said I. "I am very happy to meet you, and if I ever may be of service in any capacity, I invite you to mention it."

"Thank you," he smiled. "I will remember that kind offer. For the moment, my intention is simply to meet you and see whether I might be of any service to you. You see, I am extremely sympathetic towards you, as I am towards all who share our nature. I must say, you conducted yourself admirably at your trial. I am not sure I would have had the same presence of mind had I been in the dock. But, I am talking too much. Mr. Bartlett has news I am sure you will want to hear."

Mr. Bartlett leaned forward and spoke earnestly. "Chowder's trial was yesterday, and we knew you would want to know of it. Mrs. Cudworth stuck to her guns and repeated every word of her odious testimony, with quite the same idiotic protestations, but Hortensia did not appear. Mrs. Cudworth said she regretted it greatly, but Hortensia was indisposed, very likely, I should think, from the beating Mrs. Cudworth gave her, though I do not know it for a fact. We were not far behind the two of them when they left the courthouse following your trial, and my God, but she laid into her the instant they were out the door, with the most profane and insulting abuse one could imagine. Hortensia was an ingrate, a slattern, a foolish, damned little tart, Mrs. Cudworth would throw her wig and gown into the fire, then beat her to a bloody pulp, and much more I need not repeat. It quite put the lie to the picture of the good Christian woman Mrs. Cudworth painted of herself when in the witness box.

"I suspect in her ignorance, Mrs. Cudworth believed she would prevail with Hortensia out of the way, not knowing two witnesses are required to convict, so it was very rich indeed when the judge asked the clerk to read the transcript of Hortensia's testimony from your trial. Overbury is no friend of ours, but he upholds the process of the law, such as it is, and as he knows it, which is not true for all of them. Chowder defended himself very ably, much as you did, and would not call it depravity, which quite put Overbury out. There was no one other than Elspeth to testify to Chowder's good character, which was absurd, but the result was no different. He stands now convicted of the same two crimes as are you, with the same sentence, which we expect to be effected within a very few days. I think it very likely they will put you up together, to be done with you the sooner, and the better to manage the mob."

"Up together?"

There is a two-man pillory at Charing Cross. It rotates about a pole, and you are made to walk about so that the mob may see you from all sides. They talk about a kiss being diabolical, but here is the thing itself."

"What we want you to know," Mr. Broughton leaned in, "Is that you will not be without friends in that mob. Mr. Jackson, Mr. Duckworth, and I—yes, I am a friend of them both—are organizing a corps of mounted and armed men which we hope to interpose between you and the worst of the mob. There will be mounted military officers in authority to enforce order, but they cannot be trusted. And there are hundreds, if not thousands, of mollies in this city who are up in arms, a great many of whom will be on hand. Already there are skirmishes in the streets between them and the whores, who find our preferences insulting. Tumult and disorder are spreading, and the Crown is in a panic to get you up and back down before it spills over into general rioting."

"The Crown? I had no idea."

"Chowder and you are much in the papers, and there are broadsides and ballads circulating, and more every day. Here, I brought one." He produced from his pocket a sheet of paper, which he unfolded. At the top was a crude woodcut of two men in the same bed, looking at each other with lascivious intent, or perhaps it was merely indigestion, and below the words,

> Chowder and Joe are two pretty men,
> They lay in bed till well past ten.
> In each other's arms they find delight,
> We find, say they, buggery just right!

We have no need of the female sex,
On them we put a mighty hex
The love of men we much prefer
To a fine arse we will defer!

There were several more stanzas, each worse than the last, and by the end of it, Chowder and I were dancing amidst the flames of Hell whilst triumphant whores looked on, but I do not care to write it.

I returned the paper to Mr. Broughton. "People buy these?"

"A penny each, or nine pence a dozen, yes, and it isn't just execrable verse. The papers are full of it, too." He produced a copy of the *Morning Chronicle*, which on the first inside page featured the headline "Insolence of Degenerates" above an article making much of our lack of contrition, and exhorting right-thinking readers to turn out for the pelting. "And there are sermons." He pulled a small sheaf of printed paper from another pocket and showed it to me. Across the top was the title, *The Spreading Stain*.

"This was preached in the City just this last Sunday. The priest is emphatic the spread of unnatural vice, if not checked, will destroy England. He fails to specify by just what mechanism the destruction will be achieved, but gaps in logic are no impediment to his hostility. He is adamant we must give our all to pushing the vice back where it came from, wherever that may be, and cleanse England of it forever by whatever means necessary."

"I am speechless."

"Indeed," said Mr. Bartlett. "As an invidious popular prejudice, it has few equals. But do not be disheartened. Not everyone thinks this way, and we are here in proof of it."

"How can I ever thank you? I would be defenseless without your aid."

"Continue breathing and have faith Chowder and you will get through it. That will be thanks enough. Now we must go, but you have not seen the last of us."

I thanked them again, we said good-bye, and the two gentlemen departed. I was then conducted back to my cell, where another week passed in an uneasy mixture of tedium and disquiet. I did not know from one day to the next when I might be taken up, and had learned well enough that to query the guards was useless. One to whom I did mention it said he did not know, because it did not come through his department, but was a function of the Watch. "There's much to arrange," he said. "If they have not got everything and everyone in order, it becomes a general riot, and you would not be the only one to fail to survive."

LII

As Mr. Bartlett had predicted, I had not long to wait. Shortly after breakfast on Tuesday of the following week, a month and a day after I first had been taken, two guards entered the cell and told me to come with them. "How would you like to go home tonight?" said one of them. "There're just a few small details to take care of, then you will be free to go."

"I know what's in store," said I, rising from my cot. "You speak as if I need only sign some paper or pay a small fee."

He responded with a caustic tone. "You are the bright one, are you not? In fact, we do stop at the business office," and he led me down the corridor towards the stairs at the end.

At the business office downstairs, I did indeed sign discharge papers. I was about to pay the eighteen shillings and ten pence discharge fee, when the ancient clerk, having found me in his ledger, stopped me. "Wait, your fee is pre-paid. Very unusual. We do not see that often."

I feigned ignorance. "Indeed? I am grateful for it. But I have a question. If a man dies in prison, is there a discharge fee?"

"What? No. Who would pay it?"

"That is my point. Now, if a man dies in the pillory, is the discharge fee refunded?" I don't know what I was on about. I could not comprehend, nor bear to think on, what was about to happen and was grasping for anything to distract myself. A foolish objection seemed just the thing, but the clerk took the question seriously, scratching his chin in consideration.

"Very few die, really, although they do get fairly well banged up, you know, covered in dung and such. You'll be all right, most likely. Although buggers like you do get the worst of it. Keep your eyes closed tight."

"Ah, thanks. Very reassuring. But what of the fee?"

"It is never refunded. Cannot be. You are indeed leaving the prison. The Watch operates the pillory, so we are done with you the moment you step out of the wagon. If you then die, it is no concern of ours."

"I see. Well, what if——"

"That's enough nonsense. Come along now." It was one of the guards, who had lost patience. I was hustled to the end of the corridor and out the door into the same rear courtyard by which I had entered, where a small prison wagon awaited, just a team of four and a wagon with bars up the sides, and a narrow bench in the center of the wagon's bed, upon which sat Chowder. He looked much as I suppose I did, unshaven, anxious, and drawn. He had lost weight, and his left eye was adrift in a sea of old bruise. Despite this, he brightened when he saw me, and as I was ushered into the cart, extended his arms to me, as I extended mine to him.

"Joe, I——" he began, when the guard struck our wrists with his truncheon.

"None of your filthiness, now! Be quiet and sit back to back on the bench, so you may be tied."

Having no choice, we did as we were told, whereupon the guard tied us tightly, lashing us around the arms from waist to shoulders so we could not move, and could but scarcely breathe. No sooner were we so fastened, than two guards sat with us and prevented us from speaking. The driver and two more guards mounted the seat in front, and we began to move towards the gate, which opened before us. We were preceded and followed by pairs of uniformed, mounted guards carrying conspicuous rifles, and flanked by another pair, one on either side. Once we gained the street, the horses took up a trot, and we moved with dispatch down Old Bailey to Ludgate, where we turned and followed Fleet Street into the Strand. At first, I saw no more traffic than usual, but perhaps halfway down the Strand we began to find ourselves the target of jeers and not a few thrown bottles and stones. A hostile mob soon clogged the street, and we made forward progress only because the mounted pair in front were very aggressive, shouting out to make way and time and again cracking their whips over the heads of the mob.

After perhaps an hour, during which time the thin ropes with which we were tied bit savagely, we reached Charing Cross, where the pillory stood in the midst of a noisy and chaotic mob. It was cold, and the leaden sky threatened rain, but the mob filled the square. Thousands were present, and every one of them seemed to be in a state of agitation, gesticulating, jeering, and shouting, making altogether a roiling roar akin to that at Mr. Peevers's hanging, but sharper and more savage.

A great many carried buckets of unnamable slop, held stained, unkempt packages, or were draped with maggot-dripping braces of dead rats or cats, while numerous piemen, gin sellers, and vendors of ballads and broadsides competed with those selling rotten meat. The stench was as appalling as it was omnipresent. We reached the pillory only after much labor on the part of the guards, who alternately fired shots into the air and cracked their whips, each volley gaining us perhaps a score of yards.

The pillory was mounted on a platform about ten feet high, and consisted of a double set of boards, with holes for one's head and hands, suspended from a central pole, so they might rotate as the persons to be excoriated, facing in opposite directions, walked about in a tight circle, exposing all sides of themselves to the fury of the mob. Chowder and I were untied and taken from the cart, but remained fettered so we could take but half steps, and we were made to mount the short flight of stairs to the platform.

As we rose and came into view, the mob emitted a great roar, which grew louder yet as Chowder and I were brought to the boards and made to place our heads and hands in the lower half of the holes, so that when the upper board was lowered in place, we were caught. I thought it absurd that the man operating the mechanism lowered the top half of the boards with care, as if he wished not to pinch us, when the entire point of the exercise was degradation and pain.

Below us spread the slavering mob, an ocean of rudest clamor, shouting insults and curses, thousands of faces distorted by hatred and lust for cruelty and blood, but such was the din that we could but rarely make out just what was shouted, even by those at our feet. Nearby six uniformed men on horseback observed, and at a greater distance another six or so mounted, men, cowled and their faces black, picked their way through the mob, working their way closer to us. The base of the platform was ringed by uniformed armed guards, I suppose to keep the mob from climbing the platform and tearing us to pieces. There were as well three guards on the platform with us, but well to the side, to what purpose I could not imagine, and all the windows in the buildings nearby were crowded with people watching.

I have described the physical situation and arrangements, but these material aspects were less real to me than the hatred and rage spewing forth from the mob, which I could feel in my heart. Let them throw at me what they will, there was already a bludgeon to my soul. I do not deny I was very afraid, but fear was the least of it. The collapse of the heart, the dejection and futility, the melancholic despair was implanted and the hurt done before the first turd landed. All of the encouragement I had received from Mr. Jackson and others seemed a very frail thing to hold against the fury of these thousands, and as bad as it was for myself, it was worse that Chowder should have to endure it, and I could do nothing for him.

No sooner were we locked in, than a shot was fired, and it began. "Walk about, now," said one of the guards, and to make his point struck Chowder and I smartly on our backs with his truncheon, so we began to walk and thereby rotate. I held my head down, where I was astonished to see roses landing about my feet, and in looking up saw nearest the platform perhaps a score of young men holding bouquets, from which they were pulling red roses to toss at Chowder and me.

As I watched, however, these were set upon by screaming gaggles of rude, overly painted women wearing rags and as many rough men, quite their equal in coarseness. A brawl erupted, in which the flower bearers did no little credit to themselves, but, vastly outnumbered, they were soon beaten down and pushed aside, whereupon the victors brought forward many buckets of putrid slop and excrement, which with great zeal, they, the women especially, and using their bare hands, set flying in our direction.

I closed my eyes for fear they should be put out by a rock, thorn, or claw of dead rat or cat, numbers of which now lay about my feet, but not before I saw the mob was in great tumult, fistfights and brawling everywhere, and shouting and screams, and here and there a shot of gunfire.

Not long after I had closed my eyes, I was hit by in my lower back by what must have been a bottle of gin, as it was very solid and hurt not a little. It smashed when it bounded off me and hit one of the metal stanchions ringing the platform, and I could smell the spirits. I was increasingly hit by other hard objects, rocks and bits of cobble, perhaps, while the continuous onslaught of stinking, softer material continued unabated, thickly coating us all 'round. Something heavy, hard, and sharp hit my forehead with much force, causing an augmentation of pain that by degrees began to render me insensible, even as I began to experience a curious exhilaration that had no sense to it. I then heard a clatter and several shots very near, even as Chowder gave out a sudden "Oof!" I opened my eyes but a moment to see many rocks and broken cobbles about our feet, and Chowder slumped, no longer walking or supporting his own weight.

I cannot explain what happened next. I know only I was no longer in the pillory, nor in Charing Cross, nor in London, nor anywhere at all in this thin tissue of earthly life we witlessly accept as real. Instead, I floated incorporeal in a cerulean infinity, whilst down and to my left, radiating with stupendous intensity, was an orb, brilliant and incorruptible as the midsummer sun. I knew, without knowing how I knew, that orb was my very soul, effulgent, perfect, requiring nothing, indestructible and eternal. Though they destroy my body, they touch me not, for here is the truer reality.

And I saw away in the distance another sun, these two co-orbiting, and it was Chowder's soul. He and I were and are devoted eternally, say what you will. It changed me forever. My hurt and fear vanished, and I understood the mob as I might a raging infant that had soiled itself or a dog that ate its own spewing, knowing no better, for all of us are of this radiant, perfect, and incorporeal nature, though we know it not. I saw, too, that reciprocation of hatred is unnecessary. In spewing curses and throwing filth at me with their bare hands, the mob had become utterly bedaubed, and well enough said.

LIII

SLOWLY, AND BY MINUTE DEGREES, I became aware of the unaccountable possession of corporeal flesh, bearing its messages of pain. Hands lifted my head from the trough in which my neck had lain, and lowered my hands, no longer captured but entirely numb, to my sides. My vision was yet turned inward, witnessing the supernal radiance, and my ears thickly coated. I heard not. I did not know who, where, or even what I was. My body was carried from the platform and down the stairs, where it was lifted up and laid down in what would have been the bed of a cart, straw thrown over it. Stay down, I may have heard someone say, and the cart began to move. The jostling slowly caused the celestial vision to fade, and in reciprocation obdurate flesh to assert its claims, until concept and memory returned, and I knew wretchedness.

I attempted to open my eyes but could not. In bringing my hands to my face, I found it thickly encrusted, as was every part of me. I wiped my eyes with straw, and was able then to partially open them, but there was nothing to see, so I closed them again. In feeling about, I could find no other with me.

I may have slept, or in some other wise been unaware, as it seemed not long before the cart stopped, and the straw was pulled back. "Get up," a guard ordered. I raised myself with difficulty to see I had been returned to the rear courtyard at

Newgate. After perhaps half a minute he added, "Get out. You are free to go." And when I did not stir, added, "Don't you want to go?"

"Go ... where?"

"Anywhere you like. You cannot stay here, so you must go somewhere else."

I said nothing, extending a hand, thinking he might assist me in climbing out of the cart, but he did not take it. "Give me a moment," I said, and with some difficulty swung my legs around and over the end of the cart bed. He had opened the loading gate, at least, and I was soon standing next to the cart, holding on to it unsteadily.

"The way out is that way," said the guard, helpfully gesturing towards the gate at the entrance to the courtyard, which stood open just enough to admit passage of a person on foot. I staggered in its direction and was aware for the first time that my ankles were no longer fettered. I then stopped and turned around.

"Wait. Where is Chowder?"

"What? That other lad? I'm sure you'd like to know."

"No, please, is he alive? What have you done with him?"

The guard shrugged, as if nothing could interest him less.

"Bastard," said I.

"That's no way to talk. I brought you here, did I not? You are alive and free to go, are you not?"

"Fair enough, but why cannot you tell me the rest?"

"Suppose I don't feel like it," he said, shrugging again.

Saying nothing more to him, I turned again and resumed lurching towards the gate. The sky was darkening, and a cold rain had begun to fall. I found walking difficult, as my legs would not quite obey my mind, for the innumerable pains I felt everywhere, the clutch in my innards, and an overarching exhaustion. As I closed the few yards to the gate, I began to realize I had nowhere to go. I could not go to Mr. Duckworth's in my present state, and in any event it was nearly two miles away. I had not the capacity to walk such a distance. Mr. Jackson's, though much closer, was out of the question. Feeling in my jacket, I thought I detected coins, which made me a more than ordinarily fortunate wretch, but even with funds, encrusted with filth as I was, where could I go? I must clean myself and have fresh clothes before I could go anywhere or do anything at all.

These thoughts did not strike me with main force, but crept into my diminished mind slowly, one at a time, as I neared and then passed through the gate, which immediately swung shut behind me.

Once through the gate, I saw a small crowd across the street, which put fear in my heart, and I turned and began to run as best I could down the street in the other direction. Ever since the pillory, I have been unable to abide crowds of any size, and the more unruly they are, the less I can abide them. Nor have I returned to Charing Cross, having gone well out of my way many times since to avoid it. As I say, I turned to run, for I was certain they existed only to abuse me, but I found my legs unsteady, and I tripped on an uneven cobble and fell headlong, scraping my hands and knees in the process. I was struggling to rise and run again when the first of them reached me, inspiring panic. I was certain he held a knife and meant to slay me, but when he knelt next to me, I saw his hands were empty.

"Joseph, we are friends. You need not run. We are here to help you."

"What?" I could not comprehend it. It was only when I saw the next one to approach was Reggie that the truth of it began to penetrate.

"Hello, Joseph. Will you come with us?" I stared at him without comprehension for some moments, then said, "Oh, God. I ..."

"Now, be a good boy and drink this." Mr. Duckworth knelt and held forth a flask bearing a golden liquid. I gaped at it, fearing to soil it with my filthy lips, but he said, "No argument, now. Drink it."

"What?"

"Brandy. You need it. Drink it. Don't be a silly boy." He held it to my lips, and I pulled down several swallows, which burned like the devil, then slowly began to impart a most agreeable warmth, which by degrees spread into the beginnings of a relaxation of my terror.

After a few moments, as they helped me to get up, I asked, "What of Chowder? Do you know?"

Mr. Duckworth answered. "He is alive but was taken away in another wagon, which seems not to have returned him to Newgate. Mr. Bartlett followed it, so we ought to have news before long."

"He is alive?"

"Yes. He was taken down from the pillory breathing and moving, and was put in a wagon much as you were. Both of you were slumped over and gone by the time it was over. I'd say with luck he is in no worse shape than you."

"Mr. Duckworth ... Thank you."

"I will be pleased if you would call me Quentin."

"Ah. Thank you. Quentin."

They helped me to get up, and brought a wagonette they helped me into. I lay propped up against the bench, no straw to cover me this time, and Reggie climbed in after me. The rest of them, most of Mr. Duckworth's servants and several others

I did not recognize, piled into Mr. Duckworth's coupé and a deluxe berline, from which Mr. Broughton waved, and we set off. Reggie, bless him, did not try over much to engage me in conversation, but did offer the flask several times. "Just sip it. Not trying to make you sick, just relieve the pain. It is the most horrid thing that you have been through. You are a frightful sight, if you don't mind my saying so. No, you needn't speak, unless you want to."

"I cannot. Unspeakable. But. I saw something."

"Saw something?"

"I don't know. Can't explain."

"Of course. Another sip?"

"Yes … Thank you."

After some period of time, we pulled up at the rear of a very substantial mansion, which proved to be Mr. Duckworth's. I was helped out of the wagon and into the stable, where an enormous laundry tub full of steaming, soapy water awaited. With Quentin, Mr. Broughton, and a few of their servants looking on, Reggie relieved me of my slimed and encrusted clothing, and, wiping the worst of it from my head and neck with straw, introduced me to the steaming waters, which produced an astonishing sensation of luxurious ease even as it caused the many scratches and abrasions on my face, neck and hands to smart mightily.

I had never before had a bath, as the facilities are, of course, rare, and as everyone knows baths are injurious to the health, but here it was the perfect thing. Reggie and one of Mr. Broughton's footmen soaped me all over again and again with large sponges and poured buckets of hot water over my head, also washing my hair repeatedly. Not a little brandy was poured over me and into me, which burned like the Devil, but was good for cleaning out the cuts, Duckworth and Broughton said. I suppose it may have been, as in the days to come I suffered rather less suppuration than might have been expected.

Finally, I was declared clean and helped out, yet more steaming hot water poured over me. Several hands gently wielded soft towels to dry me, when, amidst it all, a hand I saw to be Mr. Duckworth's gripped me most intimately, at which my spirit, which from deepest insensibility had begun to dilate, reverted to a defensive posture. Mr. Broughton was by then not in evidence, and Mr. Duckworth's movement was so quick I doubt any of the others noticed, but there was no question he had taken an unagreed upon liberty, in contravention of his earlier promise.

The next thing I knew, I was wrapped in a very fine white cotton robe and led inside, following Mr. Duckworth through the blazing kitchen into the palatial drawing room, which was lit by dozens of candles. A fire roared in the enormous fireplace, and Mr. Duckworth joined Mr. Broughton, the two of them sitting in very large, plush chairs to either side of it. Mr. Duckworth gestured an invitation to stand before the fire, which I did. It was pleasant indeed to luxuriate in the radiant warmth, which soon drove the last of the dampness from me. Mr. Duckworth was clad in green velvet trousers and a maroon smoking jacket with black trim, inside of which he wore a pale blue blouse of many ruffles. Mr. Broughton was clad more conventionally in tans and black, with a white linen shirt.

"Well, Joseph," Mr. Duckworth spoke with every appearance of warm solicitude, his mincing tones more pronounced than ever. "You look rather better than you did an hour ago, I must say. How do you feel?"

In fact, I felt nothing at all, unless a great weariness and many pains be counted, but it seemed to have nothing to do with me. Everything was beyond a veil, and nothing signified. Who was Duckworth? Moreover, whom did he address? I could not have said. But somewhere within the fog of insensibility, I discovered myself to be at once grateful to and angry with him, confused as to the propriety of what he had done. Was it so very wrong? Or, even if wrong, important? Yet more things I did not know. But the fact remained, that had he asked, I would have said no, as I did not care to be intimate with him.

The clock ticked. He had addressed me, and a reply was required. How did I feel? I did not care to be impolite, and, by means of a process to which I was not privy, a facsimile self emerged that cobbled together bits of relevant information, and which, after a full minute or more had passed, answered thickly in my stead. "I don't know. I'm rather drunk, I suppose. Everything hurts. My forehead and lower back, especially. Shaky. The brandy is very good, though. Thank you."

"You are very brave. I doubt I would have survived, up there." It was Mr. Broughton. "Perhaps you do not feel like a hero, but to us you are."

He, at least, had made no betrayal, at least not yet. The facsimile self continued its regency, and it was not, in fact, for some days until I ceased to feel the separation and strange doubleness its presence entailed. "You are very kind to say that."

The two gentlemen said nothing for some moments, and then Mr. Duckworth spoke. "Indeed, my dear Joseph. When is the last time you ate?"

"This morning, early."

"And what did they feed you?"

"The usual watery gruel."

"Are you hungry? Do you care for a bit of supper? The rest of us will dine later, but we have had a proper luncheon and, needless to say, have had a rather easier time of it today than have you."

"I don't know. I ... suppose I might. Thank you."

Mr. Duckworth gestured to a young man I had not noticed in attendance. "François, bring our guest a little something, as I mentioned earlier."

"We were very worried about you," said Mr. Broughton. If it were not for Mr. Jackson and our mounted corps, I fear you might not be with us now."

"Mr. Jackson was there? After the first bit I could see nothing. I did feel especially some sharp and heavy objects."

"There was a fellow who had himself a cartload of broken bricks, and was about to heave one when Mr. Jackson put his horse in the way, and it stepped on the man's foot, giving him something else to think about. He appeared to be in great pain, and I expect his foot was crushed."

Mr. Duckworth added, "Another fellow thought it clever to throw bottles of gin, of which he had a great store."

"Ah, I felt one of those."

"I'm sure you did," Mr. Duckworth continued. "One of ours whom you have not met, Doxley, rode up next to the man's wagon containing the gin and pushed it over, smashing most of the bottles. The man was wild with rage, but he calmed down well enough when he found himself looking up the barrel of Doxley's pistol."

"I knew nothing of any of that. I was gone. Something extraordinary ..." But here my supper was brought, a lovely plate of boiled chicken and potatoes, and a pot of ale. Despite my absent mind and bodily pains, the food smelled good, and I sat at a small table near the fire and ate, while Mr. Broughton and Mr. Duckworth conversed.

As I finished up, Mr. Duckworth said, "Joe, You may consider my previous offer to assist you to be good yet. I do hope that will be to your liking. But we need not style you Archibald, nor get you out of London. As the Crown is no longer in search of you, it is not necessary."

It was impossible to refuse. The rest of it would have to be sorted out later. "You are very kind, Mr. Duckworth. Thank you."

"Quentin. You are most welcome. Now, for tonight, I would be pleased if you would sleep in the first guest bedroom upstairs. It's much finer than the groom's little chamber off the stable. Will that be all right?"

"I ... care not to spurn your hospitality, but I do not find the guest bedchamber necessary. I will say, though, that I do feel as if I ought to lie down very soon. I do not feel well."

"All the more reason for you to take the guest chamber. It is more well-fitted for your care, should you ail. I insist. François, find Reggie and tell him to escort

Joe upstairs and to bed."

I mumbled and nodded a thank you, feeling what little strength I had left to be rapidly ebbing. Reggie soon appearing, I said good night to the two gentlemen, whereupon I was led upstairs, shown the location of the W.C., and then introduced to a richly appointed bedroom. Reggie lit candles and excused himself, saying,

"Joe, I am so very happy you are safe and here again with us. I hope you will sleep well, my friend."

"Ah, yes, good night. And ... thank you so much." Speech was now very nearly beyond my capacity.

I now found myself alone in a magnificent bedchamber of rich paneling, thick, ornate carpet and high, vaulted ceiling, upon which, flanked by pink clouds, circled a flock of adoring cherubs, as unlike the cold rigors of Newgate as could be imagined, with a warm, comfortable bed, immaculate down pillows and comforters, and acres of embroidered counterpane, and it was strange and wonderful, much finer than anything I had ever had. Indeed, I could but little comprehend it, sitting on the bed in wonderment. I found myself to be trembling, and my head swimming, and soon was occupied with the worry that my dinner was going to come up, which, no sooner than I had made my way to the W.C., it did. I then pissed, which I would not mention, but that it came a bright red. Reggie, appearing, asked whether I were all right.

"I—I'm not sure. It's been ... too much. I need to lie down. A glass of water would be lovely."

"Yes, sir."

"Dear God, don't call me sir."

"Sorry. But for tonight at least, you know, as Quentin's guest, that is what you are."

"No. Joe. Please. And thank you."

"Yes, Joe, sir," he smiled, a giggle behind it that I did not have the strength to appreciate. He disappeared and I went back to the chamber, hurting everywhere and trembling anew, and crawled into the miraculous bed. Reggie brought the water and quickly withdrew. I rinsed my mouth, spat into the basin, and then lay a long time, caught between the pelting mob, the pillory, and my vision, which had never entirely left me. Finally I slept, but in my dreams it all continued, except Chowder was there, and I could talk to him, and as the night progressed hold him close, in which was healing succor like no other.

LIV

I SLEPT VERY LATE. IT was nearly eleven, and a weak sun shone through the lace curtains when Reggie rapped softly on the door, to which I responded with a croak. He opened the door an inch, and asked whether he might enter.

"Yes, please." I sat up in the bed and attempted to appear alert despite my headache, many pains, and disorientation, at least some of which was due to the after-effects of the unaccustomed brandy, helpful as it may have been the night before. Despite that, seeing Reggie lifted my spirits, and what was more, he bore breeches, a shirt, underclothing, stockings, and a pair of shoes.

"I hope these fit. I think you are about my size, but we guessed at the shoes. If they are not right, please tell me so I can get you another pair. All gifts from Quentin."

"Thank you. He is too kind. I will have to thank him."

Reggie offered a gentle chuckle, accompanied by a complex "Indeed," that was at once a statement, a question, and an exclamation of rueful irony. "And just how do you think you might do that?"

"Well, I ... I don't know. May I ask you something?"

"Anything at all, my dear."

"How do you handle him? Does he grab at you? What do you do about it? He was at me last night before I was even dry from the bath."

Reggie laid the clothing across the counterpane at the foot of the bed, furrowing his brow. "I am very sorry to hear that. I made up my mind to endure it. There are worse things, such as having no employment."

"Is that it then? You allow him whatever liberty he wishes to take?"

"Well, no. Not any more."

"How do you stop him?"

"The need does not arise. The moment he had me, he lost interest. Quentin requires constant novelty. The instant he gets what he wants, he is done and straightaway is off again in search of something new."

"Seems rather pointless, doesn't it? I find this confusing and unpleasant."

"I am sorry, Joe. It may become more so. Quentin is very taken with you now, much more than he lets on."

I made a face of puzzlement and disapproval. "So, has he had every one of you in this house?"

"You can guess the answer to that. You could say it's what you have to do to get in. But after that he leaves you alone. But—oh, dear me! I almost forgot! Messrs. Jackson, Bartlett, and Broughton are downstairs. They have been to see Chowder and wish to speak to you. May I tell them you'll be down?"

"Well, yes, of course. I will be down as soon as I can get dressed."

"They are with Quentin in the drawing room, where you were last night." He departed, and I visited the W.C. where I pissed rosy pink. The more I moved about, the less well I felt, but was just able to disregard it. I then dressed, finding the clothing fit tolerably well, but the shoes severely pinched my toes and would have to be replaced.

In the drawing room, I found the gentlemen in conversation before a bright fire. Only Mr. Duckworth, in a pink silk banyan and white linen shirt, sat. His face was unpainted, and alone of the gentlemen, he wore no wig. He gestured to the other chair, inviting me to sit, and Mr. Jackson spoke first.

"Hello, Joseph. It's a great pleasure to see you in one piece, and well looked after."

"I am ... very happy to see you, too, Mr. Jackson. I must thank you for your efforts yesterday. Mr. Broughton and Mr. Duckworth were telling me of it."

"You are welcome indeed. After much reflection, I determined I could not remain idle—not when your and Chowder's lives were at stake. It isn't as if any of that rabble will have the least effect on my shop or trade—and I don't care if it does." He spoke with much emphasis, and seemed moved to say it, as I was to hear it. "A fellow similarly convicted died in the pillory just two years ago. Had you expired up there when I might have done something to prevent it, I would never have forgiven myself. That is why we felt we must ride through the mob and break up the worst of it."

"Speaking of Chowder," Mr. Bartlett interjected, "I followed the wagon that took him away from the pillory yesterday, to his sister's rooms in Spittlefields and saw him helped inside. He was just able to walk and required help from Elspeth to get up the stairs.

"I did not speak to either of them then. I went back with Mr. Jackson this morning in an attempt to see him, but we were rebuffed. We did not get inside the door. A young man was present, who insisted on speaking to us, even though we could see Elspeth in the room behind him. He was very arrogant and domineering. The instant we asked whether Chowder were there, he told us Chowder was very ill and did not wish to see anyone connected with his trial, the pillory, the mob, or especially 'that other fellow what caused all the trouble,' as he put it. I suppose by that he means you."

"But that is impossible! Chowder would never say any such thing," said I.

"Of course he wouldn't," said Mr. Bartlett, "but this oaf pretends it or has convinced himself of the truth of it, the result is the same. This is the difficulty Elspeth is in. She works and pays the rent and buys the food, while this cretinous leech parasitizes her. He has no work or legitimate trade and is a very dangerous fellow, I believe. Elspeth is frightened of him now. I was able to gather that much when I visited her when you were first incarcerated, to inform her. He was not there then, and she volunteered a few things from which one might draw conclusions."

"I must go to Chowder. He could die there, with that fool lording it over him and Elspeth. We must get him out of there."

"Do you feel well enough to make the trip?" Mr. Jackson leaned forward.

"I do not care how I feel, and I will find the strength. But the more who go, the better. Who will help me?"

"Every one of my boys and I can be counted on," said Mr. Duckworth.

"You can count on me as well," said Mr. Jackson.

"And me and my staff, too!" added Mr. Broughton, with meaningful emphasis. And looking from me to the others, "Well, gentlemen, when shall we do this?"

"Why, now, of course," said I. "I mean, if that is to everyone's convenience. How quickly can we assemble and depart?"

"I can go home and collect my staff, and return with twelve men and two carriages, in two hours or less," said Mr. Broughton.

"We will be ready here," said Mr. Duckworth. "I have but the coupé, as you know, but it can carry four, if two perch on the outside of it. All eight of my boys will come, if a few can catch a ride."

"But of course," said Mr. Broughton.

"I have hired a gig for the day and can lead us all there," offered Mr. Jackson.

"And I will ride with you," said Mr. Bartlett, who was now standing very near to Mr. Broughton.

"Excellent," said Mr. Jackson. "I just need to stop by the shop and make arrangements to have it staffed the rest of the day. I will return here in about an hour and a half, no more than two."

And with that, Mr. Broughton and Mr. Bartlett departed together, and Mr. Jackson hastened to his gig.

Mr. Duckworth and I were now alone together. "Joseph, you look very fine in your new garb," he said. "apart from your scratches and bruises, of course. Do you like your clothing?"

"Yes, sir. It serves me very well. I do thank you."

"You are most welcome, Joseph. Can't very well have you trotting about naked, now, can we?" This was said with just enough leering forwardness to indicate it would, in fact, suit him very well. "And how do you feel now?"

"Not so very well, truth be told, sir. There is a troublesome ache in my lower back, especially. And I feel as if it might be wise to try to eat a bite, sorry. I find myself distinctly underfed. One does not sup so very well in Newgate."

"No, no sorry about it. In a moment, I will send you off to the kitchen to eat all you please. But first I would like to say some things to you."

"Yes?"

"Joseph, I find you quite extraordinary. I would like you to stay here. I don't have any specific vacancies at the moment, but there is always something needing to be done. You could begin as Reggie's assistant and fill in wherever needed. Does that please you? And please come and stand closer to me, if you would."

"Mr. Duckworth, I do thank you, and I am so very sorry, but I cannot. I don't wish to be ungrateful, but really I cannot. I do owe you the world, and yet I will not stand closer to you. I wish to be intimate with no one but Chowder. It's the same as I said to you in your carriage last June. You and I are too different in age, and I do not care to be exploited while in a position of dependency. Or at any time, actually."

Mr. Duckworth said nothing for some moments, then he compressed his lips and shook his head. "Joseph, do not disappoint me. I offer you great opportunity.

Reggie will not be here forever, and you could rise to manage the household. You may well regret your decision."

"Again, sir, I am adamant, with apology, to be sure. You have been most kind. May we please leave it at that? My heart makes the choice for me. I do not mean to be obstinate."

Mr. Duckworth's incipient frown now grew into a scowl. "Very well, then. Very well. Perhaps you will find a situation in another house. But your options are quite limited, you know. Your apprenticeship is in ruins, and given your recent history, no one will touch you except the very few of means and our persuasion. You may have inspired your diffident Mr. Jackson to step forward on your behalf, but he will not take you back, of that you may be certain. I will leave the door open for the time being. I do hope you will reconsider."

I said nothing.

He sighed deeply. "But I will not be petty. Your refusal will occasion no reprisal. If I were spiteful, it would scarcely encourage you to change your mind." He attempted a smile. "I do wish to be kind." He extended his hand.

I took the offered hand and shook it. "Thank you very much, sir. May I go to the kitchen now?"

"Yes, yes, be off with you," he said, suddenly brusque and waving his hand dismissively. "I must finish dressing, anyway."

I passed into the kitchen, where the cook, James, and his boy, Otto, bustled, and there were rich smells of the luncheon soon to be had. Reggie was waiting by the door, and clasped me on the shoulder, saying, "Bravo, my dear! You handled him as few ever have. I will miss you, though."

"Thank you. I hope I have not just cut my own throat. But I couldn't, you know? Truly, I could not."

"It's not a memory I cherish, to be sure. I expect he now will spend a great deal of time at Moorfields in an effort to forget you. It's a pattern we have seen. He brings some of them back here, and if a few are fetching, they tend to be a rough lot."

"Goodness."

"And it does go downhill from there. He's been blackmailed more than once and robbed more times than that. But I am babbling, am I not? James has prepared onion soup, roast parsnip with barley, and a bit of beef for luncheon, which is very nearly ready. Will you join us?"

"Of course, and thank you. Say, I'm very sorry, but these shoes are rather too small. Is there any chance of getting a larger pair?"

"I will see to it right away."

"Reggie, you are a dear. And what can you tell me of this Mr. Broughton? Does he also prey upon his minions?"

"If he does, I have never heard it, and I do believe I would have, as I know several in service to him very well. Mr. Bartlett is his companion, and they are very devoted. Do you know he is enormously wealthy? Much beyond our Duckworth, here. Quite possibly the richest commoner in England. He would be in Parliament, were it not for his being of our persuasion, which causes him to be shunned by the gentry. And he would be in Newgate or dead, were it not for his wealth and his discretion. His character and compassion are most admirable, and his household is impeccable. One is very fortunate to be employed there."

"Reggie, I do thank you. You are a treasure, indeed. One last thing, do you know what became of my jacket? There were a few things in the pockets I would be sorry to lose."

"Oh, dear. The stable was mucked out last night, as all the water from your bath made a fine mess, and it could not be left in that condition. Your jacket, as was all your clothing, was unrecognizable, and went with the sodden straw and dung. I'm sorry you did not say something."

"Ah … Well. I would have, had I had the capacity." Feeling I had provided spectacle enough, I thought I would not tell him the residue of my fortune, perhaps seventeen pounds, was in that jacket. I don't know why, as there would have been no harm in his knowing. His friendship had already proven as genuine as it had instrumental. "It's all right. Not your fault. Nothing for it now."

"Sorry, Joe. It's deep in a dung heap by now. I wouldn't even know which one."

LV

Mr. Duckworth's servants supped in a plain room adjacent to the kitchen, without paneling or decoration of any kind, but this was more than compensated for by the jollity of the company. Reggie presided, and the cook's boy, Otto, served. Though Reggie had listed them on the day I first visited, I was now properly introduced to James, the cook, and his boy, Otto, Josiah the coachman and groom, Françoise, the parlor maid, Peter, the chamber maid, Rudolph, Mr. Duckworth's valet, a very busy man indeed, and the Russian footman, Eugene, who was exceptionally tall, fair, and just a bit rough in his manners. Reggie quickly told them of our impending mission to rescue Chowder, to which they subscribed with full-throated enthusiasm.

"If that rude fellow tries to keep you from your Chowder, I will squeeze his head like a grape," offered Rudolph, to general laughter.

Josiah, small and wiry and of keen blue eyes, said, "I will tie him up and Otto will sit on him."

Otto, who, though styled a boy, was of considerable girth, said, "Yah, and he will be stuck good then," to more laughter.

The good cheer and camaraderie was balm to my heart, but I found I had little appetite, the pain in my back and the confusion of my mind both persisting.

Despite these impediments, I was happy to tell of where and how Chowder and I had met, and how we ended up in the pillory at Charing Cross, which story was received with rapt attention. Indeed, the luncheon was so pleasant and comforting, I confess to wondering for a moment whether I had not erred in declining to join them in Mr. Duckworth's employ, despite the price, but then as quickly thought of Chowder.

If I stayed there, what place would be for him? I realized with a start I knew nothing of how Chowder was to be supported. Mr. Duckworth had made no offer concerning Chowder, and it was now impossible to conceive that he would, whether or not he had ever had the intention. I desired more urgently than ever to leave Mr. Duckworth's as soon as possible, and resolved to make application to Mr. Broughton the instant the opportunity should present itself.

The luncheon concluding, the servants donned greatcoats and hats, as it was very gloomy and wet outside, assembling in the stable ready to depart. I waited in the dining room while Reggie was gone a few moments, returning quickly with a pair of shoes, a jacket not unlike the one I had lost, and a hat that would do well to keep the rain off. The shoes were foppish, having an absurdly large silver buckle, too high a heel, and not enough proper leather to keep one's feet dry, but I was not in a position to complain. "These are Quentin's, but he no longer fancies them, and says if they fit you are welcome to them."

"They will do very nicely. Thank you, and please thank him for me," said I, donning the shoes, which fit quite well.

"I will convey your sentiments, to be sure," said he. "And I suppose it's to be expected, given your harsh treatment of the man," and here he offered a grin, "but Quentin says he finds himself indisposed. He begs your forgiveness and trusts you will understand that he cannot accompany you to Spittlefields. He feels, moreover, his presence in any case would be redundant, given the many strong arms and backs on hand."

"But of course. You may tell him my gratitude is undiminished."

With that, Reggie and I went to the stables, just in time to see Mr. Jackson drive up in his gig and station it beside the entrance, where Reggie went to have a word with him, I presumed about Quentin's indisposition. Josiah had harnessed the two horses to Mr. Duckworth's coupé, which now sported a full compliment of young men within. In a very few more minutes, Mr. Broughton's heavy and luxurious berline came into view, pulled by four very fine and well-dressed horses, driven by Mr. Broughton himself, Mr. Bartlett at his side. The berline was also full of energetic, mostly young men, and was followed by a landau with the top up, bearing several more.

The two gentlemen's servants were, clearly, well known to each other, as there was much convivial greeting and good spirits exchanged. I did not fail to notice Mr. Broughton's staff, on the whole, like Mr. Duckworth's, was very appealing in appearance. Mr. Broughton was no Duckworth, eternally on the hunt for fresh intimacies, but if his staff might be expected to be very well dressed as a testament to the prominence of his house, they were more than ordinarily good looking for no other reason than he took pleasure in it.

Reggie spoke briefly with Mr. Broughton, then gestured to me to join him beside the berline, where he introduced me to Mr. Broughton's servants, particularly Theodore, Mr. Broughton's private secretary, a pale blond of slight build and owlish countenance, who greeted me with shy reserve and a furtive smile, and Henry, the butler, easily double the bulk of Theodore, whose penetrating gaze bespoke order and efficiency, and who offered me his hand with a precisely formulated, but not unfriendly grin. These two remained inside the coach, and Reggie then took me to the landau, where waited the footman.

"Joe, I want to introduce you to Immanuel, Mr. Broughton's first footman and man-of-all-purpose. He is a most capable fellow who has proven his worth time and again. Now, one thing you must know about him is that he does not speak. He is able to hear and understand perfectly well, however."

Immanuel jumped down from the driver's seat as we approached, offering me a broad smile and his hand, which I shook gladly. I stated how very pleased I was to meet him, and bowed politely, which he returned with pleasant grace. As he smiled I saw in the corner of his mouth and upon his lower lip a ragged scar, that was not so prominent that it ruined his features, but which certainly inspired curiosity.

As we returned to the berline, Reggie added, "Immanuel is from Jamaica, where he was born on a plantation. Mr. Broughton spent some months there two years ago to inspect his inherited properties, and returned with him. Mr. Broughton emancipated him in Jamaica and he came to England of his own free will. He is paid a proper salary same as any of us, but beyond that I know nothing of his history. Given that he cannot speak, I don't know that anyone does."

"Do you know what happened to him?"

"Only that an attempt was made to cut out his tongue when he was a slave and enough damage done that he cannot form words. I have no idea why or what any of it was about."

"How horrible," said I. "Reggie, how can I thank you? For everything. You have been so very kind. I don't know that I will return here today. It depends on the next few hours. But whatever happens, I will think of you and miss you."

"The same, my dear," he returned with an endearing smile, and we embraced with every sentiment and sensation of fond friendship.

We were now ready to depart. Mr. Bartlett was seated beside Mr. Jackson in his gig, and Mr. Broughton gestured to me to sit next to him in the driver's seat of the berline. I climbed up, and in a few moments we were off into the smoke and rain, Mr. Jackson leading the way, Mr. Duckworth's coupé following, driven by Josiah, Reggie and Theodore sitting next to him, after which came Mr. Broughton's berline, and last the landau. Mr. Broughton was very gracious as I sat down beside him, wiping the wet off the seat where I was to sit, and offering me a dry blanket he fetched from the box next his seat. He handled the reins with expert skill, a business I knew little of.

We had gone but a very little way when Mr. Broughton addressed me. "I'm glad to have a chance to talk to you, Joe. Are you feeling any better? You certainly look better."

"Thank you for asking, sir. I don't know. Things ache. I do not feel quite right, truth be told, but I expect I shall recover, given enough time. It was a very unsettling experience, to be sure."

"Indeed it was. Yes, let's hope that you will recover quickly. And your companion Chowder as well."

"Thank you, sir."

"Now, may I ask you something?"

"Of course."

"How are you getting on with Duckworth?"

"I could be doing better, sir. He is a confusing man to be around. How well do you know him?"

"Quite well. You can be honest with me, Joe. Is he treating you fairly?"

"In some ways, yes, very much so. I am destitute, and he has lodged and clothed me and asks for nothing in return. Well, except, that is, he has taken liberties with my person when I was defenseless and presses me for intimacies I do not care for."

"He ought not to do that. I am sorry to hear it, though I must confess I am not terribly surprised."

"And I am sorry to tell it, but it is the truth. He poses as kindness incarnate and speaks of respect, yet violates the very principle."

"Will you stay there? He spoke to Mr. Jackson and me of offering you a position."

"He has, just now, saying I should be Reggie's assistant, but I have declined him."

"Indeed. And what do you now intend to do?"

"That is a very good question, sir, that I do not yet know the answer to. It would be very awkward staying there now, assuming he would permit me to, which in fact I don't know he will. He strikes me as very capricious, to say nothing of self-interested, and my integrity, if I may so style it, thwarts him. If I do not let him use me intimately, then by his lights, he has no reason to extend himself further. So, that's done. I have no expectation of returning to my former situation at Mr. Jackson's, despite his recent kindness. He has made no mention of it, and reasonably so, I suppose. I cannot imagine my presence now would be any sort of enhancement to his reputation or trade. So, that, too, is done. I have not a penny, and Chowder the same. In fact, I was wondering, sir, whether it might be possible for Chowder and I to go into service to you, if you are in want of any more, that is. We are both very hard working and honest, and I can read and write very well. We would be very pleased to serve you in any capacity whatever."

Mr. Broughton said nothing for several minutes, during which I feared I had misstepped by being too forward. He did not appear to be displeased, however, and perhaps was merely giving his attention to driving, as the rain fell more heavily upon us now, and the smoke was very thick as we negotiated a series of narrow lanes and had to dodge much traffic coming the other way. I was very relieved to find, when he did speak, that he was agreeable.

"Joseph, your offer pleases me. I have been thinking along much the same lines, but did not wish to intrude upon any prior arrangements you may have made. Mr. Jackson has spoken glowingly of your character and abilities, and says he has seen enough of Chowder to say the same of him."

"Thank you very much, sir. Mr. Jackson is a most excellent man, and he has helped me enormously. I am very sorry to have lost my position with him. Chowder and I will give you our all, you may be sure of it."

"Of that I have no doubt, and thank you. First thing, though, I want to give you time to recover from your ordeal. I was speaking recently to a physician friend of mine, who told me when one has been pelted in the pillory, it is often followed some days later by a dangerous fever. Before I place you in a situation, I will want to know you are out of danger, so I will give you no duties at first. Then, as soon as you are ready, which with a bit of luck will be very soon, we will start you off with a few undemanding tasks and build you up from there."

"Thank you very much, sir. You are very kind."

"You are most welcome, Joe. I do believe our association will be very pleasant and mutually beneficial. So, when we return with Chowder, you will both come to my residence and lodge there. And we will start you both off at half a footman's salary, of course with room and board included, to be increased to full pay as soon as possible, for whichever position you are placed in. How does that sound?"

Mr. Broughton was then, as ever afterwards, careful of our sensibilities, that we should not be dependent on his charity nor beholden to him, but we would earn our keep as independent men. This did not mean that he was ungenerous, for he was never less than liberal and kind, but his greatest gift was our dignity. He was not unlike Mr. Jackson in the refinement of his bearing and the breadth of his interests, and very unlike Mr. Duckworth, being unambiguous in his transactions, restrained in his deportment, and exacting no unseemly tariffs.

"That sounds very good indeed, sir. Thank you so very much! You will not regret it."

"I have no doubt of it, and you are most welcome, Joe."

We rode on for some minutes through torrents of rain, when Mr. Broughton said, "I say, are we here? Looks like Joseph and Thomas, I mean to say, Mr. Jackson and Mr. Bartlett, have stopped."

"I don't know. I have never been to Elspeth's rooms. But, indeed, they are getting down, so this must be the place."

We were in a narrow street between two decrepit, four-story blocks of ancient, much begrimed red brick, down the fronts of which water streamed, splashing into the street. The carriages, placed as closely as possible against the left side, left scant room for traffic to pass, and though it was mid-afternoon, the street was deep in darkening, sodden gloom. Mr. Broughton and I climbed down, and joined Mr. Jackson and Mr. Bartlett beside Mr. Jackson's gig, while the score of servants gathered around.

"I believe," said Mr. Jackson, "that there is no harm in all of us going up. Joe, Mr. Broughton, Mr. Bartlett and I will go to the door with two or three others, and that ought to suffice. The rest of you may follow along and wait nearby in the hall. We can easily let you know if any more are needed inside. It's on the top floor, up a very long flight of stairs."

"Good, then, said Mr. Broughton. "I should like Eugene and Immanuel to go in at the fore with us, while the rest of you follow closely behind."

Eugene, Mr. Duckworth's tall, Russian footman, indicated his readiness, and Immanuel, now carrying a truncheon identical to those carried by the guards in Newgate, strode up from the landau to join us at the fore, and we shook hands again. He then clapped me on the shoulder, a gesture which, despite its familiarity, pleased me very much.

Mr. Jackson, eyeing the building's façade, said, "Shall we go in, then?"

With that, he led us to the building's entrance. We climbed the few stairs in front, opened the door, entered, made a hard turn to the right, and climbing the narrow, dark stairway three landings, until we reached the top, where we turned and went down a similarly dark and narrow hallway, lit only by light coming through small windows at either end, We stopped before the second to last door on the right, where Mr. Jackson rapped softly. There being no response, he rapped again, just a bit harder.

"What d'ye want?" It was the unpleasantly harsh, slightly slurred speech of a young man given overmuch to drink and his pipe, coming through the door, which he did not open.

Mr. Jackson was as unperturbed as could be. "It is the Watch. Open up. We have business with Potter Gorham."

"Not surprised to hear it," we heard the voice say, then, as if he had turned his head to speak to someone in the room, "Say, Elspeth, your damned brother has brought yet more disgrace upon us."

"Go to hell," came the rejoinder.

Disregarding the injunction, the voice said through the still closed door, "How do I know you are who you say you are?"

Mr. Bartlett exhibited a stentorian basso profundo I had not suspected he possessed. "If you do not open, we will break it down, and then you will find out!"

The increase in volume prompted several other doors along the hall to open slightly, out of which curious eyes peeped. An unshaven young man in a nightcap stuck his head out the door and said, "Probably should open it, Roddy. Buggers look like they mean business." He looked down the hall, "And there's a damned lot of them."

The door opened a crack. Roddy peered out and immediately snarled, "Why, I thought I told you—" but no sooner did he open the door than Immanuel thrust his truncheon into the gap, preventing Roddy from closing it, whereupon Eugene, Mr. Broughton, and Mr. Jackson put their shoulders to the door, which gave but little resistance before flying open. Eugene and Immanuel entered, followed by the three gentlemen and myself.

It was a tiny room, having but a single, small window admitting the waning light of a wet winter's afternoon, and on the far side an open, half-sized doorway. A tiny coal fire in the grate and a tinier lantern on a little bureau did little to relieve the gloom. Roddy, diminutive and red-haired, was now in the far corner behind the deal table, in a defensive posture, fists up, and glowering. "You can't have me, and damn you!"

"We are not the press gang, though that would suit you well. We have come for Chowder, not you." said Mr. Jackson.

Roddy spat and said nothing. Elspeth emerged crouching from the inner doorway, her eyes registering puzzlement, but her mouth smiling. "Why, Joe, however did you find your way here? It is a great pleasure to see you—and your friends." She looked at the others who had entered and, nodding uncertainly, offered a slight curtsey. "Hello indeed, and most welcome. I must beg you to excuse our indisposition." Mr. Broughton smiled and tilted his head graciously, Mr. Jackson and Mr. Bartlett bowed, and Immanuel and Eugene, unable to relinquish their positions, nodded without taking their eyes off Roddy.

Elspeth then said, "Joe, come. Chowder has done nothing but ask for you. He is in here." She beckoned as she spoke. I crossed the room and lowered myself to enter the doorway where I found find a very dim, tiny chamber and Chowder half sitting up on a horsehair mattress on the floor. He was wan and had not been properly cleaned, but was smiling broadly. His hair was matted yet, and he had new bruises about his face to keep company with his now mostly faded black eye, though in the gloom it was difficult to tell just what was what.

"Oh, Joe," said he.

"My dear Chowder." We embraced, needing no words, and simply held each other for the longest time, during which we heard scuffling and grunts in the other room.

"Yes, tie him well," Elspeth said, "and deliver him to the press gang, will you? Can you?"

"With the greatest pleasure, yes," Mr. Jackson responded.

Roddy shrieked, "Damn you! Bitch! I told you no good would come of letting your brother come here. Damn all of you!"

"No good for you, to be sure," said Elspeth, near to giggling, "but very good for me. There is a recruitment office hard by the church, just off Spittlefields's Market. If you will deliver him there, I shall be very obliged indeed. I dare say he will do better as a tar than a leech. And if he's worth a bounty, you may let him keep it." This was followed by more scuffling, grunts, and curses from Roddy which faded, I presumed, as he was hustled out the door and down the hall.

I sat beside Chowder. "Sounds like more than one good reason for us to show up."

"You have delivered the both of us, my friend. Roderick has been a curse upon Eppie since first she let him stay here. She tells me he was fairly pleasant to her in the beginning, but soon began thinking he should have say over everything she did. She humored him at first, but when she resisted, he became very ugly about it, and soon she could do no right. He has struck her more than once, and she has returned the compliment, but the situation does not improve. She has begun to doubt her own judgement and been very melancholy, despairing of ever getting him out of here. And he had no use for me at all, as you can well imagine."

I shook my head. "Very good riddance, to be sure. The Navy is too good for him."

"Indeed. But tell me, who are all these people you have brought?"

"Mr. Jackson, two gentlemen friends of his, and their servants—and most of the servants of another gentleman who is not here. They are all of our persuasion, the gentlemen and their staffs."

Chowder shook his head in wonder. "I am astonished. And grateful, of course. However do you do it?"

"I don't know. One thing leads to another. There was Mr. Jackson, of course, then Mr. Duckworth—I must tell you about him. And Mr. Broughton is a friend of Mr. Jackson's. I don't know him well, but he seems very kind. He is interested because he is sodomitical as are we, and he wishes to help, and Mr. Bartlett is his companion."

"Ah, yes, Bartlett twice visited me in Newgate."

"Right, of course. Now, my dear boy, tell me, do you wish to remain here or will you come with me? I have found situations for the both of us, in service to Mr. Broughton. He offers to pay us wages from the start, half at first, then when we are restored to health, proper positions and full pay."

Chowder grinned anew. "You are excellent, aren't you? Yes, of course, I will go with you, and very gladly. Eppie and I are very dear to each other, but I am a burden to her here. She has not the resources to feed and clothe me until I am on my feet, and what would I do then, in any case?"

I embraced and kissed him again, though he did not smell very good. "And how do you feel?"

"If it is possible to feel happy and wretched at once, then that is me. My heart is lifted as never before, but my body is half broken. I feel as if I have the beginnings of a fever, and there are many pains. But I am fit enough to go away with you now. I have waited so long to see you, I will never let you out of my sight again."

I kissed him yet again. "I will tell the others that you will come with us, while you make yourself ready."

LVI

I RETURNED TO THE FRONT room, where Mr. Broughton, Mr. Bartlett, and Elspeth sat conversing, announcing that Chowder would return with us. I had not supposed he would not, but the choice was his, after all.

"Joe, that is excellent. As I said earlier, I will be pleased to provide lodging for the two of you, in anticipation of your going into service to me as soon as possible."

"Thank you very much, sir."

Elspeth, who had patiently waited her turn to speak, now burst forth, "Joe, however did you find your way here, and where is it that are you and Chowder are going? I refuse to lose track of either of you."

"Mr. Bartlett, here, followed the wagon bearing Chowder after he was taken down from the pillory. And then he and Mr. Jackson returned this morning."

"Ah, I wondered if that was Jackson, this morning. I didn't get much of a look at him when I was there last summer. And may I ask where you are going?"

"My residence is in St. James' Square," said Mr. Broughton, retrieving a card from his inside breast pocket and handing it to her. "You will always be welcome there, and at my country house in Wiltshire." He smiled, doffed his hat and nodded his head graciously.

"Why, thank you, very much, sir." Elspeth was a determined spirit, and though she was otherwise a model of good manners, she looked him in the eye, which Mr. Broughton did not seem to find inappropriate.

Chowder now emerged from the bedchamber, wrapped in a cotton sheet that had once been white. He looked no better in the slightly brighter light of the parlor, being quite dirty and bruised and showing many scratches, but he looked very good to me.

"I, ah, actually have no clothing," said he. "No time to get any. The washerwoman was here earlier, and she would not take what I wore in the pillory. She said they would never come clean and would besides stink up her works. There would be no getting the smell out. I had a few spares at Cudworth's, but there's no getting them now." He smiled sheepishly.

"What did you do with your dirty clothes?" I asked, thinking of mine in a dunghill.

"When the washerwoman had gone, Roddy threw them out the window. They are in the street yet, I suppose, stinking up the rain. Roddy's got a spare pair of breeches and a shirt here, but they are too small for me to get into."

"We will get a riding blanket from the trunk in the coach, and that will keep the rain off," said Mr. Broughton. "And there will be clothes for you at my residence." As he spoke, Mr. Bartlett went to the door and issued the instruction.

"You are very kind, sir, and I thank you," said Chowder.

In a very few minutes, Theodore appeared, bearing a woolen riding blanket of dark blue, which he presented to Chowder.

"Well, then, shall we be off?" Mr. Broughton queried.

Chowder and Elspeth said their good-byes, vowing to see one another again very soon, and we went into the hall, where the servants broke into applause and gave several huzzahs, which caused Chowder more embarrassment than anything, as he would greatly have preferred to have been properly clad. Be that as it may have been, we were quickly down the stairs and into the street, where chill rain fell in torrents, and Chowder and I were introduced to the luxurious, padded interior of Mr. Broughton's berline. Mr. Broughton, now preferring his coachman, Edward, to drive, joined us within, as did Theodore, and in another moment we were off. Once the coach began moving, I found myself to be without strength and very drowsy, beginning to feel feverish. I rested against the comfortable seat and let my head fall against Chowder, despite the odor arising from him. He, in turn, pulled his blanket closer around himself and nestled into me, soon closing his eyes. Mr. Broughton, in the seat opposite, looked genially upon us, smiling and forbearing to speak, and in a very little while I closed my eyes as well, drowsing the way to the gentleman's city home. It seemed no time at all until Mr. Broughton gently tapped my shoulder to alert me to the fact that we had arrived. The carriage had been unhitched and now stood in the stable of a commodious carriage house, from which we were led into the kitchen of Mr. Broughton's city residence, as he styled it.

"Welcome to your new home. Henry, my butler here, will take you to your chamber and see to it you are looked after. If I do not see you again today, I surely will tomorrow. I must beg your forgiveness, but I have a some very pressing business matters I must attend to, or I would look after you myself."

We thanked and said good-bye to Mr. Broughton, who left with Theodore, whereupon Henry invited us to follow him, also motioning to another fellow to whom we had not yet been introduced, to follow. We left the kitchen and walked through a series of grand rooms, which I took to be a banqueting hall, a ballroom, and an opulent drawing room, before climbing a flight of stairs and entering a long hallway. This was a much larger house than Mr. Duckworth's, although it had rather less gilding and excess ornamentation.

Henry spoke as we walked. "There is a pleasant bedchamber in the servant's wing that will suit the two of you very well. As you know, he wishes the two of you to rest until you are free of fever and suppuration. You may take meals in your chamber or join the staff in the servant's hall, as you wish, for these first few days. We do hope you will join us for meals if you are feeling well enough, but first things first. We have arranged for a physician to examine the both of you tomorrow morning, and that will give us a better idea of how you are doing and what to expect."

The hallway turned a corner to the left, with a series of doorways on either side, and at the far end, another stairway leading down. We went very nearly to the far end, where Henry opened one of the doors on the right to a very pleasant, and pleasantly warm bedchamber quite as he had promised, with much dark woodwork, two beds, two armoires and a washstand, a cheerful fire with a full scuttle of coal to the side, and a large window overlooking St James' Square.

"Mr. Broughton and I hope you will be happy here." He paused and, looking us over, seemed to wrinkle his nose. "I say, Chowder, how would you like to get cleaned up? George, here, functions as the upstairs chamber maid, and he will be pleased to prepare a bath."

George, who had walked silently beside us from the kitchen, appeared to be nearly forty, but stood erect, still had most of his hair, and his features were open and pleasant, most notably his clear blue eyes, which were alert and friendly. "Nothing would be easier. Just downstairs is a tub. I will go now and tell the undercook to heat water and will return within the hour." He bowed and departed.

"Perhaps, Chowder, until you have had your bath, keep that blanket handy," added Henry, uncertainly.

"I won't dirty the sheets or upholstery, if that is what you mean to say," said Chowder. "I know better than that." He said this pleasantly, wanting Henry to know he had the wit to take care, but not wanting him to think he was challenging him. It was a delicate balancing act, but one which was successful, as Henry appeared pleased by the comment.

"That's a good boy," he said, smiling, then immediately corrected himself. "Sorry, you are a man, not a boy. Just a manner of speaking." He struck a light and lit several candles, as darkness was gathering outside.

"I don't mind," said Chowder.

"Thank you. I will leave you now, and George will see to your bath. May I assume you would rather take your supper in your chamber this evening? I certainly would, having been through what you two have. Tomorrow or the day after is soon enough to meet the rest of the staff, let alone begin your duties. Do take some time together and get some good rest."

We both averred that eating in the chamber sounded like a very good idea. I was finding it difficult to keep my eyes open and felt very warm indeed.

"Very good then," said Henry. "Welcome to you both. And I wish to extend my personal sympathies and welcome. I believe you will both do very well here. You will work hard, but there is nothing wrong with hard work. In exchange, you will receive above average remuneration, respect, and the freedom of not having to hide your affection while within the walls of this house, as everyone here is of the same heart. Given what you have both just been through, I need not stress the value of this, nor the importance of discretion when without the walls."

"You are very kind as well as clear, and we do understand and thank you," said I.

"Indeed, yes," Chowder added, "and thank you."

Henry smiled, shook both our hands, and departed.

Chowder and I were now alone together for the first time since the evening following Mr. Peevers's hanging, but being utterly exhausted and Chowder yet filthy, we just sat, each in our own chair, holding hands and looking out the window at the traffic in the Square. "I do believe I love you," said Chowder, gently pressing my hand.

"And I you."

Neither of us spoke for the longest time. In all the weeks since I had seen him last, I had in my mind poured out to him everything that had happened, everything I had thought and felt, but here in the flesh, words were clumsy and exhausting things we had little need of. Later, we would talk for hours, sharing and comparing our experiences, but at this particular moment, such things were beyond us. Finally, Chowder spoke.

"Nothing seems real. I feel so strange."

"It will take time, to be sure, but we will heal."

"I feel ..." He began to sob, and I got out of my chair bending to him. As my eyes filled with tears in sympathy and in concert to my own pain, I took him in my arms.

"It's all right, my love. Cry it out. We are together now, and together we will remain."

Chowder heaved several more sobs. "Sorry. It's all been so horrible. I didn't cry till now, though. What must you think of me?"

"I love you. Look at me. I'm crying too, see? You are no more a baby than I. Besides, it's natural to cry under such circumstances, I should think. And anyhow, I don't give a damn, and neither should you."

"My God, but I missed you."

"And I you." We pulled each other closer and kissed fiercely, and then he began to sob again, so I held him close as one would a child and told him again and again that I loved him and we were together to stay, tears streaming down my face the while. He slowly left off sobbing and held on tightly to me, as I did to him, and we held each other as close as we could until we heard a soft rapping at the door, and George saying,

"Hello, Chowder, will you come? Your bath is ready."

LVII

"YES, I'LL BE RIGHT THERE," said Chowder, wiping his eyes with the back of his hands as he got up from his chair. He tucked his blanket 'round himself, and opened the door. A smiling George entered and lay a set of clothing upon one of the beds, except for the shoes, which he placed near the hearth.

"These are spares and cast offs, from Immanuel and Theodore mostly, but if they fit, which I believe they ought, they will do for a few days. We will get the tailor and shoemaker in here to fit you properly very soon. Perhaps tomorrow."

"Why, thank you so very much," said Chowder, "and Immanuel and Theodore too."

"Most welcome. You'd do the same for any of us, I'm sure," said George. "Now then, love, come. Let's get you clean."

I followed as George led Chowder to the end of the hall and down the recurving stairway to another corridor, which led off the servants' kitchen. But a short ways down this hall a door opened into an unusual room, in the center of which was a large tub entirely of copper, which at one end rose head high in a very broad, fan-like appendage above a small seat. The walls and floor of this room were covered in tile of sky blue, the likes of which neither Chowder nor I had ever seen, and clouds of steam rose from the water nearly filling the tub.

"Frederick, he's the undercook's boy, is heating more water, so you may rinse thoroughly. He will bring another bucketful or three as soon as they are ready. And you needn't worry about splashing water about. Everything is tiled, as you can see, and there is a drain in the floor. The tub has its own drain, too, so when you are done, just uncover the drain, and the water will flow away, sparing the trouble of carrying it out."

We were staggered by the brilliance of it, and said as much.

"And here's a bar of soap," he said, proffering a small, brick-like object of translucent, amber-colored substance. Chowder accepted this and examined it, sniffing it carefully, then handed it to me. The bar, as George had styled it, was gummy to the touch, and had an odd, yet pleasant odor. We had seen soap before, of course, but only the soft sort used by washerwomen.

"Towels here," said George, pointing to a cabinet, "and sponges and wash cloths there," gesturing in turn to a shelf along the wall beyond the tub. "When done, you may wear a towel back to your chamber and then dress or not, as you wish. That's up to you. That old blanket can go in the laundry. Frederick will bring your supper up a little after six, and I think that about covers it. If you need anything, come down to the kitchen, and someone will help you. Very likely me, actually." He smiled, bowed, and withdrew, closing the door behind himself.

"My goodness," said Chowder. "I feel like a lord."

"Fortunately, you do not behave as one," said I, grinning. "Go on, step into it."

"Right," said he, dropping his blanket and sheet. He stepped into the tub and sat on the little seat, the warm water coming well up his thighs.

"No, go on, get right down into the water. Then, when you are all wet, you sit on the seat and wash."

"Again you are the bathing master," he laughed, lowering himself until he was almost completely covered, then he pinched his nostrils and submerged. When he emerged, he shook his head, sending water flying. "Damn, this feels extraordinarily good. Why don't people take baths, I wonder."

"Supposed to sap your strength, is what I believe people say."

"That's all right then. I haven't any strength left to sap, so there's no harm to be done." He sat again on the seat, took the bar of soap and rubbed it into his hair, producing a prodigious, if rather dun lather. Finding a bucket on the floor, I filled it with water from the tub and, when he had paused, poured it over his head. He soaped his hair again, and I rinsed him again until after several iterations, his hair lathered white and clean.

"Now stand up," said I. I took the soap and a sponge, and went several times over his entire body, rinsing between whiles, until nothing was left to wash.

"I could do this for myself, you know," said Chowder, as I very gently washed under his foreskin. "Not a little boy."

"And deprive me of the pleasure of doing it for you? I think not, sir!"

"Ah, yes. Well, I'll wash you one of these days, and you will remember it," he said, laughing.

Frederick rapped on the door and brought in two buckets of steaming, very warm water. Frederick was blond and very fair, and his round face was all pleasantness, even if it did not bespeak the most penetrating of wits. I took one of the buckets and poured it over Chowder's shoulders, and Frederick emptied the other over Chowder's head. Chowder then stepped out of the tub and began to dry himself with the large cotton towel I handed him, as Frederick reached into the tub and pulled out a wooden plug, whereupon the water in the tub began to drain away.

"Where does it go?" I asked.

"Into the cesspool," said Frederick. "There are several beneath this house. Ah, look at him," he said, nodding towards Chowder. "Clean and lovely as can be."

Chowder beamed. He was indeed several shades lighter. Despite having lost considerable weight in prison, to the point of having become scrawny, and showing yet many bruises and scratches upon his face, he was as appealing as ever to me.

I thanked Frederick for his service, at which he withdrew, saying his chamber was next to ours, and not to hesitate if we needed anything. To Chowder I said, "Come, let's go up. I don't know about you, but I am exhausted."

"Exactly so," said Chowder.

Back in our chamber, Chowder lay upon one of the beds. "It's a very pleasant sensation, being clean. I quite like it. But the inside of me is not as well as it might be, sadly. How about you?"

"Much the same, I'm afraid. I ache everywhere and am too warm. Not a feeling I'm fond of. May I join you?"

"Please."

I disrobed and lay beside him, but the heat now radiating from our bodies, we did not hold each other close. I had another headache, and I was again near to trembling. I wanted nothing other than to lie in darkness and make not the slightest movement or effort of any kind. Even to talk was now too much. Gently squeezing his hand, I said, simply, "I love you. I think I will go to my own bed, actually," but Chowder did not hear me, as he had already fallen asleep.

I slept very hard and long, quite dreamlessly, not waking until some time before dawn. Rain pelted against the windows, and I rose in dim, leaden, light to see St. James' Square as vacant as it was sodden. In taking inventory, I found myself to be decidedly feverish, but not fiercely so. Everything ached, especially, it seemed, my joints. And yet despite, or perhaps because of, the fever and pains, I was possessed of a deep and exquisitely peaceful languor. Chowder slept on, breathing deeply and evenly, and I allowed the moment to penetrate, thinking of all we had endured, for we were arrived in a safe harbor at last, if we would but survive our illness.

I was quite hungry. Wondering what had become of the dinner we had been too insensible to receive, I opened the door of our chamber to find on the floor two domed silver trays and a smaller tea tray, complete with teapot and cups. I brought these in, and placing them on the small window-side table, lifted the dome to find a dish of boiled beef, potatoes, and parsnips, with half a loaf of bread and much butter. It was cold, of course, but tasted very good indeed, as did the tea, even if it too was necessarily cold. I then built up the fire, and in mucking about with it, made enough noise to wake Chowder, who stretched and rose, sitting himself at the table, where I presented him with his supper.

"Why, thank you, indeed," said he. "First you bathe me, and now you serve me. I quite like this," he laughed, cramming a too-large piece of bread into his mouth, and following it with gulps of tea. "And, my goodness, but I am hungry."

We made comparisons, soon establishing we were feeling similarly, having mild, but not raging, fever and many pains, yet good appetites. We marveled anew at our good fortune. After finishing our repast, I placed the trays where I had found them in the hall, and then he joined me in my bed, where we soon fell back asleep, each of us cradling the other in our arms in turn, much as we had slept together when first we had met.

We were awakened not long after by a soft rapping at the door, and when I responded, "Yes, please come in," Frederick entered with a large tray containing two plates of eggs and bacon, and more bread, butter, and tea, which we found we were every bit as hungry for as we had been for our dawn repast. The day had brightened and a bit of sun was finding its way between towering clouds of brilliant white, throwing the splendid mansions on the Square into bold relief.

"Feeling all right?" Frederick asked, as he lay the trays upon our table. "I'm told a physician is expected soon, who will examine the both of you, and the tailor and shoemaker are to follow this afternoon."

We thanked him and allowed we did, in fact, feel much better, if a bit feverish yet.

"That's good then," he said, "You can just put the trays back in the hall, if you like, or if you are feeling up to it, bring them down to the kitchen. The staff who have not yet had the pleasure are impatient to meet the two of you."

We thanked him again and fell to when he had gone, soon finishing. We then dressed and carried the trays down the stars to the kitchen, where they were received by Frederick in the scullery. He introduced us to Sebastian, one of the undercooks, quite tall and every bit as wide, with a very large, full, and dark beard. He primarily cooked for the servants—this was but the servants' kitchen, after all—and at table in the servants' dining room we met Cyril, another chamber maid, diminutive and possessed of a fluttery intensity, Edward the coachman, who was unaccountably grave, Philip the pleasant and alert groom, and Jeremiah, a stable hand, who seemed rather a rustic country boy, but very appealing withal.

There were also two footmen, Sean, an Irishman, and Immanuel, of whom I have spoken. Charles, a scullery boy, and Theodore, Mr. Broughton's private secretary, as previously mentioned, completed the party. Later, Chowder and I were to meet a number of others—more than a score of servants were on staff— but as they were rarely all at table at the same time, this was accomplished over several days.

All greeted us very pleasantly, and as a whole exuded warm ingratiation and no little competence, but in comparison to Mr. Duckworth's household, they were on the whole a serious, even somewhat drab lot, apart from Immanuel, who comported himself with every evidence of an impressive acuity, and Theodore, whom I suspected of a quick, if furtive, wit. They were not unsmiling or unfriendly, but not much given to joking or fun either. I supposed it made for greater efficiency or stability, or both, and we were, after all, there to work rather than play.

Returned to our chamber, Chowder and I lay on his bed and began at last to talk of our experiences, which were necessarily similar except in certain particulars.

"That common pit was very bad," said he. "That's where I got me nasty black eye. Bastards."

"What happened?"

"It's very crowded in there, you know. Not enough room enough to turn around, and God, but it stinks. And this one oaf, he's all of half an inch away, huge, foul-smelling fellow, great stinking beard right in me face, looks down at me and says, 'Aren't you the pretty one,' he says. 'How's me molly boy?' he says, mocking like. 'I ain't no molly,' says I, 'and you can take it back.' Well, he wouldn't take it back, just kept on with it, and now everyone's watching. I couldn't let that stand, now, could I? I had to teach him a lesson, right? So I punched him in the nose."

"Remind me not to anger you," I laughed.

"Now you are just being silly," said he. "He didn't anger me. He insulted me, and was in want of correction. Not the same thing at all."

"Right. Sorry. You are entirely correct, of course. Please do go on."

"Well, it started a brawl, it did, and in another minute everyone is a-going at it. "'He's a molly,' one would say, 'Let's have at 'im,' and the other, 'No, 'e isn't, you can lay off 'im,' and 'Aren't you the fat arse,' and straightaway they go to blows. I don't even know which one punched me. Don't believe it was the fellow I hit, but whichever one it was, he got me, all right. Me eye hurt for days, and I couldn't see out of it for a long time. Seems to be doing better now, though.

"So, anyways, then, I don't know how many guards waded in, curses and truncheons a-flyin', and now everyone's fighting them instead of each other. And there're girls and women in there, too, shrieking 'Rape!' and pissing and hollering. The women had it very rough, they did, and not just then, but the noise they made was enough to drive one mad. Finally, the guards sorted it out by turning the hose on 'em. Us, I mean. I dunno, but after that no one bothered me. I did get 'im good, I did. Think I broke his nose. You never saw so much blood. And then two days later I'm in the semi-private room, thanks to Mr. Broughton."

I told him of my semi-private room, the drunkards, and the upended privy bucket.

"Damn. Well, I did not have it quite so bad, there. They were a dull and melancholy lot, though. But I will tell you one thing: do not ever ask me to play cribbage with you. I mean, not ever. I am sick of it enough to last me all my life."

"I can agree to that, if you will agree never to serve me watery gruel," I allowed, laughing.

"If you insist," he laughed in turn, and held me close.

I looked into his eyes. "I say, when was the last time I told you what a handsome young man you are? Because you are, you know."

"Dunno, but I do think you should kiss me, right now."

Which, of course, I did.

LVIII

WE WERE THUS ENGAGED WHEN we heard another rapping at the door, this time louder and more authoritative. Chowder opened the door to Mr. Broughton and another gentleman, in a claret waistcoat of many pockets.

"Ah, Chowder and Joe," said Mr. Broughton. "So good to see you up and looking better. This is Mr. Palsgrave, the physician of whom I spoke. He has much experience with gentlemen prisoners and has even attended several who stood in the pillory."

We responded appropriately to the introduction, and Mr. Broughton sat in one of the chairs at our window table, looking on while Mr. Palsgrave wasted no time, commencing immediately to look very closely at our scratches, into which he carefully rubbed tiny amounts of a scarlet unguent, saying it was the latest mercury compound, and very efficacious. He then took our pulses, examined our bruises, felt of our sore joints, and peered into our chamber pots, asking many questions all the while, until, finally, he pressed his palm against our foreheads, and bade us both to sit, each upon his own bed.

"I am very encouraged," said he. "The fever is not without danger but is mild, and we must hope it remains so. If it becomes very high, the prognosis is grave, but I do believe in such a case we would be seeing it already. I have seen a man die within four days of standing in the pillory, though he seemed to survive it well enough at first, but then the sudden onset of a very high fever rapidly finished him. I believe the difference there is that he was deeply cut about the face by broken glass, and much dirt got into the wound.

"There is no doubting the filth thrown bears much contagion. These two, to their great good fortune, have no deep gashes, and the unguent will quell the suppuration of these scratches. The bruises, though painful, are of much less concern, as nothing is broken. Now, the blood in Joe's urine, if it does not worsen, is not so very bad, really. I have seen young men recover perfectly well from just such injury, and that the boys have good appetites is a very welcome sign indeed. They have much catching up to do after a month of prison fare. Give them as much meat and drink as they will take. Now I will bleed them, which will let out what corruption may have taken residence, and then you have nothing to do but keep an eye on the fever and feed them well." He smiled.

"Thank you, very much indeed. We will feed them prodigiously, to be sure," Mr. Broughton laughed. "And when would you say they may be capable of working?"

"There is no harm in it now," said Mr. Palsgrave, "If they do not have too much pain. Very light duty, of course, not more than two hours per day to start. At first, you might have them simply accompany one or another of your other servants as they go about their duties, to give them a sense of the tasks at hand. Just a suggestion, of course," said he, bowing slightly and smiling again. "And I would not at all be surprised if in a week, or at most two, they are capable of putting in a full day."

"Ah, yes, very encouraging indeed, and thank you for the suggestion. I like it very much. And yes, please proceed."

Mr. Palsgrave took from his satchel a lancet, the sight of which made me shudder, and a small, silver bowl. I almost protested, as I had when in Mr. Peevers's infirmary, but thought better of it. I wanted nothing more than to be wholly accepted in this place, and to please Mr. Broughton. To question his judgement, or that of his physician, struck me as a poor way to begin, so I submitted to the procedure, as did Chowder.

We both looked away when the lancet was applied to our inner elbows, which did not hurt so very much, but I do not mind saying I was not at all sorry when it was over and Mr. Palsgrave bandaged our arms. His ministrations now complete, he said good-bye and departed, leaving the silver bowl of blood on the table. It seemed he had taken perhaps a gill from each of us, and Chowder and I found we felt little altered after the procedure, if perhaps slightly lightheaded.

Mr. Broughton now addressed us. "Well now, what do you boys think? Ready to get started, as Mr. Palsgrave suggested?"

We both allowed we thought it the best possible idea.

"Excellent. Joe, I have it in mind for you to become assistant to Theodore, and in time to be able to fulfill any function of his that needs doing, as he directs. He is my personal secretary, as I believe you know, and is quite overburdened, especially with my personal correspondence, which seems only to increase, leaving little time for the other projects I have put him to. Among other things, he is teaching Immanuel to read and write, and there are the scrap-books, which he will tell you of. Research and documentation pertaining to my art collection is so enormous a task, I am thinking of retaining someone just for that purpose, but in time you can help with that, too. And, eventually I will ask you to catalogue my library, which it sorely wants.

"Theodore will train you in all of this, no need to concern yourself with the details now. Much of the art is at my country estate, in any case. But to start you off, how would you like to work on the scrap-books? It is my intention to keep a record of everything in the press concerning those of our persuasion. It is just a whim of mine, but I feel it to be important. You can work in Theodore's study, which is just beside my personal office, for an hour or two every morning this first week to start. Assuming you mend as Mr. Palsgrave believes and I very much hope you will, in the weeks following we will add another task I have in mind. Over time, you will pick up more pieces bit by bit, thus relieving Theodore of the worst of his overload. Does that sound agreeable?"

I averred that it sounded not only agreeable, but I could imagine nothing better, with which response Mr. Broughton was very pleased.

"And you, Chowder, I have a choice for you. Henry tells me I am in need of a second chamber, ah, maid," and here he emitted a genial chuckle, "here on the servant's side, but it is very dull work, carrying every day water and coal, and twice a month clean sheets, up to all of the servant's bed chambers, and ashes, laundry, and water down again, day after day, to say nothing of the chamber pots, and I fear you have too much wit for it. None of my staff are dullards, or I wouldn't have them, but the work is tedious and requires no skill.

"So, the other thought I had was the kitchen. The servant's kitchen is well enough staffed, but the central kitchen, where my meals are prepared and everything is made ready for the entertainments I host, is in want of an assistant undercook. Peeling potatoes is not the most interesting work, but over time you will learn much, as the meals are quite varied, and the entertainments require broad application of the culinary art. And, at certain seasons there is extra work in the gardens, to which you may be called from time to time to pitch in." Mr. Broughton looked eagerly at Chowder, who had been listening with rapt attention. "So then, what say you?"

"By all means, the kitchen is far more interesting to me, and I do thank you, sir!" Chowder was very eager, here displaying that alert, mobile countenance I have ever found so very attractive in him.

"Excellent!" beamed Mr. Broughton, rising. "I thought so. I believe, Chowder, you will enjoy working under Richard. He is an excellent cook and manager, and I am fortunate to have him in my employ. You will learn much from him, and there is no reason why you should not in time rise to a position of greater responsibility."

He shook both of our hands, smiling broadly. "These positions will serve the both of you very well as the years pass. The truly expert cook, and the alert and well organized secretary, are much in demand. There is no end of indifferent applicants, of course, but the better ones with strong recommendation are never without employment. Not that I have any intention of letting either of you go, mind you."

"We thank you with all our hearts, sir. We will not let you down. You may be sure of it," said I, with which Chowder concurred heartily.

"Excellent," said Mr. Broughton a second time. "I will tell Henry and Theodore what has been decided, and they will take it from there. You may expect them to stop by later today, so do not stray too far from your chamber."

And he withdrew, leaving Chowder and I alone together again. With one mind, we lay ourselves down again upon his bed.

"My goodness, what do you think of that?" I asked.

"Not at all bad, is what I say," said Chowder. "But weren't we in the middle of something when Mr. Broughton and the physician wanted in?"

"Ah, yes, I do believe I recall something or other. Now, what was it?"

"Mmm, was it this?" He laughed and kissed me. Suffering this time no interruptions, we proceeded to joyous lovemaking, in which we were restrained but little by our bruises and feverish enervation, following which, we slept arm-in-arm yet again, though it was by now nearly noon, and a very bright day for late November.

LIX

WE HAD NOT SLEPT LONG when we were awakened yet again, this time by Frederick, entering with our luncheon, which proved to be bread, butter, boiled cod and cabbage, and a pot of ale. Frederick was accompanied by the tailor and shoemaker, who made a quick business of measuring us. The tailor said very little, other than, upon departing, "Be about a fortnight, I suppose," and the shoemaker said nothing at all.

We sat at our table beside the window, looked out at the Square and a great crush of traffic, brilliant in the rare, late November sun, and ate. I had not realized how hungry I was until I sat down.

"And when you were in the pillory," I asked between swallows, "what was that like? I mean, did anything unusual happen?"

"Dunno. What's unusual, I suppose, is I don't remember it. I remember being taken there and walking up the stairs to the platform, and a bit of being locked in, but then, nothing. It's a complete blank. You'd think I would remember, right? But I don't. The next thing I remember, I was in the cart going home to Eppie's, hidden under a load of straw. I remember nothing at all of the pelting, which I suppose is a blessing. Why? Do you remember it?"

"Some of it." I told him then of the mollies throwing roses, the battle that erupted all 'round, the bottle of gin, and what Mr. Bartlett had told me of the efforts of Mr. Jackson and the others on horseback to inhibit the worst excesses of the mob. But though I had determined to tell him of my vision, the words were slow to come. "And then, I don't know, it was extremely odd. You will think me daft, but I was somewhere else. Not in the pillory at all. And I saw the both of us, but we weren't as we are now. We were each as the sun, radiant, perfect, and whole, and nothing could harm us."

"Seems a very beautiful dream, and much preferred to feeling turds hit one's face."

"It was no dream. I was every bit in my senses as I am now. Not that I understand it, mind you, but it has changed how I think and what I believe. We live this life, so often perilous and grim, but there is much, much more to it, to everything, that we cannot see in the ordinary course of events. I can't explain it. I have a great thirst to know more, but I can't imagine where one goes to find out."

He had finished eating, put down his fork, and regarded me with a very thoughtful expression. When he spoke, the penetration of his intelligence was on full display. He would, at moments, sound very like a common laborer, as when telling me of the brawl in the pen at Newgate, but at other times his insight was of another order entirely.

"Do you think, then, that you were Divinely inspired? I'd say you were. Very likely, I mean. I don't know anything about it, but one morning Miss Strickenwell went off about seers, or was it saints, and the visions they would have, so I suppose it's possible."

"But I'm no saint, and you know it. I'm never more inspired than when I am naked in bed with you. And I didn't see God, just you and me, but in another place, and in another form."

"And yet you have been inspired by your experience. You just said it has changed what you believe and how you think. Now, if you raved about it all the day long and shat yourself and failed to notice, a person would say you were mad, but this is not the case. You behave normally, and you make sense whenever you speak. So what I have to say is, if God, or who or whatever, has granted you this experience, I say embrace it, as indeed it seems you have. But whether you call yourself saint or sodomite, or simply Joe, is the least important part of it, I should think."

I paused a moment before speaking, pondering his words. "Once again you have cut to the heart of things, and I am in your debt. I must think more upon it. But, I say, you haven't touched your soup," said I, gesturing towards the bowl of blood Frederick had failed to remove when he set our luncheon down on the table.

"Oh, dear. And to think I stinted myself so that you could have it, and now it's cold. Do you think Sebastian will make black pudding of it?"

"One can only hope. Would be a terrible shame to waste it."

But here Henry arrived and took Chowder with him to the central kitchen to meet Richard and be shown what was what. I left the door open, and very soon after the two of them had departed, Theodore appeared, holding in one arm a large folder full of newspapers. He hesitated for the briefest moment before greeting me, pushing his spectacles up his nose as he did so.

"Ah, Hello, Joe. And how are you?"

"A pleasure to see you again, Theodore. I suppose I am well enough," said I, smiling.

"Well enough to come with me? Henry has directed me to show you my study and a few things, which I am very pleased to do."

"But of course." I followed him into the hall, retracing the path Henry had taken when he brought Chowder and I in, but we turned down another corridor and entered a wing of the mansion I had not seen before.

We soon arrived at a very comfortable, small library, in the middle of which stood a large antique desk facing a pair of very tall windows, that overlooked an inner courtyard. Theodore lay his folder of papers atop a tottering pile of similar folders on the desk. Many such piles cluttered the edges of the room, obscuring the lower shelves of books.

"This is Mr. Broughton's personal office. He has a much larger one for his commercial interests, and premises in the City, from which a small army administers his affairs, but this is about none of that."

"This is very pleasant, I must say. Mr. Jackson's premises were but utilitarian, in comparison to this." Looking out the window, I saw the courtyard was filled by a formal garden centering on a fountain, in the shape of two cavorting porpoises and a young woman in flowing robes. The garden was dormant, given the season, but its appearance in the already waning late autumn sun was pleasant indeed. "Are those roses?"

"Yes, and a wonder to behold in June, they are. Not much to see at the moment, though. Now, over here, is my study." He showed me to a much smaller room to the side. "I gather Mr. Broughton's office was once a bedchamber, and what is now my study was a closet. But it is airy enough and has its own window."

Theodore's study was indeed diminutive. He had just enough room for a small but serviceable desk, two little bookshelves, and a tiny table and a second chair, but the ceiling was high and the window tall, just as they were in the larger adjoining study, which did much to prevent it from being close.

"I have enough other things to do that I am rarely in my study before noon, and Mr. Broughton is here no more than a few hours a week, so even if we do overlap, which as I say is unlikely, I can use the larger room in which to write correspondence or do whatever it is I need to do."

I expressed my understanding and gratitude.

"You are most welcome. Now, the scrap-books are very simple. You merely need to look through the papers and magazines, cut out any mention of mollies and such, no matter how slight, paste it neatly into the scrap-book, and then note beside it what paper and the date. Here beside my desk are the folders containing the oldest papers. It is important to place the items in the scrap-books in the correct order, so do keep an eye on that. And this is the current scrap-book. Scissors, here, and paste, there," he said, indicating in turn the items mentioned. "If there is anything at all you need, please do not hesitate to ask."

"I shan't and thank you again, very much."

We walked back to the bed chamber I shared with Chowder, and I took careful note of the path, that I might be able to find my way the following morning. As we walked, Theodore and I chatted, but beyond telling me his parents had been in service to Mr. Broughton's father, and lived yet elsewhere at Mr. Broughton's expense, his reticence offered but little satisfaction to my curiosity. I was not so boorish as to press him, and I reminded myself with a sense of wonder, this was my new employment. With a bit of luck, we would have years in which to deepen our acquaintance. From what Henry had said, it seemed safe to assume all of the servants were of the sodomitical persuasion, but such a thing was yet very new to me and seemed too miraculous to be true.

Returned to Chowder's and my chamber, I found Chowder at the table, looking at the traffic in the square. He had much to tell of the central kitchen and of Richard, with which and whom he was much impressed, and I told him of my visit with Theodore to his study. Time passed quickly, and soon darkness fell, not long after which our supper was brought. We ate it contentedly, but found ourselves exhausted by what had been, feverish as we were, a very full day.

We fell into bed, though it was not yet seven. Chowder was soon asleep, but sleep did not come for a long time for me. I would almost nod off, but on the verge of sleep find myself back in the pillory, suffering the worst of it, from which I would then recoil into full wakefulness, suffused with a dread no amount of reassurance could dispel. I thought of waking Chowder, that he might hold and comfort me, but forbore. He needed his sleep, and I did not care to tax his resources. I told myself not to be a fool, as I had survived Mr. Peevers, Rowland, Mrs. Cudworth, Newgate, and indeed the pillory, to say nothing of the earlier death of my parents, had been vouchsafed a vision, and arrived in a safe harbor at last, with Chowder beside me. Prospects were, at last, bright indeed, but at that moment my heart would have none of it. Finally I slept, only to be visited by fitful, troubled dreams of standing yet again in the pillory, and Rowland smirking.

Frederick awakened us the following morning shortly after six, wanting to know whether we would eat in our bedchamber or with the other servants. After an instant's consultation, we replied we would be down shortly.

"Very good, then. Breakfast is at seven. No need for haste." he responded.

We descended at a quarter to seven, finding most of the servants we had met previously, and several more whom we had not, already at table. They were drinking coffee and discussing any of the day's tasks that were to be out of the ordinary. We sat ourselves next to Immanuel, who greeted us most pleasantly, and listened. Mr. Broughton was to entertain several members of Parliament for a luncheon. Though Richard supervised the other kitchen, he took his breakfast in this one so as to be party to the planning for the day. He said it was to be a light luncheon and little to it, but he would not mind if Chowder were able to attend through the morning to see how it was done. Henry mentioned he had much silver yet to polish, and wanted George and Cyril to attend it to it no later than nine, which meant some of the morning's routine tasks would not be completed until later in the day, but this was not expected to present any problems.

Henry then added, "Though it is not to be for nearly a month, I will mention now in mid-December, Mr. Broughton will again host the annual Mollies' Ball, as he did last year." This was met with general approbation and broad smiles. "There will be the customary arrangements," Henry continued. "A buffet will be prepared so the guests may serve themselves, leaving the greater part of you free to attend the ball. Those whose services are absolutely required will trade off early and late shifts, so none shall be deprived of the opportunity to partake." This was met with more smiles and applause.

Sebastian then announced breakfast was ready, and we rose to serve ourselves a rich, creamy porridge, as unlike the watery gruel I had once endured as could be imagined. On the counter to the right of the stove, bangers and boiled eggs, bread and plenty of butter and jam, and yet more coffee, tea, and cream and sugar, and a pile of plump, radiant oranges, finer than any I had ever seen, were available. The large, many compartmented cast-iron stove sent forth a wonderful heat, and from

---

it wafted smells of the morning's baking. Though I had already had ample evidence the food in this house was generous and of the first quality, I thought I should pinch myself to be certain it was not a dream.

Following breakfast, I made my way to Theodore's study and began to look over the oldest papers in search of any mention of mollies or sodomites, which I soon found to be very scarce indeed. In those first two hours, I found but one such, telling of the death of a sodomite in the pillory. As the paper was dated two years previously, I assumed he was the fellow Mr. Jackson had mentioned. I found it so affecting, I quite forgot myself in reading it. This pattern was to continue, as the clippings, though infrequent and never very long, invariably made for melancholy reading, concerning as they did men and boys unlucky enough to be caught, taken to court, and sent to the pillory, or sometimes the noose, or raids of so-called "molly houses," wherein those of our persuasion are wont to congregate. I learned much over time, and not only of mollies, as in looking over the papers, I was unable to forbear reading many another article, especially in the *Gentleman's Magazine*, which offered many lengthy digressions on widely varied topics of the day.

As promised, the tailor and shoemaker returned a fortnight later with two sets of livery for each of us, appropriate to our various functions and the vagaries of the weather, from, for Chowder, heavy boots and heavy woolen trousers for laboring in the gardens, to the finest of dress in which to be seen by those of quality upon whom we might attend, and also to wear at the rapidly approaching Mollies' Ball.

LX

OVER THE ENSUING WEEKS, CHOWDER and I were introduced by degrees into the routines of the house, lengthening our hours until we were putting in entire days and working as hard as anyone. For some days, Theodore diverted me from the scrap-books to prepare and address many score of invitations to the coming Mollies' Ball, which were to be put in the post. In time, Chowder and I found ourselves healed; that is to say, no corporeal traces of our ordeal remained, but I will say our spirits persisted in reverberation. We were both subject, if at decreasing intervals, to nightmares and low spirits, but these were leavened, on my part at least, by random moments of exaltation when I would find myself on the point of re-entering my vision, which I continued to ponder.

We were grateful for the diversion offered by our employment and the camaraderie amongst the staff, which we found to be rather more of than we had at first seen. Chowder did indeed peel many potatoes, but between-whiles learned other tasks, beginning with how to fire the enormous stove. This task was not so very complex, but it had do be done just so, or the coal would not catch. The stove required over an hour to heat up properly before it could be used, and Chowder started it at four in the morning, making him one of the earliest risers in the house. He was given a wonderful clock in recognition, that would ring a bell at any desired hour if one would but insert the requisite pin in the proper spot. I came to loath it with a particular intensity, as I did not have to be up for another hour and a half, and it invariably wakened me. I often could not get back to sleep but could do nothing about it as Chowder required it for his employment, in consideration of which I resolved to not let it irk me, severely annoying though it may have been.

THE BALL, AS I LEARNED from Theodore as we sat together addressing envelopes, was an annual affair, first given three years previously by Mr. Broughton subsequent to his inheritance of his father's vast estate. The brilliance of it was, that unlike a conventional entertainment, little regard was given to the station of those invited but much to his persuasion, and whether he were known to Mr. Broughton or those in service to him and deemed trustworthy. For this one evening, those in service mingled on an equal footing with their masters, as we were, indeed, all of us equal as outcasts before the law. Thus it was beginning in the late afternoon of the chosen day, as darkness fell, many a fine carriage arrived bearing gentlemen of wealth and exquisite refinement, but also tradesmen, apprentices, men in service, young men of uncertain status, and even laborers, every one of them admitted with welcoming grace.

Chowder and I were free to disport ourselves as we liked, as we were to be celebrated for having survived the pillory, and were to be introduced to this society. As Henry had promised, most of Mr. Broughton's servants, once preparations were complete, were similarly relieved of duty. Those whose service was indispensable, tending to the buffet tables, the provision of liquid refreshments, and to cleaning up as the evening went on, were organized into two shifts, so those serving early might be free later, and vice versa.

Chowder and I dressed in our finest livery, clothing such as neither of us had ever before possessed or worn, and regarded each other for a moment. Looking at Chowder, resplendent in coat and tails, ruffled shirt of brilliant white, cotton stockings, black shoes with brass buckles, and waistcoat and breeches of the finest manufacture, my heart, and not only my heart, leapt.

"I know you have just put your new clothes on," said I, "and yet, seeing you in them, I want nothing so much as to tear it all off you."

Chowder laughed. "Will a kiss do? And later, I promise, you may have your way, if I don't tear yours off first."

I agreed, laughing, and we kissed the first of many times that night.

We made our way to the ballroom, where we were among the first to arrive, and found it brilliantly lit by many score of candles on great candelabra in the corners, and by six enormous crystal chandeliers suspended in a row down the middle of the ceiling, each bearing as many candles again. The buffet tables were laden with every conceivable type of cold meat and fish resting on beds of ice, and cheeses similarly varied, intermixed with elaborate arrangements of oranges, divers kinds of apples, plums, and grapes, whilst on tables lining the walls several hundred glasses of red, white, and rosé wine had been set out next to great urns of coffee and tea, two enormous punch bowls, and trays of pastries and small cakes iced in an infinite variety of hues. At one end of the ballroom was a broad dais, upon which chairs and music stands were arranged for the chamber orchestra to come.

Chowder, of course, had worked very hard in the kitchens as preparations were made, and proudly showed me a sugar sculpture of a diminutive church and churchyard he had made.

"I spent an entire day on this. I thought Richard would be displeased I had taken so long, but he was delighted when he saw it."

"It's magnificent. I am entirely overawed by your talent. I have done little but write names and addresses on envelopes, which any fool could do."

"Any fool that can write, perhaps, which isn't so very many. I wanted to make a little Christ on the Cross out of chocolate for the churchyard, but Richard said it wouldn't do to have it eaten."

We looked up from the arrayed confections to see guests had begun to trickle in, among them Mr. Duckworth, in the company of a thin young man I did not recognize, who immediately went to the buffet and piled a plate very high with meat and bread. Holding it in one hand, he then took a large dish of punch in the other, and sat alone at a table where he devoted himself utterly to the process of ingestion, while Mr. Duckworth, seeing me, approached. He was dressed very richly in scarlet breeches, bejeweled sandals, and a long-tailed, richly embroidered coat of sky blue, into which were worked many pearls. His wig was of the first quality and latest fashion, understated and tied with silver thread.

"Ah, young Joseph, I am very pleased to see you. Really I am." He bowed deeply with an exaggerated flourish, smiling with watery sincerity.

"'Tis a pleasure to see you, sir." I nodded my head and smiled in reciprocation.

"None of this 'sir' nonsense, now. We are all equals here. And this is your Chowder?" Without waiting for affirmation, Mr. Duckworth bowed again, now to Chowder, so low it seemed his wig must fall off or his brow scrape the floor. I laughed in what I hoped was a not unkindly manner. Mr. Duckworth took no notice. Righting himself, he said to me in his ever effeminate and precisely enunciated tones, "Well, and dear me! I must say, my dear boy, that were I you, I would have made exactly the same choice. I am but a drooling old fool, and here you have a young man as fine and fit as yourself. I can only dream of such and assure you I do understand. Please permit me to congratulate you on surviving your ordeal, your employment here, and on the aptness of your romantic attachments." Again he bowed, very low.

He seemed actually to mean it, and I thanked him heartily for it.

"And so you see," said he, "that I really am not so very terrible." He smiled again, rather too broadly, entreaty in his eyes. Safe now beyond the reach of his manipulations, I was free to be gracious in return.

"Indeed, Mr. Duckworth, you have been very kind to me, and I am most grateful to you for it. To be sure, you are not so very terrible." I bowed to him as deeply as I dared, not caring to lose my balance.

Chowder now said his piece and bowed very low, as well. "I do thank you for taking Joe in, and for everything you have done to help him."

Yet again Mr. Duckworth bowed to an absurd depth. "There is someone I would like you two to meet. Will you come with me?"

"But, of course."

The ballroom was now filling up, and the chamber orchestra had taken its places on the dais. Mr. Duckworth led us to the table where the thin young man was just finishing his meal, about to begin his second dish of punch. His clothes were clean, if very plain, but he was even thinner when seen at close quarters than he had at first appeared, and there was to him a haggardness perhaps not entirely explained by the habitual want of proper nourishment and sleep. His teeth were very poor, and his hair was graying and scanty despite his apparent youth.

"Joseph and Chowder, it is my pleasure to present Robert Bletchley. Robert, Joseph and Chowder, of whom I have spoken."

Robert offered the faintest hint of a smile. Looking at Mr. Duckworth, he seemed almost to roll his eyes, clearly having little use for formality and fuss.

"Call me Skinny. Everyone else does." He extended his hand but did not rise.

We shook hands. "A pleasure," said I.

"Robert, here, knew Mr. Peevers rather well. Didn't you?" said Mr. Duckworth.

"I did."

"Go on, tell them what you told me. Joe and Chowder met at Peevers' school in Little Eastcheap, before he went down."

"Ah. I don't envy you that." Skinny hesitated, gathering his thoughts. "I don't know ... Peevers, he was an odd duck."

"How did you come to know him?" asked I, in witless innocence.

"He, ah, hired me for an evening. A little sport, you know. He was pleased with me and hired me again on several occasions."

"He was still Governor of the school at that point, was he not?" Mr. Duckworth interjected.

"I can't say he was, as he never spoke of it. But given the date, you yourself said he must have been."

"Yes, that's right, I do believe so. But go on, tell them the rest of it."

Skinny looked at Mr. Duckworth quizzically, then shifted his gaze to me, hesitating. He then regarded Mr. Duckworth again, saying nothing.

"Yes, yes, very well," said Mr. Duckworth, reaching into his pocket and dropping a sixpence into Skinny's hand.

"At first he wanted only the usual sort of thing, but it wasn't long, I think the third time, that he gave me three pounds to beat him. He brought the switch I was to use on him. I don't mind saying I gave him his money's worth. I beat him quite severely, and he cried, he did. Tears. Said he was a very bad boy, he did." Skinny said this without looking at any of us, but straight ahead, his countenance without expression.

"Yes, and then, tell them the rest of it."

"Not long after that, he came to me again, and when we had finished our business, complained of a toothache that was rapidly worsening. I told him I could get him something to help it. It was very dear, but would quell the pain like nothing else. He said he didn't care what it cost. He must have the tooth out and would I please obtain it for him as soon as I could." Having said this, Skinny reverted to obdurate inarticulation, staring blankly ahead.

"Go on, tell them what it was," said Mr. Duckworth, but Skinny remained unmoved until Mr. Duckworth reprised his offering of silver.

"Opium. A great ball of it, enough to put even one as great and fat as Peevers right out. Told him to bite it, right on the tooth, and then suck on it till it was gone. Well, at first he was merely very fond of it, as people are, and then he refused to live without it, as people do, and before long he wanted nothing else, as people will. So then there were no more beatings nor buggery, but plenty of opium. Nothing but opium. I wrote him bills for cabinetry, but it was opium he got. Wasn't long before he was spending ten pounds a day on it and living in a back room of the brothel, for which he paid even more. All of which, of course, is what put him in the Fleet. I signed the instrument myself." He said this flatly, again looking at no one.

I knew nothing of opium, but it sounded very dangerous. Mr. Peevers was most unfortunate to have encountered it, and a fool at best, for having entertained it, assuming he had had any idea of what he was getting into, which perhaps he had not. Looking at Skinny, who, having drained his dish of punch, looked impatiently in the direction of the punchbowl, I thought to myself Mr. Peevers had more than met his match.

"Ah, extremely interesting," said I. "I had no idea. I do thank you, and you, Mr. Duckworth, for that intelligence." Chowder and I took our leave of them, as I had just espied Reggie across the room, where he stood in conversation with Theodore, and was eager to introduce him properly to Chowder.

The ballroom was now filled nearly to capacity, and the chamber orchestra had begun to play. Reggie greeted us with warm effusion, saying to Chowder once I had introduced them, "Oh, my dear, you look ever so much better than you did the last time I saw you, when we all came to fetch you from your sister's. I cannot stand it, I must hug you both!" Which he did, first hugging Chowder and then me, with sincerest affection, while Theodore, having let go his reserve, looked on, smiling broadly.

"Reggie, you are the dearest thing," said I. "Were it not for you, I might be starving in the street."

"Not at all," said he. "I merely introduced you to Quentin. And besides, I cannot imagine you ever at a loss. Look at how you have done here. I had nothing to do with it." As he said this, he stood nearer to Theodore and took his hand. There was no show to it. The gesture was entirely natural, but it was evident they were more than friends.

"Well, in any case, I will ever think of you fondly and with gratitude." I bowed, and on rising said, "Am I to gather, then, that the two of you … ?"

"Are companions, yes. It's been over a year, now." Reggie leaned over to Theodore and kissed his cheek for the briefest instant, causing Theodore to giggle, then blush.

"He's a silly goose, and you must forgive him, as we all must," laughed Theodore.

"Indeed we will," said I. The four of us then chatted happily for some minutes, and we told Reggie of our progress at Mr. Broughton's, what we were being trained to do and everything that had happened. I then shared with him the intelligence Skinny had imparted regarding Mr. Peevers. "And what is this opium? I have never heard of it."

"You want nothing to do with it, I will tell you that. I have never tried it and will be sure never to try it, but I hear it is entirely beguiling at first. The problem is that very soon it becomes impossible to leave off, as one suffers unspeakable torments if one cannot have it, and one will then do anything at all to get it. It becomes one's entire life."

"Dear me, I have never heard of such a thing. Perhaps in a way not unlike tobacco, but worse, from the sound of it. I do thank you."

Scanning the room, I saw Mr. Jackson seated at a table with someone looking very like Dudley Bostok, and a gentleman whom I did not recognize. "I say, that's Mr. Jackson, there. Come, I will introduce you."

We crossed the room, navigating our way between a great many men of nearly every age and description, eating, drinking, conversing, laughing, and in many cases, flirting. Mr. Jackson greeted us with warm enthusiasm. I introduced Reggie and Theodore to Mr. Jackson, who introduced Dudley Bostok and Mr. Doxley, who had been instrumental in protecting us during the pelting, and whom I had not yet met. Reggie and Theodore graciously excused themselves, saying they were sure we had much to catch up on, and would not interfere. "I will allow you to part," said I, "but not before another hug," with which request Reggie happily complied.

Mr. Jackson invited us to sit. "Dudley, here, is my new employee. I've had enough of apprentices," he said, laughing, "if you don't mind my saying so. I find this modern arrangement has much to recommend it."

"Not at all," said I. "You might say I did not work out so very well."

"Not in the least due to any fault of your own," said Mr. Jackson. "I found you superb in every respect."

"You are, as ever, very kind, Mr. Jackson, and perhaps you are correct. But in future I shall err more on the side of discretion, if I am to err at all. But, Dudley, what a pleasant surprise."

Dudley smiled and nodded his head.

"You two have met?" Mr. Jackson was puzzled.

"Indeed," said Dudley.

"The Society for Moral Improvement," said I, laughing. "And I believed every word of it, that is, until you said it was all cant."

"It's a great pity you ran off so quickly," said Dudley. "I might have introduced you to a few friends who could have helped you."

"A lovely thought, and I thank you, but given I was to meet Rowland the next day, and he and Mrs. Cudworth were determined to seize me, I'm afraid the result would have been the same."

"We could have fought them off, you know. I would have enlisted dozens of sturdy young men, all the very best friends of mine, each one of whom would have wielded his massive cudgel."

We all broke out laughing. "Oh, dear me! Cudgels, indeed," said I. "And your hundreds of old ladies would have been right behind, swinging their pockets with lethal ferocity."

"Exactly so," laughed Dudley.

Mr. Doxley, who was as short as he was round, and rather older than Mr. Jackson, was one of Mr. Jackson's most capable printers and bookbinders. Chowder and I thanked him profusely for his efforts on our behalf, and the mood pivoted from levity to the very grave.

"A very dear, young friend of mine was pelted to death ten years ago," said he, "and I will never recover entirely from that blow. I would, and will, if necessary, give my life to prevent such a thing from happening again. Riding a horse through that mob and taking out the worst offenders was the least I could do. I swear, if that bastard had defied me and thrown another bottle of gin, I would have blown his brains out, and been very happy to answer for it."

"We are forever in your debt, sir," said Chowder.

"You are both most welcome, with all my heart. My greatest recompense is to see you both here, healthy and whole and together."

"I do thank you, again, sir," said I. "And I thank you again, Mr. Jackson, for everything you have done, but especially for standing up for me. I did put you in a difficult position, which I understand, and yet you were there when it mattered most."

"As I have said, in the last analysis, nothing was more important to me."

"Mr. Bartlett has told us that you and Rowland are at quits because of it."

"Indeed we are. His betrayal of you was as unforgivable as it was unnecessary. I will never see him again," he paused, "and now there is no possibility of it." His expression was very grave, much tinged with sadness.

"None at all, sir?"

"Rowland is dead. Several days after you were taken and he and I had had that great and final row, I received a letter from him telling me he was very sorry for everything, and begging me to reconsider. I answered I could not, as I now found him and his acts entirely odious. It was two days after that, his body was found. He had hanged himself from a joist in a cellar room he had taken for the night. My reply was found in his pocket."

"Oh, sir. I am so very sorry. He was unkind to me, but I would never have thought he should die because of it."

"Indeed," said Mr. Jackson. "Nor did I. We would not have gone back to what we were before, but even so, I was hasty, and a fool. And now nothing is to be done."

I took Chowder's hand in mine. "There was no cause for his jealousy, to say nothing of his treachery. None at all. I wonder why he took us so."

"I don't know," said Mr. Jackson, eyes downcast at the table. "But," he said, looking up, "I do know one thing. You and Chowder will ever be welcome at my premises. Give me a day or two's notice, and we will take a meal together. It will be my pleasure and my treat. I do hope you will take me up on the offer."

"We will indeed, sir," said Chowder, and I heartily assented.

But here Mr. Broughton appeared. He greeted Mr. Jackson and Mr. Doxley with the affection reserved for the oldest and best of friends. "I wonder if I might steal these two away. I want to see that they eat something, and then it will be time to toast them."

We took our leave of Mr. Jackson, and of Dudley and Mr. Doxley, with much protestation of our eternal gratitude and highest regard for Mr. Jackson, who returned every fine sentiment with exquisite grace.

We followed Mr. Broughton to a table just in front of, and a little to the side of the dais on which the chamber orchestra played, where sat Mr. Bartlett, Henry, and Immanuel. We greeted them, then went to fill our plates. Returning to the head table, as Mr. Broughton described it, we sat and ate, and very good it was.

"I want you to know I am extremely pleased at your progress," said Mr. Broughton, to Chowder and I. "Not that I had the slightest doubt you two would do well. Each one of my staff is excellent in his own way, and I take great pleasure in it."

"Your care and encouragement mean very much to us both," said I. "We cannot thank you enough."

"Keep on as you have been, and I shall be thanked very well indeed," said he. He then turned to Immanuel, who held a pencil and had before him a sheaf of paper. "Immanuel," and he winked to him as he said this, "has learned much from Theodore lately." To Immanuel he said, "Would you like to say anything?"

Smiling, Immanuel began to write in a large, loopy hand, at first uncertainly, then rapidly. When he had finished, he held up the sheet of paper for us to see. The spelling was erratic and the hand unrefined, but the sense of it was, *Hello! I congratulate you both. Now I must tell you and everyone, my name is not Immanuel. My name is Olu.*

"Indeed, it shall be our pleasure, Olu," said I. "How grand that you are now able to express yourself."

He wrote again, then held up the paper, which said: *Thank you. It is a great relief.*

Mr. Broughton now spoke. "It is my intention to have Olu advise me on what to do with my plantations. I am very much opposed to slavery, yet I inherited from my father three very large sugar cane plantations in Jamaica, upon which reside over a thousand Africans. I could sell the plantations and wash my hands of it all, but that would do nothing for the Africans themselves, who would be no better, and, quite possibly, worse off. So, we will see what can be done, starting with legislation, and of course we will ask the Africans themselves what they require. I am fortunate I do not need the income, if it comes to it. My other interests are sufficient to maintain me. What say you, Olu?"

Olu wrote: *I will be very pleased to assist. There is much to learn and do.*

"Exactly so, and thank you, Olu," said Mr. Broughton. "Now, Joe, it is time to present to you your next task, if you are amenable. Actually, Olu has the identical task, but he already knows of it. Quite simply, I would like you to take an hour or two every morning, following your work on the scrap-books, and write your life out for me."

"My life, sir?"

"It is my intention to collect and preserve the life stories of as many of those of our persuasion as I am able to induce to be written. They will serve to prove we are unjustly maligned, and not in the least the monsters we are held to be. I do believe a more enlightened age will arrive, though none of us may live to see it. Does that interest you, Joe?"

I had never considered any such thing and was tempted to regard it as an exercise in vanity I could well do without, but the more I thought of it, the more I warmed to the idea. "I believe so, sir. There is indeed much to tell. But I have not the capacity to bring any art to it. "'Twill be a very plain tale, I fear."

"That does not matter. If you will simply write what happened just as you remember it, veracity will prove the very art, and the rest is of no concern. So you are agreed?"

"Why, yes, sir. Do you want me to start at the very beginning of my life, or ... ?"

"Yes, let's have as much of your life as you can tell. The whole thing. All the better."

"Then I shall be very pleased to do it. Thank you, sir."

"Excellent. And while you are doing that, Olu will be doing the same. Now, I do believe a toast is in order." He gave a signal to the orchestra to cease playing at the conclusion of the present piece, and when they had stopped, he stepped up to the dais, rang a hand bell several times, and when all were silent, began to speak.

"It is my great pleasure to welcome you all to the third annual Mollies' Ball. I am, as most of you know, William Broughton, and this is my home. Now I wish to propose a toast." He paused, and there was a fair bit of shuffling as those who had not any drink in hand went to fetch one. " As most, if not all of you know, we have here this evening two young men who have recently endured the worst, short of the noose, that this Kingdom in its wisdom offers to those of our persuasion. I speak of Joseph and Chowder, or Potter, as he is properly known, loving companions whom it is my great pleasure to have now in my employment. If the two of you would please join me up here." Chowder and I readily complied. "To Joe and Chowder. Hear, Hear!" roared Mr. Broughton, and the responding " To Joe and Chowder," was deafening.

I felt as if in a dream and next held up my glass, and said, as loudly as I could without actually shouting, "To Chowder!" And again came a deafening response.

Chowder was next, saying, "To Joe!" And a third time the room roared.

We drained our glasses. From the room came shouts of "Kiss! Kiss!" and we happily complied, the result of which was a great "Huzzah!" and greatly protracted applause. Chowder and I bowed very low and shook hands with Mr. Broughton, and then it was time to get down. I felt very giddy and took great care in stepping down from the dais so I should not fall. The instant Chowder and I had descended, the orchestra began again, playing now a jig. Chowder, much to my surprise, danced very creditably and entirely for my benefit, though of course others were watching. I had never seen him dance, and he appeared to me even more beguiling, and I will say beautiful, than ever he had before.

"Utterly splendid!" I enthused. "Where on Earth did you ever learn that?"

"Richard has been instructing the kitchen staff," he laughed. "In odd moments, he will have us put down the work for a few minutes. He plays a little pipe and shows us how to do it, then lets us each give it a try. You could learn, too. I could teach you."

"I should like that, but I fear my feet are all thumbs," I laughed.

The orchestra now began to play a minuet, and many lined up to dance. Neither Chowder nor I had the slightest idea of how to dance the minuet, though there did not appear to be much to it, if one could keep straight in which direction to flounce and twirl, and to whom to bow next. We were pleased to look on for a while, until Chowder turned to me and said, "I say, may I take you up on your earlier offer? I think I've had about enough of this. It's wonderful, but my head is swimming."

"Offer … ? Oh, yes! I promised to tear your clothes off!"

"Yes, and I shall be very hurt if you do not," he laughed. "Perhaps not the best idea to do it right here, though."

"Indeed. To our bedchamber, then!" We took our leave of Mr. Broughton and the others, and to our bedchamber we went, where I will say only that we were both true to our word and more.

There is little more to tell. Four o'clock the following morning, Chowder got up and went away to the kitchen. I, for once, had no trouble falling back asleep, and was, in what seemed but a moment later, shaken out of the deepest sleep by that infernal alarm clock, that Chowder had thoughtfully reset. The morning proceeded in the ordinary manner, except that at ten, after having read old newspapers and magazines, and cut and pasted clippings for two hours, I began the new task. Taking a sheet of paper and dipping the quill, I began to write: *When I was small, I assumed I would grow to be a waterman like my father …*

Author's Note

THREE OF THE CHARACTERS IN this work are based, to varying degrees, upon actual persons. The inspiration for Mr. Jackson was Joseph Johnson, a progressive bookseller and publisher who kept premises in St. Paul's churchyard. He was a member of the founding Unitarian congregation, published Benjamin Franklin, Mary Wollstonecraft, and Joseph Priestley among many others, and was friends with William Blake, lending him money on several occasions. He never married, and did adopt a young man, Roland Hunter. While there is zero concrete evidence Johnson was gay, it is an intriguing possibility. Johnson did not live above his shop, but maintained a substantial residence elsewhere in London.

Mr. Broughton is based loosely upon William Beckford, who was indeed the richest commoner in England in the late eighteenth century, owned plantations, and who does seem to have been gay or bisexual. Beckford, however, inherited a million pounds when he was but ten years old, not thirty, and married and fathered two daughters. He chose exile from English society in 1784 after his letters to a boy in his early teens were discovered by the boy's uncle. Beckford had an estate in Wiltshire, amassed a significant art collection, and, a little later than did the fictitious Mr. Broughton, kept scrapbooks which included magazine and newspaper articles pertaining to mollies, transvestites, and other so-called deviants. He also wrote a gothic novel, *Vathek*.

There is a rich tradition of female bare-knuckle fighters in London in the eighteenth century, beginning with Elizabeth Wilkinson in the 1720s. Figg's Boarded House existed, but I have invented its layout and manner of operation.

Gay men did die in the pillory in that era. The Bridewell records office, on the other hand, is pure invention.

Several of the places described existed earlier in the eighteenth century, but had been substantially altered or ceased to exist by the late 1770s, such as Moorfields, the Timber Yard, and the Fleet ditch.

Finally, in London at that time there was no systematic law enforcement or police force as we would think of it today. There were parish watchmen, but these were famously ineffective. It was typically the responsibility of the victim to apprehend the evil-doer, and to address this need there existed professional "thief takers," such as the hired muscle Rowland and Mrs. Cudworth employed. Obviously, this was a very unsatisfactory system, and crime was rampant. Policing in the modern sense did not begin until the 1830's.

Made in the USA
San Bernardino, CA
13 April 2019